10-17-20 11

Bryon
"Peace"
Bielyjsh

My Name is Cougar

Bill York

iUniverse, Inc.
New York   Bloomington

My Name is Cougar

iUniverse books may be ordered through booksellers or by contacting:

iUniverse
1663 Liberty Drive
Bloomington, IN 47403
www.iuniverse.com
1-800-Authors (1-800-288-4677)

Because of the dynamic nature of the Internet, any Web addresses or links contained in this book may have changed since publication and may no longer be valid. The views expressed in this work are solely those of the author and do not necessarily reflect the views of the publisher, and the publisher hereby disclaims any responsibility for them.

ISBN: 978-1-4401-9496-2 (sc)
ISBN: 978-1-4401-9497-9 (ebk)

Printed in the United States of America

iUniverse rev. date: 2/8/2010

Other books by Bill York

Fatal Encounters
Fatal Ambition
Reflections of the Great Spirit
Valley of Silent Drums
Episodes of Revenge

This book contains the most complete alphabetical compilation of Indian tribal names and Indian Chiefs' names, with their tribal affiliations, ever published in one book

DEDICATION

To my wife, Dot, who understands my eccentricities.

Observations of the author

America would erupt into anarchy if it were not for the thin blue line
of law enforcement

While researching material for this book I interviewed policemen in various departments. I also attended the 12th Annual Citizen's Police Academy in Gwinnett County, Georgia where I was privileged to go out on live emergency calls with patrolmen during the most dangerous time of night. I experienced first-hand the terror-engendering dangers confronting police officers when assigned to investigate actual shoot-outs after dark between rival gangs, (gangs being defined as three or more people banding together to commit a felony.) Gwinnett County has documented one hundred twenty three gangs, a phenomenon that has increased in the past ten years. If it were not for our first line of defense, the police departments across the country, people would be even more at the mercy of killers, pedophiles, corruptors, merchants of filth, swindlers, drug lords, rapists, looters, conmen and thugs. America is suffering meltdown.

When I was a youth growing up in Indiana I slept with the doors unlocked. During WW II, I witnessed maniacal acts of inhumanity. Similar behavior is infesting our society on an increasing scale. At four o'clock in the morning I sit before my computer writing with a 38 revolver on my desk. When driving I have a 32 automatic in my car. This nation is developing character flaws that would have been denounced as outrageous just forty years ago. The Boy Scouts have a motto each American should adopt; Be Prepared.

Over 17,000 citizens are murdered annually in the United States. Every year one and one half million people are victims of violent crimes. Prisons burgeon with killers and rapists. Home invasions, robberies, drug related crime is pandemic. Senior citizens are targeted for crime on a level unparallel in history. We see increasing psychosis infecting the nation during spring break when young people flaunt the same decadence of the Roman Empire just prior to its collapse, girls shaking their asses and grinding their hips like they were achieving stand-up orgasms. We watch looters and crooked contractors preying on victims of natural disasters. Guns are the weapons for hoodlums preying on people without protection. A weakness in our criminal justice system was highlighted in Atlanta where a murderer remained alive for three years, at the expense of taxpayers, while the people he shot had been dead that same period. We know he killed them. There were witnesses to two of the shootings. An indication of how fragmented this system has become? The man wasn't guilty? How? Why? He did it. Witnesses saw him murder the Judge and the reporter. The killer stood with the attorneys assigned to represent him and with a straight face one of his lawyers declared him not guilty. Why will a lawyer say that the killer is not guilty when dozens of people witnessed him killing two of his victims? And why is the killer entitled to free representation that cost taxpayers three million dollars? His trial was finally held with the killer convicted and sentenced to three life terms, which in itself makes the criminal justice system seem moronic since the man can't live more than one life. The system is riddled with a mish-mash of asinine sentences. A man butchers his wife and two daughters and is sentenced to thirty years to life. Absolute idiocy. Years later that murderer will still be alive. Meanwhile, his victims are dead! A review court will likely find a technical violation of the trial procedure and will reverse the decision and we'll have one more trial. With plea-bargaining to avoid more burdensome costs, the murderer will be sent to some over-crowded prison even though his victim's bodies will have decomposed. In the meanwhile his attorneys are still attempting to bankrupt the system by demanding more money for his appeals. There is another case now where a cop was shot while trying to protect a vagrant from a gang attack. The shooter was identified by several people who were present. The murderer was convicted and sentenced to death. Twenty years later that cop shooter is still alive and surprisingly garnering expressions of support from two world leaders, and others, with some of the witnesses recanting their testimony. Where is the intelligence in a system that allows a murderer to stay alive twenty years while the policeman he killed in cold blood has been dead for twenty years? Where is the justice in the criminal justice system? A rapist mutilates two roommates after murdering them. He is convicted of 1st degree murders and sentenced to life in prison. There was irrefutable evidence. Why wasn't the rapist shot right after the trial?

Another flaw in the criminal justice system is the use of testimony by expert witnesses. Attorneys will find hired-guns who get paid handsomely to testify for the defense or the prosecution, whoever gets to them first or offers the largest reward. They will sit and spiel what the lawyers want them to spiel. They will take a fact and make it a non-fact. A fact is interpreted two ways until the fact is no longer a fact but opposing theories. Those experts are skilled as testifiers but are compensated to have opinions favorable to the side that paid their tab; mauve is not mauve but claret, burgundy is not burgundy but wine colored. This system has been bastardized over the years until criminals who can afford the most syrupy-tongued lawyers and the most slick-tongued experts are able to usurp the system. Lawyers develop reputations by winning cases, whether the defendants are guilty or not. The more cases they win, the more will be their future opportunities and fees.

The normally achievable middle-class dream is becoming a myth at the present rate of change. The wealthy class purchase private jets, yachts, exclusive country club memberships, mansions and live ostentatious lifestyles while the middle class survive by working at two or three jobs, maxing their credit cards, closing their savings account and obtaining home equity loans that lead to an inevitable economic collapse. An example of the income inequity is the flood of scandals on Wall Street, the banking industry and throughout the business world, where the rich become richer by way of intricately complex financial manipulations while the poor become poorer. The American dream has become an illusion for millions of people. We are seeing disruption of families as the economy falters because fewer people are prepared for the fact that our established way of life is under attack and there is the painful reality that more productive people will be forced to join the ranks of the helpless homeless.

As the disparity between the rich and the poor widens the deepening abyss will reach cataclysmic proportion, and is already indicating evidence of violence and discord and as we descend toward anarchy our homes will need to be barricaded like medieval fortresses to guard against the disenfranchised people who are already reacting in desperate ways in order to survive in an increasingly inhospitable world.

Synopsis

YEARS 1819-2009

Cougar is the story of a Nez Perce Indian boy who witnesses the destruction of his village by the United States 7th Cavalry, in 1819. Returning from hunting in the mountains he watches in horror from a bluff as soldiers on horseback charge back and forth through his village hurling torches into teepees and indiscriminately firing at old men, women and children trying to escape the attack. He watches his father decapitated by the slash of a saber. He sees his brother killed. He sees his mother shot through her back. Given the name Cougar by his grandfather because of his interest in pumas when he was young, the boy escapes the carnage by hiding in the forest. After the soldiers leave Cougar walks around the compound. He picks up a long knife and an Osage bow from his father's bloodied hands. He studies the faces of his dead family. Tears flood. His horse nudges his elbow. Cougar spends two days burying the bodies of the villagers in the sacred burial grounds. When he is finished he stands in the middle of the compound, lifts his arms to form a circle, then begins chanting to the Great Spirit, his cries carrying into the trees on the hillside, up across the boulder strewn escarpment, up into the snow-covered mountains, echoing and re-echoing the agony of his torment. The Great Spirit hears the funereal lamentation of the Indian. Cougar constructs a travois and piles it with furs. He gathers a supply of arrows. He mounts his Appaloosa. All that remains of a once vibrant native people rides away to commence a new life in a remote valley in the mountains. Cougar beckons to the cougar that he had saved from being killed by wolves. It growls then follows. Practicing Moon and Sun Dances taught to him by his grandfather the boy becomes a conjurer, given great power by the Great Spirit, finding that he can assume any visage, including making himself invisible, and able to traverse in time, so that he can observe the paleface civilization and see changes brought about by the conquerors. He discovers exhibitionism and rampant immorality with millions of aborted fetuses. He finds the relentless pursuit of materialism, alcoholism, voyeurism, gang violence, ostentatious lifestyles, unfettered sin, impoverished vagrants, squalor, pompous millionaires, political corruption, sex orgies, corporate embezzlement, Hollywood debauchery, glorification of human idols, child molesters, lurid pornography, home invasions, the pursuit of instant gratification, infidelity, the evolution of males and females into an enfeebled unisex engaged in anal penetration and insalubrious mouth-to-crotch copulation, incestuous sexuality, flaunted nakedness, sexual assaults, environmental pollution, looks of hatred and the gluttonous depletion of natural resources. Most astonishing is to see millions of people with infantile brains being de-humanized in an avalanche of mind-killing drugs. He sees fork-tongue lawyers, through the gibberish of hyperbole and deliberate distortion of truth, protect criminals from justice. Cougar sees into the ailing soul of a decaying society. He decries the murder of millions of indigenous people to make room for strangers that four hundred years later are destined for oblivion as the result of unwholesome priorities and a flood of wickedness he sees sweeping across the land.

Just as firewood turns to embers,
Embers then become ashes.
There will be just minute traces,
Of those bereft of civil graces.

WARNING

The average lifespan of a society is 200 years. Nations wealthier and more powerful in their day than we are now have fragmented morally, been sabotaged from within, defeated by circumstances beyond their control and then disappeared into the annals of time.

Visigoths	Mayans
Saxons	Phoenicians
Wallachians	Polynesians
Celts	Goths
Franks	Abyssinians
Normans	Incas
Athenians	Mycenians
Trojans	Aztecs
Philistines	Macedonians
Hittites	Assyrians
Spartans	Persians
Babylonians	Etruscans
Carthegenians	Moors
Mesopotamians	Medes
Romans	Vandals
Vikings	Khmer
Mongols	Canaan

Huns	**Ming**
Byzantines	**Shang**
Ottomans	**Xia**
Olmecs	**Yuan**
Toltecs	**Zhou**
Sumerians	**Nazis**
Maoris	**Jomons**
Clovis	**Judah**
Nubians	**Mesopotainians**
Minoans	**Native Americans**

IS AMERICA NEXT?

THE AUTHOR'S OPINION

*History cannot be modified but people should be guided by
knowledge gleaned from the experience.*

During the time, from 800 to 400 B.C., spanning a 400 year chronicle, the world witnessed the destruction of Jerusalem because of corruption and wickedness in the city. The end was assured when they became idolaters. If we do not learn from history it is bound to repeat itself. This society is self destructing with adulation of Hollywood fetishes and contrived sports idols. We grovel in supplication for an autograph. We blather in reverence at screaming people on stage. We are being anesthetized by drugs and alcohol. We are mesmerized by pornography. We lust for immediate gratification. We are drowning in materialism. We are obsessed with orgasms and lewd nakedness. We are brainwashed by purveyors of decadence. We are trained like Pavlov's dogs and too many of us respond like mindless herd animals. We are breeding a lower-culture of strange humans, including thugs, crooks, con-men, killers, pedophiles and rapists. At this present rate of putrefaction we will replicate the cataclysmic end of Jerusalem in less than three-hundred years. Two centuries have gone by since the beginning of our end. Less than one hundred years remain for the nation that was once considered a beacon of hope in a troubled world.

WHEN GOD IS FORSAKEN
IDOLATRY WILL REIGN SUPREME

WHEN IDOLATRY REIGNS SUPREME
EVIL WILL FLOURISH

WHEN EVIL FLOURISHES
THE END IS NEAR

PROLOGUE

200 YEARS AGO

Those Remarkable Early Americans

Year 2005 marked the 200th anniversary when the Lewis & Clark expedition first encountered Nez Perce Indians in Idaho. 70 years later saw the abject surrender of Chief Joseph, with his starving and freezing band of old men, women and children at Bears Paw in the north of Montana. The surrender was the end of an era on this continent, punctuated by three centuries of a cruel campaign of killing, unparalleled in the modern world until Josef Stalin and Adolf Hitler unleashed their dementia. Columbia Encyclopedia estimates that there was an estimated seventeen to nineteen million natives living north of the Rio Grande valley before Columbus arrived. Four centuries later only 250,000 remained. The people were outgunned by the invaders. They were ravaged by diseases brought from overseas, for which they had no immunity, then starved by the wholesale slaughter of buffalo, on which they depended for food and clothing. Crops were burned. Millions of Indians froze because, in the panic of trying to escape being killed, there was no time to make clothing. Along the coastlines Indians were taken aboard ships and sent to Europe to be sold into slavery.

In the final stages of the Pleistocene Era that began two million years ago sheets of ice covering this continent from north Greenland to the Missouri and Ohio rivers began melting with the last vestige of the Ice Age occurring about 11,000 years ago.

As the ice receded northward, people who had migrated to what is now the southwestern United States, began migrating East and North, and thus became the first people to exist north of the Ohio River valley. Discovering abundant wildlife and fishing, they moved into the southeastern area of the continent about 9000 years ago. They were gatherers and hunters. When the earth was fertile they became farmers. Where there was a confluence of rivers and streams the natives established villages. There was water, eels, fishes, crawfish, turtles, and sturgeon. During migrations, wildfowl were abundant. Farming was productive so villages became an important part of native life reducing the need for nomadic wandering. Animals played a major role in the existence of the natives.

Villages thrived and when the population became too many for the environment to sustain, the people held a powwow and decided that some of their people should move farther up or down the river and set up another village, thus assuring that there was never a problem of over-population. At no time were natural resources depleted.

Unlike present civilization Native Americans did not experience alcoholism, drug addiction, road rage, corruption, taxes, pornography, over-crowded-prisons, carbon monoxide, acid rain, denuded forests, utility bills, depraved television, and mounds of garbage, diesel fumes, and deadly pollutions. Instead of the internet and telephone indigenous people communicated by using environmentally friendly dugouts, smoke signals, canoes, trail trees, drums, runners, and horses.

With a life expectancy of forty years, while Native Americans nurtured this land, it is estimated that eight billion indigenous people lived and died here. When forced to relocate farther westward, away from their homes, the sacred burial grounds of their ancestors became overgrown and lost forever. Sadly, it is a rare Indian burial ground that is excavated now when preparing a site for commercial development or roadbeds.

REFLECTIONS OF THE GREAT SPIRIT

An Epic poem by Bill York

From the frigid Atlantic Ocean
To the might of the Pacific
Stretched a land of wondrous bounty,
Filled with deer and ponderous bison,
Rich with fur and open prairies,
Tinged with wild flowers in profusion,
Painted green with towering forests,
Crowned with snow-capped fortress mountains,
Washed with pristine rushing rivers.

Nights were cooled by gentle breezes
Days were long amid the wonders,
Fiery gusts swept through the deserts,
Stars like diamonds glowed in heaven,
Rainfall soaked the fertile valleys,
Caressed by seasons ever changing,
Abundant fishes teemed in waters,
Maize and berries filled each harvest.

In this place so filled with bounty
Lived the Indian, tall and stalwart,
Lived in peace with all their Spirits,
Hunted buffalo when needed,
Took the wild-fowl for their larder,
Raised their young with wise contentment,
Loved their land and to their bosoms
Held nature's treasures for the future.

Around the night fires fabled stories
Passed among them rife with wisdom,
Tales of glorious hunt adventures,
Tales of things beyond horizons,
Things experienced in other seasons,
Facts of truth and yarns of fiction,
Late into the night narrations
Filled the children's minds with wonder.

Tawny men bedecked in deerskins
Smoked a peace pipe filled with birch bark,
Chanted songs of bygone ages,
Danced the dance of generations,
Ate the bear meat from the fire pit,
Bragged and boasted of their prowess,
Flaunted dress with flowing feathers
From the loons and golden eagles.

Younger ones in robes of beaver
Snuggled warm inside their wigwams,
Teased and taunted in the darkness,
Laughed in mirth at senseless prattle,
Pinched and frolicked with each other,
Told of dragons in the swampland,
Talked of ghosts in hidden places,
Whispered secrets not for others,
Until sleep removed the mischief
Replaced by dreams of new tomorrows.

In the warmer days of sunshine
Children romped and chased each other,
Climbed into the tallest aspen,
Tried to imitate the marten
Darting through the lofty branches,
Gathered pebbles from the beaches,
Threw them at the great horned owl,
Scared him deep into the forest.
Shot their arrows at the rabbits,
Chased them into hidden burrows.

They watched the otters in the river,
Skipped flat stones across the surface,
Watched them sink in roiling currents,
Saw the hummingbirds assembled,
To partake of flowering sweetness
In their coats of mauve and emerald.
They gathered nuts and hazel berries,
Cracked them with the larger pebbles,
Ate the fruits and fed the ponies,
Swam in brooks of cool fresh water,
Lived as the Great Spirit wanted.

As the season changed from summer
Cold winds blew in from the Northlands,
Whipped the waters to a lather,
Carried spits of snow and hailstones,
From the sounds of far off thunder.

Squirrels took nuts from giant oak trees,
Stored them in each nook and cranny.
Warriors hunted for more deerskins,
Took the coyote from deep canyons,
Captured beaver from the marshes,
Dried and tanned the skins for lap robes.
Women dried the meat from bison,
Made more clothing for the village
And moccasins to thwart the coldness.
Living things prepared for winter.

The blizzard came with blasts of fury,
Swirled the falling leaves of autumn,
Faded memories of summer,
Froze the surface of the waters,
Drove the birds away for winter,
Drove the marmot into hiding,
Forced the bear to hibernation,
Piled snow deep inside the forest,
Filled the trees with glistening hoarfrost,
Painted scenes of frigid splendor,
Banked snow high upon the wigwams,
Chilled the people with its frenzy.
It made the ponies stamp and shiver
With their tails turned to the north wind,
Suffering long into the winter.

In the early days of spring time
All the warriors took the young men
Out across the open meadows,
Taught them use of bows and arrows,
Showed them water in the cactus,
Showed them how to catch the groundhog,
Taught them how to shoot the pheasant,
Showed them how to race the ponies
Riding swift on lathered bare backs.

They taught them how to track each other,
Showed them things to eat from nature,
Let them hear the piercing war cries
Echoing across the barren canyons,
Let them skin the ponderous bison,
Made them race for far horizons,
Told them to beware of wolf packs,
Told them not to challenge panthers,
Made them climb the steepest hillsides,
Let them feel the haunting stillness,
Let them slumber bathed in moonlight,
Helped them learn for their survival.

All the women took the maidens
To the center of the village,
Taught them how to shell the maize seeds,
Taught them how to bake the corn-pone,
Taught them how to flint the firewood,
Showed them how to chew the deerskin,
How to cut it thin for bow strings,
How to make it strong and supple,
How to sew the robes for sleeping,
How to cook the meats and berries,
How to make them last the winter,
How to tend the new papooses,
How to set the broken leg bones,
Showed them how to be a midwife,
Helped them learn for their survival.
The Great Spirit loved his people
Lived beside them, moved among them,
Gave them life and inspiration,
Told them how to solve their problems,
Showed them rules of limitation,
Taught them how to fill their larders,
Kept them from life's bad beguilements,
Gave them knowledge of the seasons,
Told them when to plant the maize seeds,
Showed them how to trap the beaver,
Helped them learn for their survival.

When the Indian faced temptation,
Succumbed to lust and provocation,
Caused for others agitation,
Broke the bonds of long duration,
Committed sin among his people,
The Great Spirit chose the judgment.
It was firm, uncompromising,
Meant to warn the misbehavers,
Revealed his will with great vexation.
The Great Spirit took strong measures
To influence the errant parties.

Sent out visions from the heaven,
Meteors and bolts of lightning,
Searing hot volcanic ashes,
Earthquake tumult in the mountains,
Monsoon rains across the valley,
Turned the streams to raging rivers,
Turned the day to cavern blackness,
Sent down floods on haughty people,
Fiery maelstroms on the prairie,
Swirling dust storms in the village
Gave them drought and burning tempests,
White hot heat and plagues of locust,
Brought seething anguish to the sinners,
Made them suffer chills and fever,
Quelled aggression, made them humble.
Such was the power of the Great Spirit.

When the sun dropped from the heaven
And the day had turned to darkness,
And the village was all sleeping,
There were some with eyes wide open,
Thinking of loved ones departed
Who remained so clear in memory.
Thoughts alone late in the nighttime
Feeling how their heart is aching,
Knew that there was no relieving,
That the pain was now eternal,
Knew that never prayer or signing,
Could erase this great affliction,
And the mind would always wander,
When it was the time for sleeping,
Longing, craving, yearning, grieving,
For ones who now are only vapor,
And the tears rolled down in silence
In a private world of loved ones.

*One remembered always laughing
Had a face so young and tender,
One that loved the whole creation,
One that smiled at tiny pleasures,
Spread her goodness to all others,
Gave to all who needed solace.*

*Now is left just minute traces
Noticed still as time is passing.
Like blue beads and ermine sandals
Words still seen high in the aspen,
Carved are words of adoration,
Words of hope and expectation,
Fainter foot prints on the beaches,
Scent of jasmine on the lap robe,
Leather dress with sea shell necklace,
Dried wild roses from her tresses,
Touched to lips that still remember.*

*One recalled so reckless daring
Tawny face with dark eyes flashing,
Strong and agile like the puma,
Wise and clever like the snow owl,
Tall and stalwart now a warrior,
Wore a neckband made from talons,
Wore a loincloth made of wolf hides,
And moccasins from rugged bison,
Wore a head band made from feathers
Taken from the highest aerie
While facing danger from the eagle.*

He swam across the mighty rivers,
Captured pike with bow and arrow,
Ensnared wolverine and badger,
Chased the foxes into burrows,
Caught the eyes of all the maidens,
Thinking far into the future.
But it was not bound to happen.
Lurking in some dismal darkness
That came in silence on the east winds
Was a strange and unknown illness.
It spread its tendrils filled with toxin,
Found the young and daring warrior,
Took his power and made it weakness,
Forced his manhood into frailty,
Thrust his flawed and failing body,
To the other side of shadows
To the land of the hereafter.

One young maiden most affected,
Walked in mournful meditation
Where they strolled before as lovers
Thinking of the missed tomorrows,
Thoughts benumbed by flaming sorrow,
Exists each day with muted ardor
Until the time to be together.

At a time when all were sleeping
Came the sounds of violent thrashing,
Came the noise of grunts and snarling,
Came the ponies' neighs of terror.
Men and women grabbed their torches,
Dipped them in the slumbering fire pit
Filled with still hot glowing embers.
Lighted torches laved with deer fat,
Ran to see the loud disturbance.
Found a grizzly raging fury,
Standing high upon his hind legs
Twice as tall as any warrior
Rending logs to bits and pieces.
Savagely it smote the ponies,
Raking, biting, slamming, charging,
Breaking down the wood enclosure,
Dealing death and wanton slaughter.

Determined men with burning passion
Attacked the bruin with their spear points,
Darted at him throwing torches,
Shot him with their flint stone arrows,
Hit it with the broken timbers
As he ravaged other ponies.
When its red blood began pouring
From the eyes and mouth and spear holes,
Glistening in the flickering firelight,
Then the bear rose up in panic,
Tried to scramble through a thicket,
Ran into a stone outcropping,
Crushed his head which sent him reeling.
When the giant omnivore
Fell with breath and heartbeat failing,
Then the people started dancing,
Yelled with joy their jubilation,
Gave up thanks to their Great Spirit.

All the people in the village
Gathered round their mighty Chieftain,
Waited for his words of wisdom,
Watched the smoke drift from his peace pipe,
Listened to his incantations,
Patient while he meditated.
Then he stood tall like the fir tree,
Spread his arms with one great motion,
Formed a moon then spread arms outward,
Then he spoke, his words like thunder.

"We are the people, a supreme nation,
Spread across the northern woodlands.
Many are our lakes and rivers,
Many are our plains and mountains,
From the land of the Ojibwa,
To the home of the Apache
We share our crops in times of hardship,
Share our fish with loon and osprey,
Share our fur in coldest winters,
Share our wigwams with the traveler."

He told them of old deeds and daring,
Told them of loved ones departed,
Extolled the joy of past adventures,
Rekindled visions of their legends.
They listened to his truest wisdom.
All the chiefs from all the nations
Must abide the Mighty Spirit.

Came a time when all the warriors
Took up spears and bows and arrows,
Burnished knives and wooden war clubs,
Did a war dance to the Spirits,
Plotted vengeful retribution,
On a sudden raiding party,
Who had kidnapped one young maiden?
That had stolen from their larder,
And had burned too many wigwams,
Causing hardship for the people.
Out across the darkening prairie
Rode the warriors, faces painted,
Gleaming in the dimming sunlight,
Minds intent upon one purpose,
Seek revenge upon the raiders,
Save the maiden from tormentors,
Burn the village of the robbers,
Display the might that all should witness.

Furiously they rode their ponies,
Black eyes glowering in the sunset,
Evoking yells of righteous anger,
Attacked with vicious indignation,
Stormed the village, killed the Chieftain,
Made the bandits flee in terror,
Left nothing standing for the outlaws.
Killed enough to leave a message,
Leave in peace this mighty nation.
Rode back to their safe encampment
With the young and smiling maiden,
Divided things among the people,
Held a night long celebration
Until from the east horizon
Arose the bright sun from its resting.
Gave fervent thanks to their Great Spirit.

Into this land of wondrous bounty
Came a people pale in skin tone,
Came from great potato famines,
Came from tyrant persecutions,
Came from poor and arid countries,
Came from lands of yellow faces,
Came from places of great hardship,
Came from toil and virtual slavery,
Came from tropical diseases,
Came from virulent oppression,
Escaping from demonic terror,
Came at first in tiny trickles,
Came at last in teeming masses
To a melting pot of races.
Came to find a land of respite
Where to rest their weary bodies
Came to find a better future
Praying for a place to prosper.
Came to find religious freedom
Where to love their own Great Spirit.
Came with threadbare coats and trousers
Came with knapsacks filled with trinkets,
Found a land of trusting natives
Who shared their larder with the strangers,
They traded beads for lands and forests,
Forced the natives from their homelands,
Set up forts and strong defenses,
Fired with vengeance on objectors,
Slaughtered proud and peaceful natives,
Murdered women and their children
In the name of their Great Spirit.

Pushed them from the fertile valleys
Forced them from the mountain forests,
Chased them from the Mohawk basin,
Hounded them like so much cattle,
Razed and burned their rightful village,
Lowered them to destitution,
Tore asunder family unions,
Shot and lynched the strong protestors,
Robbed and plundered all possessions,
Raped and maimed the fairest maidens,
Assassinated once proud Chieftains,
Subverted laws among the people.

The Eastlands saw the forced migrations.
The Northlands witnessed mutilations.
The Southlands pulsed with depredations.
The Westlands suffered subjugations.

Drove them from the coastal lowlands,
Pursued them through the Smokie Mountains,
Pushed them westward, ever westward,
Tracked them down like beasts of burden,
Herded them with calloused venom,
Spit and hurled insults upon them,
Changed the robust native people
Into beaten serfs and vassals.
Crushed them all in reservations
Void of trees and vegetation,
Gave them land both dry and fallow,
Doled out food not fit for eating.
Swathed in rags and tattered clothing
Natives stood with spirits broken,
Voices low in lamentations
Without hope or expectation,
Fading like a blurry sunset,
Waiting for the time of darkness
To be with their own Great Spirit.
During thoughts in watchful silence
The Great Spirit saw new changes,
Larger wigwams full of wonders,
People living longer life spans
Because of medicine and science,
Telephones and transportation,
Leisure hours for all the workers,
Added time for rest and pleasure,
Abundant hours for meditation,
For the pale face and his offspring.
All these things should make them happy.
Why then are they not contented?

The Great Spirit now will ponder
How to aid his faltering people
To regain their one time greatness.
Just by watching modern progress
He believes the time is coming
That will see a great uplifting
To the olden times of greatness
Those who suffer scorn and hatred
Just existing on the pittance
Rationed out to reservations.

There are harbingers and omens
That refutes a healthy image,
Of a land so filled with promise.

The Great Spirit senses reasons
Why a place with much abundance,
Shows increasing social discord.
People stacked on one another
Much like firewood used for warming,
Much like boulders on the levee.
Sees division in the families
Over half of them divorcing.
Sees contempt for law and order,
Sees the fear that comes with darkness,
Lust and rape and dreadful beatings.
He sees the turmoil overpowering,
Hears the constant din of noises.
Sees pollution ever growing,
Acid rain now killing forests.
Hears the clusters in rebellion.
Sees the drugs and wild defiance.
Sees revolting sin with children
Sees the unrelenting violence,
Sees the wild salacious dancing.
Sees the rampant fornication
With its virulent diseases.
Sees the wigwams, old, decaying
Filled with frightened huddled people
Preyed upon by savage hoodlums.
Sees the glaring looks of hatred.
Sees the riots and the looters
Victimize defenseless people.
Sees a world so full of sadness
Sin and mind defying madness.

Sees evil greed and strange perversions,
Lurking harm in cities dying,
Intolerance and child abusing,
Sees a world beset by terror,
Neighbors killing one another.
Sees the millions of abortions,
Sees the death row executions,
Countless lost and wayward children.
Sees the hungry looks of people,
Feels the pain of those despairing,
Feels sympathy for old and feeble.

Sees corrosive radiation
With its lethal power for killing
Hidden in the land and waters.
Sees suffocating tax oppression
Piled upon a weakened people.
Sees men divided based on races,
Sees vast marauding armies
Slaughter people by the millions
At the will of men demented,
Heard a term called ethnic cleansing,
Knows it as an act of murder,
Just to steal the land and wigwams
Of the ones exterminated.

Sees the mansions for the rulers
Safe in fortress like enclosures,
Use of dogs and stockade fences,
Chains and bolts to thwart intrusions,
And ward off the desperate masses.

All these things spell ruination
For the land seen as a beacon.
These are frightening indications
Added to those dire predictions
Of a world so much in turmoil
That there may be no tomorrow.

What the Spirit sees will happen
As it did among the Mayans,
As it did among the Aztecs,
As it did among the Romans,
As it did among the Mongols,
As it did among the Incas,
As it did for the Phoenicians,
As it did for the Mycenaeans,
Too, the Carthaginians,
As it did for other people,
Decaying from internal weakness,
Seen throughout the darkest ages.
So will other dwindling cultures,
Who have lost their true direction
Fail and falter in the twilight
Of their zenith, now declining.

Just as firewood turns to embers
Embers then become ashes.
There will be just minute traces
Of those bereft of civil graces.

Then restored will be the Natives
Rising to the great occasion,
Back upon the open prairie,
Deep inside the darkest forest,
Riding fast across the meadows
With their ponies in full gallop,
Building up a land of wigwams
For an ever grateful people,
Taking back the land of plenty
That belonged to those departed,
Taking bison just when needed,
Taking wild fowl for their larders,
Restoring pride among his people.

Finding need for restoration
Mighty Chiefs from all the nations
Sent out word to every village,
Saw the need for one great Powwow,
Sent out word with swiftest runners,
Sent messengers on fastest ponies,
Sent smoke signals from the hilltops,
Gave notice with the deerskin tom-toms,
Sent birch canoes along each river.
Emissaries traveled widely
To announce important meetings.
Came powerful leaders from each homeland,
Towering men so dark with sunshine,
Robust men with forceful voices,
Fervent men with dark eyes burning,
Dressed in flowing feathered bonnets,
Riding ponies swift and eager,
Sure hoofs pounding, thick manes shining,
Bringing more important Chieftains,
Meant to save their plundered nation.

All the Chiefs now came together
Came to hear the wisest message,
Came to give their sage opinions,
Brought with them sagacious counsel,
Carried gifts for other Chieftains,
Brought their peace pipes for the Powwow.

Came together, gave the peace signs,
Sat on deer mats in a circle,
Pondered long and smoked their peace pipes.
Cherokees from southern mountains,
Seminoles from distant swamplands,
Senecas from eastward forests,
Arapahos from western deserts.
Came Dakotas from the north plains,
Came Mohicans and Algonquins,
Came the Crow, the Ute and Cheyenne,
Came the Delawares and Blackfeet,
Came the Ottawas and Hurons,
Came the Choctaws and the Shawnee.

Came the Mandans and Snohomish,
Came the Erie, Cree and Piaute,
Came the Mohawk and Apache,
Gathered all in one great union,
With the Sioux and with the Pawnee,
With the Creek and the Shoshoni.
Spoke of things that had to happen,
Talked 'til sunlight lit the heavens,
Made plans for a brighter future.

Found there was no opposition
Unified for endless effort,
Spreading out across the prairie,
Traveling to each distant valley,
Every lake and every river,
All the forests, every mountain,
Every place with hope for dwelling.
Cast new seed on barren hilltops,
Seedlings to renew the forests,
Plan to save the giant Sequoias,
Aid the failing coastal Redwoods,
Build new herds of mighty bison,
Clean up all the lakes and rivers,
Cleansing all the air for breathing,
Blowing smog from off the mountains,
Give the land a chance for healing
So that in the promised future
With firm resolve and dedication
They will witness as they labor
From horizon to horizon
Again a land of wondrous bounty.
All convinced that this will happen.
Such are the plans of the Great Spirit.

Chapter One

After two hundred years of existing in seclusion, secure from the palefaces who had torched his village and killed his family, Cougar decided to leave the valley and visit the land of the paleface to see how they had fared since the murderous attack so many moons ago. He also wished to visit those sacred burial grounds of his ancestors and find where he had lived as a youth.

After riding the Appaloosa up to the plateau where it could roam until they returned Cougar and the cougar left the valley, ascending above a covering of gossamer clouds. A storm cloud loomed in the distance with brilliant flashes of lightning. A chill breeze blew down the side of the mountain. A condor spiraled above searching along the edges of bluffs, eyes focused, seeking a carcass. Two Golden Eagles soared alongside in concert with the duo, yet keeping a cautious eye on the cat but feeling safe since the predator was now in their domain.

Traveling invisibly, Cougar and the cougar followed a valley to its confluence with a stream that had a strangely familiar look to Cougar. He recognized rugged arroyos that led to a meadow. Everything was different though. He saw no evidence that a village had existed where the two rivers merged together. Instead of trees Cougar remembered having covered the earth; he saw big buildings rising to the sky and roadways of concrete running in all directions. People scurried amidst the sprawl. Automobiles, belching noxious vapor, roamed the asphalt trails. Where were the horses? The river was filled with ships spewing smoke. Where were their dugout canoes? It was difficult to remember the exact location of his compound, but he studied one point of land where his village was probably situated when the soldiers began hurling torches into teepees while the people were sleeping and shooting them as they tried to escape. Now there was concrete and asphalt covering the entire area. He could not find their sacred burial grounds where he had buried his family.

He patted the cougar's rump. The feline twined itself around Cougar's leg. It growled. They rose above the jumble of concrete. A surge of sadness swept over the Indian when he stared down, realizing that he had no past. Evidence of his childhood was buried under man-made clutter. It was as if the Nez Perce Indians had never existed. Yet the memories were acute.

Observing from above the jumble Cougar was astonished by the barren scars on the mountains where verdant forest once grew. Buffalo and other wildlife no longer wandered the lands. The city was covered with clouds of pungent fumes indicating the palefaces were ruining the atmosphere by the over-consumption of natural resources. He could see mountains of garbage littering the hillsides and valleys. Cougar recalled the sagacious words of his grandfather when he had said that a man can only ride one horse at a time. Palefaces were living as if nature's resources were without limit. The words '*wasteful*' and '*greed*' came to Cougar's mind.

Moving slowly across the city he was astounded by the congestion of people existing on top of each other like maggots on a carcass. He wondered why palefaces lived in teepees so much bigger than they needed. Again the word '*wasteful*' came to mind. He recalled how frugal his people lived and with respect for nature when he was young. He also recalled one more astute counsel his grandfather always emphasized; that you never take from nature more than nature can replace. Palefaces were using up the earth by the over-consumption of natural resources.

Cougar and the mountain lion found themselves above a golf course where a tournament was being played. On the few occasions Cougar had left the valley he had watched other golf tournaments and was intrigued by the outdoor activities. He was curious about the throngs of people that followed golfers around the course like trained sheep. They applauded when a golfer made a good shot. They applauded when the player made a bad shot. They *oohed* and *aahed* when players adjusted their balls or scratched their butt. They followed the golfers like Pavlov's dogs sticking their faces in front of cameras trying to get just one golfer to smile their way so they could smile knowingly to him. When more golfers smiled their way their spirit was lifted even though the smiles were not intended for them. They pretended the smiles were just for them anyhow and they were emotionally and spiritually fulfilled.

The spectacular sickened Cougar. Why were individuals so dependent on the activity of others? Cougar and the cougar wandered invisibly, in and out, among the fawning worshippers. Cougar smiled, knowing that those spectators would be stricken if they were aware a 200 pound mountain lion was near them. Cougar noticed one downcast golfer ambling slowly along the last fairway. The Indian decided to become that golfer to find out why the man was so despondent. Cougar became Jack Gresham.

Chapter Two

It was the fourth time Jack Gresham had missed the cut in one season. During his extraordinary career Jack had won many tournaments including the Masters but he knew his game had begun going to hell the past seasons. During the last year while he ambled along to the final green he wondered why he was becoming tired so fast. His normally easy repartee with the gallery had slowed. His lively banter was gone, replaced by pre-occupation. His legendary shot placements were gone, with his long irons causing the balls to stray into sand traps and shorter irons missing the green or leaving him with impossible putts. He hadn't eagled one hole in the last four tournaments.

Jack Gresham was known for destroying the myth of course invincibility with a display that had elicited screams of adulation for a decade. His scores were now soaring above par and his earnings were plunging. He would be happy to get the last hole over with and go back to the resort. His embarrassment had grown until finishing the last hole was humiliating. He had become annoyed with spectators clapping when he made great shots, but also yelling enthusiastically when he made a triple bogey. Spectators were puppet-minded-idol-worshipping, pain-in-the-ass nuisances.

That night, in his resort room, Gresham again felt that itch coming. With such a heavy schedule and prize money reaching asinine amounts, creating more pressure to perform, milling minions of sucker-uppers looked for golfers to perform sensational shots then, between holes, they would shove pens in his face for his autograph. He had begun to feel like he was playing for cultists.

A seeping lesion underneath his tongue was sore and it seemed to be getting larger. His tongue explored the pustule. Make-up hid the open abrasion on his lower lip. There was a sore place under the foreskin on his penis. Neosporin had not eased that discomfort. He decided to see a physician when he returned home. He pulled down his pants and checked the soreness. He knew he had gotten something from one of the sluts.

Sleep would not come that night. Lying restlessly in bed he glowered at the clock. It was early evening. Jack put in a phone call to his wife. She wasn't home. He missed his wife. He turned on the TV and watched a stupid sit-com with a machine creating laughter. After failing to pound his pillow into submission he decided he couldn't endure the tossing and turning. His sheets were damp and he couldn't find a comfortable position.

His flight out was not until the following morning. He took out the notepad from the zippered pocket in his golf bag and looked up a number. Dialing, he waited impatiently, tapping his finger on the phone. She was home. Yes, he could come over but wait a couple hours. As a matter of fact, she would come over and pick him up in her new convertible. She said that Arthur was on location on a shoot in Mexico. She purred she had seen him on TV, hoping he would phone. She said she wanted to show him the Oscar she had gotten last week for *The Uprising*. She asked why he had not called early in the week. She sounded annoyed.

Not only was Jack Gresham recognized as a world-class golfer while he was in high school but within two years after graduation Jack was the father of adorable twin cherubs, Tina and Tana. The girls were the result of the union of teenagers who dated during high school. From the seventh grade friends assumed that Jack Gresham and Gini Molinara would be paired forever. Jack, the star athlete, and Gini, winner of two Miss Georgia pageants, fulfilled a marital union designed in heaven. Tina and Tana were approaching their puberty years and Jack had begun to find himself aroused when the girls snuggled on his lap. Occasionally he noticed one of their budding nipples and his heart would pound. Sometime he would rub their bellies under their pajamas and his heart would thud even harder and he would have to adjust his erection. Tana would laugh and move her body to enable him to touch her *down there*. Tina kept her legs closed tightly together.

Jack glanced again at the telephone numbers. He had Lydia listed as Lydia_*Nymph*. There was no other identity. There were the initials of ten other tour golfers who had used Lydia at one time or another. Phone numbers passed among good friends. Lydia had been married when he first met her at a pro-am in the valley. With the tour in California, it was amazing to know how many Hollywood starlets were ready to screw professional golfers. The fact that they have wives made no difference. To hell with morality, this is today.

Jack lay nude on his back, with moonlight streaming in the window. He could hear sounds of the ocean in the distance. Gossamer threads of lightning illuminated the bedroom.

Like a hovering wraith Lydia positioned herself above his body, clutching at him with nails like stilettos.

Jack had had sex with Lydia four times prior, after meeting her during a golf tournament. She'd been in the gallery. Now, he was once again exposed to the magic of her naked artistry. He would not think of Gini and the twins. Jack would not worry about his failing game. He would be taken to a plateau of orgiastic ecstasy found only in the phone numbers listed on his notepad.

He watched as she raised the gown up over her head, throwing it casually on the rug. Her breasts swayed as she arched her back lowering her scented vagina to his lips, gyrating like a dancer. His tongue probed upward, seeking, then penetrating the deep recesses of her body as he pulled down on her thighs. Pubic hairs moistened by the application of FDS, and the ejaculations of the basketball player she'd been fucking when Jack called, gently wetted his face and neck. Lydia was the master of feminine talent. The FDS masked her need for a douche. There wasn't time. An application of Vagisil protected the abrasion on her anus left by the basketball star's penetration and his roughhouse antics.

Along with her movie contract, Lydia's income was well above a million dollars providing her service to the visiting football, baseball and basketball teams. She thought of the funny story told to her by one of the Atlanta Braves players, about the little Georgia woodpecker that was visited by a friend from northern California. The California bird derided the tiny pine trees in Georgia, telling the Georgia woodpecker that he should visit him in California, that he would find giant redwood and sequoia trees where pecking was pure delight. The Georgia woodpecker flew to Eureka and his friend pointed out a 200 feet tall redwood, suggesting that the Georgia bird fly up to the top and peck to his heart's content. While pecking the redwood a storm came over the coastal range with lightning hitting the tree, splitting it, and knocking the bird to the ground. The California woodpecker flew over, asking what happened. The little Georgia woodpecker explained that he was up in the tree pecking away when all of a sudden he split the tree right down the middle. "It's amazing how much harder your pecker gets when you get out of town."

Jack's heart started pounding while his tongue began a flicking exploration. She was releasing a musk scent which cart-wheeled his brain into an incredible world of fantasy. He could sense the wetness flowing from her. It ran down his face as his lips synced with the slamming of her thighs and his tongue explored her yeast infection and vaginal warts. Lydia swiveled in a frenzied undulation as she reached behind, taking his hardness in her hand. A particle of feces, expelled by her stuttering release of bowel gas generated when the basketball player had probed in her anus lodged behind a molar. A chancre in the vestibule of her vagina oozed infectious pus.

For some reason, his reflections went back to Gini. Every time Jack had interludes he felt guilty, knowing that Gini was waiting. After some years of disagreement on sex experimentation he knew that it was her religion that had kept her from approving of oral copulation and other deviances. Jack loved Gini but his propensity for variety was something over which he had little control. That was his rationale for hiding the notebook with the phone numbers in the cities where he was scheduled to play.

Lydia's fingernails dug torturously into his penis as she slithered lower on his hips, inserting him into her vagina. There was some burning sensation where his foreskin curled back. He relished the feeling knowing that they would soon have an orgasm so satisfying that she would scream, "Oh God! God!" as their sweat-soaked bodies writhed in unison slamming meat against meat, lusting animals seeking release, surrendering to the battering cadence as old as the sea.

"I will be playing at Pebble Beach one month from now," he said as he exited her convertible in front of his motel. "I'm in the Crosby"

"I have a cottage in Carmel," Lydia said. "Phone me in advance and I'll plan on driving up for a couple of days."

"I'll let you know,"

"You won the Crosby a few years ago, I recall," she said.

"No. I was ahead by three going to 18. I hooked my second shot down onto that dammed beach."

His forehead twisted into a scowl as he recalled. "I lost in the playoff. It was about the time my whole game started going to hell."

"I will encourage you good next time," she smiled, reaching, walking her fingers down to his zipper.

They parted, having generated magic. Undetected on his tongue was a particle of feces. Moving into the opening under his foreskin was the HIV virus which had been deposited by the basketball player. Seeking open lesions was the spirochete Treponema Pallidum that was transferred from her vagina onto his tongue. The virus found the sore under his tongue, and entered his blood stream. In turn he'd infected her with herpes simplex. With Lydia's exposure to sexually-transmitted-diseases, by the time they would tryst again, in a month, the pair would have transmitted their viruses to more sex-crazed people, acquiring other diseases in return.

Cougar quickly left from what had been a disgusting experience. He figured people were enroute to hell with such conduct. He wondered if the girl's husband had knowledge of her sexual indiscretions. Cougar decided that he would go find the woman's husband and determine if he knew about his wife's out-of-town meeting. He recalled the comment about her husband making a movie in Mexico. He willed himself above a restaurant in Cancun where Lydia's husband was enjoying lunch with another guy. He hovered nearby listening to the enlightening conversation between two men.

Chapter Three

Arthur Model ordered two more tequilas with another basket of tortilla chips with salsa. He couldn't recall how many drinks he had consumed since he and Ed entered the Rio Bravo lounge. He was aware his tongue was thick and his concentration fuzzy.

Ted Ketterman took out a legal pad from his attaché case and positioned it on the table. "I hope you're not a jealous man, Arthur," he said.

Arthur Model rubbed his unshaven face. "I used to be jealous. It doesn't mean crap anymore," he stated emphatically "This is money. What do you have?"

Ted Ketterman was a close friend of Art Model. Ted had retired from the San Francisco police department after ten years running the homicide department. Four years into retirement a mutual fund, in which his retirement account was invested, went belly-up. Ted's instinct was to locate the bastards who had embezzled the money and kill them. Instead, aware of danger inside a jail and needing to supplement his social security income, he became a private detective. One of his first fees came from Art Model with his cheating wife, Lydia.

"She's a busy woman." Ted scanned his notes.

"I know that," Arthur said. He sipped his tequila. "How busy?"

"Busy. Averaging three each day since you came down on the shoot three weeks ago. She was with a golfer and a basketball player in Portland yesterday."

"Two tricks at the same time?"

"No, a couple hours apart."

"Jesus!" Art frowned. "You get graphic shots?"

"A gold mine. You won't have a problem with her."

Arthur took another drink and exhaled noisily. "The power of women, can you believe it? They spread juice everywhere and believe they can control the world with what's between their legs. I found that broad just in from Boise. She was about twenty and set on becoming a movie star. Had been married one time. I took the broad and made her a star. They come here from Cincinnati and Butte, fondle several producers, get bit-parts in B-movies, use their mouth and fame is theirs. My daddy used to call that being pussy-whipped."

"You're not fond of females, huh?" Ted said.

"Not much," Art said.

"I shot her on telephoto. I have a friend who owns a helicopter. We flew his chopper up a couple thousand feet away; mansion under construction. It looked like we were checking a home site. I aimed the camera over your wall, and shot into the enclosure and I got some superb outside footage. You will see great resolution. I filmed it with the brand new gyro-stabilized camera, the same equipment used by big producers when shooting movies from a helicopter."

"How explicit?"

"You don't want to know, Art," Ted said.

"I'm paying you good money, damn it, and little you can reveal will upset me. What happened?"

"I'll show you. I cut a few shots out of the film." He positioned a number of pictures on the table. They were ultra pornographic. It was Lydia with friends.

Arthur's face took on a scowl while he scanned the photos. There was one picture of Lydia going down on a muscular stud as another muscleman got involved. The disturbing photos had been shot around Arthur's pool.

Art put the photographs in his lap. They were distressing. He gazed out over the incoming rollers. Far out to sea a convoy of navy ships was heading northwest, maybe to San Diego or Seattle. The sun was a slice of orange near the horizon. He thought of Sonja wishing she was with him. He began to feel badly, even despondent.

"See the guy on the ground?" Arthur pointed.

"Sure."

"He is one of those Hollywood studs you see all the time with a different broad. He worked a race scene for me a few years ago. He has the reputation for rooting around like a pig rooting for acorns. What germs that son-of-a-bitch gets he deserves. I hope his tongue rots off."

"Your boys know about your problem, Art?"

"Sure. Both of them left home after jokes started buzzing around about their beautiful stepmother. Jake is crabbing in Alaska. Art, Jr. flies a bush plane in British Columbia. I seldom hear from them. They were upset when I left their mother for that broad." Art scratched at his forehead. "I wouldn't tell anybody else but you this, Ed, but I think both of them were bangin' Lydia after we were married."

"You're kidding."

"No. They were teenagers chasing around with hard-ons all the time. I saw Jake in the pool with her one night when I came home early. I drove back to the office. Sonja yelled I was a dumb schmuck for becoming involved with someone young enough to be my daughter. Sonja was right. One time I got up to piss. Arthur was being hand-stroked out by the pool."

"You did nothing?"

"No. By then I knew it would stop sometime soon. I had to find out about property laws. Enough porno pics and she'll lay off the big money demand. Patience will save me a few million bucks. I've kept her much longer than I should have. Men get cowed when they are young. Don't want their broads to find out that there are bigger-built things around."

"You're sure down on women, aren't you?"

"I've found there is nothing special about females. Errol Flynn opined, 'If you turn them upside down they will all look the same'. Imagine the smiling manikins hunched down on the crapper straining to eject a brick instead of a banana. The aftermath is swirling stuff whether it came from Roast Venison Loin Trattoria from La Bodeguita de Pico's or soup beans and hog jowls from Bennie's hamburger joint. They need toilet paper like everybody else. And for the same purposes."

They ordered another tequila.

"You ever get your pecker in trouble, Ted?"

"Yep. Once in Palermo, while I was in the navy. I got a dose of clap. Back in those days you washed up, got a syringe of burning gunk from sick-bay, squeezed it in your pecker and then worried your butt off for a month that your pecker might fall off. I wanted no more of that so I keep my plaything in its nest."

"Promiscuity is out of hand," Art said. "I'm in a business where I see it, watch the broads in their designer's gowns, swivel-hipping down the carpet during the Academy Awards banquet, expecting to be anointed for their B-rated performance. Hollywood is little more than society's self-lionized crème de la crème staring into cameras with that attitude of superiority. Everyone is screwing everyone else, posing, demure, kittenish, with exaggerated smiles, showing their capped-teeth to their wide-eyed minions. It's a known fact that crap in Beverly Hills and crap in Hog Waller, Arkansas has exactly the same aroma. They are convinced that their play toys are the center of the Universe."

"You are pretty vehement on the subject," Ted said. "Knowing you, I guess I'm not surprised."

"Damned vocal. I'm sickened by what is happening in Hollywood. I knew everybody at the Screen Actors Guild Awards. Some of them have kids out of wedlock. Some of them have phony tits. Hollywood is an unending orgy; ménage ET beaucoup. They gape in the cameras with smiles of piety convinced that if they drop their Kotex on Sunset Strip in the middle of July it won't begin to stink. I see Hollywood couples breaking up after having been shacked up for years. I have stopped watching TV, a lot of crap, not worth seeing. I see programming with some guy hammering nails or sawing a 2X4, or some broad covering her pimples with face paint. Watching a tomato being sliced is not too scintillating either. How often do we need to watch our hairy ancestors still swinging from trees, or the ones we work with who haven't completed the evolutionary cycle?"

Arthur grimaced. "The ones that sicken me are the nearly naked broads, gyrating their fat asses in front of a camera with the lens focused up their crotch. Lenny Bruce wrote a book several years ago titled *Fuck*. Every word in his novel was *Fuck*. He would get a Pulitzer Prize today."

"When I began detective work my initial client had a problem like yours, perhaps worse, but he handled it real smart. She was a starlet when he married her. She had the goods on him screwin' around, and was going to take him to the cleaners. But he was sharp. He got her soused one night and was in the sack with her, then got up to take a leak and left the light off. He had hired some dude to hide outside his doorway when it was dark. He let the stud in. He zapped him with Old Spice, the same perfume he used. I was inside, too. Instead of hubby back in bed, the dude went in, crawled in with her and started screwin'. No covers. Thrashing bodies with good ole' doggie-style movements. Using my infrared equipment I shot some fantastic, full-face, bared-ass pictures. You should've seen the look on her face when she saw them. I recorded her moanin' and groanin' on tape, also."

"Jesus, Ted. Where's your ethics?"

"Ethics-schmethics. I got eight grand for the job. Ethics will improve with improved payments. That's the way democracy works. She went away quietly."

"I'll admit it was a good idea," Art said.

"I have to get going, Art. My flight is in an hour. I'd like to spend a month here but duty calls. When'll the movie be finished?"

"Another couple weeks. Get me some more pics of the tramp. How much do I owe you now?"

"Don't worry about it," Ted grinned. "I'll bill you when I'm done. What kind of movie you doing? "

"Movies suck today. Writers continue writing after they have run out of talent. Actresses and actors are arrogant and overpaid. I'm making crappy, short, B-flicks. You know, dark-tanned cowboy chasin' wetbacks across the border trying to get back the virginal girl and a wagonload of stolen gold bars. Not my best work, but low budget."

Ted studied Art's eyes for a moment. "Because we're friends I have got to ask you, Art, and I don't want you to get pissed." He hesitated.

"What?"

"Have you caught anything from Lydia?"

"Maybe. But after I discovered she was screwin' some clown in town I visited my doctor and got some doses of antibiotics. From then on I stopped dippin' my tool in her pool. I am too old for that bunk-buddy crap anyhow. Too sweaty. I've had to restructure my priorities."

"You're lucky."

"I suppose. Some of that crap is incurable and will kill you. I've got a friend who believes he is Jesus. It's syphilis. That stuff destroyed his mind. He used to have a business back east. Now he walks around mumbling to himself, smelling of urine and preaching to trash cans and telephone poles."

"Wouldn't you think people would be concerned?"

"Apparently not. It's insipid. I am convinced this country is headed the same way as the Roman Empire. When they began having sex in the Coliseum while gladiators killed each other and then decided that homosexuality was good, it wasn't too long before they were gone. I believe we are headed that way. It seems like people's brains have been relocated between their legs."

"I'll see you in Beverly Hills."

"Yeah. Ted, I want to talk to you when I get back home."

"You want me to just bring the bill over to your house?"

"I'll call you."

"What's it about?"

"I know we're being swindled by politicians, and by bureaucrats. Lawyers double-talk juries and let killers back on the street. Scammers are hustling the public, selling overpriced gimmicks on television. Getting drunk and acting stupid is cool. Kids are being brainwashed that there is safe sex so schools pass out condoms to elementary grade children which give kids the idea that sex now is okay. The public is so stupid that they're not aware that wrestling is a first class scam. We have cage fights where Neanderthals attempt to seriously injure each other. Sit-coms are idiotic. Entertainers scream filth while grabbing their crotches. America has its priorities backward. We gawk at females with silicone tits, insane movies and television crap. We have carnival barkers selling God. With many around us living in poverty we idolize purveyors of evil instead of admiring those people who have benefited society."

"I agree."

"Do you know Johnny Fellino, Ted?"

"A small-time hood?"

"Yeah, he wanted to be the head Mafioso a few years back. Wanted to take over when Bugsy Siegel got it. New York told him to tone it down or die. He took up making flesh flicks, and hustling drugs to pushers."

"You interested in him?"

"Yes. He is why Lydia is the way she is. Just after she and I met she was struggling for bit-parts. Fellino conned her into doing pornography flicks. Drugs were part of his tactics. She got caught up in the Hollywood cocaine merry-go-round. By the time I knew what was happening she was a lost cause. I owe the bastard, big time."

"How'd she get the Oscar?"

"Good typecasting. She played the part of a drugged whore."

"I gotta' run. See you in L.A."

Listening to their scurrilous revelations Cougar confirmed what he already knew to be a fact from his previous visitations to California. For some yet unknown reason the residents of Hollywood, and most of the major communities in the state, were the fore-runners of a climate of decadence that was beginning to contaminate everybody. With the unending publicity that the movie colony receives from the networks it was not difficult to understand that Hollywood had evolved into Sin City with a capital S. He could not wait to get back to the sanity of his wilderness. He was disgusted by the filthy language he had heard the men using. That same filth was being spoken on the networks and on television, but bleeped as if that was an acceptable method for uttering trashy language on public airways. Cougar knew that what he had just heard was more evidence that paleface society was headed downhill.

Chapter Four

My wife, Pat, and I sat out on the deck enjoying iced tea, relaxing in the sun. A cool wind had begun blustering down the slope signaling the likelihood of rain. I lay in the hammock watching a red-tailed hawk that was perched in the poplar up on the hill. It was eyeing one of the remaining chipmunks that scurried around underneath our deck. Over the past few weeks the hawk had about cleaned out the small rodents. Such is nature.

Pat was engrossed in one of her novels. She is an avid reader.

"I want to go to Idaho," I blurted.

She closed her book to stare at me. "You want to go where?"

"I want to go to Idaho again."

"Go for what?"

"You remember when I went there a few years ago. It's beautiful country, particularly when you get up in the mountains. I love it there."

"You showed me some pictures of Indians," Pat said.

"When I spent a month on the Nez Perce reservation four or five years ago, doing research on Thundering Drums, I heard about an old Nez Perce Indian who lives in the wilderness of the Bitterroot Mountains. People who live there talk about an Indian that has been seen on several occasions for over two hundred years living somewhere up in the mountains. I want to interview him. I wanna' speak with him. I need more material for my book. I am stymied. I need inspiration."

"How do you know an Indian is there?" Pat said.

"People who live in the Pacific Northwest say they have seen him over the years. Loggers, who stripped the mountains of trees, claimed to have spotted the Indian just watching them near their logging operations. They say he has a large mountain lion with him. When one guy tried to go near him, he and the cougar just disappeared. There used to be millions of Indians all over the Pacific Northwest perhaps three hundred years ago, and for over twelve thousands years. No reason one isn't still there."

"But two hundred years old? No way. It's probably a myth, like Bigfoot, or that Yeti creature in the Himalayas, or that Loch Ness thing." Pat grinned, devilishly.

"Perhaps not, the Nez Perce Elders I talked with on the Nez Perce reservation are convinced he exists. Maybe he's a Shaman with unusual powers."

"It'll probably be a wild goose chase."

"I don't know. Their Great Spirit did cool stuff. Wouldn't it be a coup if I'm able to communicate with an Indian who's lived for two hundred years? Anyway, I haven't been in Idaho for years. I need to go. I want to go. The old wilderness bug has bitten me again."

"Aren't you a little too old for that stuff," Pat said, a look of concern spreading across her face.

"Eighty-two is not that old. It's all in the head. I'm in great shape, kiddo."

"Hey, if your life insurance premiums are paid up, then sure you can go," she chided.

"Honey, since I have been doing research on Native Americans I have often thought about how terrifying their lives must have been when their villages were attacked by heavily armed cavalrymen and all they had to defend themselves were bows and arrows and spears."

"The truth is sometime sad," she said.

"My ancestors committed murder on seventeen million people. Today no one wants to talk about it. I get some people pissed when I try to discuss genocide. They say Indians fought among themselves. I agreed, but not the virtual extermination of a culture. It was the most ruthless genocide in history until Josef Stalin and Adolf Hitler. And the sad part is that the genocide was endorsed by the highest office in our government. When Andrew Jackson approved his removal order he noted: if those savages refuse to leave their villages willingly, they are to be shot. *'The only good Indian is a dead Indian.'*"

"That is sad," Pat said. "So when are you going?"

"I'm checking Google for weather conditions in the Bitterroots. I can fly into Lewiston. I've been there before. I'll rent a car. I will take highway 173 to a place called Lowell, a small town. I'll leave the car with someone and head up a logging road to the Selway-Bitterroot Wilderness. The Indian has been reported in the foothills, and into the Nez Perce National Forest. It's a huge wilderness. I'll get a horse."

"You got everything you'll need?"

"I think so. Last night I checked my survival kit. I have quinine pills, trail mix, venison jerky, nasal spray, fire sticks, mosquito netting, matches and a GPS. I'm taking the bow so I can hunt quietly. I also have a foil blanket in case it's cold, fishing tackle, a sleeping bag rated at 20 degrees, some plastic garbage bags and my survival kit."

"Why take garbage bags?"

"I learned in survival class that I can make lean-to shelters, make a hole in the bottom, and put it on like a nightshirt, stuff it with leaves and grass to keep me warm, make boots, not for walking, but to keep me from getting frostbite by stuffing them with dead grass and leaves. And then if I hollow out a concavity in the dirt and cover the hole with a garbage bag, pushed down into the hole, I get some pure water from dew falling during the night. It collects in the bottom."

"That's nice."

I detected some sarcasm. "Wanna' go?"

"No!"

"We can both get into my sleeping bag."

"For what? You're 82." She grinned.

"So, you're no spring chicken," I said.

"How about a grizzly bear chewing on you?"

"I'll take my Ruger 30-06. Not a problem. I'll need some topography maps. Mountains go up to 9000 feet."

"How long will you be gone?"

"However long it takes to find him — two, possibly three weeks."

"Seriously, what if you don't find the Indian?"

"Then my story will be mostly fiction."

I hate long flights on airplanes. Because of congestion on the highway I arrived late at the airport and hurried through the concourse in order to catch my flight. Boarding, I was one of the last to locate a seat. It was a Boeing 727 with a heavy load. The last remaining seat was between a Sumo-wrestler and a Texas cowboy with the rancid smell of cow shit on his boots. Tex wanted to discuss his recent conquest of a female but I wasn't interested. I don't know why people want to talk all the time.

Jets fly so high you cannot see anything. I could soup-up my piper tri-pacer and pretend to be a crop-duster. As we cleared SEA-TAC, I could see Mount Hood near Portland. The prop-jet from Seattle to Lewiston allowed me to see the scenario down below until I got a kink in my neck. The peanuts were too salty.

Lewiston Idaho is a sun baked town on the Clearwater River across from Clarkston, Washington, which is also unimpressive. Named after Lewis & Clark, of the famous Lewis & Clark expedition, it lays stricken in the heat waves of the Northwest. A couple trees. A drab hue of brown, located before climbing up into the wilderness elevations of the Bitterroot Mountains.

On my way out highway 173 I stopped to see Jim Cook who operates the Clearwater Camp on the Nez Perce reservation where I had spent four weeks, two years ago. I wouldn't forget the 20 lb. steelhead that I hooked when canoeing the river near the rapids where Lewis & Clark crossed to meet the Nez Perce in 1805. It proved to be a fatal meeting for the people in the Northwest. During the next 70 years of lop-sided battles the natives were almost exterminated.

As usual Jim was out front with his guests. Some Nez Perce Indians, who work for Jim, were showing the art of bow making. Others were chipping on obsidian for arrowheads.

Jim saw me and hurried over to my car.

"Why didn't you call me before coming," Cook said. "Why're you here?"

"I didn't intend to stop. I just remembered as I was making the bend and saw your sign."

"Where are you heading?"

"Up in the National Forest."

"What for?" Jim said.

"I'm going to look for some ancient Indian that I hear lives by himself in an isolated valley up in the mountains. You heard of him, or ever seen him?"

"Everyone says they've encountered some native in the wilderness between here and Missoula. Some say it's a hoax, like Bigfoot. That story has been around for many years. It's a fable that a lot of folks keep alive because it's good for business, like having you out here spending money."

"Maybe. I'm still gonna' search a little."

"Some of the Nez Perce on the reservation believe that story. One of them who works here told me he had seen an Indian with a cougar, crossing the Clearwater River last summer. Floating in the air then disappearing. He said it looked like a young brave. Not too old, dressed up like he was headed to a powwow."

"I hope I find out. I gotta' meet him."

"You recall that professor you pissed off when you were here the last time?"

"Vague memory. Why?"

"He was here last year. I have three of your novels. He started reading *Reflections of the Great Spirit*. He handed it back. He's still upset because you write complimentary stuff about Indians. He hates them."

"I remember he provoked me to the point where I was about to kick his ass. If it hadn't been for you in the way, I might have. He was an arrogant prick. He's also irritated because Indians can seine for salmon and he's not allowed to. They have a casino, too. I recall him moaning about the Indian having everything. I told him that they owned the whole fuckin' continent before his ancestors come over here and stole the place and killed most of them."

"We've got a lot of his kind. How long will you be gone?"

"Month, maybe. Until I decide he's not there, that maybe he really is a mythical vision."

"You a little old for such strenuous activity?"

"Maybe. I'll know when I get back from out there. In the meantime I'll see beyond the horizon again. It has been a while since I escaped from our fantasyland with all that crapola that goes on today. Memory of my wilderness trips often keeps me from sleeping at night with great images in my head, satisfying memories, as compared to the reality of today."

"Want anything to take with you?"

"I'm an old Boy Scout. I'm prepared," I said. "I have a cell phone. Where's the closest tower?"

"Orofino. Deeper in there you will likely have to climb a mountain to use it. Of course, you are gonna' be in high elevations most of the time anyway. If you find who you're looking for be wary of his puma. Those that reported they have seen the Indian say the cougar is a huge, mean bastard. Protects his pal. You gonna' stop by on the way out?"

"Sure. See you, Jim."

"Mike, you may run into something awful strange if the story proves to be true. I heard that four loggers were looking directly at an Indian with a cougar lying near him, real close. One logger wanted to move closer to speak with him but as he started walking down the hill toward them, the Indian, who was riding an Appaloosa, and the mountain lion, just disappeared. All three vanished."

"You mean they went back into the trees?"

"No. Just kinda' dematerialized, kinda' faded away. The logger said it was eerie. Up northeast of Wieppe."

"I didn't intend going into that area but an Indian has been reported seen in a number of spots. I plan on going due east from Lowell. Maybe I'll have luck, we'll see. It will be an interesting experience. I have never been in Lowell."

"You cannot miss it. Take 173 on out, then cut off on 12. Quaint village. Little place. A resort called Three Rivers Resort. Nice people, good food. You can get something in there to eat. Maybe forty residents. Good trout fishing in the rapids."

"I'll hunt. Nature's been good to me in my life."

"Want some coffee to take along?"

"Sure. Plain."

"I'll get some for you. You got a GPS?"

"Sure."

"That'll help you. They positioned a satellite up above the Rockies. You can know exactly where you are all the time. I'll send your coffee out. Stop by when you're heading back home. Good luck."

Chapter Five

I've been through many tiny towns in my life. As a matter of fact I was born in a crappy town in the coal mining region of South Central Indiana. My town was so tiny that when some folks suggested building a one way road to get out of town they realized if they did that nobody would be able to get back into town.

Lowell, Idaho is kinda' like that. A little glitch on Highway 12, between Kooskia and Missoula. Perhaps forty residents living there. On the confluence where the Selway and Lochsa Rivers become the Clearwater River. Near to where Lewis and Clark explored westward in 1805 to the sorrow of the Native Americans who had lived there for thousands of years. Part of the Lolo Pass.

From Lowell the mountains go upward toward heaven. After a hearty breakfast at the Three Rivers Resort, I went over to see about renting a horse. Suzette Nigard showed me an Appaloosa stallion that I felt like I had known my entire life. We made a deal after she determined I was experienced with horses. "We had a swayback mare which my grandfather let me ride after my chores were done on the farm," I told her. "I still have great memories of her. We had a lot of good times together."

I got my gear from the car and checked the stuff I would need. I mounted the stallion and cantered around a ring on the property. Two circles around was enough, we meshed perfectly.

The eastern sky was afire with a tiny sliver of the early sun silhouetted by jagged peaks of the Bitterroot Mountains, appearing like the scutes of some primordial dinosaur. We moved out.

Crossing over the river through a shallower section we began riding up into the cedar forest. The Appaloosa felt easy between my legs. Even though I had not ridden a horse for many years, it's kinda' like a bicycle, you never forget. He had unusual tufts of brownish hairs on the tips of his ears. Pink palm prints had been painted on the stallion's rumps. I had made a friend out of the animal in the corral when I handed him a clump of crisp redtop clover, then two apples and two carrots. We were already buddies.

A silver salmon, perhaps a six pounder, leaped from the water and sucked up a gadfly that had ventured much too near the surface. A Golden Eagle soared across the sky, undulating, and spiraling, seeking prey.

I stopped the stallion just inside the trees. I sat perfectly still in the saddle and listened to the quiet of nature broken only by wind whispering through the tops of the cedars. Below, the river gurgled. In the distance a woodpecker pounded out his rhythm, extracting grubs. Some squirrels cavorted up in the trees. I was in a place of mystical beauty, like a natural cathedral. Through the leaves I could see the vaporous contrails of military aircraft lacing the sky. The silence was awesome. There was an aura of tranquility. The stallion snorted.

In the distance I could see snow-covered mountain peaks rising up into the bluest sky I had ever seen. It seemed like all the smog in the world had been washed away. Trees mantled the foothills. High up, I could see eagles riding thermals, searching below for lunch. Gossamer clouds misted over the terrain. There was an incredible silence. The tarn, reflecting the sky, was a deep cobalt color. The horse felt easy between my legs. I reached around its head and handed it two sugar cubes.

I suddenly sensed an uneasy feeling like I was being watched. I scanned a 360 degree perimeter. Nothing. Maybe my nerves were acting up after all; I hadn't been in the wilderness for four years. Maybe I needed more time to adjust. I kneed the Appaloosa. We climbed deeper among the trees. It would be a great week. My mind inventoried the items of survival gear in my saddlebag. I was prepared. The feeling of being watched went away.

I studied my topography map and decided to explore the area between the Lochsa and the Selway rivers, the original Nez Perce homeland, hundreds of years ago. It was a big wilderness. To my south was the Salmon River. I figured I would not be able to find a crossing so my best bet was to continue climbing east, slowly working my way up to the higher elevations of the Bitterroots. The Indian had been reported seen a number of times in that section of the wilderness.

We climbed upward for maybe an hour. I spoke to my horse and patted his shoulder. The saddle creaked. Two reddish foxes with fur the color of flames fled across our path. The Appaloosa sometime lowered its head to munch something succulent. I chewed on a strip of venison jerky. I was in awe of the beauty around me. These were invigorating moments.

After a few hours the trees began thinning out and I could see obscure evidence of logging trails from long ago when a gluttonous population began scalping nature. I'd read where a hundred years was necessary for the planet to renew itself. Animals had been following the trail keeping it from becoming overgrown. I brought the Appaloosa to a halt, climbed down from the saddle, and dropped the reins. I bent over to study the tracks left by passing animals. I saw the fresh tracks of a panther. Again, I had a disquieting feel we were being watched. I slowly scanned the woods again. Nothing. Lichen and moss were heavily laden on the trunks of the trees. There was absolute quiet. I listened.

The air chilled with a promise of rain. I wondered if I had been too impetuous in coming at this time of the season. Mother Nature displayed her eccentricities at higher elevations. My horse felt warm between my legs as I re-mounted.

The terrain was getting steeper with craggy knolls breaking the sloping hillside. My stallion was getting skittish on occasion. I could feel his shoulders tense, and then relax. He shook his mane, snorting. I thought of my old swayback mare when I was a kid in Indiana doing the same thing when a bear was in the forest. I became more watchful. We stopped beside a giant boulder where water trickled out from a crevasse. I untied my pack and used a bottle to catch some water for me and the stallion. The taste was incredible. If I drank ground water back in Georgia my guts would develop cramps and my teeth would glow in the dark.

I topped a slope and looked down into a tiny valley. I brought the horse to a halt and dismounted, dropping the reins. The valley in the distance was narrow with verdant forested slopes rising sharply to a backdrop of snow-covered mountains. I was spell-bound. I breathed deeply. My sea-level lungs were not accustomed to the thinner air at this elevation.

This is nature's cathedral, I decided. I stood with my thoughts for a long time. I wished my wife were with me. I listened to the wonderful silence. Here and there wildflowers swayed in profusion. I saw a worn path used by elk and deer when migrating to their different grazing fields as seasons changed. A gentle mist began. I flicked a horsefly off of the ear of my horse.

Periodically, I dismounted and cut a Y in the bark of a tree along the trail. In case of an accident, a good tracker could follow my marks. I cut one fork of the Y a little longer to indicate the direction I was headed. As we crossed a plateau, I carved a Y ever so often in the cedars along the trail. When following a ravine to a higher elevation I continued to carve the Y.

The stallion suddenly reared, snorting loudly as a bear appeared, coming out from the tree line. The beast stood up and stared at us. It apparently decided that the Appaloosa's slashing hooves were too dangerous. It turned and disappeared back down the hill. I gentled the horse.

My mind went back to Atlanta. I thought about the people packed into smoky cocktail lounges bullshitting each other with stupid conversation, the men ogling female breasts, the females becoming more inebriated so that they could later blame their sexual dalliances on being intoxicated. Night Clubs have become flesh markets. I wondered why people had nothing better to do.

A Great Horned owl, on silent wings, drifted down from the tree line, disappearing over a rise in the terrain. Grouse chattered noisily in the underbrush. Winds played melodies far out among the cedars then flirted with my unkempt beard.

Chapter Six

I thought about when I came to Atlanta in 1962 from the wonderful City by the Bay when clouds of marijuana smoke drifted over the region while seminal fluids were being exchanged in the Tenderloin bathhouses. A sign on a transient hotel on Peachtree Street showed fewer than a million people lived in the metropolitan area. Now it is nearly six million stressed out citizens stacked on top of each other like boulders on the levee. And drinking water contains a disturbing amount of chemicals.

Being an avid fisherman I backed my bass boat in the Chattahoochee River below Roswell when I first arrived in Atlanta. I ran wide-open down to Bull Sluice where I had been informed big yellow perch abounded. My depth finder indicated over fourteen feet deep in the channel. Inside a metropolitan city the area reminded me of some wilderness scenarios I had visited in my wanderings. Bull Sluice really was a honey-hole for perch. Tossing number 6 gold hooks with minnows into areas adjacent to submerged grass beds produced forty yellow perch with over half of them keepers. I wondered about the contamination of the river in a metropolitan city. Could I eat them? I decided that since they were caught before the water swirled through the toilet bowls of thousands of homes that they were probably safe to eat. Thirty years later I was asked by the producer of a wildlife series on Georgia Public Television to host a documentary showing the abundance of yellow perch in the Chattahoochee River.

To my surprise my propeller got stuck in mud flats several times on our route downstream. The depth finder indicated that the river channel was only a few feet deep, filled with muck from the out-of-control residential and commercial construction boom. I called the director of the Department of Natural Resources, and bitched. I asked why they did not dredge the channel so that it would be a lot deeper. He said it was not possible because dredging would stir up layers of pesticides, mercury, arsenic, cadmium, PCB's, DDT, lead, chromium, dioxins and herbicides, creating a lethal potion that would poison half of the people down the Chattahoochee basin. He asked me to forget what we had discussed.

I recalled finding three-legged frogs in Minnesota ponds and curved spine bass in Lake Lanier, caused by acid rain drifting down from industrial plants up north. I wondered how long people can live being deluged with deadly chemicals. I remember oil spills off the California coast. I had devoted days cleaning the gunk from seals, sea otters, pelicans and cormorants.

I tried to calculate how many people could occupy this continent before quality of life began to deteriorate and was suddenly shocked to realize we were probably already there. I wondered how many people could be piled on top of each other in Atlanta before unexpected repercussions would commence. Upon reading the daily killings in the newspaper and watching anti-social conduct on television I knew we were already encountering problems stemming from overpopulation. When I arrived in Atlanta you could walk downtown at midnight without being mugged. Today people can get shot seemingly just for being around, like it's joyous entertainment for some social misfits. When asked by a passenger seated next to me if I was afraid of bears, wolves and wolverines in the wilderness I explained that if I did not encroach on their domain or threaten their young they were predictable, unlike the two-legged animals roaming Atlanta looking for victims. She stated that she would be afraid of animals in the wilderness. I suggested that we make a bet. I would spend a month out in the wilderness where wolverines, grizzlies, and wolf packs lived and she would spend a couple nights camped-out on Peachtree Road in downtown Atlanta and we would see who lasted the longest. She conceded that I made a good point.

Chapter Seven

I filled two canteens from the trickle. I knew it came by way of a hundred miles of filtering and purification before seeping out from the boulder. The stallion and I drank again, deeply. I filled another canteen.

From far up the mountain I heard the howls of wolves on the hunt. I wondered if they were the packs recently re-introduced into the homeland of the Nez Perce.

When following a bubbling stream coming down from a bluff we came upon a small lake created by industrious beaver. As the sun began sinking below the cedar forest I figured it was a good time to set up our camp for the night. I searched for an outcropping, where it would be simple to make my lean-to. I tethered the horse near the bank were rich grasses grew. He began to graze. Up the lake I saw some ducks splashing in the water, scuffling and making quacking noises, perhaps mating. I put on moccasins and my camouflaged outfit. I took my Bear bow, attached the retrieval reel, and slipped back into the trees. After crawling abreast of the birds I mounted a broad head with blades that open on piercing the target. I waited for the right moment.

On down the stream a mother elk with a frisky calf was mincing through the water. They stopped, glanced around and stooped to drink, wonderful nature, thrilling.

The ducks were keeping their eyes on the elk while feeding. I was able to crawl somewhat closer. Having won seven medals back home in the Gwinnett Olympics, I was ready. I drew back on my recurve then waited until one of the fowl turned butt-up to feed on weeds on the bottom of the stream. The arrow swished into the duck. Eureka! With the bird impaled, I reeled it in.

Building a fire the old way is fun. Using shavings from a dead branch and spinning a dried stick into the pile of tinder causes the tip to become hot eventually glowing reddish and by blowing on the litter a fire is soon ignited. A magnifying glass would be easier. I had brought one just in case shavings would be wet.

I cleaned the duck on the shore. Minnows gulped the scraps as I threw them in the water. Brightly colored feathers floated downstream. Across the stream I saw a bobcat leaping up onto a boulder. I heard wolves howling farther up the valley. From somewhere up on the plateau I heard replies. I wished I could understand the magic of their mournful calls.

The bird was a tasty treat even without my wife's seasoning. I tossed the remaining scraps in the underbrush and heard rustling noises. Dessert was a square of caramel

I gave the horse a ration of oats and walked him to the stream for a drink.

A huge bear ambled from a cedar thicket followed by two rowdy cubs. She stopped and stared in my direction then growled a warning. Heeding maternal admonitions the cubs followed her back into the undergrowth. I had experienced one encounter with a grizzly in Canada. I listened until the sound faded. Bears with cubs can be mean. A chance encounter with a mother grizzly bear with two cubs while I was canoeing the Mackenzie River in the Northwest Territory caused me to have to shoot the mother bear to keep from being killed. Unfortunately, the young cubs were collateral damage.

Remembering that gold had been discovered, downstream at Orofino, on the Clearwater River, I began to think I might find a mother lode. I got a pan from my back pack and found a small, rocky rill. I began panning for gold my mind excited by the possibility that I might strike it rich, like at Sutter's Mill. I wondered if I had been born much earlier if I would have had the guts to give up everything and traipse over mountains to seek gold. After one hour I had a few specks of fools-gold and one piece that might be 24 carat but a tiny fleck wasn't going to make me rich. My back was aching. Two river otters rippled the surface a few feet away and eyed me curiously. One was munching on a sizable brook trout. They stared at me I guess because I was the intruder. I asked if they knew where a large nugget was located. I stared back. The pair submerged and apparently left the area. I didn't see them again.

Chapter Eight

By the time twilight drew near I had my lean-to made of heavy-duty garbage bags secured on the slanted edge of an outcropping. I anchored the bottom edges with large rocks. I cut off some limbs from a shrub and piled them inside my make-shift bedroom. The aroma of nature would cause magical dreams. I wondered if my wife was worried about me.

Once again I had an unusual feeling that something, or someone, was close by. I made certain the rifle was loaded with the safety off. I stared into the darkness and saw gleaming ovals. I knew I would be under surveillance through the night. I was in their realm. I prayed that they were tiny and not hungry. A breeze picked up in the treetops playing a super-sweet song. I thought of my wife and I began to doze off. Something scurried close to my lean-to. Blackness kept me from seeing. I had a chilling premonition of danger and wondered why any 83 year old, supposedly intelligent person, would explore this wilderness when the comforts of home were back home. I was consoled by the realization that in a few weeks I could go back home. My muscles hurt from the ride. I sucked on one more nougat. Wind whispered to me from the treetops. My hands remained on the rifle as I tried to sleep.

My brain kept reflecting on things from my past. I thought about my only brother, killed in the Battle of the Bulge. Not quite 21. I would like to have gotten to Hitler before that insane son-of-a-bitch shot himself. I could have killed him in increments. I thought about my first wife with her eccentricities. . I felt a sigh of relief knowing that I didn't have to put up with her foibles. I wondered why more people were not up here in these lush mountains pigging-out on nature.

Off in the distance some doves cooed. A woodpecker pounded for grubs.

Even though tired, I found it difficult to go to sleep.

I heard unexplained noises up and down the valley. I felt strangely uneasy.

I grabbed another caramel and just held it in my mouth, like a baby with a pacifier.

I heard something move near my shelter. I flipped on the flashlight. Nothing.

I reflected about Harry Truman and the decision which he made that saved thousands of military lives when he ordered bombs dropped with many Japanese being killed. But *they* started the fuckin' war. I remembered Pearl Harbor and the Bataan Death March. I read about the raping of Nanking. I recalled the arm-wrenching fight after I hooked a trophy northern pike on the Wolverine River in Nunavut. It was still pulling me across the river when I finally dozed off to sleep. Strange, woodsy sounds kept waking me up to a half-doze. If I was at home I could turn on the television and watch elephantine broads attempting to dump manatee pounds and dysfunctional people exchanging their odd-ball philosophies on life.

I went out and got the Appaloosa and brought it to my shelter. It lay down with its head inside my lean-to. I thought of my wife working the cross-word puzzle knowing she needed me to help.

I began thinking about the Indian. Would I find him? Would he be a simple native person? Would he be aware of the enormity of those changes that had occurred throughout the world during his supposed two hundred years of living, or even locally? Would I learn something I could use in my story, to impart something educational to my readers?

Would he know, for instance, about the potential death of the world when the nuclear submarines that had been sunken off Murmansk finally imploded releasing nuclear materials into the oceans? Would he be aware of the potential for a planet-wide fire-storm from the inevitable maelstrom, with earth turning into a giant cinder floating around somewhere out in the universe, devoid of life? Scary. I wondered if he would know how to control teenagers who were already showing indications of killer mentality.

A zillion questions flooded my brain. I hoped he really existed. It would be an extraordinary coup if I could actually interview someone who had lived for two centuries. No other writer had ever done that. And then maybe he would be a savage like Hollywood portrays and I would be scalped in my sleep.

The stallion was snoring. I didn't know that horses actually snored. But why not? Stranger things happen in life. They're entitled to snore.

Sometime later I finally dropped off to a fitful sleep.

Chapter Nine

Sometime during the night, I awakened with a start. I had been having scary little vignettes of a nightmare. I was a caveman during the era of dinosaurs cowering in a cave with a huge lizard attempting to claw its way into the back where I was hiding. I could see its claws digging closer then I realized that I had backed in as far as I could go and I was doomed to be consumed by some prehistoric carnivore. My bladder got me fully awakened. I sighed with relief. Then I heard a low growling just outside my lean-to. I grabbed my flashlight and aimed it through the mesh toward the sound. The light revealed the blackest eyes of the biggest wolverine I had ever seen. Its lips were drawn back. I could see razor-sharp teeth. I cleared my throat loudly and screamed, Boo! The king of weasels turned tail. I heard it crashing through the underbrush. I raised the flap and crawled from under the outcropping. The horse whinnied. A breeze whipped through the branches up above as I relieved myself. I shuddered with the chill. My stallion took a noisy piss then turned and wandered down to the river. I started to crawl back inside my lean-to for one more hour of catnapping, waiting for dawn's light, rapidly appearing over the mountain.

I heard the Appaloosa stomping near the stream. It shook its mane, looking in my direction. A movement to my left caught my eye. I cringed. From the forest, three forms like whitish, spidery wraiths, like gossamer vapor started taking form. There were three clusters of vaporous mist moving up closer to my campsite. I reached for the rifle.

"That's not necessary," a resonant voice said.

The forms were now visible. There was a huge cougar and another Appaloosa horse. Between the animals walked the most impressive Indian I had ever seen. He was over six feet tall with wide shoulders. He was wearing a sleeved white ermine mantelet that covered him to his moccasined feet. He wore beaver moccasins. His jet black hair cascaded down over his shoulders to his waist. A full headdress covered his head. Over one shoulder was slung an Osage bow. A quiver of arrows lay across his back. A gold ringlet pierced his nose. The Indian's deep-set eyes were ebony toned. For some reason his skin reminded me of the wonderful color of cedar I had used in the seventh grade to make a blanket chest for my mother.

The Indian looked at me with an intensity I had not experienced before. I felt like I was visiting with royalty.

He said, "My name is Cougar."

I said, "My name is Mike Hayden. I have been looking for you. I didn't know your name." My mouth felt as dry as a Mohave Desert sand dune.

"I know," the man said. "I've been tracking you ever since you arrived in my land."

"Why?" I struggled with the question.

"I have read your books. You speak good words about my people. I want to know you," he said.

I looked toward the mountain lion. It sat passively with its lips drawn back revealing four large flesh-ripping teeth. "He looks mean, and powerful," I said. I had determined that it was a monstrous size male, maybe two hundred pounds. I could see its muscles.

"If I approve of you the cougar also approves." The Indian smiled.

I started to feel comfortable in his presence. "How do you accomplish that materializing feat?" I said.

"The Great Spirit has given me miraculous, unlimited power."

"In my world we do the same thing, but artificially, with tricks, with electronically sophisticated cameras, gimmicky."

"I do that, and much more, by the will of the Great Spirit. I have traveled in time and visited your people on numerous occasions. I can become any visage of your society, live that life until I tire of it then return to my way of life. In the course of my journeys I have learned many things."

"Your headdress is amazing. Nez Perce usually have only two feathers in their hair," I said.

"I traded Sioux Chief, Sitting Bull's descendants, obsidian to make arrows when I visited the Pine Ridge reservation last year. This is usually plains Indian headdress," he said.

I said. "I need some coffee every morning before I'm fully awake."

"Let's mount up and ride farther up on the mountain to my home." The Indian gestured.

"You have a teepee, a lodge?" I said.

"Not exactly, we live in a natural cavern which is deeper in the mountain wilderness. My friends and I have been here for over two hundred years," he said.

We mounted the Appaloosas. His mare was white with some splotches of brown and tans. Hand paintings adorned her flanks and muzzle. Even though he might have been aware of the atrocities the 7th cavalry had committed in his village, he seemed to harbor no resentment. I felt at peace riding into the back-country with him.

"Appearing so youthful and muscular how could you live for so long?" I said, as we moved out. "And just how old are you?"

"I was born in 1789. Chronologically, I am over two hundred years old. Visually, I'm the age I was when the Great Spirit granted me eternal life."

"When was that?" I said in wonderment.

"The Great Spirit can do amazing things," he said. "I was twenty years old when my family was killed in 1809. I am two hundred and nine years old."

We climbed upward over some rocky terrain with the cougar criss-crossing our path. Sometimes it would disappear, like a ghost, and then unexpectedly, re-appear.

"Practicing his hunting skills," Cougar said. "By the way, how old are you?"

"I was born in 1926, during the Great Depression. Of course you already know that, don't you?"

"Just testing your honesty," Cougar said. "Yes, I knew that."

"Have you always been in this valley?" I said.

"Ever since our village was destroyed, I needed to hide from the soldiers. I avoided being killed because I was hunting when the cavalry attacked. The cougar and I luckily stopped to bathe in a mountain stream, or I too would have been murdered. Also, I did not want to assimilate into a society so hell-bent on killing. So we came here and have remained here ever since. The Great Spirit has granted me power to traverse in time, so on occasion I have visited places where the palefaces live. Quickly I have returned to the tranquility and stability of this isolated region."

We passed through a narrow defile and came out into a remote valley, thick with cedar and grass. A bubbling stream rippled out from under a towering plateau on one end of the valley then emptied into a larger stream down the valley, and disappeared below a bluff at the other end. The area was verdant. We rode up to the entranceway to a grotto that was hidden from view under an outcropping of boulders. The opening into the cave was wide but if anyone found the defile into the valley, or flew over the mountain, the entranceway wouldn't be visible. Across the river rising two thousand or more feet were snow-capped mountains which shadowed the entire region, until late morning. The water was jade green roiling swiftly around enormous boulders that had catapulted down during a past earthquake. They had been polished to a glistening sheen from flooding and small pebbles that scoured them over the centuries. Some boulders were striped white by guano deposited over the years by migrating wildfowl. Beaver had built a sizable dam farther down the river, creating a deep mountain tarn. Trout winnowed in the shallows. The valley was a sanctuary of incredible isolation and serenity."

"Anyone ever come here?" I asked.

"Seldom," Cougar said. "But on that rare occasion when a trapper or a hunter entered our valley they elected not to stay here very long because they discovered that this place is haunted. Arrows fly and a mountain lion roars, yet no archer or cougar is ever spotted." Cougar smiled devilishly.

"Back your stallion up a little." The Indian motioned, as he urged his horse a couple of steps backward.

The reason for the urgency became apparent as several thousand bats flew out from the cave, darkened the sky, and disappeared over an escarpment. Soaring high above the vale were two bald eagles, riding strong updrafts, searching along the valley rim for their breakfast.

"The bats are friendly," Cougar said. "Because they live in this valley we have no mosquitoes. When the cougar is out of sight hunting, the eagles will descend to the valley and spend time with me. I have flown with eagles. They do not come when the cougar is here because they have seen him leap to catch ducks and geese. We also have ospreys that fish this river. This valley is full of animals; martens, otters, beaver, elk, deer, black bear, and an occasional grizzly bear. The cougar surprisingly scares the grizzly away. We have had herds of buffalo that found their way through the defile and into the valley. The cougar chased them away. They would have eaten us out of house and home if they stayed longer. We even had a pack of timber wolves. The cougar proved his worth then, also."

I removed the saddle and halter from the stallion, patting him for the nice ride. We freed the two horses to roam. They headed for the stream.

Upon entering the mouth of the cave, the opening spread out wider with towering stalactites and stalagmites. There was a well-worn pathway that disappeared toward the back. Coming from somewhere in the blackness I heard the sound of a waterfall. The temperature was comfortable eliminating a need for heating or air-conditioning. There was a thick pile of moose hides on a ledge

"That is my bed," he said. "I have some jerky if you are hungry. I'll have the cougar round us up a deer for dinner." We sat down on a mat, facing each other, with light coming in from the outside.

"I am curious as to exactly why you decided to find me," the Indian said.

"Well, as you already know I have written two books about your people and I have a third book almost half written. I'm curious about your observations of the way this society has evolved since your ancestors were killed by my ancestors. I want to write some of your impressions in a book I'm presently working on, like, for instance, what you think of this paleface society now?"

"That is not a simple question, it is very complex. There are so many ramifications resulting from behavior of your people with which my people were unfamiliar. I honestly wonder if you really want my observations. I would like you to understand that my comments can be construed as an indictment of your society. For three centuries after the

Europeans began over-running this land staying alive was impossible for my people. Ninety-eight percent of my people were either murdered, starved to death, frozen to death or died from diseases, brought to this land from Europe, to which they had no immunity."

"I intend to write the truth as I see it, from the mind of a thinker who has lived 83 years and has witnessed the insidious fermenting of evil, particularly in the past forty years."

"Well, as a starter to my lengthy observations of the pluses that made your country the land of opportunity and a beacon of hope for millions of oppressed people around the world, your country has become the land of desperation filled with opportunists who prey on the uneducated. Humility, morality, ethics and integrity are being replaced by incivility, exhibitionism and unprincipled business practices. It is like the Serengeti plains in Africa. When an animal becomes weak, a condition I see occurring among your people, hyenas, lions, cheetahs, jackals and vultures have a feast. When a citizen from your society shows some indication of weakness they are preyed on by determined opportunists. It's a sickness that is fragmenting the United States."

I nodded in agreement, making some notes. "It reminds me of a situation when I was in the navy. We had young kids in service who were from the farms and backwoods across the country and many had not finished high school. Needless to say they were unsophisticated. While overseas the youngsters would run out of money and still want to hit the cathouses when off duty. One older guy, who may have been in banking before the war, lent money to the kids to be repaid come payday. He charged them 50% interest for a month. That's 600% per annum. If the kid borrowed the money two weeks before payday the 600% became 1200%. If it was just a week the interest was 2400% and if was just one day the charge was now 16,800 %. The older fellow came back from overseas a millionaire and the sailors had no idea they were being royally screwed. That's kinda' how it is in banking and finance today."

"Why do people remain stupid?" Cougar said.

"Too many school drop-outs. One parent homes. Peer influence. Drugs. Many reasons."

"You wisely said that by not pursing an education drop-outs would be flippin' hamburgers for pissy wages the rest of their lives. Further, when calamities strike, hurricanes, tornadoes, earthquakes, volcanic eruptions, floods, forest fires, concerned citizens turn out to help in the clean-up and assist the victims but that group is integrated by looters and opportunists who prey on the victims of the disaster. That's the same people who can't speak intelligible English or can't get a decent job."

"In Gwinnett County where I live," I said. "Crimes increased by 3.7% last year. It is across the board in type of crime. Home invasions are maybe the worst when old people are terrified in their homes. The next are merchants being robbed in their business and then shot so there will be no witness. While I am on my computer it's usually early in the morning before daylight and, even though we have a security system, I work with a 32 firearm on my desk. I'm too old to fight with thugs so I'll have to shoot them. I agree with your assessment. Also, twenty seven thousand people were murdered last year."

The mountain lion went to Cougar entwining himself around the Indian's legs.

"My friend is getting hungry. What would you like? Wildlife is abundant in this valley."

"What does he hunt?"

"Anything, he can take down a goose before it gets five feet in the air."

"Roasted goose sounds good."

"He will get two. He can eat one all by himself and finish up the scraps." Cougar murmured something to the big cat. It loped off toward the river.

"Where are the Appaloosas? My horse is not familiar with the region."

"My mare is familiar. Your stallion is following my mare. You can bet on it." Cougar smiled knowingly.

Astonishingly the cougar was back in less than ten minutes, dragging two plump Canadian geese. He dropped both at Cougar's feet. A puma is the only wildcat that purrs. I could hear his sound.

Cougar said, "I'll make the fire and you can clean the geese down at the stream, or vice versa."

I picked up the two geese and headed down to the stream. They must weigh 20-25 pounds each I decided. How can a cougar consume that much? I wondered. The cougar had a rich brown coating of fur and rippling muscles. Having spent my entire career in the fur business I knew what a great man's coat he would make. I soon changed my thought pattern. Perhaps that cougar was mentally gifted like the Indian and might read my brain. Maybe I would be its dinner as payback for my thought transgression. The idea was chilling.

I watched as the man wrapped the geese breasts and thighs in reed grass in which he had added wild onions and chokeberries. He wetted the grasses and raked back the coals in the fire, putting the meat in the fire pit covering it with grass and fiery coals. Everything else he threw to the cougar. "I discovered a beehive yesterday," he said. "Along with an assortment of nuts, honey will make a fine dessert."

"I'm pleased I came out here. It sounds better than the Ritz Carlton," I said.

We sat back against a grizzly hide covered boulder. Cougar lighted a pipe. "You smoke?"

"No."

"Your loss," he said. "So what else do you want to know?"

The cougar got up, stretched, looked at Cougar then loped off toward the tree line carrying scraps from the geese in his mouth.

"I think he has a girl-friend around here somewhere. He leaves too often."

A magnificent red-tailed hawk settled down on Cougar's arm, staring at him with piercing eyes. It turned toward me and stared. Its eyes were as black as obsidian. I stared back.

"It only comes down when the cougar leaves," Cougar said. He handed the hawk a piece of jerky.

The hawk was huge. Back in Georgia I had seen them in my neighborhood but not two feet away.

"I'm curious. I think I know, but just what kind of food did you people eat?"

"The same as you eat with some differences."

"But you didn't have refrigeration," I said. "You didn't have grocery stores."

Cougar moved his hands around in a sweeping motion. "Our grocery store was nature. It was open twenty-four hours a day," he said.

"Except for winter we never had refrigeration. When food was needed we went out and opened Nature's store. Everything was always fresh."

"How about the variety in your food?" I said.

"My people ate much the same as you; wild onions, berries, khouse-khouse, honey, sassafras, apples, and much more. We had an unlimited supply of animals which provided meat year round. We had migratory birds, more fish than you, because our rivers and lakes were pure. Now many of your rivers are polluted, with a dwindling supply of fish, and many are unfit to eat. Instead of going daily and getting a supply of meat, you buy pre-packaged meat that has been injected with preservatives like sulfur dioxides, growth hormones, antibiotics and chemicals. Your fruits and vegetables are sprayed with insecticides and pesticides. It's no wonder you people are getting sick. Our foods were natural and my supply here in the valley is the same."

"It is hard to defend against your concept because I know you are so right," I said.

"Mike, just to show you how backward your professional people are I read where your scientists have discovered that dried prunes and berries are good meat preservatives. My people were using those 5000 years ago."

Cougar grabbed his pipe and tamped in a supply of aromatic tobacco. He lighted the briar pipe and smiled in my direction. A cloud billowed up around my head. I slowed my breathing until it swirled on by.

"Thanks, friend," I said jokingly.

"Just teasing," he smiled. "Want some?" His eyes wrinkled into a grin, aware that I really did.

"No," I said.

"Mike, we knew many centuries ago that by rubbing salt on meat it was partially cured. Then by smoking it we found that formaldehyde emitted by the burning cedar halted the development of bacteria."

"What do you think of my society, generally?" I still had much to learn from this remarkable man.

"A society of extremes," he said quickly. "Those citizens are consumed by lust, greed and rage. You are being rapidly seduced into paganistic idolatry because of having looser morals, drugged minds and little self confidence. Your brains are weakened by meth-amphetamines cocaine, opium, heroin, and alcohol. Your people are being destroyed by merchants of death. They sell misery to your masses. You are obsessed with the adulation of the false idols of drunkenness, nakedness and debauchery. Yours is a society of sheep, obedient to manipulators. You claim to be creating quality life for people. How can that be when you are building too many factories, clogging roadways with monoxide-spewing fuel-guzzlers, stacking people on top of each other like maggots on a decomposing cadaver, polluting the environment, becoming addicted, giving birth to millions of toss-away babies? You are aware of the quality of life we have here in my valley, watching eagles ride the thermals, enjoying falcons in flight, abundant food, no expense for air conditioning or heating, no suffocating exhaust fumes and solitude like no other place in the world. Notice the cherry tree, there are several hummingbirds sitting side by side. I could never find another place in the world to compare."

"Amen, brother," I said.

"So be it." Cougar smiled.

"Amen," I repeated.

Cougar looked at me intently.

"Let me clarify my comments. If your country truly is where quality of life is supposed to exist, then why are there so many psychiatrists and psychologists with a constant stream of sufferers? If your nation really is providing quality of life for its citizens then why is there a big market for depression and anxiety pills? I see that as the opposite of quality life. Your prisons burgeon with hardened inmates who obviously didn't have quality life. You have people on television who fondle their crotches in sickening displays of contempt. There are many people screaming obscenities on camera for the world to hear. In America, quality of life is certainly a contradiction in fact disputed by a breakdown in social order that seems to be accelerating. You have attorneys via television, attempting to convince everybody to file a civil lawsuit against everyone else. You have televangelists preaching that if you don't alter your ways, you will go to hell. But if you send in enough money you will get a new automobile, a new house, or a high-paying job. You have scammers trying to sell overpriced gimmicks. Am I saying too much? Your divorce rate is over fifty-percent, and the primary reason for splitting-up is infidelity. Why experiment? You asked my opinion.

43

Why get married in the first place if your eyes are going to wander the next day. Marriage shouldn't be taken lightly. I think your people are suffering from mental incapacitation."

"But there are some great people in this country, proud, honest, humanitarian, predictable, and industrious, but they are being overwhelmed by hordes of corruptors, interventionists, opportunists and debauchers. The moral majority that nurtured this country since it was founded is being engulfed by an immoral minority. Unfortunately, those opposite philosophies are being reversed. We are being exposed to an avalanche of disgusting sins that would have elicited screams of outrage just a couple decades ago. I don't hear outrage anymore. "

"Perhaps I can come up with a solution for you," Cougar said

"That's why I came to find you. There is so much to be learned from your vast knowledge. My readers need to know the truth," I said.

"That is the truth," Cougar said. "This is also the truth. Famous entertainers have stopped singing and now simply jump stupidly around the stage screaming at the top of their lungs, making lewd gestures and breaking their instruments, grabbing their crotch with female singers repeatedly poking their finger at the audience as if transmitting some kind of mystical message. People with enfeebled brains consider that stomping and screaming as fantastic entertainment."

"I deplore the changes in entertainment," I said.

"Honestly, Mike, and you might not want to hear any more."

"I'm here to learn what you know, so shoot."

"Well, I truthfully believe your country is heading toward a cataclysmic end. Your liberty is in peril. You are wallowing in materialism, addicted to credit cards. Sex orgies are a disgusting way of life. Attorneys are greedy, encouraging everybody to sue everybody else so they can become wealthy in the process. You have sicko people preying online. Want me to go on?"

"I'm not sure. But, yes, go on." I needed to know.

"Your people are much too active having their brains deadened by screamers at football games, bowling, golf, basketball, hockey, soccer, boxing, races, card games, tennis, wrestling, darts, pool and other equally meaningless activities. Audiences scream too much. Why scream and cavort up and down shaking their fist as if involved in the sport. How satisfying can it be to see gladiators in a ring brutalize each other? How frequently do want to watch Hippopotamuses scattering their dung in the river? How enlightening is it to watch fishermen kissing fish they have hooked, puncturing their eyes and gills with barbed hooks while grinning at a camera, assuring that the fish will bleed to death or die from a buildup of lactic acid caused by struggling to escape death while the fishermen scream idiotic redneck inanities? What's intriguing about seeing some Aussie repeatedly duct-taping some crocodile, hearing RAP with its filth, watching Komodo dragons devouring a goat carcass, cobras spitting venom, fat people trying to get rid of fat, pathetic males discussing erectile dysfunction, mental retards spilling their guts on talk shows about their sexual transgressions, compensated shills hawking pain killers, people repossessing cars, oil rig workers fighting or oversexed housewives trying to figure out which friend's husband to screw that night, and more women advocating marriage to other females. Why the fascination for raw sewage? How many trucks do you need to watch settling through ice in the Arctic before it's no longer entertainment? They produce programs which are so insipid, so empty of interest that I wonder why any business buys advertising on them. Many of those programs are intellectually effete as if somebody employed fleas to develop their plot. The most amazing fakery is wrestling where every movement is a sham yet people sit in the arena screaming as if the scam was real. Cheering as players pour ice water on the coaches or slosh champagne all over each other boggles my mind. How can crabbing be entertaining? Producers are using the deposits in septic tanks for new material. Some of you will be nothing more than spectators in life."

"Hollywoodites could puke on themselves and there would be admirers applauding. You should remove specific words from your language; stars, legends, idols, icons, heroes, celebrities, hall of fame, super-stars, champions, debutants and all-stars. That identification sets those individuals apart from the rest of you; creating the illusion that they are superior to everybody else, when in fact many of them are not the kind of individuals with who you'd want to spend time. I hear comics mouthing dirty jokes with the audience roaring and applauding as if filthy words were the essence of cultural enlightenment."

"Some people have outhouse mentality," I said.

"Some people have outhouse morality," Cougar said.

45

"Why do so many people worship so many celebrities?"

"They have empty lives. My people had no celebrities," Cougar said.

"Your people were fortunate," I said. "I am amazed at people scrambling around sports arenas following some player to get a signature. What's wrong with admiring yourself? I would not care if the Atlanta Braves, Hawks, Falcons and others involved in hustling tickets moved to Canada. Stopping the World Series, Wimbledon, French Open, Super Bowl, U S Open, Crosby Classic, Australian Open, and Bass Masters would send shockwaves across the world but it won't cause a blip on my emotional chart. They haven't benefitted me an iota but my eyes become moist seeing grown men kissing smelly fish and trophies. I have been in the Atlanta stadium once and that was the first year it opened in 1967. I got sick of the stench of drunks and strangers screaming in my ears. I might not choose to stand up for a seventh inning stretch. I might want to stretch in the sixth or the sixteenth. I refuse to be a marionette or perform like a puppet. NASCAR should close all of the race tracks saving millions of gallons of gasoline to slow pollution. A problem with sports is that there is a winner and everyone else is a loser. I play some sports but I will not bow down to anyone who becomes a contrived hero playing a child's game. Also, I'm not prepared to buy products which some sport personality endorses, so I threw my Gillette Fusion razor in the garbage can and quit buying Buicks. If I need healing for athlete's feet I won't get Tinactin or buy a Rolex to find out what time it is, because I won't allow millionaires in the sports world influence how I spend my dollars. That's how I get even with companies trying to play with my brain. I stopped buying Kellogg's a few years ago. I can't stand being jerked around and manipulated. Rankings mean nothing to me. I do not give a damn who is ranked number one or number thirty-seven. Ranking has not made me financially secure. I don't care whose face adorns product packaging; I won't buy the product because I know it is priced higher as the result of big bucks paid for their endorsement. Someone won the Masters, so what? The Celtics had a good team, so what? Buffalo won the Super Bowl, So what? Americans are being hammered with sports of every kind to the exclusion of satisfying simplicity. I'm not going to be jerked around by promoters. Promoters and politicians have Americans so wrapped up in multiple sports that they are able to empty their victim's pockets without them becoming aware until it's too late. I prefer having hummingbirds buzzing around my head, performing aerobatics, in the solitude of my upper deck than listening to screaming fans. And my hot dog and coke costs maybe fifty cents for both. I have little appreciation or admiration for those who can afford private jets and ostentatious mansions. Recipients of national acclaim for hitting a ball or making a crappy movie defile my mind."

"You're pretty convincing, Mike," Cougar said.

"There are too many football stadiums. There are too many baseball games. There are too many tennis courts. There are too many golf matches. There too many basketball games. There are too many races. There are too many soccer games. Now we have dart games on television. We have poker games. People are brainwashed to watch rather than to do. All of that is to get into the pockets of the people and make fortunes for promoters. And people become fatter just from from sitting and watching. And then we are expected to listen to groups in a studio attempting ineffectively to be clever explaining what occurred and what should have occurred and what is expected to occur next time."

"I'd rather be canoeing on a remote river or backpacking into a wilderness rather than listening to a bunch of pseudo-experts screaming inanities. Communing with nature is better."

"There is something rejuvenating about being away from crowds," Cougar said.

"I am also not impressed with famous personalities. Who won the Masters is unimportant to me. I don't care how many times somebody won at Wimbledon or the Indianapolis 500. Some person hits home runs. Big deal! Tell me how that benefits me. Some participants make millions playing a game. So what? Why is it considered beneficial for me to see players grunting on the tennis court when they serve a ball? None of them have improved my life. If they had accomplished nothing, my lust for life would have been no different. They emit bowel gas the same as I. I'm not impressed when a player pumps his fist, snarling and spraying spittle on the court. I'm not entertained when a player wins the match then flops flat on his back, mouth agape, shrieking in ecstasy. Eisenhower did not sprawl on his back when he was elected as

President. Thomas Edison didn't do that when he invented the light bulb. The puppets watching applaud and scream as if flopping down on the court was some admirable accomplishment. I'm irritated by tennis commentators who are so marvelously observant that when a player gets up a game, astutely remark that the pendulum has swung to that player, and two points later comments that the pendulum has swung the other way, then two points later the other commentator says the pendulum has swung the other way. I'd like to watch the match quietly without all the vocal interference and I can see for myself how the match is progressing. If they would just stop saying anything, the match would be much more enjoyable. I don't understand why television commentators are there in the first place. It's as though I have no idea what's going on and need to be spoon-fed innocuous details about the game. If you want to be bored out of your mind just listen to sport commentator dialogue. "

"It's like the clever golf announcers who hazard their astute guesses about whether a player will make or miss a putt. **I think he will make that putt. Of course, he could miss it**. <u>Duh!</u> And when that player misses a critical putt they offer their pearl of wisdom, **I will bet he would like to have that putt back**. <u>Duh!</u> Commentators interfere with sports. What is wrong with being quiet and letting me quietly enjoy the game?"

"I admire your uniqueness, Mike," Cougar said. "Somewhat graphic though."

"Other programs on television that irritate me are African Safaris that film hunters hidden from animals and killing them with high-powered rifles from long distance then gawking into a camera while holding their horns, expecting everybody that views the photographs will be convinced that that man is a great hunter having exposed himself to danger when in fact all that the hunter did was to kill a defenseless creature. At one moment in time an innocent buffalo was feeding, unaware that a man was hiding behind a knoll. One micro-second later the creature was shot so its plastic eyes can gaze from the hunter's wall for everybody to ogle. *Wonderful horns*, hunter shows his guests. *Look at the size of its head*, hunter says proudly. *I suffered from sand flea bites while sneaking up on this dangerous beast.*"

"My people killed only for food," Cougar said.

"I eat what I shoot. No heads on my wall," I said.

"I see you're sympathetic with wildlife. There was a tourist attraction recently built in downtown Atlanta. Some wealthy businessman paid for a fish tank costing a reported half-billion dollars. Then they kidnapped fish and turtles from the ocean and stuck them behind glass for people to ogle 24 hours a day. It'd be like kidnapping me from my wilderness and shoving me into a glass bowl for people to stare. I'd spend 24 hours a day, walking around in circles doing nothing. I'd rather stay in my valley rather than be put on display. Those fish would probably have chosen their natural environments rather than swimming around in circles. Many of the residents living near the fish tank cannot afford an admission. Some of the fish died, probably from homesickness. That money could have fed many starving people. Traffic is now more congested downtown, too. And parking prices went up."

"I haven't been to the place yet," I said.

"When you've seen one fish tank you have seen them all," Cougar said, as he lighted his pipe.

"So what's your take on our future?" I said.

"Your people are being hustled by clever promoters into spending too much money watching games and movies that make fortunes for their clients while you perform like organ-grinder monkeys," Cougar said. "Credit card companies and banks are sucking suckers into financial quagmires, screwing them with fees, account origination fee, maintenance fee, late payment fee, low balance fee, non-usage fee, over-the-limit fee; cash advance fee, universal default fee, outstanding credit card debt fee, credit card replacement fee, convenience check fee, foreign transaction fee, duplicate statement fee, telephone payment fee, and customer service fees. Customers are getting fee'd to death."

"Can you be even more explicit?" I said, smiling. "I'm not sure I should put that remark in my book."

"Then let's get back to people being trained to sit and watch like Pavlov's dogs."

"Why not, Mike? It's the truth," Cougar said. "You are supposed to genuflect in reverence when any sports figure appears. People are expected to *ooh* and *aah* and scream with the rest of their mindless minions."

I thought about his opinion. I suddenly realized that there isn't a man who plays professionally that I cannot live without. I could not care less who wins the Masters. I don't care who won the French Open. I don't care how many home runs some stud has hit. Golfers hit balls. Baseball players hit balls. Tennis players hit balls. Great! I have not profited a dime. I don't care who was awarded the Heisman trophy. It simply guarantees that the person will become a millionaire. Baseball is boring. Watching a pitcher scratching and spitting on the mound is boring, with others players slouched in the dugout with fingers up their nose, spitting seeds. The Indianapolis 500 is a waste of vital resources, burning fuel and contaminating the earth. I bow down to no sport icon. I prefer genuine people like Jonas Salk and Harry Truman because they benefited most everyone. Charlton Heston was the most talented and charismatic character actor in Hollywood. When he portrayed Moses, Heston actually became Moses. In spite of all the showboating and hoopla, no limber-dick in Hollywood can come close to his talent.

Cougar raised his hand, looking off over a rise in the margin. Both horses suddenly reared up, whinnying loudly, hooves flailing. A large bear appeared, coming from the tree line. The Appaloosas stamped their hooves. The bruin raised and stared at us, decided the flashing hooves were too perilous then disappeared into the forest. We gentled the horses.

"So, where were we," Cougar said.

"You indicated that this nation was going to hell," I said.

"Looks that way," Cougar said. "America has become like a rudderless vessel maybe like the Titanic. I see numerous programs on television where grinning females discuss how much larger they need to have their sexual partner's prick in order to be orgasmed by intercourse. Men on the program pretend to be devastated by the smaller size of theirs. Of course, you must purchase a bottle of pills to enhance the size of your dick. The sad part of it is that gullible suckers watching that tripe actually get taken in by the scam. Poachers in Africa shoot the rhinoceros in order to grind up its horn and sell the powder as an aphrodisiac. I expect to see people here poaching sex organs from cadavers and grinding them up and selling the powder to wackos who are desperately attempting to get one more erection. I'm convinced the entrepreneurs will make a fortune. Based on gullibility, Americans appear retarded in the eyes of the rest of the world."

"I think you're right," I agreed.

"There is no limit to programs to lose weight, get rid of pimples, retard aging, hide crotch odor, stifle farts, dry up snot, become an Olympian; all of those are symptomatic of a society succumbing to delusions. Promoters are now introducing shows that are insanely dumb with nearly naked women and foul-mouthed males, shoving each other with aggressive actions, slapping the women's asses, spraying champagne, shoving people into a swimming pool, jerking their braziers off, assuming coital positions, rubbing their pubic areas together and mouthing the most nonsensical diatribe you will ever hear. It is an exhibition of wild decadence. Defying cultural norms. And that's considered entertainment."

"What do we do?" I said.

"Take your television set to curbside for garbage pickup. Or, do you prefer watching some guys fighting with owners while repossessing their car or truck? Or you can view some card shark rubbing his nose while studying the possible value of two pairs."

"Boy, you are really graphic. What else?"

"I mentioned the Titanic. The company deluded their passengers into believing that the vessel could not sink and they put an incompetent Captain in charge. A good comparison is the United States. During the 60's you experienced the massive control OPEC had on your gas pumps, long lines and high prices. You got gas-pump-shock. But you did not learn. You kept right on purchasing those extravagant gas guzzlers and look what has happened a few years later. The oil producers have you by your testicles and are squeezing them. They have the United States in a stranglehold and are bankrupting the economy while Americans are attending parties. Congress obviously has limited insight because they did not plan ahead. The Boy Scout's motto is to plan ahead so why not expect the identical mentality from people in Washington. You expect those people you elect to man the helm to competently man the helm, but like the Titanic, America has hit the proverbial iceberg and you now find gaping holes in the vessel with the USS America settling down in the water and you don't have enough life jackets on board."

"Is it that those people do not care, or are they simply inept? And what can we do?"

"Give Washington a douche and an enema, both at the same time."

"You certainly are a graphic one," I said. "After flushing the crap out of Washington, what can we do?"

Cougar appeared thoughtful for a moment. He seemed lost in thought. Petting the cougar lying at his feet, he finally said, "There were guys vying to be President of this country. For the life of me I do not understand why anyone would want the job. The candidate who lost could have won if he had announced during the campaign that, as his first act in office, he would pardon the border agents, Ignacio Ramos and Juan Alonzo Compean, who were jailed for doing the job they were hired to do, by a prosecutor who was either using drugs or was politically motivated to advance his career opportunity. He got things backward; he's supposed to jail the bad guys not the good guys. There are millions of Latinos who would have voted for the candidate who stated he would release the agents."

"We often get zealots elected to office wanting to establish their credentials," I said.

"The people trying to become President are spending money trying to discredit each other rather than using the hours to acquaint voters with their experience for the job. As it stands, neither of them are qualified to be President, according to their negative advertising. One is depicted as a crazy militarist and the other is accused of camaraderie with a despicable character who despises America. Odd bedfellows, I'd say. It isn't any wonder why so few people vote. Listening to the two candidates accuse each other of being embezzlers, of fondling little girls, of selling votes, of being consummate liars, of cheating on their taxes, of infidelity, and every other kind of negative crap, is enough the keep the voter at home. And the likelihood is that many of those accusations are unfortunately true."

"I'm getting some really great stuff. What else?" I said.

"Improve your antiquated philosophy about punishing criminals."

"What do you mean by that?"

"Since children who are victimized by pedophiles suffer life-long emotional damage execute the convicted pedophiles immediately.

Have those fork-tongued lawyers ostracized who, through hyperbole, and the deliberate distortion of fact get a psychotic pedophile released back into society to commit more rapes, and recommend procedures to have the lawyers disbarred. Restore vigilantes. They really enforce law. Reduce trials to just one week and hang those found guilty immediately. When a psycho violates the sanctity of a young body he should have his genitals tied to a stallion with his head tied to another horse, then the horses forced to gallop in opposite directions."

"God, that's brutal," I exclaimed.

"It's guaranteed to stop pedophilia." Cougar said. "Raping a child is one of the most barbaric atrocities imaginable. My people experienced those same awful crimes when the European barbarians invaded our land centuries ago,"

"Yes, it is barbaric. Victims will be emotionally disturbed their entire life after being raped. I have read about some who committed suicide. I talked with one who said she could not bathe away the memories of the brutal attack. She was fifty years old and the horror of that rape returns repeatedly when she is alone. No wonder so many rapes happen though. Females have been provocatively showing more and more of their breasts recently and with single threads in the crack of their ass while wearing g-string bikinis that brings out the bestial traits in males, who have nothing more on their minds than getting laid. Also women hang out in bars, strip-joints, cocktail lounges and flesh markets, where alcohol and drugs are consumed in quantities sufficient to cause impaired judgment, then expose themselves to males who are rapists and killers. Some of the females are nymphomaniacs and others are searching for love in the wrong places and being raped and murdered as the direct result. When alcoholics are drunk they're capable of unconscionable behavior."

"You'd think women would learn sooner or later," I said. "Apparently not, though."

"It is deeper than just learning, though," Cougar said. "Women are being commercially exploited while allowing themselves to be demeaned to market merchandise. Female meat is promoted the same as Sani Flush and Tidy Bowl."

"Magazines display female bodies in nude poses. Nudity brings attention to products and in the process arouses prurient instincts in most men. Males ogling exposed tits bulging out of dresses, seeing cleavage down to pubic areas, and the cracks of asses, will have thoughts of rape. Exposing outrageous nakedness at swimming pools encourage rapists. I know when female bodies are exposed, with alcohol limiting inhibition, rape occurs. Alcohol, drugs and nudity cause rapes. Women think they can associate in that environment with men, tempting suggestively, teasing, then cease when they decide to. Sexually aroused drunks will become savage killers and rapists. They will rape, and murder and continue to rape their dead victims, even sodomizing the corpse. That is bestiality at its disgusting worst... It's caused by women's' pants and shorts down to where their pubic bone is exposed, shaved crotches and strings in the cracks of their ass instead of swimsuits. When will women learn that flaunting nakedness is insanity and that it unhinges warped minds and warped minds find bestiality pleasurable? Even standing in line at the checkout counters in grocery stores you are exposed to magazines with pictures of women with their tits bulging out. Their crotch and nipples may be covered but they might as well be naked. Commercials on television show scantily dressed females demonstrating Rube Goldberg contraptions for weight loss. A normal male can't help but be sexually excited when sweating female meat is practically naked. Change channels to find more nakedness, with groups of females twisting and turning like they were in orgiastic ecstasy. Cameras focus in on tits and crotches. It's like the red-light whorehouse districts throughout the world. Cultured females are embarrassed by the nakedness of those slatterns. The beauty contests, Miss America, Miss World, Mrs. America, and Miss Teen-age America are venues to display practically undressed female bodies for every sex-maniac on earth to ogle. Drunken nudity on beaches contributes to the decline in morals. Imagine how many sex-addicts masturbate while staring at the nearly naked tits and crotches of massed females, envisioning him screwing all of them."

"I'm almost sorry I asked," I said.

"Commercials now depict men having to piss every few minutes. However, they can buy a pill and stop the problem. Women, at a much younger age, are apparently leaking urine for there is a diaper being hustled so they can take a leak in the diaper and keep on playing tennis. The world has amazingly changed since my people were here."

"You worry me, Cougar," I said. "How do you know so much?"

"My mind isn't cluttered with tripe. I meditate. You people stay in constant motion, racing from one unimportant thing to another unimportant thing, never slowing enough to enjoy the really rewarding things in life."

"I slow down all the time to reflect on the past, to see if my life is really fulfilled and headed in the right direction."

"You're the exception," Cougar said. "Now let me ask you a couple questions, okay?"

"I'm supposed to be the interviewer," I said. "But go ahead."

"I am aware of several activities in which you are involved. From what you've said you don't seem to be a spectator, with your life dependent on sports and movie idols as it is with so many people, right?"

"True," I agreed.

"If Follywood was consumed by flames and all of the artificiality incinerated would your life be lessened in any way?"

"You mean Hollywood?" In my opinion Hollywoodites appear superficial: saltwater tits, nose jobs, capped teeth, perfumed crotches, you name it. Little is what it seems to be. I would not give you a nickel for an Oscar or Emmy award. Award extravaganzas go on where millions of dollars are wasted on show-boating while millions of kids are always hungry in this prosperous nation. I recall one story about Hollywood kids at a party. One asked another how he liked his daddy. When the other kid asked why he was so interested, the boy said that that he had not liked him when he had him as his daddy the previous weekend. They sometime swap-out husbands overnight. That ambience in Hollywood shows a marked degradation of our culture."

"I really do mean Follywood. Again, if Follywood disappeared would you be stressed out, your life effete, and you emotionally disjointed?"

"If you mean the absence of sports and movies, no, my life would stay the same, because neither of those entities improves my life. I won't accept being manipulated by promoters. I look at the fantasy in Follywood as you call it and I wonder why people allow themselves to be taken in by super-hype unless they are born just to be adulators of fakery. Those people pass gas and leave skid marks the same as we common folk except their farts escape through I Magnin's silk panties and Rodeo Drive Designer shorts. They have hemorrhoids, just like we common people. I wonder, as they are swiveling into the Academy Awards, which ones have genital infections. For generations women remained clean because of the fear of unwanted pregnancies. Birth control pills unlatched Pandora's Box and females began hanging out in clubs and becoming flirtatious in their search for a relationship. That contributed to a spread of sexually transmitted diseases. People, who are involved with multiple sexual partners, will inevitably become the carrier of crotch disease. I see immorality glorified in Hollywood. They produce babies' out-of-wedlock and pretend something wondrous has occurred. We need to return to fidelity or we are going to hell in a hurry."

"You're a perceptive man. Mike. You are unusual for a paleface. You could qualify as a Shaman with the Nez Perce." Cougar smiled, reaching for his pipe once again.

"Remember I'm four times your visual age." I said. "I've developed a lot of insight in eighty-four years."

"But you are really different," he said.

"In what way?"

"As you know, I can read the mind of anyone. I was in a paleface church a few years ago and was curious as to what palefaces ask for in their prayers. I was surprised. Some older men were on their knees praying and I was curious so I intercepted a prayer from one of them. I expected him to be praying for the world's salvation and food and health for the people. Instead I was astounded. His prayer was avid; *God, I have been a dutiful adherent to your teachings. I have tithed abundantly, and have never taken your name in vain. I have practiced the Old Golden Rule and I might have sullied a commandant or two, for which I am humbly repentant. Please, dearest Lord, I beseech you, please grant me one more opportunity to get into my computer, and open my treasury of pornography so that I might spend time with my naked children, and I will remain your faithful follower, forever. Amen.* That is sorrowfully indicative of the direction your people have taken," Cougar said.

"Is it okay if I'm a little agnostic?"

"I like people who are who they are," he said

"My cathedral is on a wild river, somewhere away from the fakery of this make-believe crap."

"You're a lot better off out in the wilderness than being involved in contemporary society. You're better off right here. Sanity prevails here. Some time ago I considered associating with palefaces without them knowing about my past. I read extensively so I would be more knowledgeable about the foibles with which you contend. One fact I fortunately discovered was that intimate relationships between women and men are fraught with deadly danger. Enough that it caused me to quickly reconsider."

"What happened," I said. "What fact?"

"In wildlife Mother Nature allows association among animals of different genders. Animals do not become sexually involved however until it is time to reproduce. So that occurs for example with the grizzly about every two years. Among humans sexual involvement is excessive and as a result sexually transmitted diseases are killing billions of people all over the world."

"I have read the figures on AIDS. And syphilis used to be a real destroyer of humans. I knew one wealthy banker from back home who would leave our town and go to Florida on vacation several times a year. He would acquire the services of hookers, often three or four at the same time. His Florida vacation was devoted to disgusting debauchery. He died at fifty years of age ravaged by syphilis. His mind failed and his physical appearance was appalling, sores, pustules, eyes rheumy, mouth drooling, hands shaky. I saw him a week before he died. I didn't recognize the man. Can you imagine how many other men those hookers have infected? And syphilis is on the increase again with unhealthy sexual practices."

"That's terrible but there is even worse conditions. Sexual relations today is like playing Russian roulette," Cougar said. "There are over a dozen sexually transmitted diseases and with promiscuity on the rise, and with your liberal, 'I have to get laid now', lifestyles the future of your society is precarious."

"AIDS and syphilis. What others that I don't know about?"

"I'll just give you a run down of what I learned. Plagues of syphilis alone have been responsible for million of the world's crippled, blind, insane and dead. Obviously, your banker included. AIDS will surpass the devastation of syphilis. Gonorrhea infection in the blood associated with birth canals causes blindness in babies being born. Chancroids are painful lesions and are spread by unhygienic sex practice.

"Genital herpes is incurable and sexually transmitted. Hepatitis B causes jaundice and liver enlargement. Protozoan Trichmoniasis is a frothy, odorous greenish-yellow discharge, causing itching of the genitals. Symptoms are usually absent in males yet they can transmit that disease to their sexual partners. Fungal candidiasis causes intense genital itching, a thick curd-like, whitish discharge, inflamed dry vagina and inflammation of the vulva genital area."

"I think you should stop. I've never heard of those diseases. It sure kills the idea of fun-time."

"Monogamy prohibits the advance of sexually transmitted diseases. Promiscuity advances the diseases. That's why it's like Russian roulette. Keep pulling that trigger and you will definitely catch something, probably fatal."

"I knew some guys in the navy that caught the clap in cathouses overseas."

"There are many more venereal problems; pubic lice, genital scabies, Chlamydia trachomatis, granuloma inguinale, yeast infection, Gardnerella vaginitis, lymphogran uloma venereum, shigellosis…"

"Will you stop? Please."

"It's beyond belief that an orifice in the female anatomy that is intended by Mother Nature to be used for the propagation of the race has been promoted beyond recognition to where it now is used for every conceivable promotional gimmick everywhere from odor suppressors to expensive yachts."

"Cougar, please. You make my skin crawl with your analysis. Will you stop?"

"Sure. But some advice, Mike. Condoms don't protect you from venereal diseases. Fool around long enough and you'll have it. Sexual diseases are transmitted by both males and females. Women just have a more secretive cavity in which to grow the little bugs. At the rate people are infecting each other everyone in the world will be dead. Ladies have a jewel between their legs. Promiscuous females have a conduit for the elimination of noxious wastes."

"If I were single I would remain celibate. I've had the same wife for forty years."

"You should keep it that way," Cougar said. "One other thing. You should tell your friends who have uncontrollable hormones that I saw a doctor's report indicating that he is seeing a huge increase in men patients who have pustule chancres and lesions in their mouths. That's from what's called oral sex. And that can be the beginning of a terrible death. Men have to be retarded to do that."

"Why does society accept promiscuity as healthy, when it is so damned unhealthy?"

"Prostitution is out of control. Your streets are filled with women trying to survive by any means. It's sad. Whores will have intimate contact everyday with any amount of males. The uncleanliness of that contact assures the spread of diseases. There is no way of keeping tabs on that scourge. With birth control pills normally chaste females began screwing promiscuously like men so the scourge is doubling now."

"After the invasion of Southern France was over and the Germans were in full retreat northward I was assigned to Marseilles with a patrol of Shore Patrol. Our job was to pull American military personnel out of the cathouses. Venereal diseases were destroying our ability to conduct the war. I checked records of some of the harlots. Some screwed as many as forty males each day, four an hour for ten hours. Many were infected with virulent diseases. Imagine those who got the diseases taking the diseases home to their wives and girlfriends or husbands. I like Mother Nature's policy. Sex is for propagating the species."

"Getting laid has become an obsession with your people," Cougar said.

"Homosexuals are most at risk but some of them also engage in heterosexual behavior and so the diseases spread like wildfire. When people have one-night stands neither one knows who's infected so it's kinda' like shooting craps. The probability of boxcars or snake-eyes is always there."

"It's either that they are stupid or just don't give a damn," I said. "Screw now, worry later."

"So, I take it you aren't impressed by Follywood's imprudent practices," Cougar said.

"Right on."

"So, I guess you're really a true individualist. Welcome to my world," Cougar said.

"One other question," he said. "Who's going to win the World Series this year?"

"I have no idea who's playing," I said.

Cougar grinned. "And neither do I."

We clasped hands, smiling, in a show of mutual admiration.

"Let's get something for dinner," Cougar said

Chapter Ten

I have dined in several of the great restaurants in the United States. No one prepares food with the taste of wild Canadian geese out in the wilderness eaten with a remarkable Indian by the name of Cougar, and a huge cougar gulping scraps. Now that is real atmosphere. The cougar wrapped itself around my legs then stretched. I saw its talons. I hoped we had become friends. Hesitantly, I rubbed his ears. He stared up at me with mysterious eyes then began to purr. I had apparently made a friend. Thankfully.

Up to that moment, I had been enormously impressed with the depth of thought the Indian had obviously given to critiquing the descendants of the Europeans who had cruelly destroyed the indigenous way of life which had thrived on this land for several centuries, a simplistic way of life but one that was workable, without polluting the environment beyond resurrection, as contemporary knuckleheads seem to be doing, without a major fragmentation of the pattern of consideration for the rights of others to exist and remain independent. During those thousands of years prior to the paleface incursions and conquest of the land the people maintained a good relationship with their neighbor with consideration and understanding that conflict was the formula for eventual societal destruction.

Cougar lighted another pipe. He blew three rings of blue smoke in my direction. It smelled good. I figured he was getting sweet revenge for the transgressions of my ancestors. I was envious. "From the look of envy on your face I have the impression that you would enjoy smoking again," he said.

I decided Cougar really was clairvoyant. "Yup," I said. Then, immediately, I said, "Nope."

"If you'd move here, away from the carbon monoxide and diesel fumes that's killing millions of people in your congested areas you could smoke again, as I do."

We moved back from the ledge. Nature took over the job of cleaning up as ravens and rodents attacked the last few scraps. The mountain lion moved aside.

Understanding that I only had a few days remaining to ask several important questions, I said, "Cougar---." He interrupted me.

"Before we continue the interview I have something I'd like to show you," he said. He put his fingers to his mouth and sounded a shrill whistle. From down the ravine his mare trotted and as he had predicted, followed by my stallion. "I told you. That's nature." He grinned.

The Indian took me to a grotto hidden behind a big boulder at the headwaters of the stream. He pulled back on the rock. Extending his hand inside the opening, he got a handful of shiny gold nuggets. They glistened. I got a covetous feeling immediately. It was a fortune.

"These came from this stream many years ago. If prospectors had discovered this mother-lode my valley would now be a large wasteland. They would have come to this place in hordes, cutting down trees and digging in the ground until only a pile of rubble remained. I decided to hide the ruination of mankind. If I had been like most palefaces I would have taken this gold out into your world and bought a mansion and several gas-guzzling chariots. I would have invested in the stock market and worried about the ups and downs affecting my bullion. I would have begun spending my fortune on expensive cuisine. I would have gotten a big gut and arteries clogged with cholesterol and likely had mental breakdowns associated with money. I would have hired psychiatrists to help me keep my sanity. I would have obtained too many credit cards. I would have met over-sexed women, engaging in daily sex orgies. Like other studs I would have deposited my sperm in every crotch I could seduce. I would have taken vacations to exciting places with attractive females and caught several virulent genital diseases which would have damaged my brain and ravaged my body. Like everybody else, I would've embarked on buying binges spending prodigious amounts of money. I would have coveted the gold and looked with disdain on the peasantry around me, but to make me feel good I would have donated money to charities, not enough to lower my extravagant lifestyle but just enough to be able to smile piously on the masses. Instead, I hid the root of all evil from ever being found. I like simplicity. It's best."

"Boy, can you make a point," I said. I was tempted to sneak one nugget for my wife.

Cougar grinned. "I know what you just considered. I can read your thoughts, you know." He handed me a golden nugget. "For Pat," he said.

I continued the questions.

"I'm curious about a situation that occurred out in California during the trial of O. J. Simpson. I am one who believes he was guilty and that the result was a travesty of justice. What is your opinion?"

"That's easy. I've read the transcript of the trial and I'm convinced the prosecutors were inept."

"In what way?" I said.

"They blew the summation. If I had been prosecuting the case instead of permitting myself to be bogged down with mind-numbing data on DNA, I would have emphasized facts. That glove was soaked in blood. Any idiot knows leather shrinks as it dries so during that charade of the defendant trying to put on the glove the prosecutors said nothing. When the design of a unique shoe came up where the shoe was recognized as one of a few sold in California, one of which was bought by the defendant, the prosecutor said nothing. There was the defendant's blood, smeared on the gate near the victim's home, with drops leading to the defendant's bedroom. The split-tongue lawyers were able convince a simple-minded jury that the officers mishandled evidence and wanted the defendant convicted for a reason which was never fully explained, Finally, the inept prosecutors were blind-sided by the introduction of *the inflammatory word* by one of O J's fork-tongued lawyers. Unfortunately that witness was short a fuse in his fuse box and blew the case when he denied having used *the word* when everyone knows most everyone has said *that word*. It is like my people being called savages when the only moments we were savages was when defending our wives from being raped, our children from being killed, our lodges from being set on fire, our crops from being destroyed, and our homeland and horses from being taken by real savages. If I had been prosecuting that case the defendant would be on death row. If that crime had occurred during my youth the butcher would have been dead by the next day. Your people coddle criminals too much. Also, that jury got confused by the mind numbing scientific explanations of DNA and made a mistake. Juries aren't infallible. A forked-tongue attorney can do a snow-job on a jury and have guilty people acquitted. That is what happened in this case. Four slick lawyers were able to mesmerize a puppet-minded jury and permit the murderer back on the street."

Four days visiting with the dynamic Native American was definitely one of the rewarding times of my life. I have met many famous people, including Ernest Hemingway. Hemingway was the closest kindred spirit to Cougar that I have known. Ever since I played with my brother near to two Potawatomi burial mounds back in Indiana I have thought about major travesties committed on those, whom I have learned to respect, who were annihilated by soldiers of the 7th cavalry. On my travel into the wilderness to get information about Early Americans to use in writing I have met the descendants of the stalwart people who nurtured the land for 10,000 years before the arrival of Europeans. My friend personified the nobility of a regrettable era in paleface history.

"How would you like to go back two-hundred years in time and visit with my family as they were in 1819? We would see my village, before the 7th cavalry came. Visit with my mother and father. Find my brother. See my brother and father build a birch bark canoe. Learn how unsavage my people really were."

"How can we do that?"

"Remember, the Great Spirit gave me unique powers."

"And me?"

"Yes, when you are with me."

"Do we take the horses and the cougar?"

"No, they'll be fine here. I've left them before."

"How long will we be gone?"

"A coupla' days," Cougar said.

As we descended the mountain across the territory that at one time was the land of the Nez Perce people, we passed villages along the

Lochna and Selway rivers slowly settling down to where those rivers became the Clearwater. The terrain was different than I had seen just four weeks earlier. Trackless forests mantled the hills and valleys. Enormous herds of bison grazed the hills. Wildlife roamed. Following down the Clearwater we passed several villages. Cougar waved welcome. I marveled at how friendly the waves were. On occasion a villager called to Cougar by name. There were no roads or towers. I saw none of the commercial blight I had seen on my way from Lewiston up the mountains. It was as if the world had gone back in time.

Cougar pointed to one village below. "That's where the Lewis & Clark Expedition came across in 1805. They were hungry and had scurvy and dysentery and were ill. Twisted Hair, Chief of the Nez Perce people, was sorry for the explorers and gave them food. He did it for the main reason that a Shoshone girl was with them. Her name was Sacagawea. She had a baby. After the expedition the favor proved to be an enormous mistake. It was the beginning of the end for our way of life."

We continued on down the Clearwater. Four Nez Perce were constructing a weir below rapids. It would be filled with Chinook and silver salmon upon completion. Between the occasional compound was a rugged wilderness with only a trail visible between the two. Up two tributaries moose and elk grazed. A cougar leaped from a dense thicket in pursuit of a young moose. Off in the distance a storm was forming, dark clouds roiling, moving up the valley. A light shower of chilly rain began.

"My village is just ahead," Cougar said.

As we moved over Cougar's village I could see cedar lodges and Tule teepees extending along the margin and on up around a bend in the river. People were busy tending the garden near the village. Flowers bloomed in profusion in a meadow. In a fire pit I could see meat roasting on a spit. It was a busy scenario. Children scampered down a hillside. Down the margin two figures were busily constructing a birch bark canoe.

"That is my father and brother," Cougar said. "They are building a canoe for me to celebrate my acceptance into the Counsel of Elders."

"I thought you used dugouts."

"My father hunted one year with the Iroquois where the Great Lakes are located. Those people in that part of the country had learned that the canoe handled more easily than our dugouts. He brought that idea back with him and our people were beginning to change."

"Will we visit with your parents, Cougar?"

Again Cougar pointed. "The woman in the tan ermine skirt and capelet is my mother."

"What is she doing?" I said.

"She's teaching the young girls how to prepare deer hides as blankets, scraping the sinews from the hide and tanning the leather."

I noticed that he had avoided my question. "Are we going to visit with them?"

"For a number of years I came back and visited with the people you see below, as they were a day before the annihilation of the entire population, by the soldiers. Three hundred Nez Perce were killed that day. It became more troubling each time I visited knowing that my family is dead and will always be dead and for what, a few hundred acres of land?"

"I would like to meet your family," I said.

Cougar continued to look down, his eyes focused on his brother and father at work on the birch bark canoe.

"It will be doubly painful after so long," he said.

I saw tears forming in Cougar's eyes. I remembered that death notification, when my brother was killed in Bastogne. "Maybe we'd better not," I said.

"No. I think it's time again."

We lowered down to the bank where the two Indians were busy with the canoe. One more canoe drifted nearby, tied to a sapling.

They looked up simultaneously. Grins spread over their faces. They reached for Cougar's hand and embraced him. I stood and smiled. The young Indian was an exact replica of Cougar, the same ebony eyes, the same wide shoulders.

Cougar turned to me. "I would like you to meet my father, Greybeard and my brother, Hunter."

I immediately sensed for whom the second canoe was being constructed. I extended my hand to each. "I am delighted to meet such talented craftsmen," I said.

Cougar's father was an impressive Indian, strong hands, stalwart, sunbaked, handsome, ruddy complexion, with eyes the color of obsidian, the same glistening black hair as his son's.

"I'm pleased to meet you," I said.

"Any friend of Cougar is welcome."

"Beautiful canoe," I said.

"It's steady even on fast water," Greybeard said, a look of pride on his face. "One canoe is for Cougar and the other is for Hunter. They'll be the envy of the race next week. I glanced at Cougar. He motioned me to one side.

"They are not aware they'll be dead tomorrow," he said. I could see the pain in his eyes. "The race was to be held in two more moons. Everybody was killed the next day. No one remained alive to know I survived. They think it is still 200 years ago. You see why it is so painful?"

My heart went out to Cougar. "We had better go," I said.

"First, I want you to meet a beautiful woman." We walked up into the compound.

Cougar's mother was bent over deer hides. She was removing drying sinew from the inside of the skin. She turned toward us at the sound of our approach. She was an exquisite woman, wearing an ermine capelet over her matching skirt. There was one rose in her hair. It was pure white. Her eyes were the color of pewter, flecked with silver dots. Her nose was finely chiseled. She smiled as she arose to hug her son.

"Mother, this is Mike, my friend. My mother's name is Morning Dove," Cougar said.

"Welcome, Mike." Her smile was warm. She reminded me of my mother.

"We are having ptarmigan and venison stew for dinner," she said. "Will you stay?"

"I like venison," I said. "We have whitetail deer from where I came," I said. "I tasted ptarmigan one time in Canada. Wonderful bird. Tasty. Never as a stew though."

"Where do you live?" Her smile was radiant.

"A place called Georgia," I said.

"Where is that, Mike?"

"Along the East Coast. Warmer climate than here," I said.

"I have never been there but my sister married a Shawnee Indian. They live in a region called Indiana."

"I was born in Indiana," I said.

"We'll be back shortly," Cougar said. He motioned for me to follow, tugging my sleeve.

"I cannot take it anymore, aware that my mother will be killed in one day and I can do nothing about it. We must leave now."

We turned. "I'm glad you came, Mike. Now you know what wonderful people my people were, contrary to the Hollywood portrayal of Indians. You have a history of men whom your people idolized, Bill Cody, Kit Carson, and George Custer. You read about them as great heroes. I know them as those killers of my people. Bill Cody acquired the name of Buffalo Bill Cody by killing the buffalo on which my people depended for food. After trains began crisscrossing the prairie passengers shot buffalos from the windows as sport. They left the dead carcasses for the scavengers. At one time one hundred million buffalo thundered across these vast prairies, unimpeded by fences, as far as the eye could see. Suddenly they were gone."

"Unfortunately, rampant killing is the history of the world," I said.

"I would let the crazies kill each other if they must," Cougar said. "They've been at it since the beginning of time."

"We seem to have been appointed as the defenders of the world. We have troops spread much too thin; Europe, Korea, Afghanistan, Iraq and other places where lunatics are killing each other."

"You have even more problems. You people constantly boast about defeating the Russians during the cold war. If I were responsible for the safety of the United States I would keep an eye on Russia. They have found some of the largest oil reserves in the world, and now your friends in NATO are dependent on Russia for a larger percentage of their needs. Those are your allies. You proclaim the United States as the most powerful nation on earth. I wouldn't be so vocal. You might remember that dinosaurs were the most powerful creatures on earth, and look what happened to them."

We took one last look at Cougar's village below. "The thrill of killings and torture was instilled in Britishers early in life," I said. "The London Tower was built in the 12th century just to torture and murder anyone that disagreed with the ruling party. There was a dungeon in the basement of the Tower where torture was committed on a massive basis. The victims were chained to racks and their bodies stretched until their arms broke loose from their torsos. Iron masks were placed on a victim's, heads with screws tightened until the victim's brains oozed out from their eyeholes. Thousands were tortured. By the time the English invaded this land they were indoctrinated to kill. The Spanish and Portuguese were equally ruthless killers."

"I wonder why it is so," Cougar said.

"I watched you suffering during the visit," I said.

"I loved my family," he said.

"I, too, lost my only brother in a war I neither saw coming or wanted."

"Tell me about your brother," Cougar said.

"It's painful, much like I felt your pain when visiting your family."

"The pain remains the same. I learned to cope. I had to cope," Cougar said.

"Two weeks before General McAuliffe said nuts to the Germans in The Battle of the Bulge on December 19, 1944 my brother was killed by a German 88. I lost my fishing buddy, who was also my friend. Johnny was a Sergeant in the 101st Airborne Division, and two years older than I but not twenty-one when he died."

"At that moment I was in the Mediterranean aboard an amphibious craft. We had just returned to Sicily after the invasion of Southern France. V-mail was our way of communicating during the war and mail was often as much as three months late but his messages were uplifting at times when my spirit was being hammered. He joked about me floating around in bathtubs. I told him it was funny to jump out of perfectly good airplanes. Often he would ask if I had learned anything yet about China."

"Johnny had a craze about Asia, with an emphasis on China. He knew about the Boxer Rebellion and the Opium War. He'd get a world map and show me the Great Wall of China and the Yangtze River. Johnny knew lots of stuff including the fact that were more Chinese people than any other nationality on earth. I knew my brother was the smartest brother in the world."

"I could find fishing worms by digging near the creek where the cows grazed and locate crawfish before the raccoons got them."

"He used his knowledge against me all the time. When I killed the first squirrel he would invariably ask me some question about China to show me I was not so great. When I held my breath under water longer than he, Johnny would ask me to explain what years the Yuan Dynasty ruled China. He would smirk when I didn't know the answer."

"There is a distinct advantage to being smarter. You always get to decide stuff. Like wolves, Johnny and I established our pecking order early. When Johnny was the Cowboy I had to be an Indian and be killed. When he was the General I had to be a private. That did not bother me because I had the smartest General in the world. I understood that when we grew up he would be a Sheriff and I would be his Deputy, which was okay with me."

"It seemed when living was difficult during the Great Depression we could depend on each other. Many dads during the 30's were hitching rides on railroad cars going to cities like Chicago and Gary trying to find work. We felt sorry for dad because he wasn't able to go fishing with us. Survival was hard for him. When the time came when we could have gone fishing, my brother and I were in the war somewhere in Europe."

"In spite of rugged times, our futures seemed assured until the smart half of our team went down in killing panzer-tank fire in the Battle of the Bulge."

"My brother and I made youthful plans during the mid-30's, in a coal-mining town in Indiana, during those times when the union kept miners out on strikes until there was little money for food. The Great Depression was in full swing. My brother had a talent for innovation that emerged early in our life when it was needed most which permitted us to survive even in tough times."

"By the time I was eight and Johnny was ten we helped in our grandfather's garden and raided the woods for walnuts and hickory nuts, with mushrooms in the spring and hazelnuts and blackberries in the fall. We'd set box traps that produced rabbits all year long. Frequently we cleaned a rabbit and sold it to a teacher who was one of the few people that had money. We could buy more rifle shells. We gigged frogs in a slough and seined turtles and fish in creeks and ponds."

"After the plowing was done we could saddle up two old horses and go into the woods and live off the land day and night for a couple of weeks. We took fishing poles and single shot Springfield rifles. We lived on fish and squirrel and sometime we stole some watermelons and a couple ears of corn from a nearby farm. We cooked our meals in a rusty bucket."

"We climbed gnarled vines that tangled up high in the canopy and gave Tarzan's yell as we swung over the pond and let go, plunging buck-naked into the old swimming hole. We slept up in the boughs of big old oak trees."

"'Liberty' magazine was a major publication when we were young."

"Johnny read where a leather dealer in Terre Haute wanted to buy furs and hides. We knew where foxes and muskrat could be trapped. We knew about beaver dams. We knew where wild minks lived. We stayed away from the swamp, said to be the home of a panther although only the town drunks had seen it. The rest of us heard scary screams sometime at night."

"We hitchhiked to Terre Haute and spoke with the skin merchant. He sold us some traps and taught us how to set them. By the time I was eleven we were checking traps every morning before school. We got a quarter for a muskrat pelt and one dollar for a beaver. If we got a mink it was worth four dollars. Johnny took care of the money explaining that he was our accountant even though I wasn't sure what that meant."

"Maybe our trapping and hunting together when we were young was the reason I devoted forty years in the fur business. Over the years, when cutting and sewing a fur garment, I would pretend Johnny was helping me. Invariably, I would create a work of art."

"I guess Johnny teased me about floating around in bathtubs in the Navy to get even for the fact that I always caught the biggest fish when we were young."

"He also got even by asking me a question about China that he knew I couldn't answer. I didn't think it was important. With his keen intellect and my luck with a rifle, the Great Depression was not that difficult."

"Sometimes, late at night, when memories flood in unannounced, I get up and get the box from the shelf in my office and take out his Bronze Stars and two Purple Hearts. I polish them. I read the letter from President Roosevelt and I feel the Screaming Eagle patch. I study a picture of his young face and I wonder if he knew his death was imminent and if he felt lingering pain. With my eyes blurred, I put his mementos back in the box. I go back to bed and stare at nothing with tears running down my cheeks and dawn still long hours away."

"I still spent time fishing, with less enthusiasm. The pain was always there and sometimes I would feel a close presence and often an unexplained question would pop up in my mind like what is the Capitol of Mongolia? I would ponder for moment then find myself saying that I didn't give a darn about Mongolia. Then it was hard to tie on a hook through misted vision."

"I retired in 1991 at the age of sixty-four. It occurred to me that my brother would have been sixty-six and maybe President of the United States, although Johnny always seemed much smarter than that. More than likely he'd have headed up some University. I decided to take up fishing, and write adventure stories about my experiences. Instead of bass and crappies, I often spent weeks in the Canadian wilderness catching pike, trout, char and muskellunge."

"On my vacation one year I went to a remote river in Western Ontario. It is the home of Muskies in sizes that will make you stare in disbelief. I caught ten Muskies, including three at over thirty pounds. I knew Johnny would have been proud of me."

"Sleep was elusive my last night there. I took a canoe out and canoed a few miles downriver. I lifted my paddle and drifted. The silence was peaceful. I thought about how our plans had been radically altered, and how reality was so different than our teenage dreams. I lay on my back gazing at the heavenly panorama in the vista which my brother had explained to me fifty-some years ago."

"The Big Dipper was still there. The moon was full and looked the same. Even though I could not see it I remembered that Johnny had told me Haley's Comet would travel back around about now. The spectrum was like a dome of precious jewels, reaching from horizon to horizon, and perhaps to infinity. I figured Johnny knew I was there, wishing he were with me."

"Echoing across the tundra I heard the howls of timber wolves possibly foretelling the death of a moose or another of wildlife's wonders. A snow owl on silent wings ghosted between the moon and me. Loons exchanged haunting messages from upriver. A swirling bank of fog enveloped my canoe."

"I drifted off to sleep. In the darkness Johnny came out of the vapor and into the canoe with me. Our embrace was long and tender. I wanted it to never end. I felt the love and respect I had for him from a long time ago. I held a hand that I had not held in fifty years. I saw the same smile and blue eyes I'd looked into with awe as we became teenagers. He asked me if I knew anything about China."

"I explained that China had a land area of 3,691,500 square miles including Taiwan and Tibet. I told him their population was well over a billion and that they were from Tungus, Chinese, Mongolian, and Turkish ethnic origins. I said their capitol was Beijing and that Shanghai had twelve million people."

"I wanted so desperately to impress my brother information just kept gushing out. He stopped me and said. "I'll be darned, my little brother finally got even with me, didn't you?" I told him I had attended college because I wanted to be as smart as him."

"My finest Muskie rod, with the tip bouncing, appeared in his hands. He was engaged with a large fish. I watched the scene unfold. He was the master angler practicing the art of catching a trophy fish. He lifted the Muskie into the boat. It had to be a world record. He grinned that same crooked grin I remembered from our youth."

"You were right little brother." Johnny said. "China isn't that important. Catching the biggest fish is what counts."

I smiled, "I'll be darned, and you just had to get even again didn't you?" He said he had learned the technique so he could catch a fish bigger than mine."

"I awakened with the sun coming over the top of the trees and felt a kink in my neck. I glanced across the river and realized I was alone. I couldn't explain that feeling that came over me, but I knew, somehow, I had been fishing with Johnny again."

"Fog lingered a few feet from my canoe. I spoke aloud to a vaguely discernable figure and I thanked him for fishing with me. I said I wanted him to go with me again, very soon. Slowly, my brother faded away."

"For some moments I had to keep my eyes closed to hold back fifty years of pent-up emotions. After a while I knew it wasn't possible. The dike ruptured."

"Later I returned to the lodge to the smell of frying bacon. I was hungrier than I had been in five decades."

I saw a grown man crying.

"I felt the same way when I saw your family," I said. "But with those powers the Great Spirit granted you why don't you just bring your family back to life?"

"The Great Spirit is wiser than that," Cougar said.

"What do you mean?" I said

"The Great Spirit loves everyone equally. He shows no preference. So, if he allowed my family to come back he would have to permit every family that had died to come back. My people have been on this land for 14, 000 years. That's 56,000 generations. Before Columbus arrived there were 18 million of us living here. That means that 1 trillion, 8 billion of my people have lived and died here. Mike, you and I know Mother Earth can not support even 10 billion people. We've talked about it earlier, so you see how impossible your suggestion is in spite of the Great Spirit's power."

"You did those multiplication figures in your head?" I said.

"Of course," Cougar said.

"Are there any of your people that you admire above others?" I said.

"Yes. Nez Perce Chief Joseph. Sioux Chief Red Cloud. Sioux Chief Sitting Bull. Crazy Horse. Suquamish Chief Seattle, Cochise, Geronimo, Osceola, Pontiac, Quanah Parker, Sequoya. Mike, I could sit here for days tolling the names of great Indians. You listed all of them in your last book. Do you have any heroes among your people?"

"A few. My only brother is my #1 hero. Johnny would have been 21 years old in January when he was killed December 19, 1944, in the Battle of the Bulge. As kids on the farm in Indiana I always knew Johnny would become a paratrooper because he was always jumping out of somewhere: the apple trees, the hay maw, the roof of the barn. He was joyful when jumping from the highest limb of the oak tree into the creek below."

"Sixty-five years later when I still see heroes departing the airport for the Mid-East I think of Johnny. I walk through the shopping malls and see military personnel having a meal. I walk over and extend my hand and thank them for what they are doing and tell them that I was doing the same thing in the Mediterranean in World War Two. I notice their looks of appreciation. We become kindred spirits. When standing in line, waiting for my order, I sometime pay for their lunch."

"I know a man who has macular degeneration. You can't tell that six decades ago the man was flying fighter aircraft into combat in the Pacific. He is one of my heroes. True heroes are found, not on golf courses or baseball diamonds, or race tracks nor in Hollywood, but in nursing homes and veteran's hospitals or streaming through airport concourses on their way to or from zones of danger. Heroes wear firefighter and police gear. Those nurses that tended to the wounded on D-Day are my heroes. Rosie the Riveter was my hero. Heroes are parents who dutifully nurture their kids through troubled times. Heroes are those teachers who endure the restrictions of a dysfunctional system. Heroes are the FBI. Heroes are Border Patrol. I have never seen a hero on a football nor baseball diamond. Doctor Jonas Salk and Harry Truman are heroes. Heroes are those rare people worthy of emulation."

"When finding some military medals at a flea market, I worried about what would happen to my brother's medals after I'm gone. Upon visiting the museum of the 101st Airborne at Fort Campbell, KY, I designed a shadow box, constructed from eternal wood, and placed my brother's Purple Hearts, Bronze Stars, his dog tags, his paratrooper insignia pins, a yellowed letter from Franklin Roosevelt and offered it to the curator at the Don F Pratt museum, on base at Fort Campbell. My gesture was accepted. Now, my number one hero is featured in the Battle of the Bulge Pavilion at the 101st Airborne Division museum. True heroes are born, not created by publicity agents or promotional stunts."

Chapter Eleven

With a couple days remaining before I needed to go back, I had gleaned valuable information for finishing my 3rd book on Native Americans. My friend had been a reservoir of details about the history of Indians that were never recorded and without Cougar's knowledge and experience significant parts of my nation's past would have been lost in time.

The Appaloosas and the cougar came to attention as we descended into the valley. They moved up toward the entranceway into the cave and waited.

I figured I could milk him for a few more opinions of what seems to be a continuing problem in the United States, high school drop-outs and unenforceable law. I asked Cougar for his observations on those subjects.

"I'll take the State of Georgia where you live. I'm familiar with that area. Your schools' drop-out rate is 30%, unbelievably high when you consider that the ones leaving school are consigning themselves to a career of flipping hamburgers, robbing banks, and welfare. As far as unenforceable laws, you only have to see the traffic on your metropolitan interstate system where your speed limit is 55 MPH, with cars and truck careening by at 70 to 95 MPH, and with no police cars in sight. Why pass a law which can't be enforced? There's a law against bank robberies, yet bank robberies are on the rise. There's a law against rape, yet rapes are on the rise. There's a law against murder, yet murder is on the rise. In my world when those false idols of greed and lust emerged as the dominant force among my people the Great Spirit sent bolts of lightning, raging floods, fiery zephyrs, painful pustules and periods of famine until idolatry was vanquished and the aberrant conduct righted."

Cougar scratched his head for a moment and said, "There is one other confusing thing that is occurring all over this country and that is violent gangs scrawling graffiti. I know it's like lions pissing a scent around their territory and defying any other animals to cross. But I cannot understand why anyone can feel so useless and disappointed with their lives that the only way to compel the world to know they exist is to spray-paint graffiti. Graffiti, along with their caps on sideways, and boom boxes, is a way for embittered wastrels to demonstrate contempt for everyone else."

"How do you stop it?" I said. "How do you stop the senseless acts like destroying mailboxes, turning over tombstones and dropping rocks down from overpasses that results in people having wrecks and being killed?"

"Such lunacy never occurred among Indian people. It's a sign of the lack of discipline and too much idle time. I would put every idiot to work cleaning up the mess they had created, then have them stand day after day in public with signs on their head admitting that they are idiot-minded. They would remain there until they promised to not be stupid again. If it happened again it would be mandated that they remain standing without water or food until they seriously promise to get over being ignorant."

"That's rather severe," I said.

"Whatever it takes," Cougar said.

"What about the breakdown in law and order? What is your opinion of the major reasons for the increases in violent crime against innocent people, particularly old people who can't defend themselves?"

"Your officials in government boast about creating millions of new jobs because of the reduced taxes. What you don't realize is that while your Federal government may have lowered taxes your States have jacked up their taxes even more, to the point where workers are bringing even less money home to pay bills and buy food. Your middle-class, and low income citizens, is getting hammered. It all started during the Carter Presidency when inflation hit 14% and interest rates went to 21%. Carter went on TV and stated the problems were caused by some mysterious kind of malaise. Before his faux pas, only one person in the family needed to work to support the family. After that mysterious malaise spread, it took both parents working to support the family. That is where your real problems hit the fan when economic shock-waves had a devastating impact on families, with kids unsupervised by a parent. You called them lock-key children. When a parent can't feed their children or pay bills and house payments or rent, they become desperate and begin to rob others to feed their kids. Desperate people are desperate people and will do desperate things just to survive including murdering others. It is when anarchy ferments. That is what's facing your society now."

"What's the solution?" I asked.

"It may be too late. You first would have to get rid of greed and stupidity. Those two banes are at the root of your trouble. The problems were first caused by unions demanding more money than the profit on the product would permit. Then the government wizards piled on confiscatory taxes, then the company executives gave themselves salaries too high, plus bonuses and other perks. That greed permitted foreign manufacturers to beat up on American companies competitively causing them to have to move offshore to remain in business and costing American workers' jobs. Then NAFTA, endorsed by the highest office in the land, caused the loss of more jobs. Ross Perot stated that if NAFTA was approved the country would hear one giant sucking sound as American jobs went down the toilet. American workers now have to compete with the wages paid to workers in third world countries but it's too late. At one time America manufactured everything that is now being made offshore. You have a perfect example playing out right now in the automotive industry. Greed from every angle has killed a once vibrant car industry. China has benefitted most from the greed in America's industry."

"Everyone wanted to live too well, I guess," I said.

"Gooder than they could afford," Cougar said. "Pardon the word creation."

"People in Congress should have recognized the emerging calamity but they were all too busy shoving money into their pockets," I said. "Actually, I believe those in Washington are aware of real problems but in addition they intentionally create artificial crisis after artificial crisis to keep the voters mentally and emotionally distracted while their pockets are being emptied. Professional pickpockets do the same thing."

"I hear leaders in Congress explaining flamboyantly that their basic responsibility is to protect citizens in their homes and businesses. Washington has been an abysmal failure since home-invasion is increasing and business owners are being killed on a scale unparalleled in history. No witnesses."

"I've seen it coming on," I said.

"It's becoming worse," Cougar said.

"Want to come up for air?" I grinned at Cougar.

"Not yet. I am on a roll," he smiled. "Your people are bombarded further by malpractice and class-action lawsuits with grotesque settlements by mindless juries which send prices skyrocketing even more. Attorneys become wealthier and others poorer, forcing more people to improvise by robbing and killing just to survive. You have law firms advertising on television now attempting to get people to let them sue someone, particularly insurance companies. They talk about enormous financials settlements. They never discuss the portion of those settlements that the lawyers get."

"Your explanation sounds really ominous. What would your answer be to our problems?"

"That is easy. Stop breeding and send the adulators of artificial idols off to their Happy Hunting Ground and ship the graffiti sprayers' back home. Hire your next President and the gurus in Congress so that when they are found to be helplessly inept they too can be sent back home. It takes firm measures to correct stupidity, including the nuts that needlessly destroy property."

"Vandalism is caused by inactivity. No sense of direction. No respect for others."

"Also contempt for society," Cougar said.

"It shows in statistics," I agreed.

"One situation I think you should mention in your writing. That's the crisis in the Middle East. I spent some time in Israel. Those people are industrious. Proof is that they acquired a desert and turned it into an oasis. Millions of Arabs now want the place back. And of course the Israelis, understandably, are not going to give it up. They are being threatened with extermination by Iran. That region is potentially a flashpoint for World War III. Israelis are not going to remain sedate and let the Iranians beat-up on them. They have suffered incredible terror for years with the Arabs around them raining rockets on every kibbutz near Gaza and infiltrating out of the West Bank for the purpose of killing Israelis. If I were President of Israel I would unleash devastation on my enemy in one massive onslaught and stop the rockets and to hell with world opinion. They have nuclear capability and well trained military. It would be the death knell for the Iranians. Look what happened three times to overly aggressive Arabs. Israel will survive. The Iranians should remember that the flea caused the Black Plague, ticks cause Lyme's disease, the mosquito causes Dengue Fever, encephalitis, West Nile virus and malaria, and a mouse can panic an elephant. Small does not mean weak. I would incinerate the two areas where Iran is manufacturing death for Jews and make the regions uninhabitable for years. Look what occurred at Chernobyl after a nuclear disaster."

"But there could be catastrophic consequences in the Persian Gulf in that event," I said.

"That's true," Cougar said. "The Russians would like to see the Persian Gulf closed. With their vast reserve of oil and gas they would then control the world market for energy and the price of a barrel of oil would skyrocket creating financial tremors in the industrialized nations. If you think you are suffering a recession now wait until oil hits $400 to $500 per barrel. The Russians will conquer the world without firing a shot."

"But what if Israel does conduct a pre-emptive strike for their survival?" I said.

"With Russia providing arms to Iran, that is their exact expectation, the Gulf gets closed and they own the market for oil and gas."

"Take the opposite side. What if Israel does not pre-emptively take out Iran."

"You have heard the Iranian leader declare that Israel should be wiped off the face of the earth. Their intentions are perfectly clear. Either way the Persian Gulf gets shut down and the Russians win."

"It seems an unsolvable dilemma."

"Probably," Cougar said.

"Quirky rulers sometime come into office," I said. "Fortunately, they are not eternal."

"Netanyahu opined probably the truest truism ever expressed when asked why the Jews and the Arabs couldn't live in peace together. He stated: *if the terrorists put down their weapons there would be no violence. If the Jews put down their weapons, there would be no Israel.* Some lunatics are dedicated lunatics."

"Lunatics can be the downfall of a country. Look at Hitler. Gone. Look at Stalin. Gone."

"Unfortunately, it takes too long for them to self-destruct," Cougar said. "In the meanwhile the world suffers."

"You have knowledge of everything, don't you?"

"Almost. For example, I wish sports figures would simply fade away. Enough is enough of faded personality's way past their prime. Wrinkled golfers and stoop-shouldered tennis players should just stop hanging on."

"I worry about companies taking their manufacturing facilities to other countries and causing the loss of jobs for American workers. It's hammering the economy and hurting the work force."

Cougar smiled and said," I have a suspicion you know how the problem began."

"Again you're observant," I said.

"You likely know more about that than I do," Cougar said. "How'd it happen?"

"Maybe," I said. "Mostly greed. Gluttony is one of our major social problems."

"Tell me."

"I recall when it began back in the 40's and 50's; unions striking; forcing management to accept higher wage and benefit demands. At first that was good for the workers but then gluttony took over: demand became too costly, corporate executives began taking higher salaries and too many perks and bonuses that put industries in economic danger. Politicians began sticking their fingers into the cookie jar. Costs skyrocketed. Profits plummeted as greed bloomed; appliances, apparel, steel, leather, porcelain, jewelry, electronics, etc, etc, etc. The choice for industries was simple; reduce quality, lose market shares to foreign competitors, who made a better product, or locate out of the country, in order to survive the three-pronged assaults; Another consequence of the offshore debacle, we now have Internet technical support coming from foreign countries."

"To escape the economic chokehold that unions held on business many companies moved from northern states, where unions were healthy, to southern states where the right-to-work laws helped keep costs lower. But that was only a partial remedy. The other two thirds of the problem, excessive taxes and gluttonous executive compensation continued to reduce industry's ability to pay for modernizing, resulting in shoddy products and further decline in market share. The survival instinct in business resulted in locating offshore where cost could be controlled. Every time a business was forced to locate offshore, America's work force shrank accordingly. Those lost jobs never returned."

"Politicians who were too busy arranging their own financial future allowed this calamity to occur We now have 10% plus unemployment due to these conditions and I don't hear anyone suggesting what to do about it. We have a job-loss crisis. Maybe we have passed the point of no return. But I believe there is a way to reverse the trend."

"Instead of wringing our hands in stupefied resignation let's find a candidate with guts for President, somebody smart enough to admit the errors of the past, sufficiently compelling to coerce compliance, and dedicated to removing avariciousness from this economy. Unions shot themselves in the foot and lost millions of jobs. Executives enriched themselves but depleted the cookie jar. Politicians contributed to the death knell. We need to bring back jobs to America by whatever means necessary; lower taxation, lower payroll-lower executive salaries. Restore fiscal sanity to business."

"Is it Gingrich? Is it Huckabee? Is it Palin? Is it Romney? Is it Glenn Beck? We need a visionary who is not concerned about purchasing a re-election but willing to get down into the trenches and take on the enemy, which is increasingly from within."

"In the meanwhile I feel uneasy, like I'm aboard a cruise ship, adrift in towering waves, the engine room awash, the rudder broke, with the Captain asleep in the conning tower, and with the stewards looting the passengers' safe in the Captain's quarters."

"That kinda' spells it out accurately. I just wanted to see if you knew, too," Cougar said.

We were sipping warm sassafras tea laced with honey. Its taste was a virgin experience for me. I complimented Cougar on his cougar. I began. "One of the major enigmas in our society is the rejection of integration by ethnicities," I said. "Nobody seems to be interested in establishing a bond between them and it is remaining in stasis. In 1964, President Johnson passed his grand revolution and announced that his great society would be the hallmark of his Presidency, and citizens in the future would live and work together in harmony. It hasn't happened that way."

"It'll never work," Cougar said. "Mother Nature does not allow it simply because every unique species wants to maintain its own identity. That is why polar bears do not co-habitate with the grizzly. Deer don't cross-breed with elk. Ducks don't migrate with geese. Cougar don't breed with wild cats of any kind, only their own. Nature is aware it doesn't work. The Great Spirit believes in Mother Nature. I recall a tragedy that occurred in New York years ago. A girl in Alabama was born in a black family. For some unknown reason, her coloration was pale and her features Caucasian. Being unhappy at home she decided to leave home at an early age. She went to New York and became a top fashion model. When a renowned physician, the member of a prominent family, attended a fashion show, he became enamored with her beauty. They dated. A relationship developed. They were married and she became pregnant. The girl did not tell her husband of her ethnic background. Wanting to witness the birth of his baby and while serving on the teaching staff at a maternity hospital he invited one student to witness the birth of his baby as a part of the study. When the child was born it was black. The doctor hurried from the room convinced that his wife had been unfaithful. The day she arrived home he filed for divorce. That's the reason Mother Nature does not condone any cross-breeding. Those relationships are cultural anomalies from which many unpredictable consequences will transcend. Nature is determined the zebra keep its wonderful stripes. It's an undeniable fact that if you mix black and white the result is a shade of gray. Individuality will be gone. I would be called a racist by Afro Americans or those politicians double-talking voters to guarantee their tenure in office. In speaking with cultured Afro Americans though, I know that they choose to keep their unique ways. People are entitled to be different. We may not like the same food. I might not enjoy RAP. You may not like the sounds of flutes. Nothing wrong with that except in the stunted minds of those who like to keep things agitated. With my people I'd be known as a realist. Practice the Old Golden Rule."

"I recall when the fur industry began trying to develop new colors of minks. We only had brown mink and they did not sell well. Some furriers and ranchers formed a Breeding Association with the idea of breeding specific colors to get other newer colors. It was hit or miss. Eventually, with keeping records of certain colorations bred with other strains we produced predictable mutation colors. It required a great amount of record keeping. And yet, mistakes were made with undesirable results. To perfect colors took years. We got a lot of peculiar shades in the process. I agree with Mother Nature that uniqueness must be maintained. You do not want to dilute the gene pool of unique species and have unusual appearing results. The aberration will transcend through succeeding generations of mutants, and by the reason of continued breeding between the descendants' appearance will be unforeseen and maybe undesirable. The worst part is that the children evolving from those unions have no say in the tribulations related to cross-breeding."

"Mother Nature is always right," Cougar said.

After visiting four weeks with Cougar, I had to agree with him but I pressed him for additional information.

"You people have a much greater problem than social discontent," he said. "The moral sickness you project over the world does your image irreparable damage. The filth you televise and show in your movies has foreigners thinking that all Americans are over-sexed, overweight, overpaid, and obsessed with an attitude of superiority, looking down on the uneducated in the world. Even where you live in Georgia, you have laws against gambling, punishable by punitive fines, yet your State promotes lottery tickets that appeals to that segment of your population that can least afford the costs of gambling. They promote how simple it is to become fabulously wealthy just by buying lottery tickets. Those hustling the pitch smile and grin and talk about the millions of dollars to be had from just one purchase and the life of abundance to be lived. The program is pitched to sucker in poor pathetic people who are living below the poverty level and believe they can own yachts, mansions, and glitzy cars so they take money that should be spent on food and utilities and piss it away on the lottery, again, and again. It is a devious technique to get more taxes from gullible citizens, and is profoundly hypocritical."

"Taxes are excessive," I said. "You are really conversant on that subject.

"As well as others," Cougar smiled. "The problem with taxes enacted by inept politicians is that the politician has no accountability. He either does not stay in office, by his own choice, or he is not re-elected, leaving taxpayers burned by his bungling. Taxes are rarely removed, being tightly interwoven in the fork-tongue hyperbole of the politician's agenda."

"You're an amazing intellectual, you know," I said.

"Few people realized the constrictive enormity of taxes," Cougar said.

"We also have, potentially, a severe problem with Atlanta's drinking water supply. When I first arrived in Atlanta in 1962, the population was somewhere less than a million. Atlanta had Lake Lanier. Atlanta now has nearly six million people. Finding a Chamber of Commerce report I read where Atlanta is projected to be the most populated city in the country in ninety years. There's no barrier to expanding from Alabama to South Carolina and from Florida to Tennessee. I fished in Lake Lanier and during one moderate drought I watched the water level drop dangerously low. As the population grew I spoke with some officials about one more dam above Duluth. There's a location on Peachtree Industrial Boulevard where one more dam could have been built when the farmland was still affordable. I recently flew from Peachtree DeKalb to up over the dam: golf courses, large industrial complexes, mansions, concrete and asphalt roads, shopping centers and warehouses. The acreage would cost too much. With a population of six million in Atlanta, if we have an extended drought and when the lake dries up, we will see an exodus which will make the escape of Jews from Egypt seem like a Boy Scout's outing. Then if that projection proves to be accurate there is no way in hell to supply water requirements. Atlanta will cease to exist."

"That situation exists in more places than Atlanta. I've seen the problem developing for years across the planet," Cougar said. "And no one appears to be concerned. Population growth outstripping available water supply guarantees social upheaval."

"Some Judge has decided that in three years people living in Atlanta can't drink water from Lake Lanier. How's that for arrogant idiocy. People have been drinking water from the Chattahoochee River long before it had a name and Lanier is nothing more than a wider and deeper place in the Chattahoochee. The Judge must be smoking something or power has gone to his head. Apparently he is uneducated about the Grandfather Clauses and Riparian Rights. Grandfather clause says if you have been doing it long enough you can keep right on doing it. The Indians living here drank water from the river for 10,000 years. Riparian Rights is spelled out in the Real Estate Manual. It says I can drink water from this side of the river and the other side is for folks living over there. And I can visit over there and drink some of their water. As I see it, that's the law, is spite of some confused Judge. My great granddaddy stood stolidly with his Winchester in Wyoming to defend his right to some water flowing in a stream. I hope it doesn't come to that."

"But he's faceless and I'm not fond of people I can't see. My computer is filled with faceless people aggravating me as much as this Judge."

"But then I wondered what would happen to all that water if Georgians can't use it. My Angel Trumpets would die. And I'm sure not going to pour bottled water into a number three galvanized tub just to take a bath. I did that during that last Depression out on the farm. I got to bathe after my Grandfather, my Grandmother and my Aunt and my brother. By then I could plant potatoes in the muck. Not again."

"With grids criss-crossing the land carrying oil and natural gas to where it is needed, it seems to me that another grid could be put in place to pipe water from flood areas to drought-stricken areas. No community can last without water. The vision of government officials seems to be limited."

"Slowing down population growth which will curtail consumption is a partial solution. During the fourteen centuries Early Americans nurtured this land we maintained a practical and workable ratio between supplies of natural resources and the requirements of the people. Your problems stem from too many people over-utilizing finite resources. The practice doesn't work."

"You're an observant man, my friend," I said.

"I speak what I know to be the truth," Cougar said.

Chapter Twelve

"Cougar," I said. "On the internet where everybody is able to communicate with everybody in the world our nation is at a crisis with deranged pedophiles preying on young girls, even boys. What would you do?"

"I'll take you back to my childhood. If anything like that occurred, and I remember very few, the punishment was instantaneous, and severe. My people believed that when an eye was taken an eye should be sacrificed. There was never a time when the victim waited to have retribution for such a hideous crime. Immediately, the guilty person was taken, his cloths removed, and he was spread-eagled between two ant colonies, honey was dribbled on his body and the ant colonies were agitated. The man was left to endure the same agonies as that suffered by his victim until he was stripped of his flesh by the ants. We had few pedophiles, you can be certain."

"That's severe punishment," I said.

"But it worked to keep our crime rate low. Look at the enormity of your crime rate and prison population. I will give you another example. One man, hopped up on peyote, tied up a girl and raped her and shoved her in a river where she drowned. He was tied up the next day and shoved in the same river where he drowned. That is the way to keep crime at a minimum."

"How'd you know who did it?"

"The Elders had a good idea who savaged the child and they questioned him without the protection of your idiotic Miranda Decision. He confessed."

"But if you torture a man he'll confess to a crime he didn't do just to stop the punishment."

"We did not just beat a man to get him to admit his guilt. In the process the suspect must reveal something about the rape that only the perpetrator would be aware of. Then, we knew we had the right man. You need to get rid of your Miranda Decision and the ACLU."

"Two centuries ago the British merchants introduced opium to the Chinese peasants in order to destroy their minds and gain a foothold in world commerce. Within a decade many Chinese were raging potheads. That identical situation is happening in the United States. This nation is on the verge of being destroyed by drugs. What would you do?"

Cougar seemed thoughtful for a moment. "I read the reports of illegal drug interdictions on the coasts. People are now searched in airports where Federal agents find caches of mind-altering substances hidden in travel cases, soap, cameras, bodily cavities and a host of places expected to fool customs. A smuggler hires morons to consume capsules of drugs in attempts to dupe custom officials. The mules die when a capsule ruptures in their stomachs. It is estimated that less than 2% of drugs are intercepted with the rest ending up inside addicts. Between the origin of illegal drugs and the users are billions of dollars in profit. There-in lies the reason your drug program in the United States is an abysmal failure."

"Comparisons have been made between law enforcement and Prohibition. After Prohibition was enacted people who wanted to drink continued to drink. Cost of enforcement rose. Smugglers and agents died. Consumers prevailed and the law was rescinded. The change didn't make more drinkers. Legalizing drugs won't cause a large surge in drug usage. With millions in profits removed, drugs, like Methadone, will be dispensed by those agencies whose purpose is to satiate those cravings of addicts. An immediate benefit will be the reduction of gang competition where thousands have been murdered or imprisoned in the carnage."

"The facts learned from those experiences were that alcoholics continue to be alcoholics until they decide not to drink. Numbskulls will be exploited as long as they allow themselves to be exploited. Drug addicts will be addicts until they decide to not be users. Billions of dollars are spent attempting to alter the attitudes of stupid people."

"The United States needs an immediate rapprochement to the problems of illegal drugs. Illegal drugs should be legalized and sold under government supervision. The profit enjoyed by smugglers and pushers would disappear and prices would be controlled at a low rate with taxes levied on drugs at the same level as beverages."

"Addictions will increase only among people with a proclivity to fry their brain. Prisons will be emptied of those whose infractions were as a user. Pushers would not be able to control neighborhoods. Crime related to drugs would cease and those enforcement agencies which have spent decades failing to control smuggling would be assigned to other areas of criminal behavior. Pushers would no longer have a reason to have children hooked. The idea is a realistic approach to an obvious failure. The only people who'll yell at the change are smugglers, pushers and those, behind-the-scene, financiers who have made millions from the misery of beleaguered people."

"Money saved should then be expended in a concerted promotional campaign to instruct youths, starting with children that experimenting with mind-destroying drugs is a stupid decision, and potentially lethal, and that self-destructing in the quagmire of illegal dope is only one danger in a world plagued by pitfalls."

"There will those snivelers with opposing views but if intelligence should prevail then the billions being squandered could be used in needed places then, permit alcoholics to drink and druggies to die, and stop your futile attempts to mandate human idiocy."

"Would you consider running for President?" I said. "We need somebody a hell of a lot smarter than we've had lately."

"And live in Washington, DC? I may have to question your sanity, Mike."

"Other problems are developing from drug trafficking," I said. "Gangs are becoming habituated with killing until shooting somebody is considered entertainment, like shooting rats in a garbage dump. The carnage is spreading like wildfire until the police departments even in major communities are being overwhelmed. We are really headed toward anarchy."

Chapter Thirteen

"I'm hesitant to ask you this question but did your people actually engage in scalping?"

"After the Spanish taught us how, we did. Scalping was introduced here by the invader in order to terrify and intimidate my people so we would give up our lands without a fight. Finding that the ghastly act actually worked my people began removing the scalps of the people who were murdering us. That's where our practice started. I find that Hollywood has a fetish for portraying us as blood-thirsty savages with scalps on our belt. Never do they show soldiers shooting Indian babies and cutting off body parts, as grisly souvenirs. I buried hundreds of my villagers with intimate body parts missing."

"From where did the designation, Indian, arise?"

"An adventurous idiot by the name of Columbus was looking for a country named India. When he landed in the Caribbean he thought he had discovered India, so he figured we were Indians. The name stuck. It's okay."

I was getting a library of revealing information.

Cougar again lighted his pipe. The wonderful aroma of tobacco drifted in my direction. I was very tempted to join him, but then I recalled my cousin who had his voice box removed as the result of smoking tobacco too long. Instead, he remarked, "I think America is falling apart with too many people walking around in a trance. Not only drug-addicts, but imbeciles popping pills like there's no tomorrow. You have become a pill-popper's-paradise. I do not see an end to your sickness. I do see the end to your society."

"Why has the problem proliferated?" I said.

"It is an indication of your decline," Cougar said. "You have insipid laws. When some murder is committed in your nation, the victim is dead, and yet the murderer much too often is sentenced to a prison for life. Why is that considered equitable? In my life we practiced an instant eye for an eye. If somebody killed another, if not in defense of his life, then he was killed by a member if the victim's family or absent the family, he was dispatched by an Elder. Understandably, we had few murders. Even your sentences for murders sound stupid to the public. What does a sentence of four life times mean? What does a sentence of life plus twenty years mean? I know there are legalities involved but the public doesn't understand that. Why is there a distinction about pre-meditation? If you have a gun and pull it to shoot someone willfully that is premeditation whether you decide in eight seconds or two days. The victims are dead. Why is there plea-bargaining when the victim is dead. Plea- bargaining is a gimmick to make defense lawyers look like they did good work. When a murderer hides the victim's body to hide the crime why isn't the killer taken out to the firing range and forced to be the target, being told that his eyes will be the ultimate target with shots getting closer and closer until the location of the body is revealed. I guarantee that location will be forth-coming. Use a bow and arrows. When the deceased is dead the killer should be dead, too. You have prisons overflowing with people who should be dead, also. Family members of the murder victim suffer the rest of their lives when the killer refuses to tell what he did with his victim. Stake the murderer on the shore of a swamp where alligators exist. Before night begins they will be screaming to tell the location of the body they dumped. Bet on it!" Cougar said.

"Man, that's tough," I said.

"You people are wimps. We had few murders." Cougar said. "When we actually had a murder, not a killing in self defense, we dealt with it immediately and effectively. When the victim is dead, the murderer should be dead, too. We believe that's rational."

"Another tough question. What do you think of pornography?"

"Easy question. People who photograph it are sick. People who look at it are sick. People who pose for it are sick. People who profit by it are sick. People who are embroiled in the porno industry, in any way, are in desperate need of psychiatric care, including those who fondle themselves while ogling that filth."

"Right on the head, I agree. What is it about this country that disturbs you the most?"

"There are severe problems in your country, some of them are likely insurmountable. There has been too much procrastination fixing fractures until they became huge fissures," Cougar said.

"What does that mean exactly? I said.

"Well let's take them in order of the relevance to your country remaining viable. Your borders are porous to the point where the country is being taken over by foreigners. At the present rate of immigration you will become the minority in your own country. Soon after that happens, you will have no control over your own destiny. Foreigners will be in total control. Just look at what happened to my people."

"So how would you fix it?" I said.

"Take your cues from Mother Nature. Animals piss a scent around their territory. Any animal which crosses that line is either killed of chased away. You're going to have to begin shooting people who illegally cross your borders."

"But that's inhuman," I scowled. "Civilized people don't just kill other humans."

"Then suffer the consequences," Cougar said. "When you become the minority you will become subservient to the dictates of the majority, and you will wish you had made effective corrections sooner. If we had practiced that philosophy several centuries ago my people would still be the dominant force on this continent."

"What's next?" I was hesitant to ask.

"The gluttonous depletion of wildlife in the seven seas. Every country is using nets that sweep the ocean clean of major aquatic species."

"But people have to eat." I attempted to justify the fact that I already knew to be ominous.

"Too many people on earth," Cougar said. "I already told you that humans must quit breeding like bedbugs."

"Okay. What else?"

"The pollution of your waterways. Chemical run-off from farming, industry, and the discharge of human waste is polluting the lakes and rivers, killing fish and irreversibly contaminating your water."

"How do you fix that?" I said.

"Stop breeding. Let Mother Nature catch up," Cougar said. "The Great Spirit made one mistake. He made animals and he made man. He should not have made man. Animals breed only for perpetuating their species. Man breeds just to be breeding."

"What other observations have you made?" I got another notepad from my pack.

"I think it's your older people being victimized by marauding hoodlums just to steal their social security checks. I've seen massive brutes attack defenseless old men and women, as bestial as anything I have ever seen. I have witnessed defenseless merchants killed in their place of business by armed robbers to steal their money and leave no witnesses. Your country is close to anarchy. It is accelerating, too. You need to exact instant retribution and more severe penalties in order to reverse the problems."

"How about the world AIDS epidemic?"

"Some say it originated in a colony of monkeys in Africa, then maybe in the Caribbean. No one knows for sure. Some theorized that it was spread by the bites of mosquitoes. That theory has now been debunked. What is known for certain is that in only twenty years the plague has overtaken most of the world killing twenty-five million people and infecting another forty million with perhaps hundreds of millions unaware they have the infection, which makes them spreaders of the virus and with no cure in sight. I recently read a revised figure from the CDC showing that their latest estimate was as much as 40% off, that there may be another forty or fifty million carriers of AIDS."

"In the United States the deadly disease began in the steamy bathhouses in major cities where males engaged in orgies, exchanging seminal fluid with other males in a disgusting inter-play that is not part of Mother Nature's plan. Probing into body orifices that are intended as conduits for releasing feces contributes to the spread of other diseases. Males who participate in that lifestyle are pathetic. And now women are acting the same, involved in unnatural sex orgies. It is all part of a morality deterioration in this country, that insatiable quest for orgasms."

"There are millions of future victims for sure by the exponential spread of the killing virus, via behavioral patterns that flourish because of raging immorality and the absence of knowledge required to constrain intimate contact with those already infected. AIDS will continue burgeoning, unabated, under those circumstances. It's now killing 6000 victims each day and it infects 7000 more every day, mostly attributable to unconstrained sex acts. Then your people refer to mouth-to-crotch copulation as oral sex. There is no such thing as oral sex. Companies that manufacture tampons and sanitary napkins emphasize that their product contains odor blockers. Why on earth would anybody want to place their mouth at the source of odor? No one would stick their tongue in a sewer pipe repeatedly so why is it normal to place your tongue in an orifice where toxic waste is excreted. To do that is to assure you will eventually come into contact with yeast infections, genital warts, infectious vaginal pustules including syphilis and AIDS. If producers of tampons and sanitary napkins are not hoodwinking the public when they are aware that women need odor blockers then the manikins in Hollywood with their décolletages down to their asses have to use odor blockers, too. They can't be exempt just because they are in Hollywood."

"Additional millions can become victims of AIDS simply by their extraordinary involvement in promiscuity. Sex with multiple partners assures an ultimate contact with an infected person, with both of them becoming carriers of the viruses. By the logic of extension every carrier can become the infector of more victims with every encounter and with the compulsion for frequent exposure a proliferation of sex related diseases is assured. Other victims of sexually related viruses are babies infected during birth, and hemophiliacs who receive contaminated blood."

"Sociologists are attempting to find ways to constrain the advancement of AIDS. The solution is simple: wildlife is an ideal example for controlling the spread of AIDS: use sex only for the propagation of a species as Mother Nature intended, and AIDS would not have started in the first place. Simply stop promoting promiscuity. Stop AIDS."

"How about the loss of personal freedoms to government dictates?" I said.

"You're virtually slaves to governments now. You are losing more freedoms to government each day. You are victims of deliberate brain-training."

"How so?" I said.

"A backwoodsman was asked how to kill feral pigs. He said it was easy. He put out some corn and let the wild pigs eat it. Then he put up one fence. The pigs got used to the one fence and continued to come for the corn. He put up another fence. The pigs got used to that so he put up another fence and then another fence without a gate. Over time the pigs got used to the fences without a gate. While they were busy pigging out on free corn the man added a gate. Then he could then simply slaughter them, one at a time. That is what the government is doing to you folks."

"Government can become all-powerful when citizen's minds are distracted by intentional diversions by those wanting total power. It has happened to nations throughout history. We now have people trying to take away our guns. If sanity prevails, that won't happen. History proves that with the removal of defensive weapons the average citizen is in peril. Guns were banned by rulers in the Soviet Union, Turkey, Germany, China, Guatemala, Uganda and Cambodia. After their protection was taken away over 56 million citizens of those countries were exterminated by authorities or were murdered by thugs. When gun control takes effect only the honest people are without guns. Hoodlums still have them. After discovering that most Americans owned guns the Japanese decided not to invade after Pearl Harbor."

"I have a high powered rifle, a 38 police special, a 410 single-shot shotgun, a 20 gauge pump gun, a 32 hammerless revolver and a 22 magnum pistol. I love guns. I have never killed anyone. Certain screwballs in the country want to take away everyone's guns. The membership in the NRA is on the rise. When a murderer tries to enter my house or break into my car I must be prepared to shoot him. By law, I'm entitled to do that."

"Defending yourself is a right that can't be abridged," Cougar said. "I suppose the wimps would want you to use a baseball bat if attacked by a grizzly."

Chapter Fourteen

"How about a swim, I feel grungy?" I said.

"Stream is cold, but it's our bath. Let's go."

We stripped and jumped in the water. It was *cold*.

I struck out, swimming upstream, Cougar keeping up alongside me. It felt great. Soon I began to tire. The water was roiling and 83 years is aged. My friend kept abreast then began pulling ahead. I tried valiantly to keep up with him. I fell back, and swam to the bank. I understand why a youthful Indian could beat me. Then I realized the Indian was perhaps two-hundred years old. Puzzling. Unlike a tiger or jaguar a cougar has little appreciation of water. The cougar loped along the bank and occasionally stopped to bat at a butterfly.

We climbed out and sat on a boulder deciding to dry off in the warm sunshine. Again he lighted his pipe and began drawing deep lungs-full of the tantalizing smoke. I was by then about to succumb to the temptation but I remembered my decision. A decision is not a decision if it is rescinded.

"Cougar, I know this subject may be beyond you," I said.

"Few subjects are beyond me," Cougar smiled.

"Okay. What about America's involvement in Iraq?"

"Simple. American officials forgot the conundrum of Vietnam when they became enmeshed in a controversial decision to control the domino effect of communistic influence in the sub-continent of Asia. Faking a shelling at sea in the Gulf of Tonkin as the excuse to commit more troops they were responsible for the death of 55,000 American military, and you may remember the sight of hysterical people clinging to the undercarriage of helicopters in a last-ditch attempt to escape the death throes of Saigon."

"I was too old for the Vietnam War but I recall the nightly death toll," I said. "And you're right."

"Someone forgot the tragic mistake Russia made when they invaded Afghanistan and committed a huge force for the attack. Afghanistan is a mountainous country where no modern army can maneuver efficiently. They lost thousands of troops killed, plus massive equipment before they retreated back into Russia. Afghanistan has been invaded many times by enemy forces throughout history and the invaders always lost. You are encountering the identical conditions and your losing should have been a foregone conclusion. Alexander the Great discovered the sounds of a sucking quagmire, to his regret. Alexander was wounded in battle and died away from home. You should have learned from ancient history."

"Some officials have short memories," I said.

"Some officials are arrogantly stupid. Look what happened to George C. Custer," Cougar said.

"Little Big Horn was a big mistake for the 7th cavalry," I said.

"Hitler should have read about the ill-fated attack Napoleon made into Russia before he did the exact same thing with the same loss of thousands of troops who would rather not have been there. Hitler was demented. Japan should not have attack Pearl Harbor. Mussolini should not have invaded Ethiopia. Militarists are crazy, too. Big-shot military people sit home and let the troops die. They should think of troops as human beings rather that disposable collateral. Big-shots should be at the front getting killed. Wars would be fewer. George Custer should have reconsidered attacking Crazy Horse. Way too many Sioux and Cheyenne warriors that were well armed, although too late in the general scheme of history. Genghis Kahn loved killing people. Kahn did that all over Asia and Europe. Attila the Hun murdered people all over the known world. Macedonians killed Athenians. Athenians killed Trojans. Throughout six centuries, wars infected the Middle East. All considered I understand what happened to my people. Foreigners learned from infancy to kill people and plunder everything they possessed."

"You have remarkable insight, Cougar," I said.

"Iraq is little different. George Bush Sr. made a dumb mistake in not allowing Schwarzkopf to go on into Baghdad and kill Saddam Hussein. While he was visiting his son, George Sr. expressed regret for not finishing the job. George Junior said he would be happy to finish the job. Since Saddam Hussein had used poison gases on the Iranians, Kurds and Shiites, George Junior agreed that that would be sufficient reason for an attack to be launched to save the planet from Weapons of Mass Destruction. Now you are bogged down in another lethal quagmire. What people should realize is that fanatics have been killing other fanatics since the beginning of history and nothing will change their demented zeal. Russia killed thousands of Finns. China slaughtered Tibetans. Idi Amin murdered Kenyans. Pol Pot exterminated half of the population in Cambodia, Pizarro killed Incans, Cortes massacred Aztecs, Japanese killed Koreans, Mongols and the Chinese. English invaders killed people all over the world, New Zealand, India, South Africa, China, Yemen, Rhodesia, Lebanon, Iraq, Egypt, Uganda, Sudan, Malaya, Australia, Hong Kong, Nigeria, Sierra Leone, Ivory Coast, the Bahamas, Zanzibar, Tanganyika, Nyasaland, Bechuanaland Canada, Tasmania, and Southwest Africa, Swaziland, Rwanda and Burundi. Meanwhile, the Portuguese were killing people in Mozambique, Angola, Gambia and South America. Belgians were killing people in Zaire and in the Congo. French were murdering people in Dahomey, Madagascar, Algeria, Cameroon, Equatorial Africa, West Africa, Mauretania, Upper Volta, Ubangi Chari, Ghana, Gabon, Guinea, Togo, Guinea-Bissau, Senegal, Chad and some Islands in the Caribbean. The Spanish were killing people in Rio de Oro, Rio Muni, Tunisia and Philippine Islands. Germans slaughtered people in Liberia, Abyssinia and Eritrea. England, Italy, and France killed people in the African Horn when carving up Somaliland. Brutal, imperialistic, marauders slaughtered millions of people during centuries of conquests. It is still going on constantly, crazy people killing people in Algeria, Morocco, Sudan, Sri Lanka, Ethiopia, Chechnya and others, and now suicide bombers with their dementia. Some people lust to kill other people. With North Korea rattling sabers and Iran threatening to erase Israel from the globe, if I were President of the United States I would order nuclear submarines be submerged in the Persian Gulf and in the Sea of Japan. Since Israel is the primary target for radical terrorists with funding from Iran, who has repeatedly called for the extermination of the State of Israel, I would suggest that the Israelis submerge some nuclear subs near to Iran. With the first threats by their cadre of goose-stepping soldiers I would order the nation charcoaled. Years ago when my village was confronted with aggressors who intended to kill my people we sent out warriors to kill their Chief. When you cut off the head of the serpent the snake dies. Thinking that snakes grow new heads is a myth. Something I do not understand about the United States is that you continue to feed hungry people in North Korea while Kim Jong IL spends millions of dollars on his military. You're supporting your enemy. That's a stupid foreign policy."

"His threats are becoming more bellicose," I said.

Cougar said. "A lion will be a lion until action is taken to turn them into pussycats. It is going on in many places in the world. I've been around the world visiting with people and I'm convinced that they are not going to change. It is in their psyche." Cougar paused, reflectively. "One consolation I see is that there are some intelligent people. Unfortunately their voices are overwhelmed by radicalism. What I do not understand are politicians and newscasters using moderate terminology in describing terrorists. Why refer to genocidal extremists as insurgents and rebels? Killers are killers. You have a peculiar obsession with political correctness in your society."

"We are known as a peace loving country. We abhor the prospects of war."

"But you also must face reality. If a grizzly cub is in your area, you need to be careful because a cub can hurt you. But if you wait until the cub is fully grown and still is aggressive you will be dead. So what I would do if I were President would be to destroy the cub before it gets so big it is lethal. The same applies to the Iranians, and any other country that shows signs of wanting to eliminate the United States. Israel did that to Iraq when Hussein was building his nuclear reactors. I would reconsider everyone who potentially could become a full-grown grizzly. It was an asinine mistake to go into Iraq in the first place. You should never send in live troops to attack people who are guerilla warriors, suicide bombers, crazy maniacs who thrill to die in the name of some religion, particularly in that part of the world because they have been killing each other for thousands of years. The

United States is concerned about world opinion where women and children are killed in attacks but collateral damage in an unavoidable part of warfare. When Iraq was attacked this time the military experts assured Americans they would be in and out in a year. It could have been accomplished in less time than that if a consideration of world opinion was not part of the equation. When Rocky Marciano entered the ring he did not tie one hand behind his back. He did not consider the opinions of others that he might damage someone. If you go to war win it quickly or don't start the war. That way you don't commit young men to death."

I was amazed at how much he knew and his rationale for everything. His knowledge seemed inexhaustible. "How would you extricate this country from an unwinnable conflict in the Mid-East?"

"In 1979, Russia attacked Afghanistan with massive air power and ground forces. Their stated purpose was to protect Afghanistan officials favorable to the Soviets. They initially committed 80,000 troops and extensive airpower. After six months, 50,000 more personnel were sent to Afghanistan. The invasion proved to be much too costly to the Soviet Union in the amount of people killed and equipment lost. In ten years of war with Islamic Jehadists the Soviets lost 15,000 killed and 30,000 wounded. When Mikhail Gorbachev came to power in Russia he decided that the war in Afghanistan was unwinnable and that they needed to get out of the lethal quagmire."

"The United States did not learn from history; our debacle in Vietnam. plus Russia's defeat in Afghanistan. If Washington had considered the Soviet defeat in their unwinnable war we would not be bogged down in an unwinnable war in Afghanistan, Eventually we will reach the death toll in Vietnam unless we learn a lesson from the Soviets. That attack on Afghanistan contributed to the collapse of the Soviet Union."

"You are losing too many personnel; you have 44,000 troops engaged against 500,000 Jehadist warriors who are well armed, in mountainous areas where modern armies cannot operate effectively. If the Soviets couldn't defeat the Mujaheedin with 120,000 troops, and were forced to withdraw, you need to quickly reconsider your options."

"I am distressed by hearing the death count announced each evening on the news. Having served in the navy during WW II, and having lost my only brother in the Battle of the Bulge, I am aware of how painful it is to lose loved ones. I suggest we pull our people out of the Mid-Eastern morass. Not one more military person should die at the hands of Jehadists."

"President Truman decided to not invade Japan based on an assessment that millions of Japanese would be killed, and thousands of your military personnel would die. Victory was achieved long distance. You should adopt the policy of Teddy Roosevelt; speak softly and carry a big stick."

I looked at Cougar. The man had an understanding of many things. "Have you ever has a desire to wreak revenge for what happened to your family?"

"I thought about it after the troopers killed all the people living in our compound, including my parents and brother. I finally realized that it was over after most Indians were dead in a four hundred year campaign by people who lusted to kill people. Worrying about revenge would waste my time. No, I have not, because the Great Spirit knows that someday your people will be no more. When the paleface is gone the mountains and valleys will resound with the spirits of our dead who will be reborn and be again as we once were."

"You seem to know a lot," I said, admiringly.

"I have been around a long time," Cougar replied. "I know for example that there are six billion people on this planet projected to be ten billion in one hundred years. The earth can't support those here now. You see that already by the depletion of natural resources. Yet few people are talking about it. If you think there is an open borders problem now, just wait until ten-billion people begin crossing your borders to obtain food and water. It will make the Mexican fiasco look like a boy scout outing. Overpopulation by humans is the most destructive calamity on the planet. If I were charged with correcting that monumental problem I would have those sterilized those that are breeding like bedbugs."

Chapter Fifteen

Cougar stood up and stretched. "This has been a great experience for me. I haven't pondered so much in many years. You're good for me. We are good for each other. I'll cover another critical subject that's been on my mind recently and that is global warming. It is real and your people act like ostriches with their heads in the sand; the problem won't go away. It is becoming worse. The condition is likely irreversible. Too few people seem to be concerned. It's like you are knowingly, or stupidly, committing suicide. The people who could have a positive effect on global warming; oil companies, race promoters, automobile manufacturers, movie producers who create fireballs for visual effects, combustion engine manufacturers and others, could resolve the problem but when money is amassed by executives that do not give a damn, that probability is remote. They, for personal reasons, don't worry about their children and grandchildren being victims of gluttony. I'd abolish drive-thru windows where engines continue to spew out death from the tailpipe. Walk inside to make bank deposits or have lunch, install solar energy, row canoes, push lawnmowers, ride bicycles, and horses, walk instead of drive and the problem will be lessened. Dispose of extravagant houses. Build homes underground where there'll be no need for heating and air conditioning. Live in energy-efficient tipis. There are many ways to conserve natural resources."

"You are suggesting that everybody radically alter their lifestyle," I said.

"What is their alternative?" Cougar said. "Dying is not the greatest of options. At the rate global warming is increasing drought will be more frequent and severe. I see crops failing on a massive scale. I see worldwide starvation resulting in migrations on a level unheard of on earth. I see genocide over food and water. When one society is without food and water it must move or perish. And the lack of food and water is only one of those problems. Another result of climate warming is that Dengue fever and malaria will affect the planet on a level unseen before. Mosquitoes thrive in tropical weather. If you are bitten by mosquitoes carrying the diseases there is a probability of massive deaths. With global warming affecting the entire globe the amount of people dying will be staggering. With people stacked atop of each other in congested regions the enormity of the problems are increased exponentially. Global warming will create more droughts, floods, rising ocean levels, displacement of populations and billions of deaths. It could be the end of life on earth."

"That's a dire Prediction," I said.

"There's more." Cougar looked serious.

"Okay. What?"

"Nuclear proliferation has been a critical subject in the news lately. If some lunatic terrorist gains control of a government which has nuclear capabilities then the planet might be turned into a giant cinder ball floating in outer space, completely void of life."

"The future seems ominous," I said.

"There are some dedicated terrorists emerging within radical governments. The authorities have convinced gullible young radicals that if they become suicide bombers that there will be virgins awaiting them in heaven. Those overtures reminds me of the get-rich-quick schemes seen on television, scammers taking advantage of infantile minds. Besides, after one or two virgins, the remainder won't look so good."

"I'm concerned that the trend is increasing," I said.

"You must recognize that no civilization has lasted forever."

"Can the Great Spirit help?"

"The Great Spirit never interferes with the natural order of events. If you make your bed with snakes then you will be bitten while you are sleeping and you are going to die. Such is one certainty of life."

"Then, the way we are heading now, life on earth is tenuous. Is that it?"

"Yes," Cougar said.

Chapter Sixteen

"How about our television programs? We are being enslaved to filthy mediocrity," I said.

"I'm not through with global warming," Cougar said.

"S'cuse me," I said.

"The main reason for the climate becoming warmer is ignorant people. Cataclysmic climate changes will happen; droughts, snow storms, earthquakes, hurricanes, tornadoes, cyclones, tsunamis, floods, starvation and diseases will kill billions of people. During that time frame there will be massive dislocations of people and the earth will suffer destructive battles for survival. You're seeing that on a smaller scale today. The earth can support six million people but studies project that ten billion people will inhabit this planet within one hundred years under ideal conditions. After severe climate change the earth will only support two million people. That means that billions of people will perish. Even though I will not be affected I cringe when I see bombs exploding around the globe. I know absolutely that with every explosion, life on this planet is closer to ending. My sympathy is with the animals. They have no control over bombs, yet their lives are negatively impacted, and will also end. Earth has another severe problem. A substantial percentage of the planet's fresh water is frozen in the polar ice caps. Because of overpopulation and the subsequent heat being generated into the atmosphere the ice caps are dissipating. When they are gone, oceans will have sustained a twenty feet rise in water level. Imagine the disruption where communities along coasts are inundated. Entire islands will be submerged, with their populations drowned. The calamity is presently reversible but very few officials seem to be concerned about the end of life on earth so too little is happening. If they wait too much longer to react it will be too late."

"Why aren't the people charged with the welfare of society doing something about the problems? Aren't they concerned? Are they incompetent? Are they immune to the obvious fact that society is falling apart all around them?"

"Many of those government officials are so obsessed with assuring their own wealth, health and welfare that any assumption they are interested in the other problems flies in the face of reality," Cougar said.

"Enough conjecture on the end of life on earth. You certainly portray the dark side," I said.

"I'm not quit finished. Just look what happened to my people with unprotected borders. Because of porous borders you now have 385.3 billion dollars a year being spent on non-Americans; incarceration, food assistance, education, social services, suppressed American wages and Medicaid. It is bankrupting your national economy. The crime rate is two and one half times greater among illegal aliens. Over one million sex crimes have been committed by illegal aliens. Forty-five billion dollars in untaxed wages have been sent back to their countries of origin. Illegal aliens are responsible for millions of pounds of drugs smuggled into your country; cocaine, heroin, marijuana, methamphetamines. Terrorists have entered the United States through porous borders. Of course you obviously have an over-abundance of drug addicts so until those people wise up or die, a strong market for illegal drugs will continue."

"I recall similar observations after the Europeans over-ran this continent. After three centuries of my people being murdered, our homes being burned, being starved by the wanton slaughtering of animals on which we depended for food, frozen to death because in the terror of fleeing for our lives there was no time to make clothing. Our ways of life forever gone, those who escaped the massacre surrendered. Chief Joseph, leading a ragtag band of freezing and starving children, women, and old men desperately trying to escape being shot, by fleeing to Canada, finally stated:

From this day forward I will fight no more forever.

Cougar seemed disturbed by what happened so many years ago. "You know what happened to over sixteen million of my people. They died at the hands of foreigners. So you see what open borders did for us. Your officials are asleep at their post and you will be overwhelmed, too."

"And the root cause of that is?"

"Officials are too involved with lining their own pockets for their financial security. Too many of them can't keep their hands out of that old cookie jar. It's just one more sickness afflicting those in public office; Representatives, Senators, Governors, Mayors, Presidents, and candidates for President can't even keep their zippers zipped up. They apologize with all kinds of lame excuses for misconduct. **Mikie made me do it!** Of course media sharks are in that frenzied feeding mode. They seem to revel when wallowing around in slime. The slimier the more it boosts ratings. The higher the ratings the more media can charge their advertiser for sponsoring slime. Egocentric narcissism is flourishing. It is more of that slippery slide toward oblivion. More and more programs are appearing on television with scantily clad people throwing each other around, shoving others, acting insanely uncivilized, yelling obscenities that aren't even bleeped, adversarial and vilifying everyone, exhibiting contemporary depravity, undulating as if in the madness of primitive fertility dances. And what is even more strange, they have the audience applauding like this was the greatest entertainment they had ever experienced."

"Where did you get the ability to vocally castrate someone?"

"From visiting with palefaces without them knowing I'm present," Cougar said.

"How do certain people get to the higher offices in the land with withered morals?"

"Arrogance, the entrenched idea that they are somehow special and that the morality factor which applies to everyone else does not apply to them. Hence, the females who will bed down with anyone that they think will improve their lot, with no more scruples than their new bunk buddies, and without concern for the families of the over-sexed hot-shots. That's also part of the slime image in this country."

"When I was young we were too busy just surviving economically during the Great Depression to have time for screwing around. I was eighteen years old and fighting a war in Europe before I got laid the first time. I didn't even know her name, or even cared. It was in a cathouse in Naples. But no one was hurt by it. I stuck some gunk from sick-bay in my dick to keep from getting the clap, just in case."

"We were much like animals and bred only for reproductive purposes," Cougar said. "Too much importance is attached to the physically part of relationships. Today, crotches and tits are is in vogue."

"Along with increasing immorality, this country, a few years ago, was creeping toward socialism. Under the democrats, citizens were put on government dole so that the Democratic Party could depend on them for favorable votes when the elections came up. When Newt Gingrich became Speaker of the House and the republicans gained control of the senate Gingrich immediately began a program called Republican Coalition for the purpose of lowering taxes and getting people off the government's dole, plus, to stop the encroachment of socialism. Gingrich advocated entrepreneurial enterprises. A dramatic change emerged from the Speaker's ideas; those who were able to work went to work. Business became more profitable. And surprise of all surprises government tax revenues skyrocketed, going from a negative cash flow to a string of surpluses. And that was at the time Bill Clinton became President. And the amazing result was that Clinton got full credit for the surpluses and he had absolutely nothing to do with it. Clinton grinned while doing a snow-job on Americans with his clever-tongued oratory. And, of course, with Americans being so caught up with nakedness and materialism, eight years passed while terrorist organizations grew much stronger and more dangerous. America has suffered from over-sight neglect."

"You're rather observant," Cougar said.

"Doesn't mean much," I said.

"Why don't you run for a political office?" Cougar suggested.

"I can't lie with a straight face," I said.

Cougar lighted his pipe. The cougar stretched and yawned. I could see muscles rippling.

"What's your opinion on our contemporary televised programming?" I said.

He ignored my question. "It's reality," Mike. "Mother Nature is prepared to contend with natural calamities, like fires, volcanic eruptions and many others. But Mother Nature is being overwhelmed by man-made forces, wickedness, waywardness, corruption, dishonesty, greed, a loss of direction."

"Okay, back to another type of slime," I suggested, smiling.

Chapter Seventeen

"Television. Now? Okay?" I grinned again.

"Television was okay in its infancy when there were three channels. Now, it is the intellectual avenue for rancid sewage; MTV, Girls Gone Wild, Over-Sexed Wives, perverted people grabbing their crotches, licking each other's genitalia, simulating insane sex. 24 hours each day of charlatans, hustlers, liars, cheats, swindlers, flimflammers, con-artists, scams, subterfuge, gadgets and a mind-numbing fact   is that brain dead viewers sit and watch that sewage and consider it enlightenment. I wonder how people really believe that sending in money to some evangelists on television can cause them to receive a new house, a car, a job, erase their credit-card debt, receive an unexpected inheritance, a mysterious check arrives in the mail, all that from holding a piece of cloth or drinking a bottle of water. The Great Spirit never requires payment for blessings. Intellectually and morally you'd be better off if you went back to three channels and shut it off at midnight with only a test pattern until morning. That would be less time to have your mind numbed and your morals corrupted. A company now is claiming that they have over two hundred channels. Where will they find enough trash to fill two hundred channels?"

"Is there anything on which you have no opinion?" I said.

"Very few," Cougar said. "But let me ask you about the taxes you pay. What percentage of your income do you honestly believe you pay in taxes?"

I thought for a moment. "My income is lower now for various reasons. When I was still active in business I'd say I paid maybe 35% or 40%. What do you think?"

"In the first place the lowly consumer is the only one who pays taxes. Rich people and businesses do not pay taxes. They are tax collectors for governments. If you are a doctor and get a larger tax bill you merely raise your fees to offset the increase and the patient gets stuck with your tax increase. If the patient is a lawyer or a businessman they increase their fees for service or increase the price of their merchandise and again the consumer gets screwed. When a real estate owner, who has shopping centers or apartments, receives an increase on property taxes he merely raises the cost of rentals and the lessee ultimately pays the increase, then raises the prices on his products and services and the consumers of those products or services gets stuck with the tax increases. They have no one below them to which they can transfer the tax. Rich people don't pay tax. They are a conduit for taking money from consumers and transferring it to governments. If you own a business and the tax bill is higher you simply provide yourself a raise or take more perks from the company, then increase the prices on your products or services. Consumers who buy the products or services always get stuck with those tax increases. Even those Boards of Directors of any company that gets an increase in their personal taxes can vote themselves more stock options, traveling expenses or increase their per diem rates. Morticians who incur higher taxes tack that amount on caskets and service fees and the relatives of the dead are reamed. The problem is that consumers are like infants and they aren't aware they are being skewered. When a television station or newspaper gets an increased tax it jacks-up the advertisement rate and businesses that buy advertising pay a higher price. In turn, the price is raised on their products or services, sending those taxes on down the line to the lowly consumers who have no one below them to which they can transfer the tax increases so they get stuck with the total tax burden. That's the way the system works, Mike. Congressmen talking about raising taxes only on rich people and companies is one of the greatest scam-jobs on record. Only the bottom-feeders pay taxes."

"I am amazed. I never realized those facts," I said. "I guess I really am unaware of how much I pay in taxes. What do you think I pay?"

"I don't think, I know," Cougar said. "You are way off at your 30% or 40% guesstimate."

"Tell me," I said.

"Along with foreign potentates your representatives become extravagantly richer when serving in Washington. Graft and corruption are rampant. Washington is a gold mine for the opportunist who can get elected. The term *public servants* has been bastardized. You are supporting the most heavily taxed nation on earth. You just don't know it. You pay taxes to municipalities, villages, towns, cities, counties, states and to the Federal government. I was curious one day for some reason, so I prepared a list of those taxes you pay. Do you know you pay a tax on male sperm that's cryogenically frozen for future implantation?"

"No, I don't."

"That proves my point exactly. You pay taxes which you do not know you pay. In the case of that sperm you did not experience the ejaculation but you still pay a tax for it. You pay taxes on marl."

I looked confused. "What is marl?" I asked.

"Marl is decomposing seashells that are dredged up along the Gulf Coast to be used in producing concrete. An excise tax is charged by the state where the seashells are excavated."

"Excise tax?"

"Yes. When a natural resource is removed, to be used in manufacturing, it is taken from the location where it naturally exists. It is excised: removed, dug up, taken away, severed, cut, so; the excise tax. Politicians are very creative at figuring out ways to siphon more taxes from their constituents. Now that everything is taxable they've decided to add *impact fees*. That way the impact fees can be placed on every product or service you use. That way the taxes you pay can be unlimited. Everything will produce the impact fee. It's an ingenious rip off. The justification is that everything you use or do has a negative impact on the environment."

"I give up. Show me your list."

"Hold on Mike. Here goes. There are eight pages, two columns. Read them and weep. These are all taxes, in one form or another. Lotteries are merely one more form of a clever method for raising more taxes. Here's the list."

**Forced contributions for the support of governments required
of persons, businesses or groups, within the domain of that
government: duty, impost, tribute, toll, surtax, levy, payment, fine,
surcharge, excise, capitation, tariff, exaction, fees, dues, tax, license,
admission, assessment, permit, foreclosures and condemnations.**

Above proof strength liquor taxes
Accounts receivable taxes
Ad valorem taxes
Added oil company taxes
*Additional business location
surtaxes*
Additional registration fees
Additional state minimum taxes
Additional tax on oil companies
*Additional taxes on occupational
licensees*
*Additional truck, trailer or semi
vehicle brewery taxes*
Administrative fees
Admissions taxes
Adoption filing fees
Agricultural property taxes
*Agricultural purposes intangible
taxes*
*Agriculture co-operative
corporation Franchise taxes*
Aircraft fees
Aircraft license taxes
Aircraft registration fees
Aircraft special fuels taxes
Airline passengers' taxes
Alaska mining royalties' taxes
Alaska mining royalties' taxes
*Alcohol consumption on premises
surcharges*
*Alcoholic beverage gross proceeds
surcharges*

Alcoholic beverage license
Alcoholic beverage taxes
Alien insurer's insurance taxes
Alternate mileage weight bus taxes
Alternative fuel usage taxes
Alternative minimum taxes
*Amended certificate of authority
taxes*
Amusement arcade licenses
Amusement parks licenses
Amusement taxes
Annual aircraft license excise taxes
Annual aircraft license taxes
Annual certificate registration fees
Annual decal fees
Annual flat rate taxes
*Annual foreign corporation exhibit
fees*
Annual highway privilege fees
Annual liquor licenses
Annual report fees
Apportioned net capital gains taxes
*Aquaculture production machinery
property taxes*
Articles of amendment filing fees
Articles of consolidation filing fees
Articles of dissolution filing fees
*Articles of incorporation recording
fees*
Articles of merger registration fees
Articles of merger filing fees
Articles of share exchange filing fees

Artificially carbonated wine taxes
Association captive insurance companies taxes
Assumed reinsurance premium taxes
Athletic events taxes
Authorized foreign insurers premiums taxes
Automobile impact fees
Automobile inspection fees
Automobile license fees
Automobile rental taxes
Auxiliary forests taxes
Balance of unpaid loans taxes
Bank deposit taxes
Bank excise taxes
Bank share taxes
Banner display fees
Barge permits
Barite severance taxes
Bauxite severance taxes
Bed and board licenses
Beer and wine vendors' surtax
Beer taxes
Beverage bottle taxes
Biennial corporation taxes
Bingo taxes
Birth certificates
Blend stock fuel taxes
Boat inspection fees
Boat licenses
Borrowed capital taxes
Brewed beverage taxes
Brewer's license
Bridge tolls
Building permits

Business development corporation's taxes
Business equipment ad valorem taxes
Business franchise registration certificates
Business income taxes
Business licenses
Business personal property taxes
Cable installation permits
Campsite rental taxes
Campground occupancy taxes
Canal company licenses
Capital gains taxes
Capital stock taxes
Captive insurer's taxes
Car line companies taxes
Carnival licenses
Carriers fuel purchase taxes
Carrier's taxes
Casing head gasoline taxes
Casual motor vehicle use taxes
Casual trailer sales taxes
Cellular communication taxes
Cement taxes
Cemetery company licenses
Certificate of authority filing fees
Certificate of convenience and necessity special fees
Certificate of withdrawal filing fees
Certificates of indebtedness stamp taxes
Chain store taxes
Chalk severance taxes
Champagne taxes
Change vending machine taxes
Charter aircraft licenses

Charter bus licenses
Chauffeur licenses
Cheroots taxes
Chewing tobacco taxes
Cider taxes
Cigar taxes
Cigarette enforcement fees
Cigarette papers taxes
Cigarette taxes
Cigarette tubes taxes
Cinnabar ore severance taxes
Circus licenses
Clay severance taxes
Clubs taxes
Coal conversion plant taxes
Coalmine license taxes
Coal severance taxes
Coal tonnage taxes
Coal used for burning solid waste
severance taxes
Co generated electricity taxes
Coin-operated amusement
machines taxes
Coliseums amusement taxes
Collateral security loans taxes
Colorado wines surcharges
Commercial air carrier's taxes
Commercial forestry excise taxes
Commercial forests taxes
Commercial leases taxes
Commercial radio, TV and
telephonic equipment taxes
Commercial self-insurance fund
taxes
Commercial vehicles additional
taxes
Commodities sales taxes

Community antenna television
systems taxes
Commuter's income taxes
Company FICA taxes
Company social security taxes
Compensating taxes
Comprehensive enhanced
transportation district taxes
Compressed natural gas taxes
Construction impact fees
Construction inspection fees
Construction sand severance taxes
Consumer's taxes
Contemplation of death estate taxes
Contract carrier's permits
Contract recording fees
Contracting taxes
Contractors' excise taxes
Controlled dangerous substances
taxes
Convention hotel room taxes
Conversation excises taxes
Cooler beverages taxes
Cooperative telephone companies
taxes
Copper production taxes
Copyright fees
Copyright taxes
Corporate entrance taxes
Corporate franchise taxes
Corporate income taxes
Corporate organization fees
Corporate qualification fees
Corporation annual registration fees
Corporation permits
Corporations land holding taxes
County inheritance taxes

County mutual insurer's taxes
County Network Support Fund
Cover charges sales taxes
Credit union taxes
Credit unions savings accounts taxes
Crematorium company licenses
Crop dusting permits
Crossties taxes
Crude oil producers' surcharge taxes
Crude oil taxes
Crushed stone severance taxes
Custom processor taxes
Cryogenically frozen sperm tax
Dealer's license issuance fees
Death certificate fees
Debentures stamp taxes
Dedicated reserve gas taxes
Deed recording fees
Deed taxes
Deer hunting stamps
Dessert wines excise taxes
Development credit corporation's surtaxes
Development credit corporation's taxes
Diesel fuel taxes
Dimension stone severance taxes
Direct captive insurer premium taxes
Display advertising taxes
Distillate special fuel taxes
Distilled spirits taxes
Distiller's license
Distributors of beer taxes
Dividend income taxes

Dividends in trust income taxes
Dockage fees
Document filing fees
Documentary stamp taxes
Domestic corporation biennial taxes
Domestic corporation taxes
Domestic corporations earned surplus taxes
Domestic per value shares filing fees
Domestic water taxes
Draft beer taxes
Drilling exploration permits
Drilling wells severance taxes
Driveways' license tags
Driveways' vehicle taxes
Drivers' licenses
Dry cleaning and laundering taxes
Economic interest in real property transfer taxes
Education excise taxes
Electric company's taxes
Electric light taxes
Electric transmission lines taxes
Electric utility surcharges
Electric vehicles taxes
Electrical cooperative corporations franchise taxes
Electrical inspection fees
Electricity license taxes
Emergency excise taxes
Emergency medical services fees
Emissions tests fees
Energy business taxes
Enhanced oil recovery using carbon dioxide taxes
Entertainment fees

Entity controlling interest transfer taxes

Enumerated business services taxes

Environmental assurance fees

Environmental fees

Environmental impact fees

Erosion control permits

Estate taxes

Excavation fees

Excursion boat gambling taxes

Excursion boat license fees

Exotic bird importation permits

Exotic wildlife importation permits

Export licenses

Exported fuel taxes

Express company's taxes

Farm and forest land conveyance taxes

Farm equipment taxes

Farm products storage permits

Farm tractor fuel taxes

Federal gasoline taxes

Federal income taxes

Federal Universal Service Charge

Federal Regulatory Fee

Ferry tolls

FICA taxes

Financial business excise taxes

Financial institutions' franchise taxes

Fire insurance premiums taxes

Fire Marshall Taxes

Fire risks insurance premiums taxes

Firearms permits

First truck, trailer or semi vehicle brewery taxes

Fish farming licenses

Fisheries business taxes

Fishing licenses

Flat weight fees

Fleet vehicles sales taxes

Flight property taxes

Floating fisheries permits

Floodwater impact fees

Food fish and shellfish taxes

Food processors leases fees

Foreign application to transact business-filing fees

Foreign building and homestead taxes

Foreign corporation biennial taxes

Foreign corporation fees

Foreign corporation registration amendment filing fees

Forest crop lands taxes

Forest lands taxes

Forest products taxes

Fortified wines taxes

Franchise taxes and fees

Free admissions taxes

Freight car rolling stock taxes

Freight line company taxes

Fuel inspection fees

Funeral permits

Fur trapping license

Furnishing of a room taxes

Gambling casinos licenses

Gaming taxes

Garbage disposal impact fees

Gas and oil severance taxes

Gas field production pumps taxes

Gas importation taxes

Gas production taxes

Gas pumping station taxes

Gasoline taxes
General excise taxes
General income taxes
General insurer's taxes
Generation skipping transfer taxes
Genetics program fees
Gift taxes
Government property rental fees
Grain brokers taxes
Grain handling taxes
Granite severance taxes
Grantor and grantee realty transfer taxes
Grape taxes
Gratuity taxes
Gravel severance taxes
Grease taxes
Grocery wholesalers permit taxes
Gross direct life insurance premiums taxes
Gross direct premiums insurance taxes
Gross operating revenue taxes
Gross premiums taxes
Gross receipts gasoline taxes
Gross receipts taxes
Ground rents taxes
Ground water protection trust fund taxes
Guaranty fund taxes
Gypsum severance taxes
Hard liquor taxes
Hard-to-dispose materials taxes
Hardwood lumber taxes
Hardwood severance taxes
Hazard waste disposal facility taxes
Hazardous substances assessments

Hazardous waste clean-up fund
Hazardous waste generators' taxes
Hazardous waste taxes
Health and accident insurance premiums taxes
Heat and power taxes
Heating inspection fees
Heavy equipment carrier's surtaxes
Highway impact fees
Horticultural property taxes
Hospital taxes
Hotel occupancy taxes
Hunting licenses
Hydroelectric companies taxes
Hydrous silicates severance taxes
Illuminating oils taxes
Impact fees
Import licenses
Import tariffs
Imported fuel taxes
Imported motor fuel taxes
Income producing property taxes
Income tax liability surcharges
Incorporation filing fees
Independently procured insurance coverage taxes
Industrial waste impact fees
Inheritance taxes
Initial fees and taxes
Initial franchise fees
Initial registration of interstate carrier taxes
Inland protection petroleum taxes
Insecticide storage permits
Insurance company's tax
Intercity passenger vehicles age additional fees

Intercity passenger vehicles fees
Inter-county motor carrier taxes
Interest income taxes
Interstate carriers gas taxes
Interstate diesel fuel taxes
Interstate for hire carrier's fees
Interstate fuel use taxes
Interstate motor carrier's taxes
Intoxication liquor license fees
Intrastate for hire carrier's fees
Intrastate motor carrier's taxes
Intrastate private car companies taxes
Intrastate telephone service taxes
Intrastate truck licenses
Inventory ad valorem taxes
Investment of capital income taxes
Iron ore severance taxes
Issuance fees
Jet fuel excise taxes
Joint return additional taxes
Kerrite severance taxes
Lead ore severance taxes
Legacy taxes
License fees
License taxes surcharge fees
License tests fees
Lien filing fees
Light trucks registration fees
Lightning insurers taxes
Lightwood severance taxes
Lignite ore severance taxes
Limestone severance taxes
Limited partnerships taxes
Liquefied petroleum gas taxes
Liquid asphalt taxes
Liquid fuel carriers' fees

Liquid malt taxes
Liquid natural gas taxes
Liquid wort taxes
Liquor excise taxes
Litter taxes
Livestock and domestic fowl taxes
Livestock transporting vehicles taxes
Loan agencies taxes
Local admissions taxes
Local option sales taxes
Locomotive fuel taxes
Lodging accommodations taxes
Log transporting vehicles taxes
Logging dollies taxes
Logging permits
Long term care policies taxes
Low alcoholic contents beverages taxes
Low grade ore property taxes
Low-level radioactive waste management taxes
Lubricating oils taxes
Luxury taxes
Maconite severance taxes
Malt beverage taxes
Malt extracts taxes
Manganese ore severance taxes
Manganiferous ore severance taxes
Manufacturer's taxes
Manufacturing machinery taxes
Marble severance taxes
Marching permits
Marginal properties crude oil severance taxes
Maritime visitor's fees
Marl severance taxes
Marriage dissolution recording fees

Marriage licenses
Maryland oil transfer taxes
Meals and rooms taxes
Medicaid gross receipts taxes
Medical malpractice self-insurance fund taxes
Medical service corporation's taxes
Medical services licenses
Medicine taxes
Merchantable timber taxes
Merchant's taxes
Messages taxes
Metalliferous dealer's taxes
Metalliferous mines taxes
Micaceous dealer's taxes
Micaceous mining taxes
Michigan grown fruit excise taxes
Migratory bird stamps
Mine site taxes
Mined-land conversation taxes
Mineral documentary lease taxes
Mineral documentary taxes
Minerals extraction taxes
Mining gross income taxes
Mining license taxes
Mining metalliferous minerals taxes
Mining tailings deposit taxes
Miscellaneous insurance risks premiums taxes
Miscellaneous taxes
Mixed drinks at private club taxes
Mixed spirit drink taxes
Mobile home excise taxes
Mobile home taxes
Modified Kansas businesses taxes
Molybdenum severance taxes

Money on hand property taxes
Money transmitter's taxes
Mortgage registration taxes
Motel room occupancy taxes
Motion pictures amusement taxes
Motor carriers road taxes
Motor carriers certificate taxes
Motor carriers of property taxes
Motor carrier's purchase taxes
Motor carriers taxes
Motor carriers weight fees
Motor fuel importers taxes
Motor fuel taxes
Motor vehicle carrier fees
Motor vehicle registration fees
Motor vehicles taxes
Motorcycle licenses
Mountain lakes property taxes
Multi-employer welfare taxes
Multi-state businesses taxes
Multi-state income taxes
Municipal unrefined oil and gas taxes
Municipality income taxes
Mutual telephone companies taxes
National Parks camping fees
National Parks entry fees
National Parks rental fees
Native brandy taxes
Natural gas processors taxes
Natural resource severance taxes
Natural sparkling wine taxes
Net direct premiums insurance taxes
Net direct subscribers charges taxes
Net income surtaxes
Net precedes taxes

Newspaper taxes
Non commercial vehicles taxes
Non-admitted procured insurance taxes
Non-intoxicating malt liquor taxes
Nonresident earnings taxes
Non par stock value taxes
Nuclear station property taxes
Nursing homes inspection fees
Nursing homes licenses
Occluded coal seam natural gas taxes
Occupancy permits
Ocean marine insurer's taxes
Ocean marine underwriting taxes
Off shore drilling permits
Off shore fishing licenses
Offshore canneries licenses
Oil and gas ad valorem taxes
Oil and gas conservation surcharges
Oil and gas conservation taxes
Oil and gas emergency school taxes
Oil and gas product equipment ad valorem taxes
Oil and gas properties taxes
Oil companies taxes
Oil disaster license fees
Oil discharge prevention fees
Oil production taxes
Oil shale severance taxes
Oil spill contingency fees
Oil spill fees
Oil spillage in public waters fees
Oil terminal facility fees
Old crude oil taxes
On premises liquor consumption taxes

Organizational dues taxes
Out-of-state solid wastes disposal fees
Outside burning permits
Parking and storage gross receipts taxes
Partnerships taxes
Passport fees
Patent fees
Patents taxes
Pension and profit sharing plans taxes
Periodicals taxes
Perlite severance taxes
Personal income taxes
Persons distributing gas or electricity taxes
Persons supplying gas or electricity taxes
Persons transmitting messages taxes
Petroleum clean water trust fund taxes
Petroleum environmental assurance fees
Petroleum taxes
Phosphate rock severance taxes
Pickup trucks taxes
Pilots' licenses
Pine lumber taxes
Pipe dollies taxes
Pipeline taxes
Pleasure vehicle fees
Plumbing inspection fees
Pole dollies taxes
Pollution control equipment taxes
Pollution control fees
Pond excavation permits

Precious metals severance taxes
Pre-existing leases taxes
Premixed liquor taxes
Prepared food taxes
Primary forest products assessments
Printing taxes
Private car companies taxes
Private fire insurance premiums taxes
Production credit association's taxes
Production taxes
Professional licenses
Proof strength liquor taxes
Propane licenses
Propane tank inspection fees
Property taxes
Proprietor taxes
Public utilities franchise taxes
Public utilities taxes
Public utility assessment fees
Pullman company taxes
Pulpwood chips taxes
Pulpwood taxes
Purchasers of livestock for processing taxes
Purchasers of livestock for resale taxes
Pure captive insurance companies taxes
Qualified enhanced recovery project taxes
Quality air control impact fees
Radio transmission licenses
Railroad companies taxes
Railroad franchise taxes
Railroad operating over another's tracks taxes

Railroad terminal taxes
Railway express company's taxes
Rangeland grazing fees
Raw and in process materials taxes
Raw fur pelt dealer's fees
Real estate corporations franchise taxes
Real property conveyance taxes
Realty transfer taxes
Receiver's fuel taxes
Reciprocal taxes
Recycling surcharges
Recycling taxes
Refined oil taxes
Refined petroleum products taxes
Reflectorized license plates fees
Reflectorized license plates service fees
Reforestation land taxes
Reforestation taxes
Regulatory fee
Renovation additions permits
Rental motor vehicle surcharge taxes
Rental motor vehicle taxes
Rental occupancy taxes
Reserve accounts taxes
Residential density impact fees
Resources excise taxes
Retail charge accounts payable taxes
Retail license issuance fees
Retail occupational sales taxes
Retail sale of personality taxes
Retailer's occupation taxes
Retirement plans taxes
Risk management trust fund taxes

Risk retention insurance companies taxes
River quality impact fees
Riverboat gambling licenses
Room renting taxes
Royalty agreements taxes
Rural electric cooperatives taxes
Recreational Vehicle licenses
Sales and use taxes
Sales taxes
Salt from brine taxes
Salt production taxes
Salt water yielding bromine products taxes
Sandstone severance taxes
Sanitary landfill permits
Sanitary landfill taxes
Savings and loan association taxes
Saw logs severance taxes
Sawmill licenses
Scheduled route passenger carriers taxes
Sea shells severance taxes
Secured debt mortgage registry taxes
Self-propelled vehicle fees
Semi-trailer taxes
Senior Citizens homes licenses
Septic field inspections
Service occupation taxes
Service use taxes
Severance beneficiary taxes
Severance taxes
Sewage disposal installation permits
Sewage lines installation permits
Sewer utilities taxes
Shale severance taxes

Shareholder's equity attributable to Kansas's taxes
Shore based salmon canneries taxes
Shore based fisheries permits
Short-term vehicles rental taxes
Signal oil taxes
Silica sand severance taxes
Single business taxes
Skating rinks amusement taxes
Skin dealer's licenses
Sleeping car taxes
Small cigars taxes
Small winery permits
Smaller pickup trucks taxes
Smokeless tobacco taxes
Snuff taxes
Social Security health premiums
Soft woods severance taxes
Solid minerals severance taxes
Solid minerals taxes
Solid waste fees
Sparkling hard cider taxes
Sparkling wine taxes
Special fuel surcharges
Special fuel taxes
Spill compensation and control taxes
Spirituous liquor licenses
State death taxes
State dispensary beer surcharges
State gasoline tax
State income taxes
State parks camping fees
Steam companies taxes
Still wine taxes
Stocks and bonds income taxes
Stogies taxes
Stored gasoline taxes

Strip mine reclamation fees
Stripper well crude oil severance taxes
Stumpage value taxes
Subchapter S Corporations taxes
Succession taxes
Sulfur production taxes
Supplemental net income taxes
Surface mining severance taxes
Surplus lines brokers taxes
Surplus lines insurances taxes
Swimming pools amusement taxes
Switch ties taxes
Table wine excise taxes
Table wine taxes
Taconite and iron sulfides taxes
Tangible personal property taxes
Telecommunication company taxes
Telecommunication excise taxes
Telecommunication services taxes
Telegraph and cable taxes
Telegraph companies taxes
Telegraph longest wire taxes
Telegraph next longest wire taxes
Telephone companies taxes
Telephone transmitter's taxes
Television transmission licenses
Tennis court rental fee
Temporary registration fees
Thorium milling taxes
Timber products taxes
Timber taxes
Tips and gratuity income taxes
Tire acquisition taxes
Tire disposal taxes
Titanium ore severance taxes
Title insurer's taxes

To transact business in State fees
Tobacco products taxes
Tobacco stamp taxes
Toll telecommunication service taxes
Tour vehicle licenses
Tour vehicle surcharges
Tour vehicle taxes
Tourism promotion taxes
Tourist tickets taxes
Tow operators licenses
Trademark fees
Traders' license fees
Traffic fines
Trailer home permits
Transaction privilege taxes
Transient accommodations taxes
Transient lodgings taxes
Transient rentals taxes
Transient retailers' taxes
Transmission franchise taxes
Transportation franchise taxes
Transportation insurer's taxes
Trapping licenses
Tree growth taxes
Tree retention taxes
Tree severance taxes
Trip permits
Truck camper's licenses
Truck camper's registration fees
Truck-mile taxes
Trust intangible taxes
Turpentine crude gum severance taxes
Turpentine severance taxes
U-Drive-It rental charges use taxes
U-Drive-It retail sales price use taxes

Unauthorized insurers taxes
Underground fuel storage environment study fees
Underground fuel storage tank permits
Underground mining severance taxes
Underground storage tank taxes
Underwriting gross profit taxes
Undistributed earnings taxes
Undeveloped land taxes
Undivided profits taxes
Unemployment compensation taxes
Unemployment insurance taxes
Unincorporated businesses taxes
Unincorporated businesses surtaxes
Unimproved land taxes
Un-manufactured agricultural products taxes
Un-mined coal taxes
Unorganized territory taxes
Unrefined oil and gas taxes
Uranium milling taxes
Use fuel taxes
Use taxes
Utilities earnings taxes
Utilities occupation taxes
Utility gross receipts and use tax
Utility inspection fees
Utility line discovery fees
Utility regulatory fees
Utility trailer rental sales taxes
Van rental taxes
Vehicle certificate of title taxes
Vehicle document fees
Vehicle lease taxes
Vehicle rental taxes

Vehicle weight fees
Vending machine beverages sales taxes
Vending machine food sales taxes
Vending machine permits
Vermiculite severance taxes
Vessels registered tonnage taxes
Vineyard license
Vinous liquor excise taxes
Water equipment rental taxes
Water line installation permits
Water quality assurance fees
Water quality taxes
Water runoff impact fees
Water usage impact fees
Water use taxes
Water utilities taxes
Watercraft inspection fees
Well drilling permits
Wet marine transportation taxes
Wharfage fees
Wheat taxes
White pilings severance taxes
Wholesale spirituous liquor taxes
Wholesale tobacco taxes
Wholesale vinous liquor taxes
Wide load highway permits
Windfall Profit taxes
Withholding taxes
Wood treatment fuel taxes
Workers' compensation taxes
Yield taxes
Zinc ore severance taxes
Zoning application fees
Zoning permits
Zoning signage fees

"I think I will be sick," I said.

"You should, with those revelations," Cougar said. "You have the most heavily taxed country on earth and none of your citizenry seems to be aware of that fact. When you return home ask everyone you know exactly what percentage they pay in taxation and you will get answers ranging from 25% to perhaps 50%. As a matter of interest, ask them to name the taxes they pay and you will be amazed to find that they can't name more than eight or nine so you see how insidious your tax policy is. Officials are screwing you and you do not know it."

"I don't want to discuss it anymore," I said.

"I can't blame you. My people did not pay taxes to provide service or to pay some bureaucrat for making decisions. We worked together to get things done and to decide what was best for the population as a whole. Everything we did, or needed, was shared equally. No one got paid to do what was necessary. You have one of the most burdensome governments in the world, so big that one department has no idea what another department is doing. They are falling all over each other, floundering inefficiently. "

"Let's have something to eat," I suggested. "Why don't I get a deer?"

"Let's both go hunting."

"Before we go, and before I forget, there is one quick question I'd like to cover."

"The deer will wait," Cougar said.

"We have television news reporters attempting to fill up time slots with newsworthy information. You probably are not interested but I thought you might have some thoughts on the subject," I said.

"I don't see much news but when I do I see those people wearing out news by repeating it ad infinitum. News should be new but there is too much air time to be filled with new news so tired news is repeated, ad nausea."

"I agree totally. And they attempt to make every story seem sensational. Some years ago a plane developed a problem on approach to Peachtree DeKalb airport. It crashed short of the runway killing two passengers plus the pilot. Their glide path was over a residential area. After the crash a female newscaster interviewed the residents under the glide path. She asked them if they had heard screams coming from the airplane as it passed over their houses."

"She was trying to sensationalize a terrible tragedy," Cougar said.

"That's a stupid reporter," I said.

"C'mon. Let's go hunting," Cougar said.

Chapter Eighteen

We grabbed our bows and set off for the high part of the valley. The cougar loped along.

Cougar studied my recurve bow. "You go first," he said.

Spying a doe at the edge of a clearing, I fitted a broad head on the bow and sighted down the arrow shaft. It was a long shot for me. The deer began to move. A stiff breeze was blowing. I let my arrow fly. I misjudged the crosswind. The arrow missed the deer. Startled, the deer sprinted away just as Cougar shot. The animal leaped into the air then dropped dead, an arrow embedded in its heart.

"My father's Osage bow," he said. The puma raced to drag our meal back to the campsite.

"Nice size, good and tender." Cougar observed.

I field dressed the carcass while Cougar built a fire. I tossed a hindquarter to the mountain lion. I threw some scraps into the underbrush and heard scrambling as several scavengers vied for the feast. I cut some chunks to save for other carnivores waiting in the distance. I put some pieces out on a boulder and watched a hawk and an eagle descend from the sky. They feasted, too, eyeing each other but sociable.

Cougar mixed some herbs and pressed them into the meat. He put the deer on a spit.

"You're one hell-of-an-archer," I commented.

"I only shoot moving things," he said. "I give an animal a better chance for a longer life."

"With that shot I would not want to be targeted."

We enjoyed the venison cooked over open flames. I had never had venison seasoned that way. The mountain lion finished the entire hindquarter then headed down to the stream for a drink. As usual several of Mother Nature's clean-up crew finished off the scraps.

Cougar again lighted his pipe then leaned back on an elk-hide blanket. "You are the first paleface that I have invited into this valley. I have enjoyed our conversations even though it brings back painful memories. You're not like the palefaces I have watched on my sojourns. You're a realist. I hope you and I will be friends for life."

"I'm only 83 years old," I said. "How can an older fellow like you be friends with somebody as young as I?" I grinned. "Whatever you've got you should bottle it and make a fortune."

"I will be eternally young. So will you so we can forever be kindred spirits. I already possess my fortune though, just look around. Mother Nature's abundance is my wealth."

"Truthfully, Cougar, I'm glad because, except for you, I have never had friends. I know a lot of people but I've never had what you would call a true friend. That fact does not bother me at all. You are remarkably sincere, a really rare trait. My wife says that I have eccentricities and I concede that I do. But they are as the result of circumstances over which I had no control as a youngster. During the Depression liberalism was totally unacceptable but now people accept behavior that would have elicited screams of outrage a mere forty years ago. Being here is a positive experience. I'm glad I came."

"I have spoken with the Great Spirit about you so we are going to become friends. I'm happy you came, too." He smiled. "You are the first person I've spoken to, as myself, for two centuries. I have been around the world many times and have listened in on private conversations among important people and rulers of nations. Quite frankly, if I were a mere citizen of the world I would be worried about my future, but as you now know nothing can affect me personally, and now that we are true kindred spirits you will always be above the international fray, too."

"Have you ever thought about getting married?"

"After seeing what I have seen in reality and the infidelity occurring surreptitiously in the minds of people who are married on paper but cheaters in their innermost intimate thoughts, no I do not think it would be wise for me. Uniting two extremes on a contractual basis is fraught with danger both emotional and psychological. Why expose yourself to the potential deviltry? The union of marriage is such an over-rated and emotional inter-action that I've chosen to avoid it. Why suffer when you don't have to suffer?"

"During my experiences being married is good. I have been married to my wife for many years. We have rarely experienced discord, conflict or tension," I explained.

"That word *rarely* is the key. It's ambiguous. Once would be too many," Cougar said. "The Great Spirit decries dissention."

We got up and ambled down to the river's edge and watched some trout winnowing in the clear shallows. I faced Cougar again. I wasn't going to go home without gleaning every smidgen of knowledge I could from this vast reservoir.

"How about our criminal justice system, I believe it is fractured, even impotent?"

"First, I think you should warn your readers about the massive debt they are building up. It will be their eventual downfall."

"How so?' I pulled out another notepad. His knowledge was astonishing.

"Well. Most people are heavily in debt," Cougar said. "Too many credit cards. It's the cookie-jar syndrome; put a jar of cookies in front of kids who have no control and their hands will be inside the jar instantly. Credit card companies are aware of that child-like weakness, so they send out millions of cards with low short-term percentage rates knowing full well that some of the gullible recipients will accept the offer to be able to have *anothe*r credit card. It's like a fish taking bait. People have an average of thirteen credit obligations, exclusive of mortgages, some with ten or more credit cards. Total consumer revolving debt in the country is 962 billion dollars, most of it in credit card debts. The national average for debts is $1675.00 with one third of the debtors owing over $10,000. Credit card companies entice consumers into spending beyond their ability to repay with pictures of yachts, exotic vacations, Hummers; the cookie jar syndrome, things they can't possibly afford without a credit card. Then when the consumer can't pay for what they have purchased, the credit card companies tack on exorbitant fees, penalties, then jack up the low <u>come-on</u> percentage to some monstrous amount, sending their payments skyrocketing, assuring that the victims will never be able to repay the amounts to which they have obligated themselves. It is a slick trick to keep people paying for years. You would think that watching others floundering in debt, people would learn economic reality. But the old cookie jar seducer got to them. Some credit companies charge exorbitant fees just for people to have their card in addition to the charges made to businesses that accept the card. If a credit card company charges $100 annual fee and they have ten millions cards in circulation the yearly revenue generated is one billion dollars, free and clear. For what? Prestige? That's what clever promotion will cause, illusions. Shown are smiling card-holders in prestigious restaurants, sunning on the French Riviera, golfing at Pebble Beach, bobsledding in Aspen, all for weak-willed people to succumb to the lure of the card. $100? Not very bright when people shouldn't be charging in the first place."

Scribbling frantically, I said. "How do you know all that stuff?"

"I know everything, Mike," Cougar said.

"I have only one credit card. I only use it for convenience or in case of an emergency."

"Smart people use it that way. Gullible people don't."

"Don't you ever want something you don't have?"

"The Great Spirit sees that I have everything. I covet nothing."

"Then back to our screwed-up criminal justice system? I think it's broken," I said.

"One other critical consideration with which your society is confronted and that is violence. Your emerging generation is being hammered by either actual violence or a portrayal of violence on television and in the movies. They see domestic violence at home. They play violent games at arcades. Newscasters prefer reporting about the most gruesome violence they can discover. Streets are filled with violence so it is understandable that if children are exposed to incessant violence they are more likely to be violent, too. Society has been acquiescent on violence to the detriment of the future. You may already have lost one or two generations of your children to destructive influences beyond your control, perhaps beyond recovery. Unfortunately many parents and government officials seem too busy having parties to be concerned. Too busy playing golf. Too busy shopping. Too busy vacationing. Too busy. Too busy. Too busy."

"Sounds ominous," I said.

"It is," Cougar said. "And now we can get on with your fragmented criminal justice system."

Chapter Nineteen

"Your justice system has become unfair to victims of crime. There are several problems. Your constitution guarantees a speedy trial. However that guarantee is frequently circumvented by attorneys who will become wealthy by deliberate delays, disguised as necessary, but prolonging a case so that their fees become much more lucrative. Along with the retainer fees up front they are compensated by the hour so your system does not provide speedy justice. Also a killer even under a sentence of death can stay alive for decades. That is unfair when you realize that the people he killed have been dead since the murder. If I were in charge of your justice system I would purchase an isolated island some place in the South Pacific surrounded by shark infested seas. I would transport all of your criminals by helicopter and drop them off on the island along with their pistols and knives. They could have a party doing what they do best."

"You sound severe," I said.

"To reduce crime you must be hardened. If not, you send the wrong message to criminals."

"We need a more effective system," I said.

"You need a plan for the increasing gang violence or it will get further out of hand. Originally, gangs consisted of Afro Americans wanting desperately to become someone important, so they took over neighborhoods and established their realm. They controlled drug and prostitution rackets and produced a lot of money. They could purchase glitzy chains. Woe to anyone venturing into their area. Others saw the gold chains and began other gangs. Competition for control caused immediate violence. Afro Americans began shooting Afro Americans in other gangs that intruded. In defense, paleface gangs were started and warfare began. Then the Latinos moved in and formed equally vicious gangs. White gangs have become the minorities. Afro American and Latino gangs are now in a race war according to police reports. It's a troubling dilemma for America."

"Recent evidence is worrying," I said. "There are efforts by police to form new departments and combine their forces with the Feds and others in an attempt to gain control of residential neighborhoods where gangs presently dominate. I'm afraid it will be a bloody battle with gangs so firmly entrenched. We need help."

"You do, desperately," Cougar said. "One idiotic tenet of the system, causing contempt on the part of criminals, is where the punishment doesn't fit their crimes. For example; a female is raped and murdered with the killer sentenced to life in prison, without parole. What kind of a message does it send to thugs who have little fear of prison life? It says you can kill and rape until you're caught and then you get free room and board for the rest of your life. It's imperative that your parade of pacifists be replaced by realists. You people need to commence a two-eyes-for-an-eye philosophy."

"We have some insurmountable problems, too."

"Many," Cougar said. "One more obvious trend in your society is the extreme disparity between those who live luxuriously like potentates, and those who struggle every day just to survive. The rich are becoming wealthier and the poorest are suffering demoralizing impoverishment. There are thirty-seven million citizens living below the poverty level, that's in a nation supposedly the richest in the world. You have over a million people pitifully surviving in cardboard boxes, sewers and tunnels under major cities and on park benches. It is shameful. I see them scavenging in garbage cans while rich people flaunt their material possessions. They see multi-millionaires purchasing everything they want, living in luxury. That historically creates anarchy. You are watching that brewing daily in your society; robbery, fraud, home invasions, car-jackings, looting, swindlers, purse snatching, gas siphoning, shoplifters, senseless killing, and inner-city hostilities. That causes hatred between those who have nothing and those who have more than they need. It is a problem that's been emerging ever since monkeys first stood upright. Poverty and the subsequent desperation it generates are setting the stage for your demise."

I stood and stretched. Cougar got his pipe from a leather bag and began tamping is some tobacco. I got a sudden yen to smoke again. He lighted the pipe and my urge blossomed.

"You got another pipe?" I said hesitantly.

"I knew you couldn't last much longer." My friend chuckled, as he tossed me a weather-beaten corncob pipe. I tamped in a supply of tobacco from his pouch and lit it, inhaling deeply. Violent choking and coughing spasms began immediately. My nose dripped and my eyes watered. Visible spittle sprayed across the area as I gasped for air.

"That's awful," I said.

"It is not for everyone," he said, as he blew some interlocking circles that drifted slowly away. "There is still more to our previous discussion."

I wiped my eyes and regained my composure as I handed him back his pipe. "What else."

"It entails a fallacy that all people are born equal. That's just not true. Some are born more equal than others. Isn't it lamentable, in this supposedly greatest country on earth for a homeless vagrant to be burned to death in an abandoned, rat infested house, where he started a fire to keep from freezing while at the same time baseball players receive multi-million dollar contracts, live in mansions, and are driven around in limousines simply for playing a stupid game."

"Isn't it obscene for millions of children to have to go to bed with empty stomachs while golfers, wearing designer clothing and flying on their personal jet, play a game for four days for prize money that would feed hundreds of families for a year."

"Isn't it reprehensible for billionaires to live in ostentatious mansions with a fleet of limousines, while impoverished Americans are having their utility service disconnected because they can't afford to pay their bill? This is a great nation, in whose opinion, Mike?" Cougar rolled his eyes.

"And isn't it morally repugnant for a Hollywood actress to get $25,000,000 for starring in a B-movie about a whore while millions of your citizens cannot afford food and medical care. Why is that considered to be greatness?" Cougar said. "Somewhere there has been a reversal in your humanitarian priorities. Somewhere you have forgotten your original direction."

"How did you handle the situations where you had members of a family get so old and feeble that their life was nearly over?" I said.

"We continued sharing the love of caring for old people until they died."

I thought about Cougar's response.

"I read somewhere that some original societies in Alaska have a great method for allowing their members to age gracefully. We don't do that. We stuff them in nursing homes convincing ourselves that we are humane in our treatment of old Grammy and Grampy. Stick them away where we don't have to care for them. There is a better way. For thousands of years some society of Eskimos, north of the Arctic Circle, have practiced a novel method for disposing of relatives who have aged to a point where they are unable to make contribution for the welfare of the village. With carcasses unable to decompose in such frigid weather it is impractical to bury a body. Instead, when Gram'pa and Gram'ma are too old to be of any use they are taken out on an ice floe and left for nature to be humane. The bodies are quickly frozen and in the course of a few days, eaten by polar bears."

"Modern society dictates that methods to get rid of Gram'pa and Gram'ma after they've become useless, be really humane, so we trundle them off to some bleach-soaked warehouses where they can rot incrementally while continuing to shrivel piece-by-precious-piece until only a mummy remains, and we convince ourselves that we are a wonderfully humane society."

"Surgeons adore our humanitarian ways because as our old people become older more parts need repaired or removed so our opportunistic doctors keep on cutting away part after part until their gold-clad Mercedes is paid for, or the dying person fortunately dies."

"I recall the story of a hypochondriac who could not be cured by her physician. The physician's son graduated from medical school and joined his father. A year later the son happily told his father that he had cured the hypochondriac. You are stupid, the man told his son. How do you think I paid for your books and tuition?"

"After an MRI and ex-rays one orthopedic surgeon said he could repair my frozen shoulder using arthroscopic surgery. He said I would get back eighty percent of my range-of-motion I had lost because of the problem. Right after my operation he told me that it was in worse condition than he realized and after a few probes, he decided to stop. Still he received compensation from Medicare. I soon had surgery from a different surgeon that was successful. Such are the oaths of hypocrisy."

"Morticians love the family of the deceased. They have you when your defenses are down and are able to convince you that the most costly casket is the appropriate sarcophagus in which to transport those deceased relatives to eternal happiness in heaven."

"Nursing homes are packed with seniors who have not quite made that inevitable passage from a real live person to someone who is no longer able to function. Billions of dollars are spent keeping people alive who should be allowed to die. It is inhumane to compel seniors to suffer diapers and spoon-feeding. Jack Kevorkian offered a service in assisting older people to be in control of their own destiny until some prosecutor sent him to prison. So instead of being allowed to die with some dignity people are now being warehoused under conditions that we will all regret when it is our time to go. So why not be humane and send the seniors who have no awareness of life to Alaska for disposal?"

"I don't agree with you, Mike. I believe family members should be kept around, and loved, until such time for them to go to their happy hunting ground," Cougar said.

"Are you really that compassionate?" I said.

"You remember my remark about truth?"

"Yes."

"Everything I have said since you arrived has been the truth. The Great Spirit does not condone hypocrisy. You should have known my family. You would have adored them."

"You astound me, my friend. Hollywood's producers portray Native Americans as bloodthirsty savages. How incredibly wrong they are," I said.

"How would they know about truth and reality?" Cougar smiled. "Their minds are too obsessed with portraying decadence and deceit"

"I feel that all the time," I said.

"They're too involved with fantasy and make-believe," Cougar said. "Doesn't it make you a little sick to see the absurdities they produce."

"And they are acclaimed for that sewage," I said. "They get Emmys and Oscars."

"C'est la vie," Cougar said.

"I believe that's French. What does it mean?"

"Such is life."

"I'm amazed that an Indian can speak French?"

"Solder leben ist. Tal es la vida."

"I should have known."

Chapter Twenty

During my last day in the wilderness Cougar and I sat, gazing out over his wonderful valley. The horses were grazing near the river, the cougar stretched out near the fire pit his skin quivering frequently as if dreaming. I felt a deepening affinity for my newly found friend. In less than four weeks Cougar had become a replacement brother for the brother I had lost in Bastogne. Johnny would have given an instant thumbs-up for my choice to take his place in my heart.

"You've provided me your insight on a good number of problems facing civilization, particularly in the United States. I'd like your opinion on one of my big concerns and get an assessment on pedophiles preying on young boys and girls. It is getting out of hand."

"You have a crisis, I will admit," Cougar agreed.

I explained. "It is not that rare instance of psychopathic behavior infesting this country. Other instances are the nuts in chat rooms searching for some sick release. An example: they search, faceless creatures with warped minds, depraved predators, hunched in front of their computer screen, searching online for young victims, gullible, lonely children, young boys or girls, it makes no difference to such creatures. Like hunters they stay hidden from the eyes of their intended prey until their selected victim shows vulnerability, and then the demon takes over."

"Friendly conversation at first, suggestive phrases, inveigling their way in, unknown, disturbed minds secreted from friends and family. Who are they? Scumbags? Sure, but frequently with degrees in business, plaques from universities. Not known as psychopathic citizens. Sometime, fathers with wives and kids but with an evil human frailty. Surprise! My neighbor up the road is a predator? Why? I have known the guy for years. I played golf with him. He attends church regularly. How can it be? He would not perform perverted acts on little girls. He would not rape and kill little girls. But he did, preying on emotionally immature kids that were enticed onto the internet by loneliness, seeking cool friends. Not him! It must be a big mistake! He was so nice at the neighborhood party! But authorities went into his home and confiscated his computer. There were thousands of files, filled with disgusting pornography. When did he find the time to do all that? There were files of pics and DVD's all fastidiously concealed, along with pictures of naked children in suggestive poses. Why would a sane man want to have erotic photos? Where was his wife when it was being downloaded? It had to be when she was working or in those dark hours before anyone was awakened. Depravity like that must be kept a secret. He must have spent hours seeking cesspools on the internet, lining up an enormous reservoir of pornographic photos to sate a psychopathic mind. Perhaps his aberrations were nurtured by seeing scantily-clad women on TV squirming orgiastically. Perhaps he lusted to touch them, in intimate places. Maybe he fondles himself while viewing pornography. And perhaps that once nice father became another of the predators, lusting online building up nerve to binge on decadent photographs. And like with any addiction lives are being destroyed by that behavioral anomaly."

"Locked arm in arm in their sickness the sexual predators have joined in step with those sicko people who film filthy pictures for viewing online, portable cell phones, I-PODS, and X-rated movies. They crawl from every walk of life, and at every income level: bus drivers, ball players, attorneys, day laborers, bankers, engineers, politicians. You might expect it from some sleaze-bag, but to see a Judge shackled for planning to have sex with two little girls makes one wonder, as the sickness spreads like a raging wildfire, just how much longer society can survive. And how many sickos yet secreted are there, riveted before computer screens, hidden from civilized people, lights dim, eyes glazing, doors secured, mouths drooling, morals corrupting, feeding the cancer that is eating away at their brain? They are the same sociopathic nuts who roam neighborhoods late at night, peeking through slatted blinds, lusting to see something to feed the cancerous torment in their rotting brains."

Cougar smiled knowingly. "If I had not heard it from your mouth, I would swear that you read my mind. Maybe you did. We really are kindred spirits."

"I'm going to have to leave tomorrow," I said.

"I know," Cougar said. "I wish you could stay. Let's knock off for a while. There's someplace I'd like you to see."

"Fine with me," I said. "This is one fascinating place."

"Come with me." He motioned toward a knoll.

We climbed a gentle rise in the valley and stood atop the knoll. We could see our horses nose to nose down by the stream. The cougar was lying in the shade of an aspen, sleeping.

"We're going up on the escarpment," Cougar said.

I detected nothing, yet suddenly we started to rise up the face of the escarpment. I could sense nothing except a slight motion. We were side by side. It was like an elevator ride without an elevator. I glanced at Cougar and saw nothing unusual. Man, what miraculous power, I thought.

After rising perhaps 800 feet the leading edge of the escarpment appeared. From there the rocks sloped upward to a snow-covered ridge. A large boulder rested on the slope. He walked to the boulder. I followed him. It was a place of incredible serenity and natural beauty. Picas stared at us from a pile of rocks then scurried into their tunnels in the hillside.

"Let's sit here," Cougar said. "The scenario here is spectacular. If you look to the East, you will see the sun rising over Missoula, Montana. To the North is the Sawtooth Mountain range. Behind us the mountains rise to 9000 feet. In the evening when the sun sinks in the west it silhouettes the jagged scutes of the mountains. Now look down into the valley and tell me you wouldn't like living here." He smiled.

I had to admit Cougar had a good argument. But if I suggested coming here to my wife I would have my sanity questioned. "My wife's countrified," I said. "But not this much."

"We've spent considerable time together, Mike. I want you to know that I like your philosophy on life. I have met many successful people in my lifetime, of course unknown to them. Too many have dysfunctional lives irrespective of their riches, possessions and titles. You seem contented."

"I am. I'm lucky I guess. My grandfather, who was a hard working farmer, once admonished me that a man can only sleep in one bed at a time. I remembered his wisdom. I live a simple life, as I believe you do. I don't have a lot, and I don't yearn for more, as I see other people around me doing. They never seem satisfied."

"Lust enflames more lust for more stuff than they can afford." Cougar said.

"It's a fermenting sickness in our society," I said.

"I'm aware you were in the fur industry, Mike," Cougar said. "That interests me because of my people's association with wildlife. Indians and animals are kindred spirits. We hold all animals in high esteem. The Great Spirit allows us to use the animals for food and clothing."

"I feel the same way," I said. "Animals played a special role in the development of this country, particularly the beaver. The first sale of beaver skins from the New World was held in Garraway's Coffee house on January 24, 1672 by 'The Honourable, the Govenour and Company of Merchants. Adventurers Trading into Hudson Bay' in honor of which Dryden wrote: "Friend, once 'twas Fame that led thee forth, to brave the Tropic Heat, the Frozen North; Late it was gold, then Beauty was the Spur; But now our gallants venture forth but for fur."

Cougar smiled. "Your gallants were laggards. My people ventured forth 14,000 years ago."

"I just knew you'd make some remark," I said.

"It's truth," Cougar said. "And it wasn't really a New World. We were here."

"Despite the satirical remarks of Dryden, the world it appeared had more respect for furs than for gold. To the people of the New World, the beaver was literally an emblem of wealth. It was so important to frontiersmen that an emblem of the beaver was embossed on the first shield of New Amsterdam's seal. After the revolution, the eagle supplanted the crown but two beavers remained on the shield."

"Need I remind you that we were here thousands of years before 1672? The Europeans had killed thousands of my people by that time." Cougar looked solemn.

"I wasn't part of those plans," I said.

"Just thought I'd remind you of historical facts," he said.

"The story of fur trading in early America is the actuality of our expansion. Valiant fur trappers led the way into remote regions of America and Canada. Commerce naturally followed with John Jacob Astor amassing a fortune and was virtually the first man on the continent to be the employer of thousands of gainfully employed people in the various aspects of the fur trade under the name of the American Fur Company. America exported millions of dollars in furs to hungry European and Asian markets with the incomes amply funding America's initial development. We can thank the fur business for jump starting American emergence as a world financial power."

"We didn't export furs but neither did we exploit Mother Nature," Cougar said. "We used fur for warmth, to keep from freezing during winters. We wore them. We covered our teepees with them."

"I know that," I said. "But along with being absolutely necessary in frigid climates as protection against freezing to death, fur has also gained importance as one of the world's great fashion images. Fur is long wearing and fortunately for the environment biodegradeable. Synthetics, on the other hand, are made from petroleum products which, as we saw in the Bay of Valdez spill, can pollute the land and water for all eternity. Additionally, synthetics have to be burned for disposal, further polluting the environment, or piled on already overflowing landfills with long range destructive impact on the land which has very little area remaining on which to hide garbage."

"We never had synthetics. Everything was natural. And renewable."

"I'm proud of the fact that I contributed to a strong segment of the American economy with the United States' fur industry. It provided good wages for over a million of my fellow citizens. A peak $2 billion sales volume provided city, state, county and federal government annual taxes and license fees exceeding $500,000,000. Another $300,000,000 was spent by the fur industry for advertising benefiting newspapers, magazines and the electronic media, plus their employees. Additional millions of dollars contributed heavily to the prosperity of insurance companies, equipment suppliers, shipping companies, security businesses and many more."

"I see you have a prominent location in Atlanta," Cougar said.

I smiled. "You really are a visionary, aren't you?"

"You should be convinced by now," he said.

"I am."

"How were you able to do so well?"

"All you have to do is be smarter than your competition." One thing I did that assured my success was to be totally honest with my customers. While other salons were jacking-up phony prices in order to give phony discounts, I remained assiduously honest. I told my customers that if I had to screw them in order to make a sale I'd get out of the business. Integrity was important to me."

"You apparently are doing well," Cougar said.

"You know already, don't you? I've had my ups and downs."

He smiled knowingly. "I know," he said.

Out came the pipe. Cougar tamped in another bowl of tobacco. The aroma was a lure to me, but I resisted. I watched the eyes of a man who loved his smoking.

"So how is your social life," Cougar said.

"Not much," I said. "I'm pretty much a loner."

"You're better off," he said.

"I have only one friend remaining from World War II. We're the only two left from the crew of our vessel. He and I, with three other crewmen, survived overnight when our vessel went down outside Anzio. We luckily had our Mae West so we floated, worried about sharks, though. We attended college together. He's rich. Inherited a lot of money and was successful during his career. He and I sometimes played golf. We were scratch players. I invited him to play the Augusta National course. I had a friend who was a member. Ken invited me to play Pebble Beach and Cyprus Point in Carmel. He intended to play every fine golf course around the world on retirement and he could certainly afford it. He flew his own airplane. Keeps homes in Hilton Head, Hawaii, and San Diego. One time, while visiting him, Ken showed me his finances. I couldn't believe just how wealthy some people are. However, they shouldn't become too haughty because they are not eternal. The grim reaper does not care if you are rich or poor. He is the great equalizer."

"Excessive money is the root of all evil. Sounds like he had a great plan though," Cougar said.

"It was. But it didn't turn out. He had to have a hip replaced a year later. His golf went to hell. I have never seen a man fall apart so quickly. One year later his other hip required replacing. No golf, then colon rectal cancer. Ken e-mailed me and asked me if I wanted fifteen million dollars. I asked him whom I would have to shoot. He said no one. He just wanted to trade lifestyles. I felt sorry for him. Now he has been diagnosed with Parkinson's disease. He seldom e-mails me anymore. Last one said his hands shake and his footsteps are unsteady. My life is so much better than his. But I feel badly."

"Obviously you have had an interesting lifestyle for him to want to trade you so much money," Cougar said.

"I have. I have climbed Mount Rainer, Mount Hood and Mount St. Helens. I've canoed rogue rivers. I killed a grizzly in self defense. I lived in a Cree Indian village in Manitoba for a month. I have hosted wilderness documentaries for Public Television. I've been busy. I was out here before talking to some of your Elders, while I was researching *Valley of Silent Drums.*"

"As much as you enjoy the wilderness you should move out here with us," Cougar said, patting the dozing mountain lion. It opened its eyes. I really think the cougar smiled.

"I'll let you discuss that move with my wife." I rolled my eyes, giving him a knowing smile.

"This is an ideal place to live," he said.

"You really have the better of two worlds," I said. "I came through the Northern part of Idaho back in 1947. I had a friend there. I raced his hydroplane in Lake Coeur D'Alene. Motel room was $9 back then."

"You should have gotten in touch with me," Cougar said. "You could have stayed here. At least your room would have been sanitary."

"What does that mean? I didn't know you then."

"You sleep in motels where strangers have stayed, and some of the occupants do some frolicking in bed."

"But the linens are laundered," I said.

"But not the bed spreads."

"So?"

"Hookers provide their services there. You should have the spread checked for buildup of semen, likely coat after coat over the years, maybe saliva and other bodily fluids, too."

I grimaced. "God, man, I'll stay in better hotels in the future."

"High price hotels have the same problem. People get amorous on the spread. You sleep under it. Hotels have no assurance of cleanliness. Occupants of pricey hotels are convinced that their ejaculant is superior to everybody. It is still caked semen. Stay with us when you travel. You know how much simpler we live here as compared to contemporary society."

A cool breeze began. A zillion bats flew over the escarpment and swooped down into the valley. Two bald eagles rode the thermals. In the distance timber wolves howled several chilling messages.

"You seem to know everything, Cougar," I said admiringly. "What are some of the problems we have in this country? I hope I haven't asked some question that's too hard to answer."

"One great problem that is on the increase is obesity. You have millions of people who are much too overweight to be healthy, and they seem to be apathetic about their condition. They have high blood pressure because of too much fat. The body suffers lugging too many pounds around. To see what fifty extra pounds causes just get three bowling balls and tie them around your neck and walk around all day. Your whole body suffers; knees, hips, ankles, heart, it causes diabetes. The phenomenon is killing your people early and costing a fortune in additional medical care. Children are following in the footsteps of the parents. Over half of the kids are overweight by dangerous amounts. It's caused by diet and indolent lifestyles. Fast food eating habits. Cell phones, Nintendo's, Blackberry's, television, Lazy stuff."

"You present an amazing analogy," I said. "What else?"

"I hope you have a lot of time," he said. "But there is an even more sinister danger for America and other civilized countries around the world and that is the rapid advancement of terrorism."

"I've read more about them recently. Why are they so violent? Why is their hatred so fervent?"

"First you need to know how terrorism began. Studies have shown that people who have a tendency to harm others developed that abnormality early in life, unless influenced to become involved later in life. Often they are born into poverty and suffer humiliation and abuse by their peers and members of their family, to the point of budding resentment and seething hate. Most are not attractive to the opposite gender. Many are loners choosing to isolate themselves from those who chastise and denigrate them. But then they join a cadre of people who suffer the same sense of inferiority and a potential terrorist group is in place. The adage that there's strength in numbers holds true. Weapons are introduced and a terrorist organization is born. Upon getting weapons, terrorists appeal to others who have suffered humiliation and abuse during their life. They are now able to accomplish their deadly deeds of murdering with impunity and fleeing to commit more acts of inhumanity. When terrorists die, while involved in massive killings, their family is accorded national respect and compensation and the martyr's photograph is displayed proudly in his home. Acts of terrorism increase exponentially as an assurance of endless virgins and eternal adulation influences their changing morality. Killing becomes acceptable when they discover that they wield the power of life or death over their victims."

"Eccentricies are acquired early in life," I said. "An aunt, not much older than I, groped me when I was ten years old. My stepmother solicited my services when I returned from World War II. The result is my mistrust of most women, an attitude over which I have little control."

Cougar said, "Terrorists are influenced by national accolades when involved in bombing groups of people, the more deaths the louder the acclaim. Dying to them is considered an honor."

I offered my opinion. "The world is on its way to destruction when terrorism is permitted to flourish."

"My people encountered similar idiosyncrasies among certain tribes. Usually it was from the use of loco weed. People who consume Astragalus or Oxytropis develop unbalanced minds, too. It affects animals that graze on the flowery weeds."

"You're a fountain of knowledge," I said.

"Our conversation has been stimulating to me, also. As me, you are the only person with whom I have exchanged repartee in nearly two hundred years."

"It's been really educational," I said.

"I have all the time in the world if you'd like to cover something else," Cougar said.

"I have until I leave. Give me really startling facts. I write about most any subject."

"Well, there are 27,000 murders annually in your country. You kill 55,000 people on the roads every year. Drug addiction is at an all time high. People are more obese and dying earlier, plus costing more in medical care. Alcoholism is raging. Abortions are in the millions. Old people are becoming the victims of scam-artists on a level unparalleled in history. The water is polluted. Can you imagine being downstream from a city, and having to drink the water that has passed through millions of toilet bowls? Child molesters are more brazen. Corruption is rampant. You have too many homeless vagrants. Women appear so naked in public today that their seductive nudity contributes to lust-motivated behavior in men. I know that every two minutes some female is being sexually assaulted in your country. They can't even go out jogging without encountering some psychopathic nut. Just visiting a shopping center or going to a grocery store, or pumping gas at a service station exposes people to extreme danger from thugs. Sexually transmitted diseases are pandemic. Thirty million people are addicted to the Internet. You have enough guns to invade sizable countries; many of them in the hands of merciless marauders. You have thirteen hundred facilities to treat alcoholism and drug addicts. You can see how much your society is suffering from internal weakness, and that's just the beginning. Glorifying drug addicts just because they pound a guitar and sexual deviants just because they live in Hollywood is indicative of a nation gone awry."

Cougar turned and stared out over the valley. He took out his faded corncob pipe and twirled it around in his hand. He seemed lost in deep concentration. He pulled out his moose-hide bag of aromatic tobacco and tamped the bowl full. He continued to stare, looking out over his realm. "Too many of your citizens have become dependent on the government and the government has let them down." His brow furrowed as if transfixed in thought. "The people are obsessed with wealth to the exclusion of peace of mind and contentedness." He turned back toward me with a look of concern, his pipe still unlighted.

"While I was in meditation I ran through a mental inventory of problems confronting your country. Do you want to hear a worse-case scenario? It is scary. There are so many they could be insurmountable.

A few days ago I compared the United States to the Titanic. There is no reason to change my opinion. Do you want me to go on? You may have reached the point of no return. Your minds have been sidetracked by games, sports, sex orgies and so much mind-twisting frivolity that you are unaware that you're losing your country to internal extremists. Your founding fathers would be ashamed and appalled. ”

"You have mentioned problems of which I am aware. I can figure out enough dilemmas to satisfy my needs for my book. How about something positive," I said.

"I'm not sure I can project too much positive information. There are certainly some good people in your country but the trend is mystifying. Beginning about fifty years ago your people appeared to get lost. No sense of direction. No pride. No inspiration. Little motivation, so they began experimenting with mind-altering substances, apparently unaware that drugs are the great seducers. Mindlessly assuming that marijuana was harmless they began a binge smoking the drug. Quickly it had the kick they wanted. They got hooked but soon lost their elation so they started using LSD, becoming hooked and reacting strangely. That wore off and the move was to stronger drugs; opium, cocaine, meth-amphetamine. You already have millions of stricken alcoholics, but the drug insanity accelerated and now you have millions of brain-dead citizens thoroughly convinced that one more snort or injection is the solution to their failures in life, their salvation. Just the contrary, their lives continue but they function like zombies, motivated only to achieve the next highs from illegal drugs, and now even legally prescribed drugs. It is the surest avenue to endless crime, horror, suffering, impoverishment and an untimely death."

"I know that the unfunded liabilities are monumental problems for America. For years politicians voted for goodies by promising more than government revenues could afford to pay when those expenses came due; Medicare, Medicaid, Federal pensions, military pensions, construction bonds, investment bonds and many more. Always charging to the future what they couldn't afford to pay for at the time. It was no different than everybody spending extravagantly to buy stuff they could not afford. That was done to influence voters to keep those politicians in office. That's called buying votes. But now the turkeys have come home to roost, with billions in obligations due and insufficient money to pay them. Your country is bankrupt."

"Well, as Mrs. Lincoln was asked when the President lay dying, Other than that Mary, how did you like the show?"

"Not funny," Cougar said.

"What else?" I said.

I decided Cougar should have my opinion of his assessment of conditions in America so I told him of an experience I had when I was very young.

"When visiting a relative's farm for Thanksgiving my cousin introduced me to drippings from a still in the barn. I was maybe nine years old. The taste was unpleasant but I was encouraged to have some more. The end result was that I vomited on a table covered with the Thanksgiving dinner. I was too sick to be embarrassed. The experience was educational. I do not drink. I now know that I would not function dependably under the mind-altering effect of alcohol, so why do it?"

"I'm not sure I know what marijuana smells like although at sometime I likely have been where the substance was being smoked. Becoming aware early in life how consuming mind-killing substances can effectively destroy someone's entire life, I have elected to keep my brain functioning in a decisive manner. I recall Timothy Leary running around in the 1960's with his head screwed on backward. He helped me decide. It was never even a consideration for me to have my mind deadened to the point of unpredictability."

"For the past three or more decades we have poured billions of dollars into wastefully trying to control drug use through interdiction, crop eradication and attempts to educate drug users as to the dire consequences stemming from drug use."

"The massive effort has been unproductive. When illegal drugs are confiscated and availability lessened the price goes up meteorically because the demand remains the same. When the price increases smugglers and pushers reap even more in profits and their smuggling efforts accelerate. Nancy Reagan's JUST SAY NO advice did not work. Her slogan was too simplistic."

"Comparisons have been made between drug enforcement and Prohibition. After Prohibition was enacted those who wanted to drink continued to drink. Those costs of trying to enforce the law increased.

Smugglers and agents died. Drinkers ultimately prevailed and the Prohibition blunder was rescinded."

"That rescission did not create more drinkers. Legalizing drugs won't cause a dramatic surge in drug use. With millions in profit removed, drugs can be dispensed by Federal agencies whose mandate would be to modify the addiction for drugs. The immediate benefit will be reduced gang competition to generate more money by hooking more addicts. Gone would be the vast profit that has caused the death and incarceration of smugglers and pushers when in competition for the drug marketplace."

"The fact determined from those experiences was that alcoholics and addicts will continue their ill-advised behavior until they decide otherwise. Gullible masses will be exploited as long as they allow themselves to be exploited. Billions of dollars pissed away has not modified drug usage by weak-willed people."

"America needs an immediate rapprochement to the problems of drugs. Illegal drugs should be legalized and dispensed with government supervision. Fortunes normally made by smugglers and pushers would be gone and prices would be fixed at a low rate with taxes levied on drugs the same as on alcoholic beverages."

"Addiction will increase only among those with a compulsion to ruin their brain. Prisons will be emptied of people whose infraction was as a druggie. Drug pushers will no longer be able to dominate a neighborhood. Crimes, related to drugs, will slow and drug enforcement agents who have spent fruitless years failing to control smuggling could be assigned to important areas of criminal activity. The pusher would no longer have reasons to get children hooked."

"The concept is a realistic approach to the obvious failure. The only people who will object are smugglers, pushers, and the financiers who have made millions from the misery of dumb people."

"Money saved should be devoted to a promotional campaign to instruct youngsters, beginning with young children that experimenting with mind-destroying drugs is a stupid decision and potentially lethal and that self-destructing in a quagmire of illegal drugs is one avoidable danger in a world plagued by pitfalls."

"There will be strident snivelers with opposing viewpoints but if intelligence should prevail then the billions of dollars being poured into the bottomless pit could be spent in needed places. Then allow drunks to drink and addicts to suffer an early death if they so choose and stop the unsuccessful effort to influence aberrational behavior."

"When I had my shoulder totally replaced the surgeon said I would have intense pain during the rehabilitation process. A sign of the times occurred when he prescribed a pain killer. There certainly was pain but life has a certain amount of expected pain. I took none of the pills. Through vast expenditures of promotional dollars drug manufacturers have brainwashed the public into believing that chemicals are the solution to every dilemma in life, to the point where we have become a society brainwashed into popping pills every day. It has become a national pastime, an obsession."

"I'm amazed how easy it is to victimize the masses of susceptible people," Cougar said.

"Again you are certainly graphic," I said.

"Our society seems to be losing its moral direction. In your opinion what is the major factor contributing to the breakdown?"

"From what I have witnessed in the last few years I think it's infidelity in your families. There are wife-swapping clubs. I see strip joints now opening with full attendance every day. You had a club in Atlanta called the Gold Club that employed attractive women to dance nearly nude. They paraded around a stage and suggestively posed on a vertical shaft exposing their intimate spots. Checking on some visitors I found many of them were married with kids. Why were they there? Buxom young females kept the club full. Billed as exotic dancers they do not dance. They stripped down to g-strings then strolled, eyes suggestive, across a stage with wild-eyed men ogling them. They gyrate their bodies simulating the movements of sexual intercourse. I watched one girl drop down on her knees, facing the room of men, and bend backward until her head touched the floor. She then jutted her crotch as high a she could. The men stuffed greenbacks under the string covering her slit. The more she wiggled and moaned the more cash she got. One dude, sporting a huge diamond ring, pushed a $100 bill under her G-string then leaned down and kissed her on her crotch. I found the acts of both sickening. After approval of credit the men could take girls into a back room for more erotic dalliances. Several of the patrons were recognizable from sport, business and political prominence. There are shops marketing vibrators shaped like sex organs. There appears to be an increasing obsession with nudity. You have XXX-rated movies and slimy magazines. I watched a ladies golf match recently. One player wore her skirt so short that when she stooped over to pick up her ball the people behind her could see the cheeks of her ass."

"So what would you suggest?" I said, honestly concerned about our future.

"You wrote at the beginning of your book that when God is forsaken, idolatry will reign supreme and when idolatry reigns supreme evil will flourish. Evil is flourishing now, Mike, like never before. If the Great Spirit were forsaken I would not be here."

"I'm seriously worried," I said. "Maybe it'll change."

"I'm curious, Mike. What motivated you to write about my people?"

"Well. When I was young we lived near the ruins of a Pottawatomi Indian village. My brother and I always wondered who they were, how many lived there, what were they like and why did they go. While in Sicily in WW II I met Ernie Pyle and immediately wanted to be a war correspondent. Pyle got killed the next year. I met Ernest Hemingway after the war and decided to become an author. I thought it would be great to be able to live anyplace in the world and make my living writing. I always liked words. My kids and I played word games while eating. It kinda' just started. I chose Indians to write about because I went to Manitoba fishing and making wilderness documentaries for Georgia Public Television and became friends with some Cree and Inuit people. I since have visited several reservations in the Dakotas and in the Pacific Northwest. I find it's a subject that isn't taught in schools. I am asked to give seminars on the topic. No one really knows about what happened over the past four hundred years. You and I know. Hollywood portrays Indians as savage. We know better. I fished with a Cree in Nunavut many years ago and when we had dinner we played chess. I am a good chess player but I lost three games before I was able to win. He was well educated and a good conversationalist about many subjects. That is when I started writing about Indians. I really believe I was born four hundred years too late. I would liked to have met Lewis & Clark. Things might have been different."

"Maybe some time in the past you were one of us," Cougar said, smiling.

"If you were to pick some word or words to describe what is wrong with American society, what would it be? I know that's a tough question," I said.

"It's really not difficult. All you need do is read the newspaper, watch television and in a short time you know the problems stem from greed, lust and arrogance. Those are the controlling influences that have contributed to the beginning of the end for your country. It's systemic. Once out of control it snowballs, infecting the entire population. Too many people are weak, stupid, degenerate and gullible. And you could say, impressionable. Those few who do not fit the mold can't stand up against the tidal wave of evil surging against them."

"How do you know so much?" I said.

"I can see what is perfectly obvious. You people are being systematically propagandized by an onslaught of distractions, activity insidiously intended to divert attention from reality: your liberties and your freedoms are being subverted while you watch sports, card-games, naked bodies, stupid programs, unreality shows, senseless plots, glitzy ceremonies, and a mind-numbing array of television shows that have become boring from stultifying repetitiveness. How can anyone watch someone constantly running to take a piss time and again, or showing their ass on some idiotic program where dysfunctional people spill their guts about their psychological and emotional oddities, or newscasters and their guests screaming at each other at the same time until the audience can't hear what is being discussed, or some nut talking with grizzlies until one decided to eat him, or watching dung beetles rolling balls of elephant shit, or some lion screwing another lion, really special crap designed to de-intellectualize the entire population. Your people are too dependent on others for appreciation of life, sitting like zombies watching someone else entertain them, screaming when told to scream, shaking their fists when instructed to do so. What happened to the uniqueness of individuals? Audiences are like trained seals. Those people are programmed to yell insults at each other and to the audience to provoke vicious attacks. Why viewers watch the slime is beyond me."

"It's hard to grasp your explanation. How do you think of all that stuff?"

"I don't have my mind being pummeled by societal idiocy," Cougar said."

"Also, you had a recent election and as long as we are discussing problems, your country is now being taken over by radicals. You now have strangers in government in sensitive positions. With officials in Washington spending their time in self-fulfillment people with mal-intent have entrenched themselves in important posts where they can create incredible damage to your way of life. All this happened while your people were partying. You were so busy having fun and spending your way into financial oblivion that the infiltrators literally walked in through the front door. They first stole the election by presenting a glib person as the savior. Stunted minds voted for him without realizing that the man was promising them goodies he couldn't deliver and was doing so with the aid of opportunistic co-conspirators. Insidiously, I can see this nation changing forever. You are losing it by inattention to what goes on every day. The new people are cronies of the new President and mostly unqualified for the appointments to which they have been assigned, and are involved without approval of Congress and have never gone through the normal vetting process. They are deliberately sowing seeds of discontent among the people, causing hostility and resentment among the masses toward those who have worked hard and succeeded. It's a sure formula for eventual revolution."

"I guess I have been one of those paying little attention to what goes on," I said.

"That is how Adolf Hitler came to power. Josef Stalin ruled because of uneducated peasants. Let me explain how it goes. There in one glaring example of how governments are destroyed. The Attorney General is prosecuting the people in one agency, the CIA, who have been responsible for protecting your citizenry ever since 9/11. All those CIA agents did was to interrogate the terrorists who were caught in the world-wide dragnet. With crazy killers you do not use conventional methods. You get the information by what ever means is necessary when your survival is at stake. That prosecution is endangering you, your kids, your grand kids, your great grand kids and most importantly, the people in your military."

"I read about that just before I came out here and I know what I would have done if charged with that responsibility. I would have called in the crew from my ship and we would have taught the terrorists what keel-hauling is, and after acquiring all the vital information we needed, they would have walked the plank. You don't wimp around with people who intend to kill you."

"That would have worked," Cougar said. "We had another technique that was also effective. We took the culprit, from whom we needed information, out in the forest, stripped him down, washed all the alum and sulphur from him, for your information those elements were our protection against mosquitoes, and we tied him to a tree. After a few minutes the man was screaming to tell us what we wanted to know. By then his body was beginning to swell up from thousands of mosquito bites."

"That's cruel," I said.

"Be nice and die," Cougar said.

After many hours of substantive discussions we headed back to the cliff. The sun was overhead. I marveled as we floated out a few feet then began a slow descent back to the floor of the valley.

"Do you still do Sun Dances and Moon Dances?"

"Yes, regularly. I keep in touch with the Great Spirit. He is why I am able to be here."

"I still must leave tomorrow," I said. "Can I ask a couple more questions, my friend?"

"Sure."

"Gotta' hurry finishing my book. Do you know what *earmarks* are in political vernacular?"

"Yes."

"Explain it to me. I'm confused," I said.

"It is semantics, a play on words. In Washington politicians use that word so constituents will be aware of what they are doing. Monies are attached to important bills by your congressmen. Vital bills are passed including funds earmarked for personal gain. It is high-class rip-off for personal gain. The practice should be against the law but when law makers are the ones benefitting, that will never happen. Millions of tax dollars are taken from the treasury by dishonest congressmen. No other member complains because many do it. For example, one congressman purchases several farms out in the boondocks for less than one million dollars, then attached to a significant bill is the money he earmarked to build an expressway out to that property. After the highway is begun he sells the property to a developer for a big profit often making millions of dollars on that deal. That is earmarking. I wondered why candidates for the Presidency spend hundreds of millions of dollars for a job paying less than a half million dollars. It's a pipeline to enormous wealth so when you hear a term *earmark* substitute the term *corruption*. The words go together in today's deliberately confusing political verbiage. Those being elected to Congress found a goldmine, the national treasury that they could loot to enrich themselves while keeping voters mesmerized with contrived non-issues. The British were masters at disinformation revealed surreptitiously to the Nazi high command. An example was the body of a dead man dressed as a British Officer who was dropped from an airplane near the coast of Portugal, with an attaché case chained to his wrist... Upon examining the contents of the case, which contained plans for an Allied invasion of lower Europe through Greece, the Germans concentrated most of their forces along key points of the Greek coast. When the real invasion was made in Sicily there was inadequate Germans to defend, making the invasion far less costly for the Allies."

"It figures," I said. "We had a situation at home when a major highway was being built but it had been stopped for a few years because the land had not been acquired for completion of the highway. The head of the department expressed interest in acquiring some farmland but because of a conflict of interest law he couldn't own land where the roadway might be routed. However his brother who was interested in buying a farm went out looking for a farm. Amazingly, miraculously, inadvertently, unknowingly, just by chance he found a farm that straddled a state highway. He was able to buy the farm at a bargain price. As astounding, even more miraculous, the routing for completing the roadway was decided, and was routed right through the farm that had just been bought by the brother of the manager of the highway department giving him four corners which he could sell for commercial development and the rest for residential. The department manager resigned a few months before the roadway was completed.

He and his brother began developing the now immensely valuable property."

"Rampant corruption has been the downfall of many nations," Cougar said. "Among my people we shared all things. After a buffalo hunt everyone got their equal share. The Chief's lodge was the same as all others. Everyone had the same so there was no resentment among my people as there is among your people. You have a system which ferments hostility. You have people who cannot make ends meet while you have others gorging on imported caviar. It's a formula for failure. It's a reason crime is endangering your lives," Cougar said. "People come from their squalid homes to steal and even to murder in order to survive. Desperate people can be unpredictable people. They have minimal compassion and will murder in order to get what they need. I see raging crime in poor countries all over the world. It is the method for poor people to get what they need from those who have excess wealth with little consideration for others beneath their station in life. Of what benefit is success if arrogance flourishes and compassion dies? The ways of my people were best."

"Excessiveness has been one more reason," I said. "They are pissing away dollars like drunken sailors but in the wrong place. One example of extravagance is our space effort. What do you think is a rationale for such an expensive program? No sane person envisions existing in outer space. How do we reduce entrenched programs?"

"You cannot. Wealthy people are so covetous of the money they control, and their income from bureaucratic jobs, that change is impossible. They have programmed your tax laws in order for them to live in a princely fashion. Wealthy people will not permit change. Poor people will remain downtrodden. It is one of those truths with which your people are befuddled."

"How about tort reform to correct the problems," I suggested.

"You're kidding of course. As long as lawyers have access to vast sums of money tort reform is dead in the water. Congress conducts televised hearings but those are charades intended to convince their constituents that they are actually working and earning their salary and to use impressive words that they had recently learned. It's a huge, showy production. I spent one day in the Halls of Congress. Amazing is an understatement. Astonishment is a better word to describe that experience. Your Speaker of the House was debating an amendment to a bill. He spoke, 'my friend across the aisle'. I read his mind. What he was actually thinking was, 'you son-of-a-bitch, you did not vote for my amendment, so screw you, I will not vote for your amendment even if it is good for the country'. And you re-elect those people. Congress is not there to help the people, it's an adversarial relationship between the parties designed to benefit those who gave the biggest bribes. They were there to help people in the past but greed now prevails."

"The tenure of the incumbent is pretty well assured, unfortunately," I said.

"And often detrimental," Cougar said. "But a big bankroll assures continuity in office."

"So the space program is forever?"

"Yes, Mike, it probably is."

"What's the reason behind the program?" I said.

"Well, your first intent was to keep up with the Imperialistic Russians. You were in competition with them in many places in the world. After World War Two your military captured Werner Von Braun and many of his cohorts. The Russians captured a like amount, then the space-race was on. The Russians gained an upper hand with Sputnik. America increased its space program and soon caught up. By the time the race for space became stalemated, you had a huge bureaucracy by then and as you know from history, once a bureaucracy is in place, getting rid of it is almost impossible. There are salaries with big influence so the program stayed. It's ludicrous to imagine Americans really believe there is a place in which to live out there in space. The program is a waste of assets but it is here and will remain."

"I believe the same as you. It's amazing how much we think alike," I said.

"That's what Kindred Spirits do," Cougar said. "Proof that there are too many people living on the planet is the problem of contaminating the ocean. You are dumping too much garbage in the oceans and too much human waste. Scientists have found on the West Coast of the United States and in Florida that Staphylococcus Aureus is making vacationers sick. Some die. The germs are spread by fecal matter being discharged in your water systems and it ends up in the ocean. On the way in can be found in sand on the beaches and those who plays on the beaches are literally assembling in fecal discharges. It causes pusy lesions and often death. Some idiot microbiologist said that people shouldn't be afraid of the sand. That's an awfully dumb bit of advice. He is endorsing playing around in the residual of someone's bowel movements."

"Who said everyone was smart?" Cougar said. "It's overpopulation, I said earlier."

"I would like your opinion on another calamity that is confronting this country now. We are headed for another Depression. Fifteen million people have lost their jobs and it looks as if that problem will grow. Detroit, which was a bustling city several years ago, is now a stricken place with the highest unemployment of any city in America."

"The people let it happen, even participated in the beginning of the end." Cougar said.

"How did they do that?" I said.

"I remember when it began back in the 40's, unions striking, coercing management to accept higher wages and benefits. At first those agreements were good for the workers but then greed took over: demands became too costly, corporate executives began taking higher pay, and too many perks, that placed industry in decline. Greedy politicians began sticking their fingers into the cookie jar. Costs skyrocketed. Profits plummeted as avarice evolved; appliances, apparel, steel, leather, porcelain, jewelry, electronics, went offshore. Every time a union contract was about to expire, companies were threatened with strikes unless they agreed to higher pay, more vacations, more sick leave and more costly health benefits. Every time it was more-more-more. Executives continued raiding the cookie jar and government piled on more taxes and more regulations. The costs were fiscal insanity. Companies could not afford to compete."

"But workers lived better," I said.

"The choice for industry was to reduce the quality, and lose market share to foreign competition, who made a superior product, or move out of the country in order to survive the avalanche of destructive expense. The only companies to stay were those that had not yet encountered foreign competition."

"Still more greed?" I said.

"To escape the economic chokehold that unions held on business many companies moved from northern states, where unions were robust, to southern states where the right-to-work laws helped keep costs lower. But that was only a partial remedy. The other two thirds of the problem, excessive taxes and gluttonous executive compensation, continued to reduce industry's ability to afford to modernize resulting in shoddy products and more decline in market share. Add more government mandated regulation and it was no longer possible to make a profit. That survival instinct in businesses resulted in moving offshore, where costs could be controlled. Every time a business was forced to relocate overseas to survive your work force shrank accordingly. The lost jobs never returned."

"Washington should have seen that coming," I said.

"Politicians, who were too busy arranging their own financial future, permitted that calamity to happen You now have 10% plus unemployment due to these conditions and I don't hear anybody, anywhere, suggesting what to do about it. You have a job-loss crisis, maybe beyond the point of no return. But I believe there is a way to reverse the trend."

"How would you accomplish that?" I said.

"Instead of wringing your hands in stupefied resignation find a candidate with guts for President, somebody smart enough to admit errors of the past, sufficiently forceful to compel compliance and dedicated to removing avariciousness from your society. Unions shot themselves in the foot and lost millions of jobs. Executives enriched themselves but depleted the cookie jar. Politicians contributed to the death knell. You need to return jobs to America by whatever means necessary; lower taxation from cities, counties, states and the federal government, less pay for employees-lower executive salaries, with tax breaks and subsidies for rebuilding manufacturing plants in regions with highest unemployment. Return businesses back here. Employment here depends on determined action. Surviving may depend on the return of lost jobs. Right now the prospect looks bleak."

"Who's our Savior?" I said. "Is it Gingrich? Is it Huckabee? Is it Sarah Palin? Is it Romney? Is it Beck? We need a visionary who is not concerned about winning the next election but ready to get down in the trench and take on the enemy which is increasingly from within. In the meanwhile, I'm apprehensive, like I am on board a cruise ship, adrift in heavy seas, rudder gone, the Captain asleep at the helm, and with the stewards looting the passenger's safe in the Captain's quarters."

"Looks that way to me, too," Cougar said. "Remember the Titanic."

"I wonder where the leaders have gone," I said.

Chapter Twenty-One

In my peripheral vision, I studied the individual I had come to respect like no other human I had known since Johnny. He appeared to be a youthful, educated man, and yet he was reputed to have lived ever since his family was murdered two centuries ago. I decided that his Great Spirit did possess amazing power.

"There's a lot to write about the ones who nurtured this land for centuries. I could take you to the plateau at Bear's Paw Montana where the dispirited Nez Perce Chief Joseph finally surrendered his starving, rag-tag tribe of old men, women and children, to the 7th cavalry after they were attacked, again and again, with most of them killed. After one final attempt to save his people by fleeing into Canada during a frigid winter, failed, Chief Joseph spoke these tragic words."

Tell General Howard I know his heart. What he told me before I have in my heart. I am tired of fighting. Looking Glass is dead. Too-hool-hool-sote is dead. The old men are all dead. It is the young men who say yes or no. He who led on the young men is dead. It is cold and we have no blankets. The little children are freezing to death. My people, some of them have run away to the hills, and have no blankets, no food; no one knows where they are-- perhaps freezing to death. I want to have time to look for my children and see how many I can find. Maybe I shall find them among the dead. Hear me, my Chiefs. I am tired; my heart is sick and sad. From where the sun now stands I will fight no more forever.

Cougar and I stared at each other for maybe five minutes. "Sad, isn't it," I said. "Just imagine the horror of an inescapable death of your people unless you surrender your way of life, giving up everything. And even then, thousands of them were murdered just because they were Indians. Those killers were my ancestors."

"Yes, it was filled with great sorrow, but only one of hundreds of like travesties in the Pacific Northwest where several million of my people were murdered after Lewis & Clark's Expedition in 1805 opened a floodgate to immigrants pouring over the mountains seeking land they were told was theirs, free for their taking. The place had been the homelands for the Nez Perce, Coeur D'Alene, Blackfeet, Lemhi, Lapwai, Spokane, Yakama, Colville, Jocko, Crow, Kalispel, Shoshone, Walla Walla, Kalapuya, Cayuse, Modoc, Blackfoot, Umatilla, Bannock, Columbia, Tillamook, Nisqually, Kootenai, Wenachee, Palouse, Flathead, Cascade, Colville, Yakima, Molalla, Wenatchee, Salish, Paiute and so many more I can't recall them all. That genocide occurred across this land during the past three hundred years. My village was set aflame by American cavalrymen as they shot unarmed villagers who were frantically attempting to avoid being killed. My mother, father and brother were killed by troops sent to kill us if we wouldn't leave our home for some desolate reservation."

"You sound embittered," I said.

"At one time. It passed years ago," Cougar said.

Again we looked at each other, mutually understanding how incredibly cruel some people can be to others just to steal their possessions. Genocide is a worldwide evil.

Chief Joseph was never allowed to visit his homeland in Wallowa Valley in Oregon His last years were spent on a reservation in Colville Washington where he refused to live in a house but chose to spend his final years living in a teepee, a last symbol of the great Indian Chief's freedom. The Nez Perce nation was ultimately reduced from hundreds of thousands of acres, extending into Washington and Oregon to a small reservation along the Clearwater River in western Idaho.

Chapter Twenty-Two

"I need to ask two more questions," I said. "For my grand kids' sake I need to know what you think the future is for America."

"It all depends," he said.

"On what?"

"Decisions."

"What decisions?"

"Altered directions."

"What does that mean?" I said.

"It means a change of social attitudes."

"I'm not sure what you mean," I said.

"A radical transformation of peoples' philosophy of life. It must happen. If your people do not bring back truth, values and common sense, if your people continue on their present trajectory you are headed for extinction. You will not be here another hundred years. No filth-riddled civilization will last forever. The Roman Empire is a good example of a truth. When a society accepts immorality as virtuous, wickedness as admirable, artificiality as desirable, and sin as enlightenment then with anarchy on the rise you can be sure your destiny will be on the garbage dump of history. You have problems on your borders while at the same time you're being destroyed from within."

"You're serious," I said.

"I am serious. All I need do is visit Hollywood and watch TV to find how much your civilization has drifted from simplicity. I will cite one particular program; one weathered, aged crone sits in front of a camera discussing sex information and demonstrating how to suck a dildo. The scary part of that scenario is that companies are allocating advertising dollars to promote that sickness. There is a program showing scantily clad females frantically pumping their hips while graphically demonstrating a sexual orgy. That illustrates to the entire world just how far your society has sunken in a cesspool of vulgar behavior. I'm reminded of frogs during the mating season with females and males climbing on each other to ejaculate on the other frogs engaged in their orgy. Antics by sex-crazed humans reduce them to the level of frogs. You have women in Hollywood with capped teeth, wearing designer's gowns to emphasize their silicone tits and to flaunt their pubic bones. You're falling apart as a result of out-of-control searches for orgasms. America reminds me of a passenger train with faulty brakes plummeting down an incline with the bridge down at the river ahead with the passengers engaging in sex orgies while the train engineer ogles Playgirl and Playboy pornography in the caboose."

"So what would the Great Spirit recommend?"

"Get back down on your knees. The Roman Empire was nearing the brink of collapse for several years, finally disappearing because of political corruption, over-extended military, irresponsibility, fiscal irresponsibility, the inability to close their borders, out-of-control budget and raging immorality at home. Do you see the parallel?"

Lamentably, I realized Cougar was right.

"Every civilization that ever existed disappeared for similar reasons," I said. "Either they were too weak or unprepared for opposition or they were too weakened from internal disintegration that their enemy could easily overwhelm and conquer them. From what I've read those indigenous people on this continent were simply outgunned and conquered because they had never wasted their talent developing implements of modern warfare. Do you agree?"

"That's an astute observation," Cougar said. "Hindsight is always a great teacher."

"I remember from reading history books that the Europeans were heavily armed with rifles and cannons while the indigenous people only had bows and arrows. By the time your people could acquire the necessary firepower it was already too late."

"True. You must read a lot of reference books," Cougar said.

"I've always been interested in improving my knowledge. As you can tell, that's why I'm here. There is another condition in the United States that is worrisome to me and that is the emphasis on wealth rather that on integrity and happiness. What makes people contented with their life? We seem to have our priorities backward. Take for example, the stock market. We hear the daily ups and downs of the market with the ringing of a bell at closing with a bunch of people smiling into the camera. Probably they have a reason to smile, they have jobs and an income and maybe their stock portfolio did well. But everyone isn't smiling. Those people who have lost there jobs and are being evicted from their homes, who are terrified about their future, whose kids have nothing to eat, it's not the time to smile. Their guts are churning with fear about their future wondering if they even have a future. That inequality makes people desperate, and terror stricken people do desperate things. A rally on Wall Street means nothing to someone who has lost his job and is about to lose him home. I feel the dread right along with those suffering people. I am not in favor of pure socialism but a market-oriented system that has such an obvious disparity between wealthy people and poor people isn't structured right. I may run for an office where I can help be instrumental in making a change. My wife has suggested several times that I do that."

"The ways of my people was much better. We shared," Cougar said.

"We spend too much time worshipping idols created by sports promoters and publicity agents, many of whom are not worthy of emulation. Our sensibilities are twisted. We genuflect before human idols. Icon worshipping has caused the demise of countless civilizations throughout history."

"My people worshipped only the Great Spirit," Cougar said.

"My people idolize, adulate and worship false icons. It is the identical scenario as when the Jews were wandering in the desert worshipping a golden idol. They were sentenced by their Great Spirit to 400 years of strife, until they corrected their errant ways."

"Temptation to sin is always there," Cougar said. "Only wise people avoid temptation."

"We now have a new problem. A comparative unknown man was elected President by unknown methods but including buying votes by devious means. He was a persuasive speaker and appealed mostly to the uneducated people. He promised everything to get elected and now he has reneged on his promises but it's too late. The dye is cast. He promised to get rid of earmarks. He promised to allow time for people to read and understand proposed laws. He promised to balance the budget. Promises, promises, promises. I am reminded of Herbert Hoover who promised a chicken in every pot and a car in every garage. History proves what a debacle that Presidency was. This appears like the same, another Great Depression. People do it to themselves by accepting politicians at their word when history proves also that politicians will do anything, even arrange contrived emergencies to sidetrack peoples' minds while they dip their hands into the cookie jar in Washington. One of the candidates said repeatedly that '*We will fight for you*'. Now that is a completely ambiguous statement and I had no idea what the hell he meant."

"Our Chiefs cared for the people," Cougar said. "Not personal gain."

"You want to come with me and assimilate with the palefaces?"

"You're kidding of course," Cougar smiled. "I've already found my Happy Hunting Ground."

"Do you know what is even more frightening? The Democrats are using the old military ploy of diversionary tactics; emphasize something else while picking peoples' pockets. They regularly beat up on Cheney and Bush like a couple of piñatas so peoples' minds are distracted from reality. The Attorney General threatens to prosecute members of the Bush administration to divert peoples' attention from the mess the Democrats have made since getting the upper hand in government. Then we have a Speaker of the House who is third in line for the Presidency. Listening to her is scary. I pray that both the President and the Vice President remain healthy for their entire term. And with this Vice President, second in line for the Presidency, I pray that the President stays healthy. The choices are ominous."

"If you are honest you don't have to resort to dishonesty," Cougar said.

Chapter Twenty-Three

We moved down the mountain, to where the town of Lowell was in sight. "I won't go any farther because people become nervous when I'm around." He smiled.

"It's been a good visit," I said.

"Yes it has. Thank you for listening."

"Thank you for such enlightening information."

"Earlier you said you had two more questions. There is still one unanswered."

I pondered for a moment. My brain raced back to my book. What beneficial suggestion would I like to convey to my readers? It was a momentary dilemma.

"What do we do to survive?" I said.

His response was instantaneous. "Your barbarians spent hundreds of years laying waste to the continent which we had nurtured for many centuries. It won't be easy. There are monumental barriers you've raised. I would start with the fact that no person in your society is ready to accept responsibility for their actions. A woman had a deadly wreck because she never inflated her tires. The front tire on the left was down to 15 pounds pressure. On the Interstate, where the speed limit was 65 MPH, the woman was driving 85 MPH a deer bounded onto the highway. She tried to avoid the animal by swerving to her right. The left tire, because of under-inflation, succumbed to the stress. It exploded when it rolled from the wheel. When she tried to recover her car catapulted in front of a semi-trailer, which wrecked. As a result several people died. Whose fault? An attorney sued Ford and Firestone for defective tires. If she   had her tires inflated properly and driven at the legal speed limit the wreck wouldn't have occurred."

"When a man died from lung cancer, after smoking two packs of cigarettes each day for thirty years, a lawyer showed the jury a photograph of his blackened lungs. It took a brain-fractured jury just three hours to award his wife a 30 million dollar settlement. Of course, her lawyers got a whopping 15 million of that amount, which brings up another subject about the necessity of tort reform. Lawyers are becoming very wealthy via frivolous litigation."

"When a curious teenage girl gets pregnant, it is the boy's fault. When a drunk falls and breaks his toe it's the fault of the bartender who served him."

"When people become fat and die from clogged arteries, it's the fast-food industries fault."

"When a child plays Russian roulette with the pistol he found in his dad's clothes closet, it is the fault of the dealer who sold the gun, the manufacturer who made it, and the National Rifle Association that advocates private ownership of firearms."

A couple was climbing up the hill.

"Can I ask you a couple of quick questions?"

"Shoot," Cougar said.

"How about the disposal of spent nuclear fuel rods?"

"Some day it may cause the end of life on earth."

"How about water pollution?"

"Some day it may cause the end of life on earth."

"How about the massive burden of accumulated garbage?"

"Someday it may cause the end of life on earth."

"How about sexually transmitted diseases?"

"It may cause the end of life on earth."

"How about global warming?"

"It may cause the end of life on earth."

"How about the depletion of natural resources?"

"It may cause the end of life on earth."

"How about the build up of caustic chemicals?"

"It may cause the end of life on earth."

"How about air pollution?"

"It may cause the end of life on earth."

"I have read where the world's population will increase to ten billion by the year 3000. What will be the results of having that many people on earth?"

"Simple. Earth can hardly provide enough food and sustenance for the present population. With an increase of 66%, with people already starving in many regions around the globe, more will starve and those that do not will be the ones who will have become predators, migrating to countries where food and water is available. I think we discussed this earlier. You'll see genocide similar to what Indians suffered long ago. I remember the study you mentioned about a school subject involving rodents. Over-population is the same problem whether it's human or animal. Nature can only support so many species. After that it will be necessary to start over with fewer people on earth. Probably eight billion humans will die."

"How do we change so that incredible tragedy never happens?"

"As I explained before, humans will have to stop breeding like bedbugs."

"How about a world-wide nuclear war?"

"It will cause the end of life on earth."

"I think I'm depressed," I said.

"We are kindred spirits. You're safe," The Indian said.

"Thankfully. My wife, too?"

"Com'on, Mike. You said a couple questions."

"More opinions for my book," I said, smiling.

The climbers were getting closer.

"We must go, my brother," Cougar said.

"Me, too, brother," I said.

The cougar purred. Both Appaloosas whinnied and rubbed noses.

"One other final question," I said.

"What?"

"If you were to use one single word to describe the sickness that is destroying America today, what would it be?"

"Greed," Cougar said. "However, there are parallels; evil, lust and deception."

"Deception?" I had never thought of deception.

"Your entire society is riddle with deceit. Husband says he's going out of town on business. He meets some broad out of town for a sexual escapade. Politician says he's running for office as a crusader for good, when he actually wants his hands in the cookie jar. Advertising pills that don't work. Diluting paint on a paint job. Jacking up prices on merchandise in order to advertise discounts. Saying I love you in order to get laid. Disability claims. Low APR's in order to lure suckers. Conning money from gullible victims. Get rich quick schemes. Deception has become a scourge in America."

"It's chilling," I said. "What other problems confront this country?" I got out my thickening notepad.

"Spending more than revenues. Unfunded liabilities. Fiscal irresponsibility. Morality degradation. Ethnic conflict. Uncontrolled AIDS. Failure to accept responsibility for conduct. Overpopulation. Citizens being exploited by opportunists. Pollution. Idolatry. Unemployment. Gang violence. Pedophilia. Venereal diseases. Gluttony. Drug addiction. Inept officials. Loss of millions of good paying jobs to other countries where cost of payroll and taxes assure profitability, enabling companies to stay in business; the once great manufacturing miracle is collapsing into an impoverished 3rd world country. Want me to go on?"

" No. My readers will have a nervous breakdown now," I said.

"America is spinning out of control from citizens' inattention," Cougar said. "Take your mind off the road while speeding and you will have a wreck. That's what's happening in America."

"You covered problems, what about dangers?"

"Iran. Venezuela. Russia. North Korea. In that order. Reckless, irrational rulers."

"How would you handle them?"

"Take out the radical rulers who advocate your demise."

"How."

"By any means," Cougar said. "Rescind the ban on assassinations."

"When?"

"Before it's too late."

"It's scary, I'll admit," I said. "I'm worried."

"You're protected." Cougar smiled "Quickly, when you get back home if you ever need counsel or wish to powwow, simply think. From now, and forever, I will know and I will react." He extended his hand.

I took his hand in mine. "Because we are kindred spirits I will have extra-sensory perception? All I will need to do is to concentrate and you will know? You will think and I will know?"

"Yes," Cougar said. "You now have my power."

"We really are one. I'll visit you again, soon," I said.

"Peace," Cougar said. He gave me the victory sign.

"Peace," I said. I gave him a vigorous thumbs up.

Before my eyes my friends began ascending, disappearing, like thinning vapor that disperses into nothing.

I sat astride the Appaloosa, studying the climbers coming closer. The diminishing outline of my brother continued to fade up into the overcast. Three gossamer wisps. Then they were gone.

"Peace," I said. After sixty-two years of longing. I felt like I had been with Johnny again. Once more I repeated, "Peace," as burning wetness dimmed my eyes. Lifting my reins I kneed my Appaloosa and said, "Giddyup."

"Beautiful country," I said to the people who were climbing.

Chapter Twenty-Four

I stopped by the Clearwater River Camp on the way to the airport. Jim was still making his guests feel like they were visiting in old-time Indian Territory. Jim saw me as I got out of the car. He came over.

"Are you in a big hurry?"

"I got a little time. Why?"

"Let's get some coffee. You find that Indian?"

"He found me."

"Where'd you find him?"

"Up Lolo Pass at over 5000 feet, in an isolated valley."

"Is he for real?"

"Yes, he's for real."

"You talk to him?"

"Yes. I talked with him, a fascinating Indian. I learned a lot, too."

"How did you do that when no one else ever talked to him?"

"He and I are kindred spirits."

"What does that mean?"

"We are brothers," I said.

"No wonder you write fiction. You're crazy," Cook said. "What's his name?"

"His name is Cougar. It's not fiction, believe me."

"Prove it."

I removed the gold nugget from my pocket. "He gave me this big chunk of gold."

"Bullshit, you could've found that up there."

"This weighs a half pound," I said.

"So what?"

"The Indian has a ton of this stuff hidden where he lives. I saw it."

"You got to do better than that."

"Okay, buddy. Hold out your hand, palm up."

Jim extended his hand, palm up.

"An obsidian arrow will pierce your skin."

"Bullshit."

"Ouch, damn it!" Jim appeared startled. He jerked back his hand. Blood seeped from a small laceration. "I'll be damned!" he said.

"The coffee's good Jim. Thanks. I gotta' go."

"Tell me more about him," Jim said.

"Buy my book. Title is, *My Name is Cougar.*"

Chapter Twenty-Five

I sat in the SEA-TAC airport awaiting the flight. I thought of my experiences over the past four weeks. I thought of the nuggets in Cougar's mountain. All of a sudden I realized that I had been in total agreement with every opinion offered by the Native American. We really must be brothers considering our mutual understanding of the natural order was almost identical. The man was brilliant. Cougar knew everything. He was like a complete volume of Encyclopedia Britannica.

With a few hours before flight time I decided to visit the Space Needle again. I hadn't been there for several years. I thought of my mother who loved the Northwest. I thought of the 60 pound Chinook I caught off Westport years ago. I thought of the huge Steelhead I caught while float-boating on the Tracy River. I had good memories of my visits to Seattle. I remembered the hot clam chowder while awaiting a table on a cool evening at Ivar's Acre of Clams."

I ambled around the catwalk outside the Needle, stopping to view spectacular sights. To the north lay Mt. St. Helens in all its remaining glory. Of course, all that remained to be seen of the crown was now hidden by the cloud formation that encircled its peak like a spectral mantel.

Beyond Puget Sound, lay the snow-capped Olympic Mountains.

Looking over Puget Sound my mind went back three hundred years to when the shoreline was the home for Indians who lived gently on the land; Snake, Snohomish, Suquamish, Tillamook, Osette, Crow, Nisqually, Makah, Umatilla, Kootenai, Molalla, Kalispell, Bannock and Duwamish, before the incursions by Spanish Conquistadores, searching for gold, bringing with them breast-plates, brass helmets, cutlasses, cross-bows, smallpox, influenza, syphilis, and death for those indigenous people. Half of the people were dead within a few years, until the Conquistadores found there was no gold and left to plunder, murder and ravage other societies. It seemed as if all of the Europeans reveled in murdering, an insatiable lust obvious throughout their history.

I thought about a paragraph from one of my books on Indians. It was a poignant speech delivered by Chief Seattle, Chief of the great Suquamish Nation, who spoke these words to an assemblage of troops and councilmen in the newly founded city of Seattle;

> *"The Indians' night promises to be black. No bright stars hover about the horizon. Sad-voiced winds moan in the distance. Some nemesis of our race is on the red man's trail, and wherever he wanders he will still hear the approaching footsteps of the great destroyer of people and will prepare to meet his doom, as does a wounded deer that hears the approach of the hunter. A few more moons, a few more winters, and not one of the mighty hosts that once filled this land, or that now roam in fragmented bands through these vast solitudes will remain to weep over the tombs of a people once as powerful and hopeful as your own. But why should we complain? Why should I murmur words of the fate of my people? Societies are made up of unique individuals who are no better than others. Men come and go like waves in the ocean. A tear, a moment in time, a funereal dirge and they are forever gone from these longing eyes. Even the white man, whose God walked and talked with him as friend to friend is not exempt from a common destiny. We, upon our deaths, may be brothers after all. Our dead never forgot the beautiful world that gave them being. They still love the unspoiled canyons, its murmuring rivers, the magnificent mountains, its sequestered vales and forest-lined lakes and bays, and ever yearn in tender fond affection over the lonely hearted living, and often return from their Happy Hunting Grounds to visit, guide, comfort and console them. And when the last Red Man*

shall have perished and the memory of my tribe shall have become a myth among the White Men, these shores will swarm with the invisible dead of my people."

Chapter Twenty-Six

My eyes were tightly closed as I turned away from some passing visitors. My handkerchief was moist.

In my ear I heard a voice. "I've read it, also, brother. I cried, too." I recognized Cougar's voice.

I continued to stare out over the city with its overcrowded streets and edifices where people were stacked atop of each other like logs in the fire pit. My eyes swept 360 degrees as I walked on around the Needle my mind calculating just how many natives had loved this land since the time a boat first arrived from the West, with people seeking animals, followed by more migrants traversing the land bridge over the frozen Bering Sea. Recalling the history that I knew, when the first people arrived on these shores, I came to an incredible conclusion that tens of millions of Indians had lived and died since the migration of the first travelers, fourteen thousand years ago, when the planet was not polluted, water pristine, air pure, and mountains undesecrated, and with trackless trees mantling the mountains and valleys, where animals wandered, and great herds of buffalo roamed and grazed, unimpeded by fences. In three centuries these natives were well on their way to extinction. I thought of the terror of the Indians as they encountered a more powerful opponent than they could repel. My mind went back sixty years when I was heading for Bizerte and our convoy was attacked by Stukas, screaming out of the dark night, with tracers lacing the night and with bullets ricocheting down into the convoy. I was strapped into a 20 millimeter gun mount wondering why in hell I'd enlisted. I was not yet eighteen. I was terrified when slivers of metal meant to damage my body slammed down on the deck. I cried out in the night when a shard of shrapnel struck me below the knee and I could feel blood on my calf. My loader went down shrieking in agony. I continued shooting up at the flaming tailpipes as the bombers made another run on our ship. Off my starboard stern an ammunition ship exploded, sending a blazing fireball up into the night, illuminating our ship like day. Damn! I turned off my memory machine.

I watched a diesel below on the streets, belching a black toxic mixture of lung-destroying death.

I thought of Cougar's remote sanctuary.

My mind wandered back to my grandfather's farm in Indiana when as a youth my brother and I explored the forest below the farm. After chores were finished we could take a couple of swayback plow horses and go into the woods and live off the land. Often we sat by four Indian mounds, wondering who they were, when did they go and why did they depart. When the war was over I went back home to visit my Grandfather's farm. I sat by the mounds. My brother had been killed in 1944, during the Battle of the Bulge, so I sat alone feeling the pain of losing a loved one. Indians had lost most of their loved ones. The Cherokees suffered the Trail of Tears. The Potawatomi's suffered the Trail of Death when they were sent marching away in the middle of winter to a distant waste-land over the Mississippi River and told it was their home. The same fate was ordered for the Wabash, Wea, Shawnee, Kickapoo and the Chippewa. I wondered what fear Cougar had felt when returning from his hunt only to find his family being shot and his village sacked. For what reason, I asked myself? I decided it was an inborn lust for conquests among my ancestors, a real sickness that went back to the times of the Crusaders, Mongols, Huns, Vikings and Alexander the Great when killing people was the sign of gallantry to be acclaimed as *that noble deed*. I wondered just why Alexander the Great was considered *great* because what he really accomplished was to murder millions of people on his campaigns to conquer.

I felt a presence. I could see nothing. Cougar said, "I think you might benefit from seeing the last days of the Wallowa tribe of my people. You can use the experience in your book and with gifted writing let the world relive a tragedy in the lives of the Early Americans, one of hundreds but the final capitulation to overwhelming military forces."

"Where will we go?" I said.

"We will revisit the fateful journey of Chief Joseph and his people."

"I have a flight scheduled at SEA TAC."

"You'll make your flight," Cougar said.

"There's an attendant coming." Cougar smiled. "Let's give him something to talk about."

"Like what?" I said.

"He sees you now. Watch." Cougar materialized dressed in full Nez Perce regalia.

The attendant stared in disbelief and backed up quickly.

"What is he going to tell people?"

"That's his problem." Cougar had a devilish side, I decided.

We lifted straight up from the Space Needle and were instantly three hundred mile away over the Wallowa Valley in Northeastern Oregon.

The view was spectacularly mountainous. Snow capped the top of Sacagawea Peak in the rugged Blue Mountains. To the East we could see Hell's Canyon. To the south lay the Wallowa Mountain Range with Eagle Gap at 9675 feet. Buffalo roamed the vast meadows. Verdant forests mantled the foothills. We could see abundant wildlife. Bald Eagles dotted the Ponderosa pines. It was a valley of incredible beauty. Below lay Lake Wallowa. I could see into its depths. The Grande Ronde River wound up toward the basin of the Columbia River

"This was the home of the Wallowa Nez Perce tribe for over a thousand years," Cougar said. "My tribe lived to the North in what is now the State of Idaho." He pointed. "Our land extended from Oregon into Idaho and Washington. It all changed after the Lewis & Clark Expedition. Our homelands were soon overrun by palefaces who were told they could have our land. If you will look where the Wallowa River runs out of the lake you will see where Chief Joseph lived with his people. On the other side of the valley was their sacred burial ground."

"I was here maybe forty-five years ago. I brought my family to the West Coast. My mother lived in Seattle. I fished in the Deschutes River for steelheads. I thought at the time that this would be an idyllic place to live."

"It was better a hundred years ago. The air and water were not yet polluted."

"We've kinda' screwed the place up haven't we?" I said.

"This is where the end began in 1877," Cougar said."

"The end?" I said.

"The final days of freedom or death for the Nez Perce."

"I've read where those were troubled times for the Indians here," I said.

"Calamitous across this land the past three hundred years. After the Lewis & Clark Expedition, the next eight-two years were deadly for the people who lived out here, my parents included."

"What exactly happened," I said.

"The Army had been forcing Indians from their land all over the Pacific Northwest, the same as they had done completely across the continent for nearly three centuries. When people refused to go the army was ordered to forcefully remove them to reservations. The army was ordered to shoot the Indians when they didn't leave. My village was a prime example. That's what happened to Chief Joseph and his people. In 1877 there were 800 Nez Perce living here in this place. They were attacked by soldiers and a battle ensued. Even though hopelessly outgunned the Nez Perce fought off the soldiers but a lot of people were killed. Old men, women and children were killed along with warriors. The soldiers left but said they would be back the next day to enforce the relocation order."

"How many were killed?" I said.

"Too many," Cougar said. "Some soldiers were killed, too. They left until reinforcements could be brought in."

"Knowing the army was relentless, Chief Joseph held a powwow and decided to take his people to Canada where they would be safe. In the middle of the of night the entire compound pulled up stakes and left."

"Why couldn't the Nez Perce have allied themselves with other tribes to fight the army?"

"Chief Joseph's Wallowa tribe was the last holdout. Every other tribe in Washington, Oregon, Idaho and Montana had been defeated and sent away to reservations."

"How many different tribes were there?" I was curious.

"Many," Cougar said. "Walla Walla, Shoshone, Cayuse, Bannock, Suquamish, Dumanish, Crow, Umatilla, Blackfoot, Yakima, Tillamook, Modoc, Wenatchee, Palouse, Couer de Alene, Nisqually, Salish, Kalispell, Molalla, Cascade, Colville, Columbia, Kalapuya, Snake, Kootenai, Paiute, Makah and Ozette."

"How many people totally in the four states?"

"Almost one million," Cougar said.

"I read where Chief Joseph failed to get to Canada and ultimately surrendered," I said.

"That's correct. We are going to follow the escape route of his tribe," Cougar said.

We began moving eastward. We crossed over Hell's Canyon.

"Chief Joseph and his people had a three day lead on the army but they were indecisive about the route to take and lost precious time. Leaving so quickly they had to stop and hunt for food. The army had chuck wagons and could see the route the people took and could move much faster. They caught up with the people while they were camped at Tolo Lake. Another fight began and more people were killed. After one more fierce fight the tribe was down to about 700 people. He had lost over one hundred people killed. They could not care adequately for their wounded."

"It had to be desperate times," I said.

"The weather had turned bitterly cold in the Bitterroot Mountains as the tribe crossed Idaho and moved into Western Montana, near Missoula. They were short of food and clothing and running low on ammunition. It was desperation and the fear of being killed that kept them going, the sick and wounded had to be left behind to die. They had no time to build fires to heat water for baths. The elderly could not keep up. They spotted some cavalry up ahead and turned south toward Yellowstone. The army caught up with them again and in the battle at Big Hole over a hundred more Nez Perce were killed. Escaping again they went further south and in an attempt to confuse the troops turned eastward and crossed Yellowstone. Just before entering Yellowstone another battle at Camas Meadows erupted. By then the tribe was nearly defenseless. Snow was deep and impeding their movements. Also they were starving."

"How on earth could they keep going?" I said.

"The need to be free. Freedom was the great motivator," Cougar said.

"They were certainly stalwart people," I said.

"After crossing Yellowstone and the Rocky Mountains, Chief Joseph turned northward toward Canada still west of the Bighorn Mountains. They had travelled nearly 700 miles. Less than 600 of his people remained."

"I know they did not make it to Canada," I said.

"You're right. The army surrounded their encampment at Bear's Paw just 40 miles from Canada.

"Heavy snow had blanketed the area during the night and was still falling, which muffled the sound of the approaching soldiers. Early in the morning, while the Indians were still asleep, the soldiers started firing under the tipis where the exhausted Indians were trying to recuperate enough to go on. The battle lasted five days. Finally realizing that half of his people were either dead or missing, Chief Joseph surrendered. Almost 400 of his people had been killed during the 1400 miles trek, including his son, Likuta."

"How many indigenous natives died after my ancestors came over here?" I had read estimates.

"During three hundred years of warfare over seventeen million natives were either killed, starved, frozen or died from diseases carried by Europeans, to which they had no immunity," Cougar said.

I said I couldn't believe the inhumanity to humanity that occurred here.

"That horror was just the prelude," Cougar said. "The remaining 431 Nez Perce were loaded on trains and shipped to eastern Kansas where many more died from malaria and starvation."

"They were never permitted to return to their homeland?"

"No. In 1855 Old Chief Joseph signed a treaty with the government authorities who allowed his people to keep much of their homeland, but after gold was discovered in Nez Perce streams the treaty was rescinded and the size of their lands was drastically reduced. Old Chief Joseph said the second treaty was never agreed to by him or his people. He is buried in Wallowa Valley."

"I understand that many of the original treaties with other tribes were arbitrarily abrogated."

"Many. The Sioux were given by treaty most of the Black Hills in South Dakota because no one else wanted the land. After gold was discovered there the treaty was changed and most of that land taken back from them. Chief Joseph pleaded with officials in Washington to let his last few people return to the land of their ancestors in Oregon, to be near their sacred burial grounds. They were not allowed to return but were shipped to Colville Washington and interned on a reservation where Chief Joseph died from the ravages of the eight-year-long ordeal."

I stared at Cougar. My mind was numb. This history was not being taught in schools today.

"You have a flight to catch. Go. I want to stay awhile longer," he said"

I felt a hand on my shoulder. "We're closing now," an attendant said.

Chapter Twenty-Seven

We sat on the runway at SEA TAC, waiting for the fog to clear. Looking from my window I thought of the people who had lived along the lush Green River when fish were abundant in its waters, before the arrival of industry with the heartless dumping of industrial waste, before the pollution of the river to a point where the fish were too contaminated for consumption.

Finally taking off, I stared down at the passing terrain as we left SEA TAC thinking of the time when the land was uncluttered with factories and miles of tract houses looking like residential acne, and when millions of Indians nurtured their home lands with a passionate love. They are gone now. Sadly as the jet climbed up over Oregon I looked down, thinking about Cougar's homeland when the territory of the Nez Perce extended from the States of Washington and Oregon to Montana with their teepees along the Snake, Salmon and Clearwater Rivers encompassing twenty-seven thousand square miles. Now it is merely a micro-dot along the Clearwater River.

As my plane emerged above scudding clouds into sunshine, I suddenly remembered that I had forgotten to ask Cougar what he thought about the rednecks singing about Viagra trying to sell pills to limber-prick men in their desperate attempts to stiffen their dicks or to have one more erection and the women expanding their breasts with saltwater in order to seduce men into buying Viagra pills. I know what he would have told the women; '*bite size tits are okay*'. And for the men; '*forget that you are too old for mating*'.

As I walked off my flight I grinned while walking the people-mover realizing I could've willed myself back home, avoiding the frustrations of modern airports. I thought about Cougar and his friends.

It had been one of the most momentous and informative trips in my lifetime. I was already figuring out how to convince Pat to move out there.

Chapter Twenty-Eight

When my wife opened the door I stepped inside and hugged her. "Hi Minnehaha," I said.

"Hi guy, come in, my husband may not be back for several weeks. You find Hiawatha?"

"Just thinking aloud," I said and headed for my computer, my mind aflame with my fingers itching to type.

"Come sit," I said. "Let me tell you about that incredible trip. We'll have a visitor someday soon, I'll betcha."

"Who's coming?"

"Sit. I'll explain."

Since Pat's idea of camping out is at the Holiday Inn and after several minutes of describing my trip she developed that same look of skepticism which I had experienced over several years of attempting to get her to understand my lust for the wilderness areas. I asked if she was paying attention. "You do not seem to be excited about where I've been or what I did."

"You're rambling on and on about an Indian ghost, mountain lion ghost and the ghost of a horse. I don't believe in ghosts. How do you expect me to believe an Indian existed for two centuries? Your mind's working overtime just to develop your plot."

"That Indian is real. I talked with him. I lived with him and his Appaloosa horse for four weeks, and his mountain lion. That Indian and I are now kindred spirits. He has miraculous powers."

"I gotta' fix dinner." She got up to leave.

"C'mon. Stay for just a minute."

She sat down again, a look of derision on her face.

187

"You don't believe me, do you?" I said.

"No."

"You believe in Jesus, don't you?" Religion was one of our less frequent topics.

"Of course I do."

"You ever see him?"

"No."

"I've seen Cougar," I said. "He's real."

"Prove it," she said, smiling.

I showed her the nugget of gold. "I got this nugget from him for you," I said.

"That doesn't prove anything," Pat said

"Okay, hold out your hand, palm up."

"No," she said. "I don't want to play one of your dumb games."

"Honestly. It is not a dumb game hon. Cougar and I are really kindred spirits."

"I haven't been married to you for all of these years without knowing your dumb shenanigans, buddy." Pat screwed up her face in her most dubious sneer.

"Okay, stay the uniformed redneck." That comment sometime got to her. It didn't this time.

"I've got to fix something to eat," she said.

After having spent time with such an opinionated and well versed individual as the Nez Perce, I wondered what my observations might now be about the conditions of the world. I wondered if his ideas had persuaded me. I hit the TV button. I wondered if I could now find anything substantive or intelligent about television programming.

As I flipped several channels, searching for an educational show or some animal serials, I began to watch some of the programs just to see what type of idiocy viewers were being shown. I was astounded to see how insipid some of those presentations were and I wondered why anybody would waste their time watching what seemed to be dregs from some producer's faltering mind. Perhaps I should have asked my friend while we were together. Immediately my fingers flew to the keys. It was as if I had no control over them. They began to type. And then I remembered Cougar's comments about being kindred spirits and all I would have to do to communicate with him would be to think of him and our telepathic communications ability would kick in. I knew it was happening. My fingers raced across the keys to record another of my friend's insightful opinions.

"You are in a society that is increasingly poorly educated with your principle focus on television filth, interrupted by brain-stultifying talk shows with miniscule attention spans. The inability to understand, by the contemporary generation, enough to follow infantile stories and repartee between people has resulted in what are called reality shows that have elevated pre-adolescent games to adult entertainment during prime time. Even infantile stories told in three minute videos seem too much of an intellectual exertion for America's contemporary population so MTV has resorted to televising game shows where men and women have dates to go on vacations to intriguing resorts like Austin, Texas. to wallow in pig sties, devour bugs and wash down each other with slop while blathering insensible diatribe. The insanity comprises the intellect of the programs. A diminution of intellect is apparent by the proliferation of televised poker games, where paid audiences applaud every comment, movement or wager. How can poker games be considered great fun when they are not interesting? People are being trained to react like Pavlov's dogs to brain-control. Susceptible people succumb to sale pitches by snake-oil con artists on how to become a muscled Olympian with three simple payments. For hefty payments you can buy a disc that will demonstrate how to jump forward and then jump backward then jump to the left then jump to the right, dictated by rhythmic noises. When we were kids we did that free of charge. Why not jump rope again, play tag, plays hop scotch or learn military calisthenics? Before kids' brains matured they could do the identical movements without having to pay money. People are floundering in a virgin area of brain-subjugation when they sit brain-dead, watching oranges squeezed, 2 X 4' boards sawed, hamburgers being fried,

spitting cobras, screaming carnival hustlers attempting to unload last year's fuel-guzzling chariots or situation comedies where the dialogue is written by people who have suffered brain ulcerations. Television, with its screaming singers skipping across the screen making obscene gestures and mouthing decadent comments has conditioned viewers to vestal depths of brain drain where impotent males are conned into believing they will become great Lotharios by swallowing a pill. Exhibiting a puppet's mentality, people sit gaping at the TV with their mind mummified while preyed upon by salespeople promoting everything from fart pills to genital spray. Watching compensated audiences applauding when a pork roast is removed from the rotisserie indicates a deterioration of intellect and something is missing in the lives of those that are watching spellbound in front of television becoming obese and more stupid. Singers used to earn money singing. Now they make money by screaming and gyrating as if they had fire ants in their crotch. They shriek and poke their fingers at the audience as if they were sending some mystical message."

Wanting to record Cougar's opinions, I wondered what he thought about our school system and its effect students' lives. My fingers raced. Without having to think his opinions rushed out in a rapid-fire delivery. He and I actually were kindred spirits.

"Your drop-out rate is well above thirty percent, but the percentage of students who are wasting their parents' money and their own time is much higher. Those are the students snorting drugs, smoking marijuana and convincing some girl to undress so he can show what a super-stud he is by making another illegitimate baby, for which he will provide no financial or emotional support. Teenagers are becoming recklessly irresponsible. It is unfortunate, but true. Pregnancy occurs via drunkenness, lust, heat of the moment and in many cases, plain stupidity."

I had to agree with Cougar.

"The infantile reality shows have now become exhibitions of depraved violence and are now more numerous indicating the continuing trend toward televised idiocy."

I sat in front of my computer reading the evening newspaper and wondering where in hell the country was heading. Child molesters flooded the news, psycho-weirdoes coming out of the woodwork. I wondered what made men so evil as to prey on young girls and boys. Was it a recent phenomena caused by the exploitation of women by media? Was it publishers of Playgirl and Playboy filth that reveal such graphic nudity that prurient instincts take control of psychotic brains? Perhaps their sickness is inherited from parents. Perhaps pedophiles are the result of being sexually abused as a child. I remembered talking with Cougar about that aberration during one conversation, with emphasis on pedophiles. Cougar was not one to evade answers. I recalled what he believed. I wasn't surprised when his opinion flashed instantly in my brain.

Cougar acknowledged that morality is disappearing. His knowledge seemed inexhaustible. I'm convinced that he's one of the smartest humans I had ever met. With me, it is reality that, unless cured, pedophilia will burgeon. With current trends what will the world be like for my grandchildren and their children? With all the chaos and mayhem in the world I wondered what had become of common sense. Obviously Cougar was tuned in to my mind because my fingers began to type.

Common sense has become a forgotten value. People drive too fast seemingly unconcerned that speeding is the principle reason for highway deaths. During the Great Depression my grandfather was a farmer with pearls of wisdom. He told me that if you put your hand on a hot stove it would be burned. He also told me to not walk too close behind his horse. People drink too much and are apparently oblivious to the fact that their mentality is diminished exposing them to errors in judgment and unknown consequence. Practicing common sense prevents reckless misadventures. The use of mind-altering drugs is senseless. I prefer controlling my destiny. Jails are filled with people that failed to practice common sense. Common sense compels a person to check weapons before use to see if they are loaded. Playing with a gun without checking the weapon is a lack of common sense. Becoming pregnant when not yet married shows a total lack of common sense. For preservation, common sense is the guide line people need.

I suddenly sensed curiosity in Cougar's mind about what I thought of those economic and social trends resulting from the new liberal administration in Washington.

My mind said that the country is on the path to socialism. The concept of socialism sounds wonderful as an ideology, everybody equal. No one is better off than others. If you have eight potatoes you give four of them to someone else. I thought about that for a while and I figured socialism was certainly for me. I would get together with Warren Buffet and Bill Gates and we would pool our resources and then split it right down the middle, or at least three ways. My wife said that I should consider the other end of the socialism spectrum. I would take my checkbook and get together with some penniless vagrant and pool our resources and divide it right down the middle. Suddenly socialism didn't sound so enticing. I read about Russia and their adventure into socialism. It seems that socialism worked for the upper class. Somehow some people were more equal than others. While advocates of socialism drove luxury limousines and lived in dachas out in the country, with private airfields and golf courses, Russian peasantry rode on donkeys and existed in poverty. Perhaps socialism is not precisely what it is represented to be unless you are in power. Look closely at the officials who advocate socialism and see what occurs. If you have six dollars, half of it will be distributed by government to somebody who doesn't have a plugged nickel. That way you'll be equal to the other person. Another chunk will be taken to compensate those who decided to transfer money from wealthy to poor. The transferee doesn't even have to work. Russia fell apart because few people had a lot and a lot of people had virtually nothing. A revolution ensued and millions of Russians were murdered, and when the dust settled there were fewer people who had a lot and a lot of people who had practically nothing. Such are the benefits of socialism. California is a prime example of socialism in the tank. With confiscatory taxes and the influx of impoverished immigrants wanting everything for free California is bankrupt. Only government officials are immune from the axe. Critical service is scheduled for cuts and property taxes are scheduled for increases. It's the Russian scenario all over again. Jobs are disappearing and residents are jumping ship like

California is the Titanic. That rainy day is here but no one has saved for it. Everybody is scratching their heads wondering if liberalism and socialism is alike. You bet it is. The concept appears wonderful, you have one potato. You split it down the middle and you both consume half. Then gluttony creeps in and those who thought up socialism decide that they are entitled to the whole potato and they will permit you to have the peelings. And the new President is pushing the agenda further. I sensed that Cougar fully agreed with my observations. I wondered.

My Kindred Spirit typed.

"There are two truisms: for very cause there is an effect: for every action there is a reaction. Morgues overflow with cadavers of people that failed to learn about those truisms. Pure socialism is a flawed philosophy."

I pointed to bold typing on the monitor. "Those are that Indian's opinions," I said. "Cougar communicates with me telepathically. He can operate my computer. I have made a really intelligent friend."

I noticed a look of disbelief on my wife's face.

"Go ahead and doubt the truth," I said.

"I'm married to a weird man," my wife said.

Chapter Twenty-Nine

As we ate lunch, I explained to my doubting spouse some of the materials the Indian and I had discussed.

She said, "I still don't believe an Indian is two hundred years old. I don't believe you talked with a live Indian. You're pulling my leg, aren't you?" She squinted up her brow.

"I really did," I said.

"Prove it."

"Hold out your hand, palm up," I said.

She opened her hand, palm up, still dubious.

"An obsidian arrow will pierce your skin."

"Is this one of your stupid pranks?"

"You'll see," I said.

"Yeah, sure, Mike," she grinned, still skeptical.

"Ouch!" She flinched as blood began to ooze from a tiny laceration on her palm.

I had done nothing. I hadn't touched her.

A massive, tawny, mountain lion suddenly intertwined itself around her legs, purring.

She screamed.

A magnificent Appaloosa horse nuzzled her shoulder.

She yelled. "Hey, I believe! I believe! I believe! Mike! Get them out of here!"

Suspended in mid air, a handsome Nez Perce Indian said something to the mountain lion and to the horse, motioning.

"I am glad to have met you, Pat," Cougar said, as the trio began to disappear, drifting up, fading slowly away, cloud-like, through the ceiling, hazy, like thinning gossamer.

A smiling wave, a whinny, a guttural growl, and then they were gone.

My wife stood with a look of total disbelief. Not known to use profanity, she blurted out, "I'll be damned."

"You a believer, now, kiddo?"

"I would have sworn you were full of manure. He is a hunk! I'll go with you the next time." She batted her eyes, flirtatiously.

"You're pretty old to be getting frisky," I said.

"You used the words, *pretty old*. That's *pretty*, and *old*," Pat said smiling broadly.

"Now you know all the truth, sweetheart," I said.

"But you don't necessarily know all the truth, Mike," Pat said.

"So, tell me a truth," I said.

"Little do you know what goes on while you're away. The Indian and I may already be Kindred Spirits." She winked. "That is the truth."

Strangely, I wasn't the least bit jealous.

To commemorate those stalwart Indian Chiefs who guided their people through three-hundred years of tribulation after the invasions by the Europeans.

Abbigadasset (Pawtucket)
Abel Bosun (Cree)
Abis tos quos (Blood)
Addih-Hiddiseh (Hidatsa)
Adoeette (Kiowa)
Aeneas (Okanogan)
Afraid of Bear (Sioux)
Afraid of Hawk (Sioux)
Agate Arrow Point (Warm Springs)
Ah Moose (Lac du Flambeaux)
Ah-de-ak-too-ah (Osette Village)
Ahlakat (Nez Perce)
Ahtahkakoop (Cree)
Ahyouwaighs (Six Nations)
Alchesay (Apache)
Alexander (Wampanoag)
Al-is-kah (Osette Village)
Alligator (Seminole)
Alpheus Brass (Chemahawin)
Always Riding (Yampah Ute)
Amat-tan (Kashaya)
American Chief (Kansa)
American Horse (Sioux)
Amisquam (Winnebago)
Anacamegishca (Kenisteno)
Annawon (Wampanoag)
Antonio Buck (Ute)
Antonio Garra (Cupeno)
Antonito (Pima)
Apaula Tustennuggee (Creek)
Appachancano (Appamattuck)
Apache John (Apache)
Appanoose (Sauk and Fox)

Arkikita (Otoe)
Armijo (Apache)
Ash Kan Bah Wish
(Lac du Flambeaux)
Assonnonquah (Wea)
Atawang (Ottawa)
Aupumut (Mohican)
Autosse (Creek)
Awashonks (Sakonnet)
Baht-se-ditl (Neah Village)
Baptiste Mongrain (Osage)
Barboncito (Apache)
Bashaba (Penacook)
Batiste Good (Kiowa)
Bear Bird (Comanche)
Bear Claw (Lenape)
Bear Cut Ear (Crow)
Bear Ribs (Hunkapapa)
Bear's Ear (Comanche)
Bear Tooth (Crow)
Bedonkohe (Apache)
Bel Oiseau (Osage)
Bellrock (Crow)
Benito (Apache)
Berht Chasing Hawk (Sioux)
Bich-took (Waatch Village)
Big Bear (Cree)
Big Bill (Paiute)
Big Bow (Kiowa)
Big Eagle (Mdewakanton Sioux)
Big Elk (Omaha)
Big Foot (Miniconjou)
Big Horse (Missouri)

Big Mouth (Arapaho)
Big Mouth (Brule' Sioux)
Big Razor (Sioux)
Big Snake (Winnebago)
Big Star (Comanche)
Big Star (Walla Walla)
Big Thunder (Sioux)
Big Thunder (Wabanaki)
Big Thunder (Nez Perce)
Big Tree (Kiowa)
Big Tree (Blackfeet)
Big Wolf (Comanche)
Billuk-whtl (Tsoo-yess)
Billy Bowlegs (Seminole)
Black Bear (Arapaho)
Black Beard (Comanche)
Black Bird (Potawatomi)
Blackbird (Omaha)
Black Bob (Shawnee)
Black Buffalo (Teton Sioux)
Black Cat (Mandan)
Black Crow (Sioux)
Black Elk (Lakota)
Black Eye (Sioux)
Blackfish (Shawnee)
Blackfoot (Crow)
Black Fox (Cherokee)
Black Hawk (Sauk)
Black Hoof (Shawnee)
Black Horn (Sioux)
Black Horse (Seneca)
Black Kettle (Cheyenne)
Black Mocassin (Haida)
Black Moon (Hunkpapa)
Black Rock (Teton Sioux)
Blue Jacket (Shawnee)
Blue Tomahawk (Kiowa)

Bone Necklace (Yankton Sioux)
Bow and Quiver (Comanche)
Brave Bear (Cheyenne)
Bright Horn (Archaic)
Broken Arm (Comanche)
Broken Hand (Cheyenne)
Broken Arrow (Coweta)
Buckskin Charley (Ute)
Buffalo Eater (Comanche)
Buffalo Horn (Bannock)
Buffalo Hump (Comanche)
Buffalo Medicine (Teton Sioux)
Buffalo Piss (Comanche)
Bull (Wea)
Bull Bear (Comanche)
Bull Chief (Cheyenne)
Bull Chief (Apsaroke)
Bull Elk (Comanche)
Bull Head (Pawnee)
Bull Snake (Crow)
Cadette (Mescalero Apache)
Calero Rapala (Comanche)
Callicum (Nootka)
Cameahwait (Shoshone)
Canonchet (Narragansett)
Canonicus (Narragansett)
Cany Attle (Mouche)
Captain Elick (Creek)
Captain Jack (Modoc)
Captain Johnny (Archaic)
Captain Logan (Archaic)
Cashwahutyonah (Onondago)
Cayangwarego (Tuscorora)
Cayatania (Navajo)
Chacapma (Potawatomi)
Chad Smith (Cherokee)
Charger (Yankton Sioux)

Charging Bear (Sioux)
Charging Hawk (Osage)
Charles Shakes (Kwaguitl)
Charley Amathla (Seminole)
Chato (Mescalero Apache)
Chawookly (Coweta)
Checalk (Potawatomi}
Cheebass (Potawatomi)
Cheeseekau (Shawnee)
Cheetsamahoin (Clallam)
Chetopah (Osage)
Chetzemoka (Clallam)
Chewago (Potawatomi)
Chief Aslo (Ashochimi)
Chief Beaver (Delaware)
Chief Blinds (Columbia)
Chief Bones (Palouse)
Chief-Comes-In-Sight (Cheyenne)
Chief Egan (Paiute)
Chief Escumbuit (Abenaki)
Chief Garfield (Jicarilla)
Chief Grass (Blackfoot Sioux)
Chief Horseback (Comanche)
Chief Illiniwek (Illinois)
Chief Michel (Kootenay)
Chief Moses (Modoc)
Chief No Shirt (Walla Walla)
Chief Oytes (Paiute)
Chief Pot Belly (Palouse)
Chief Sagamore (Sagamore)
Chief Sar-Sarp-Kin (Salish)
Chief Timbo (Comanche)
Chief Tonasket (Salish)
Chief Yelkis (Mollala)
Chief White (Chippewa)
Chihuahua (Comanche)
Chihuahua (Apache)

Chilliwack (Comox)
Chinnabie (Coweta)
Chittee-Yoholo (Seminole)
Chochise (Chiricahua)
Chomoparva (Comanche)
Conge (Potawatomi)
Chono Ca Pe (Oto)
Chou-man-I-case (Chickasaw)
Chu-gu-an (Kashaya)
Clam Fish (Warm Springs)
Clermont (Osage)
Coast-no (Molalla)
Coboway (Clatsop)
Coloraw ((Ute)
Comcomly (Chinook)
Connessoa (Onondago
Conquering Bear (Lakota)
Cordero (Comanche)
Corn Planter (Seneca)
Cornstalk (Shawnee)
Cornstalk (Huron)
Counisnase (Molalla)
Crazy Bear (Oglala Sioux)
Crazy Horse (Oglala Sioux)
Crooked Finger (Molalla)
Crooked Legs (Wea)
Crow (Cheyenne)
Crow Dog (Oglala Sioux)
Crow Feathers (Kiowa)
Crow Foot (Blackfoot)
Crow King (Hunkpapa Sioux)
Crow's Breast (Gros Ventres)
Cuampe (Ute)
Cuffey (Poosepatuck)
Cunne Shote (Cherokee)
Curtis Zenigha (Delaware)
Custologo (Delaware)

Cut Finger (Arapaho)
Cutshamekin (Agawam)
Cyrenius Hall (Nez Perce)
Daht-leek (Osette Village)
Dan George (Salish)
David Vann (Cherokee)
David Williams (Nespelem)
Dead Eyes (Kiowa)
Decanisora (Onondago)
Deer Ham (Ioway)
Deer Horn (Ponca)
Delgadito (Mouche Apache)
Delshay (Tonto Apache)
Diwali (Cherokee)
Does Everything (Apsaroke)
Dohosan (Kiowa)
Donacoma (Huron)
Duggins (Molalla)
Dull Knife (Cheyenne)
Eagle (Nez Perce)
Eagle Chief (Pawnee)
Eagle Drink (Comanche)
Eagle Elk (Oglala Sioux)
Eagle Heart (Kiowa)
Eagle of Delight (Cheyenne)
Eagle Ribs (Piegan Blackfeet)
Edward Bullette (Creek)
Egan (Paiute)
El Albo (Mouche Apache))
El Sordo (Navajo)
Elizabeth Job (Poosepatuck)
El Sordo (Comanche)
Encanaguane (Comanche)
Enias (Entiat)
Esazat (Comanche)
Escumbuit (Penacook)
Eshcam (Potawatomi)

Esh-sta-ra-ba (Maha)
Eshtahumleah (Teton Sioux)
Eskaminzin (Anaviapa Apache)
Eskelteslan (Apache)
Essiminasqua (Pawtucket)
Estrella (Mescalero Apache)
E-TAA-NA-QUOT (Chippewa)
Fast Bear (Kiowa)
Feeble One (Comanche)
Fish Hawk (Umatilla)
Five Crows (Cayuse)
Five Wounds (Nez Perce)
Flat Iron Mela Blaska (Oglala)
Foke
Luste Hajo (Seminole)
Fool Chief (Kansa)
Fool Dog (Kiowa)
Fools Crow (Crow)
Four Bears (Mandan)
Four Bears (Sioux)
Fragrant Eagle (Comanche)
Frank Fools (Crow)
Fuskatche (Cusetah)
Gall (Hunkpapa Sioux)
Garfield (Jacarilla)
Garry (Spokan)
Gatebo (Comanche)
Gem-le-le (Kashaya)
Georgia White Hair (Osage)
Geronimo (Apache)
Good Heart (Crow)
Goose (Wea)
Gotokowhkaka (Wea)
Grande Corte (Piankashaw)
Gray Iron (Mdewakanton Sioux)
Gray Wolf (Piegan)
Great Bear (Delaware)

Great Eagle (Caddo)
Great War Chief (Navajo)
Green Horn (Comanche)
Greenwood Laflore (Choctaw)
Grey Beard (Cheyenne)
Grey Eagle (Apache)
Grizzly Bear (Menominee)
Guadalupe (Caddo)
Haatse (Makah)
Hah-yo-hwa (Waatch Village)
Hiachenie (Cayuse)
Hairy Bear (Winnebago)
Halletemalthle (Cusetah)
Hamli (Walla Walla)
Handsome Lake (Seneca)
Hatalakin (Palouse)
Hawk (Paugussett)
Heavy Runner (Piegan)
He Bear (Comanche)
He Gnaws his Master (Comanche)
He Who Saw Fire (Comanche)
Head Carry (Blackfoot)
He-dah-titl (Neah Village)
He-Dog (Oglala Sioux)
Herrero Grande (Apache)
Hiachenie (Cayuse)
Hiawatha (Mohawk)
Hichonquash (Tuscarora)
High Hawk (Sioux)
High Head Jim (Creek)
High Horse (Omaha)
Hillis Hadjo (Seminole)
Hoarse Bark (Comanche)
Hobonah (Wampanoag)
Hole-in-the-day (Chippewa)
Hole-in-the-Forehead (Pawnee)
Hollow Horn Bear (Brule Sioux)

Homatah (Coweta)
Homily (Walla Walla)
Hoowanneka (Winnebago)
Hopothe Mico (Tallisee)
Hopoy (Coosade)
Horse Back (Comanche)
Horse Chief (Pawnee)
Howeah (Comanche)
Hustul (Nez Perce)
Ignacio (Weeminuche)
Inkpadutah (Iowa)
Iron Bull (Crow)
Iron eye (Omaha)
Iron Hawk (Cheyenne)
Iron Mountain (Comanche)
Iron Plume (Sioux)
Iron Shell (Brule' Sioux)
Iron Shirt (Comanche)
Islander (Apache)
It-an-da-ha (Makah)
Itcho-Tustennuggee (Seminole)
Jacco Tacekokah Godfroy (Wea)
Jack House (Ute)
Jack-O-Pa (Chippewa)
Jacob Thomas (Cayuse)
James Perry (Archaic)
Junaluska (Cherokee)
Jason (Nez Perce)
Jim Henry (Muscogee)
Jim James (Sinkiuse)
Jo Hutchins (Santiam)
Joc-O-Sot (Mesquakie)
Joe Capilano (Squamish)
Joe Moses (Sinkiuse)
John Grass (Sioux)
John Homo (Chickasaw)
John Hoyle (Chowan)

John Ridge (Cherokee)
John Ross (Cherokee)
John Wooden Legs (Cheyenne)
Johnko' Skeanendon (Oneida)
Johnson (Swinomish)
Johnyellow Flower (Ute)
Joseph (Nez Perce)
Joseph Brant (Mohawk)
Joseph LaFlesche (Omaha)
Joseph Perryman (Creek)
Josua (Cowichan)
Juh (Apache)
Julcee Mathla (Seminole)
Juleetaulematha (Coweta)
Jumper (Seminole)
Kabay Nodem (Chippewa)
Kah-bach-sat (Makah)
Kah-ge-ga-bowh (Ojibwa)
Kahlteen (Kalapuya)
Kai-kwt-lit-ha (Waatch Village)
Kal-chote (Makah)
Kamiakin (Yakima)
Kanacamgus (Agawam)
Kanagagota (Cherokee)
Kanakuk (Kickapoo)
Kanapima (Ottawa)
Kanaretah (Comanche)
Kan-hahti (Tejas)
Kape (Quinalt)
Katawabeda (Chippewa)
Ka-ya-ten-nae (Apache)
Ke Wish Te No (Lac du
Flambeaux)
Keesheswa (Fox)
Keesis (Potawatomi)
Keh-chook (Makah)
Kekequah (Wea)

Kemwoon (Whuaquum)
Kennebis (Pawtucket)
Kennekuk (Ioway)
Keokuk (Sauk and Fox)
Kets-kus-sum (Makah)
Kicking Bear (Oglala Sioux)
Kicking Bird (Kiowa)
Kientpoos (Modoc)
Kiesnut (Wishram)
Kilcaconen (Yeopim)
King of the Crows (Crow)
King Philip) Wampanoag)
Kinkananqua (Tulalip)
Kishekosh (Sac and Fox)
Kishkalwa (Shawnee)
Kitsap (Muckleshoot)
Kiwatchee (Comanche)
Klah-ku-pihl (Tsoo-yess)
Klah-pe-an-hie (Makah)
Klaht-te-di-yuke (Waatch Village)
Klakaghama (Siletz)
Klart-Reech (Kilikitat)
Klatts-ow-sehp (Neah Village)
Kleht-li-quat-stl (Waatch Village)
Koon-Kah-za-chy Kiowa-Apache)
Konoohqung (Oneida)
Koomilus (Tchulwhyook)
Koostata (Kootanai)
Kowa (Comanche)
Kwah-too-quahl (Tsoo-yess)
Kyoti (Tsawatenok)
Lame Deer (Minneconjou)
La Mouche Noire (Wea)
La Peau Blanche (Wea)
Lappawinsoe (Delaware)
Lattchie (Molalla)
LA-WA-TU-CHEH (Archaic)

Lawyer (Kwakiutl)
Lawyer (Nez Perce)
Le Soldat du Chene (Osage)
Leahwiddikah (Comanche)
Lean Bear (Cheyenne)
Lean Elk (Nez Perce)
Lean Wolf (Gros Ventres)
Lechat (Ute)
Ledagie (Creek)
Leepahkia (Peankashae)
Left Hand (Cheyenne)
Legus Perryman (Creek)
Leschi (Nisqually)
Little (Oglala Sioux)
Little Big Man (Oglala Lakota)
Little Carpenter (Cherokee)
Little Charlie (Wea)
Little Crow (Mdewkanton Sioux)
Little Edward (Hunkpapa Sioux)
Little Face (Wea)
Little Hawk (Oglala Sioux)
Little Horse (Cheyenne)
Little Mountain (Kiowa)
Little Pipe (Chippewa)
Little Pipe (Coyote)
Little Prince (Creek)
Little Raven (Arapaho)
Little Robe (Arapaho)
Little Rose (Cheyenne)
Little Six (Kaposia Sioux)
Little Thief (Oto)
Little Thunder (Brule' Sioux)
Little Turtle (Miami/Mohican)
Little Wolf (Cheyenne)
Little Wolf (Lakota)
Little Wound (Oglala Sioux)
Locher Harjo (Creek)

Loco (Apache)
Logan (Huron)
Logan Fontenelle (Omaha)
Lollway (Archaic)
Lone Man (Teton Sioux)
Lone Wolf (Kiowa)
Long Jim (Nez Perce)
Long Mandan (Kiowa)
Looking Glass (Nez Perce)
Low-Dog (Lakota)
Luther Standing Bear (Oglala Sioux)
Macasharrow (Huron)
Macota (Potawatomi)
Mad Bear (Sioux)
Madokawando (Drake)
Mahaskah (Iowa)
Mahtoree (Yankton Sioux)
Majectla (Makah)
Major Ridge (Cherokee)
Makhpiya-Luta (Lakota)
Malatchee (Creek)
Mamanti (Kiowa)
Man Afraid of His Horse (Sioux)
Man and Chief (Pawnee)
Man-chap-che-mani (Osage)
Mangas Colorados (Membres)
Manhawgaw (Iowa)
Man-in-cloud (Cheyenne)
Manitou (Umatilla)
Manitou (Spokane)
Mankato (Santee Sioux)
Manteo (Croatoam)
Manuelito (Navajo)
Many Horns (Sioux)
Many Horses (Apache)
Maple Tree (Minneconjou)

Maquinna (Nuu-chah-nulth)
Markomete (Menominee)
Ma-sha-ke-ta (Maha)
Mashulatubbe (Choctaw)
Massasoit (Pokanchet)
Matoonas (Nipmuck)
Mato-Tope (Mandan)
McGillivray (Creek)
Mebea (Potawatomi)
Mecina (Apache)
Medicine Arrow (Cheyenne)
Medicine Bottle (Santee Sioux)
Medicine Crow (Crow)
Medicine Horn (Crow)
Medicine Horse (Coyote)
Meetenwa (Potawatomi)
Mehskehme (Blackfeet)
Menawa (Potawatomi)
Menomene (Potawatomi)
Mescotnome (Potawatomi)
ME-SHIN-GO-ME-SIA (Archaic)
Metacomet (Wampanoag)
Metacoms (Pokanchet)
Metea (Potawatomi)
Metchapagiss (Potawatomi)
Miantonomi (Narragansett)
Miconopi (Oconee)
Micanopy (Seminole)
Miitsisupukwuse Pitun
(Comanche)
Moanahonga (Iowa)
Moara (Ute)
Mo-Chu-No-Zhi (Ponca)
Mocksa (Potawatomi)
Moise (Salish)
Mokohoko (Sauk)
Moless' (Sac & Fox)

Momee-shee (Maha)
Mon-Chonsia (Kansas)
Monaco (Nipmuck)
Mona (Potawatomi)
Monkaushka (Sioux)
Moon Day (Chippewa)
Mope-Chu-Cope (Comanche)
Mo-pe-ma-nee (Maha)
Moses (Sinkiuse)
Mougo (Teton Sioux)
Mougo (Miami)
Moukaushka (Yankton Sioux)
Mountain Chief (Blackfoot)
Mowa (Potawatomi)
Mow Way (Comanche)
Moxus (Abnaki)
Moytoy (Cherokee)
Much-kah-tah-moway
(Potawatomi
Mumagechee (Oaksoy)
Mushalatubee (Choctaw)
Muttaump (Nipmuck)
Muthtee (Coosade)
Nachite (Apache)
Nah-Et-Luc-Hopie (Muskogee)
Naiche (Chiricahua)
Nana (Apache)
Nanawonggabe (Chippewa)
Nanamocomuck (Penacook)
Nanapashemet (Nipmuc)
Nan-Nouce-Rush-Ee-Toe (Sauk)
Nanouseka (Potawatomi)
Nanotomenut (Penacook)
Napikiteeta (Piankashaw)
Natsowachehee (Natchez)
Nautchegno (Potawatomi)
Nawapamanda (Wea)

Nawat (Arapaho)
Nawkaw (Winnebago)
Neamathla (Seminole)
Neamico (Muscogee)
Neathlock (Cusetah)
Neebosh (Potawatomi)
Necomah (Siletz)
Nehalam (Siletz)
Nehemantha (Apalachicola)
Nelson (Muckleshoot)
Nemantha-Micco (Creek)
Nenchoop (Neah Village)
Neomonni (Iowa)
Nesourquoit (Sac & Fox)
Nicaagat (Ute)
Nicameus (Kwantlens)
Ninigret (Narragansett)
Ninusize (Cilan)
Nittakechi (Choctaw)
No Heart (Sioux)
No Shirt (Walla Walla)
Nobah (Comanche)
Noon Day (Chippewa)
No-taw-kah (Potawatomi)
Notchimine (Iowa)
No-Tin (Chippewa)
Numphow (Pawtucket)
Nutackachie (Choctaw)
Ocheehajou (Natchez)
Ohequanah (Wea)
Ohiyesa (Santee Sioux)
Oh-Ma-Tai (Comanche)
Oho-shin-ga (Maha)
O-Hya-Wa-Mince-Kee (Chippewa)
Okee-Makee-Quid (Chippewa)
Old Bear (Comanche)
Old Bear (Cheyenne)

Old Crow (Crow)
Old Grass (Blackfoot Sioux)
Old James (Nez Perce)
Old Joseph (Nez Perce)
Old Looking Glass (Nez Perce)
Old Man Afraid of His
Horse(Sioux)
Old Tobacco (Piankashaw)
Oliver Lot (Spokane)
Ollikut (Nez Perce)
Olyugma (Costonoan)
Onasakenrat (Mohawk)
One Bull (Hunkpapa Sioux)
One Eye (Comanche)
One Eyed John (Simcoe)
One-Eyed Miguel (Sierra Apache)
Oneka (Mohican)
Oneyana (Oneida)
On-Ge-Wae (Chippewa)
Ohyawamincekee(Chippewa)
Ongpatonga (Omaha)
Onondakai (Seneca)
Onoxas (Potawatomi)
Oobick (Waatch Village)
Ooduhtsait (Oneida)
Opa-lon-ga (Maha)
Opay Mico (Tallisee)
Opechancanough (Powhatan)
Opotheyahola (Tuckabatchee)
Opothle-Yoholo (Creek)
Opototache (Tallisee)
Oquakabee (Natchez)
Orono (Penobscot)
Osceola (Seminole)
Oskanondonha (Oneida)
Otsiquette (Oneida)
Otsinoghiyata (Onondaga)

Otter Belt (Comanche)
Ouray (Ute)
Over The Buttes (Comanche)
Ow-hi (Yakama)
Oyeocker (Appamattuck)
Paddy Welsh (Creek)
Pahayuca (Comanche)
Pah-hat (Neah Village)
Pahkah (Comanche)
Pai-yeh (Osette Village)
Papakeecha (Miami)
Paranuarimuco-Jupe (Comanche)
Pareiya (Comanche)
Paruaguita (Comanche)
Paruaquipitsi (Comanche)
Pa-she-Nine (Chippewa)
Pashepahaw (Sac and Fox)
Passaconaway (Penacook)
Passaquo (Agawam)
Patkanim (Snoqualmie)
Pawnawneahpahbe (Yankton Sioux)
Pawnee Killer (Oglala Sioux)
Paxinos (Shawnee)
Peamuska (Musquakee)
Peaneesh (Potawatomi)
Pebriska-Rubpa (Hidatsa)
Pedro (Apache)
Pee-Che-Kin (Chippewa)
Pee-pin-oh-waw (Potawatomi)
Peo (Umatilla)
Peo-peo-thalekt (Umatilla)
Perig (Potawatomi)
Perits-Shinakpas (Crow)
Pernerney (Comanche)
Peskelechaco (Pawnee)
Pesotem (Potawatomi)

Pessacus (Narraganset)
Peta Nocoma (Comanche)
Petalesharo (Pawnee)
Peter Chafean (Kalapuya)
Peter Cornstalk (Archaic)
Peter Wapeto (Chelan)
Peu-Peu-Mox-Mox (Walla Walla)
Phil Peters (Saginaw Chippewa)
Philip Martin (Mississippi)
Pine Leaf (Gros Ventre)
Pinnus (Nanimoos)
Pinto (Ute)
Pisumi Napu (Comanche)
Pleasant Porter (Creek)
Plenty Bear (Arapaho)
Plenty Coups (Crow)
Pocatello (Shoshone)
Poker Jim (Walla Walla)
Po-lat-kin (Spokan)
Pomham (Narraganset)
Pontiac (Ottowa)
Poor Coyote (Comanche)
Pope (Tewa)
Poteokemia (Sac & Fox)
Poundmaker (Blackfoot)
Powasheek (Sauk and Fox)
Powder Face (Arapaho)
Powhatan (Powhatan)
Pretty Eagle (Crow)
Propio-Maks (Walla Walla)
Pteh Skah (Assiniboin)
Puckeshinwa (Shawnee)
Pushican (Shoshone)
Pushmataha (Choctaw)
Pushmataha (Fox)
Putcheco (Potawatomi)
Quai-eck-ete (Molalla)

Quaiapen (Wampanoag)

Qual-chan (Yakima)

Quanah Parker (Comanche)

Quashquame (Sauk/Foxes

Quatawapea (Shawnee)

Quia-eck-ete (Molalla)

Quick Bear (Sioux)

Quil-ten-e-nock (Yakima)

Quiniapin (Narraganset)

Quinkent (Ute)

Quiziachigiate (Capote)

Qwatsinas (Nuxalk)

Rabbit's Skin Leggins (Nez Perce)

Rainbow (Nez Perce)

Rain-in-the-Face (Sioux)

Red Bird (Chippewa)

Red Bird (Winnebago)

Red Chief (Palouse)

Red Cloud (Lakota)

Red Dog (Sioux)

Red Eagle (Creek)

Red Echo (Nez Perce)

Red Fish (Oglala Sioux)

Red Grizzly Bear (Nez Perce)

Red Heart (Nez Perce)

Red Horse (Sioux)

Red Indian (Ute)

Red Jacket (Seneca)

Red Leaf (Brule'

Red Nose (Fox)

Red Owl (Nez Perce)

Red Shirt (Sioux)

Red Thunder (Yanklonai Sioux)

Red Whip (Gros Ventres)

Red Wolf (Nez Perce)

Renville (Sisseton Sioux)

Returning Wolf (Comanche)

Richard Ward (Poosepatuck)

Robbinhood (Pawtucket)

Rolling Thunder (Comanche)

Roman Nose (Cheyenne)

Rouensa (Kaskaskia)

Rouls (Nuchawanack)

Roving Wolf (Comanche)

Runaawitt (Pawtucket)

Running Antelope (Hunkpapa)

Running Bear (Sioux)

Running Bird (Kiowa)

Running Fisher (Gros Ventres)

Running Rabbit (Blackfoot)

Runs The Enemy (Sioux)

Rushing Bear (Pawnee)

Sa-da-ma-ne (Maha)

Sagamore John (Nipmuck)

Saggakew (Agawam)

Saghwareesa (Tuscarora)

Sah-dit-le-uad (Waatch Village)

Sahhaka (Mandan)

Sakuma (Kiowa)

Salmon (Salishan)

Sam Jones (Seminole)

Samoset (Abknaki)

Samuel Chocote (Creek)

Sanaco (Comanche)

Sanhyle (Sanpoil)

Sanilac (WyanPatte)

Santa Anna (Comanche)

Santana (Kiowa)

Santank (Kiowa)

Santos (Aravipa Apache)

Sapo-Noway (Yakima)

Sargerito (Comanche)

Sar-sarp-kin (Salish)

Sassaba (Chippewa)

Sassacus (Pequot)
Saturiwa (Timucua)
Scal-le-tush (Palouse)
Scarrowyady (Oneida)
Scatchad (Neetlum)
Schonchin (Modoc)
Schwatka (Tulalip)
Scitteaygusset (Pawtucket)
Scituate (Agawam)
Seattle (Suquamish)
See-non-ty-a (Iowa)
Selocta (Creek)
Sequoya (Cherokee)
Severo (Ute)
Shabbona (Ottawa)
Shabonee (Potawatomi)
Shakopee (Santee Sioux)
Shahaka (Mandan)
Sharitarish (Pawnee)
Shauhaunapotinia (Iowa)
Shavehead (Potawatomi)
Shaumonekusse (Oto)
Sheheke (Mandan)
Shenandoah (Onieda)
Shenkah (Paiute)
Shingaba W'Ossin (Chippewa)
Shon-gis-cah (Maha)
Shooter (Teton Sioux)
Shoshanim (Nipmuck)
Short Bull (Brule sioux)
Shot In The Eye (Oglala Sioux)
Shot In The Hand (Apsaroke)
Showaway (Cayuse)
Shustook (Tlingit)
Sianton (Kitchie)
SidpminaPata (Iowa)
Sinnahoom (Waskalatchat)

Siskiyou (Siletz)
Sitting Bear (Kiowa)
Sitting Bull (Hunkpapa Sioux)
Skemiah (Simcoe)
Skimia (Walla Walla)
Skowel (Skokomish)
Sky Chief (Pawnee)
Sleeping Wolf (Comanche)
Sleeping Wolf (Kiowa)
Slockish (Walla Walla)
Sluiskin (Skykomish)
Smoholly (Simcoe)
Smoke (Ponca)
Sobotar (Capote)
Soholessee (Natchez)
Soko (Comanche)
Sonikat (Snoqualmie)
Sopitchin (Teitton)
Sorrel Horse (Arapaho)
Sparhecher (Creek)
Spencer (Cheyenne)
Spirit Talker (Comanche)
Spotted Bear (Kiowa)
Spotted Crow (Sioux)
Spotted Eagle (Nez Perce)
Spotted Leopard (Comanche)
Spotted Tail (Brule Sioux)
Spreckled Snake (Snake)
Spring Frog (Cherokee)
Squagis (Nanimoos)
Squanto (Pawhatan)
Standing Arrow (Mohawk)
Standing Bear (Lakota Sioux)
Standing Bear (Ponca)
Standing Buffalo (Kaposia Sioux)
Standing Elk (Brule')
Standing Turkey (Cherokee)

Stan Waite (Cherokee)
Steencoggy (Molalla)
Steep Wind (Lakota)
Stic-cas (Cayuse)
Stilnaleeje (Coosade)
Stimafutchkee (Coosade)
Stone Calf (Comanche)
Stone Eater (Wea)
Storm (Arapaho)
Striker (Apache)
Struck By The Ree (Yankton Sioux)
Stumbling Bear (Kiowa)
Stumickosucks (Blood)
Stwyre (Simcoe)
Sun Eagle (Comanche)
Surrounded (Kiowa)
Swan (Wea)
Swell (Neah Village)
Swift Bear (Brule')
Tabbananica (Comanche)
Tabbaccus (Unkechaug)
Tack-en-su-a-tis (Nez Perce)
Tah-a-howtl (Makah)
Tahalo (Neah Village)
Tah-Chee (Cherokee)
Tahrohon (Iowa)
Tahtahqueesa (Oneida)
Tahts-kin (Neah Village)
Talankamani (Khemnichan)
Tall Bull (Cheyenne)
Tall Eagle Blackfoot Sioux)
Tall Tree (Comanche)
Tallassee (Creek)
Tamahay (Sioux)
Tammany (Delaware)
Tamulston (Skam Swatch)
Ta-noh-ga (Maha)

Tarantine (Penacook)
Ta-reet-tae (Maha)
Tarhe (Huron)
Tascalusa (Mississippian)
Tasunkkakokipapi (Oglala Lakota)
Tatubem (Pequot)
Tawny Bear (Comanche)
Taza (Chiricahua)
Tcheenuk (Sanutch)
Tchoops (Pellault)
Tchoo-quut-lah (Neah Village)
Tecumseh (Shawnee)
Ten Bears (Comanche)
Ten Sticks (Comanche)
Tenaya (Ah-wah-ne-chee)
Tendoy (Lemhi Shoshone)
Tennowikah (Comanche)
Tenskwatawa (Shawnee)
Te-sha-va-gran (Maha)
Tet-li-mi-Chief (Yakima)
The Brass Man (Comanche)
The Crafty One (Comanche)
The Crow (Comanche)
The Dog (Comanche)
The Prophet (Shawnee)
The Six (Ojibway)
Theyendanega (Mohawk)
Thockoteehee (Natchez)
Thomas (Walla Walla)
Thomas Hoyle (Chowan)
Thomas LeFlore (Choctaw)
Three Feathers (Nez Perce)
Three White Crows (Atsina)
Thunder Chief (Blackfoot)
Thunder Cloud (Blackfeet)
Tiamah (Fox)
Tiema Blanca (Mouche)

Tilcoax (Palouse)
Timothy (Nez Perce)
Timpoochy Barnard (Yuchi)
Tin-Tin-Meet-Sa (Umatilla)
Tishcohan (Delaware)
Tlah-Co-Glass (Tlakluit)
Tochoaca (Ute)
Tochoway (Comanche)
Togulki (Creek)
Toion (Kashaya)
Tokacon (Yankton Sioux)
Toke (Snoqualmie)
Tomasket (Colville)
Tomason (Nez Perce)
Tontileago (WyanPat)
Too-hool-hool-zote (Nez Perce)
Too-whaai-tan (Waatch Village)
Topinibe (Potowatami)
Tortohonga (Yankton Sioux)
Tortongawakw (Yankton Sioux)
Tosa Pokoo (Comanche)
Tosacowadi (Comanche)
Tosawi (Comanche)
Toshaway (Comanche)
Totkeshajou (Tallisee)
Touch-the-Clouds (Minneconjou)
True Eagle (Missouria)
Tsah-weh-sup (Neah Village)
Tsal-ab-oos (Neah Village)
Tsawatenok (Kwakiutl)
Tse-kauwtl (Makah)
Tuckabatchy (Natchez)
Tuekakas (Nez Perce)
Tuko-See-Mathla (Seminole)
Turkey Leg (Cheyenne)
Turning Hawk (Sioux)
Tushanaah (Coweta)

Tustennuggee Emathla (Creek)
Tuthinepee (Potawatomi)
Two Belly (Crow)
Two Guns White Calf (Blackfoot)
Two Hatchett (Kiowa)
Two Leggings (Northern Cheyenne)
Two Moons (Cheyenne)
Two Strike (Brule Sioux)
Ugly Game (Comanche)
Umapine (Cayuse-Umatilla)
Uinta (Umatilla)
Unanquoset (Penacook)
Uncas (Mohegan)
Unkompoin (Wampanoag)
Untongasahaw (Yankton Sioux)
Utina (Timucua)
Utsinmalikin (Nez Perce)
Victorio (Membres Apache)
Vincent (Coeur d' Alene)
Waapashaw (Sioux)
Waa-Top-E-Not (Chippewa)
Wabasha (Santee Sioux)
Wack-shie (Neah Village)
Waemboeshkaa (Chippewa)
Wahangnonawitt (Squomsquot)
Wahmeshemg (Potawatomi)
Wakaunhaka (Winnebago)
Wakawn (Winnebago)
Wakechai (Sauk)
Wak-kep-tup (Waatch Village)
Walamuitkin (Nez Perce)
Wallace Charging Shield (Sioux)
Wallachin (Cascade)
Wamditanka (Mdewakanton Sioux)
Wa-Na-Ta (Yankton Sioux)
Waneta (Iowa)

Wangewa (Iowa)
Wants To Be Chief (Sioux)
Wa-Pel-La (Musquake
Wapello (Sauk and Fox)
Wapowats (Cheyenne)
Warawasen (Setalcott)
War Bonnet (Cheyenne)
War Captain (Nambe)
War Cry (Kiowa)
War Eagle (Yankton Sioux)
War Eagle (Comanche)
War Shield (Crow)
Ward Coachman (Creek)
Washakie (Shoshone)
Wash-ca-ma-nee (Maha)
Wa-shing-ga-sabba (Maha)
Wasitasunke (Sioux)
Watchemonne (Iowa)
Waukesha (Ute)
WAY-WEL-EA-PY (Archaic)
Weasel Tail (Piegan)
We-du-gue-noh (Maha)
Weetamoo (Pocasset)
Wegaw (Potawatomi)
Wellamotkin (Nez Perce)
Weninock (Yakima)
Weshcubb (Chippewa)
Wetcunie (Otoe)
Wey-ti-mi-Chief (Yakima)
Weuche (Yankton Sioux)
White Bear (Kiowa)
White Bird (Nez Perce)
White Buffalo (Blackfeet)
White Bull (Minneconjou Sioux)
White Bull (Comanche
White Crane (Comanche)
White Eagle (Pawnee)

White Hair (Comanche)
White Hair (Kansa)
White Hawk (Minneconjou Sioux)
White Ghost (Kiowa)
White Horse (Kiowa)
White Horse (Yankton Sioux)
White Loon (Wea)
White Path (Cherokee)
White Shield (Comanche)
White Shield (Cheyenne)
White Swan (Yakama)
White Swan (Sioux)
White Thunder (Sioux)
White Wolf (Comanche)
Wickaninnish (Clayoquot)
Wicked Chief (Cheyenne)
Wild Cat (Seminole)
Wild Hog (Cheyenne)
Wild Horse (Comanche)
Wilford Taylor (Choctaw)
William (Neah Village)
William McIntosh (Creek)
William Weatherford (Creek)
Winamac IPotawatomi)
Winemakoos (Potawatomi)
Winriscah Dagenette (Wea)
Wishecomaque (Sac and Fox)
Witsitony (Comanche)
Wizikute (Sioux)
Wogam (Potawatomi)
Wogaw (Potawatomi)
Wohawa (Pawtucket)
Wolf Chief (Cheyenne)
Wolf Chief (Mandan)
Wolf King (Upper Creek)
Wolf Necklace (Palouse)
Wolf Road (Comanche)

Wolf Robe (Cheyenne)
Wolf tied with hair (Comanche)
Woman's Heart (Kiowa)
Wompatuck (Agawam)
Wonalancet (Penacook)
Wooden Leg (Cheyenne)
Woosamequin(Wampanoag)
Wopigwooit (Pequot)
Wovoka (Paiute)
Wyandanch (Montauk)
Xinesi (Tejas)
Yaha-Hajo (Seminole)
Yalukus (Molalla)
Yamparika-Povea (Comanche)
Yelleppit (Walla Walla)
Yellow Bear (Comanche)
Yellow Beaver (Wea)
Yellow Bird (Walla Walla)
Yellow Bull (Nez Perce)
Yellow Bull (Palouse)
Yellow Hair (Sioux)
Yellow Thunder (Ho-chunk)
Yellow Wolf (Nez Perce)
Ymipazo (Yakima)
Yonaguska (Cherokee)
Yoholo-Micco (Creek)
Yonipaw Camarake (Yakima)
Yooch-boott (Tsoo-yess)
Young Black Dog (Osage)
Young Chief (Cayuse)
Young Mahaskah (Iowa)
Young Tobacco (Piankashaw)
Young Whirlwind (Cheyenne)
Zele (Apache)

Dedicated to those millions of native people who nurtured this land for fourteen thousand years before the invasions by the Europeans.

Aamjiwnaang	Afognak
A'aninin	Afton
Aasao	Afton Mi'kmaq
Aassateaque	Agaiduka
Abchas	Agawam
Abegweit	Agdaagux
Abeka	Aginaa's
Abenaki	Agonnousioni
Abihka	Aguacaleyquen
Abitibi	Agua Caliente
Abitibiwinni	Ahantchuyuk
Absarokee	Ahopo
Absentee-Shawnee	Ahousaht
Acadian	Aht
Acadian Metis	Ahtahkakoop
Acahono	Ahtena
Acaxee	Ah-wah-nee-chee
Accohannock	Ais
Accominta	Aishihik
Acho Dene Koe	Aisious
Achumawi	Aivilivmiut
Acjachemen	Ak Chin
Acolapissa	Akainwa
Acoma	Akhiok
Aculhuas	Akiachak
Acuera	Akiak
Adai	Aklauik
Adams Lake	Akutan
Adawa	Akwaala
Adena	Akwesasne
Adiisha Dena	Alabama
Adirondack	Alabama-Coushatta
Adnondeck	Alabamus-Koasati

Alachua

Alakanuk

Alamo

Alaska

Alatna

Alberta

Alcatraz

Alderville

Aleknagik

Alexandria

Alexis

Alexis Creek

Algaacig

Algonquian

Alibamu

Alibamous

Alickas

Alkah

Allakaket

Allalie's

Alleghan

Alleghenny

Alliklik

Alnombak

Alonas

Alpowai

Alsea

Altamahaguez

Altmautluak

Alturas

Aluet

Aluque

Aluste

Alutiig

Altamuskeet

Amacano

Amacapiras

Amah

Amahuaca

Amalecite

Ambler

American Indian

Americone

Amonsoquath

Anadaca

Anadahcoe

Anadariko

Anaktuvuk Pass

Anasaguntacook

Andastonez

Andato honato

Anderson Lake

Androscoggin

Angoon

Anhawas

Aniak

Anisazi

Anishinaabe

Anishinabek

Aniyunwiya

Annapolis Valley

Annette Island

An-stohin/Unami

Antelope Valley

Anvik

Aondironon

Aosamiajijij

Apache

Apalachicola

Apalachee

Apineus

Applegate

Aposkwayak

Appomattox

Appomatuck
Apsaaloke
Apsaroke
Aquelon
Aquidneck
Aquinnah
Aranama
Arapahoe
Arapaja
Arapooish
Arawak
Archaic
Arctic
Arikara
Arkansas
Arogisti
Aroland
Aroostook
Arosaguntacock
Arsenipoit
Asa'carsarmiut
Asapo
Ashaninka
Ashcroft
Ashepoos
Ashiapkawi
Asilanapi
Aslatakapa
Asnon
Assateaque
Assinais
Assiniboine
Atahun
Atakapa
Atakara
Atamauluak
Atasi

Ataxam
Atfalati
Atgasuk
Athabasca Chipewyan
Athapaskan
Atikamekw
Atka
Atlatls
Atlin
Atna
Atsina
Atsugewi
Attikamekew
Audusta
Augustine
Auk
Aunie
Avavares
Avoyel
Awaitlala
Awani
Awasis
Awatixa
Awatobi
Awaxawi
Ayotore
Ays
Aztec
Baada
Babine
Bad Faces
Bad River
Baffin Land
Bahwetig
Baisimete
Bannok
Barona

Barona Capitan
Barren Lands
Barriere Lake
Barrio Pascua
Batchewana
Battle Mountain
Bay King
Bay Mills
Bayagoulas
Bear Lake
Bear River
Beardy's & Okemasis
Bears Paw
Bearskin Lake
Beaver
Beecher Bay
Bejessi
Belkofski
Bella Bella
Bella Coola
Benton Paiute
Beothuk
Berengia
Berens River
Berry Creek
Betatakin
Betsiamites
Bidai
Big Bend
Big Cove
Big Cypress Seminole
Big Grassy
Big Island
Big Lagoon
Big Meadows Lodge
Big Pine
Big River

Big Sandy
Big Valley
Bigstone
Bigstone Cree
Biidaajimo
Biinjitwaabik
Biktasateetuse
Bill Moons Slough
Biloxi
Birch Creek
Birch Narrows
Birdtail Sioux
Bishop Paiute-Shoshone
Bithani
Black Hill Sioux
Black Lake Denesuline
Black River
Black Sturgeon
Blackfeet
Blackfoot
Blewmouths
Blood
Blood Tribe
Bloodvein
Blue Lake
Blueberry River
Boca Jhaon
Bodego Miwok
Bois Forte
Boise
Boneparte
Boothroyd
Boston Bar
Bow
Brandywine
Brevig Mission
Bridge River

Bridgeport
Brighton Seminole
Brokenhead Objibway
Broman Lake
Brotherton
Brule'
Brule Sioux
Bruneau
Buckland
Buctouche
Buena Vista
Buffalo Point
Buffalo River
Bull Head
Bungi
Burns Lake
Burns Paiute
Burnt Church
Burt Lake
Bussenmeus
Cabazon
Cabinoios
Cachil De He
Cachil Dette
Cachipile
Cacores
Cadboro Bay
Caddo
Caddo Adias
Caghnawaga
Cahinnio
Cahita
Cahokia
Cahto
Cahuilla
Cajuenche
Cajun

Calamwas
Calapooya
Calaveras County
Caldwell
Callipipas
Caloosa
Calusa
Cambas
Camin Lake
Camkuota
Camp Verde
Campo
Camuilla
Canabas
Canarsee
Cane Break
Canim
Canoe Creek
Canoe Lake
Canoncito
Canoyeas
Cantwell
Caouachas
Capachequi
Caparaz
Cape
Cape Fear
Capiga
Capinan
Capitan Grande
Capote
Carcross/Tagish
Cariboo
Carlin
Carmel
Carmel Mission
Carrier Sekani

Carrizo
Carry The Kettle
Carson
Carson Colony Washoe
Cascade
Cascanque
Casco
Castachas
Castasue
Catabwa
Cathlacomatup
Cathlakaheckit
Cathlamet
Cathlanahquiah
Cathlapotle
Cathlathlalas
Catowbi
Cattaraugus
Caughnawaga
Cawittas
Cayoose Creek
Cayuga
Cayuse
Cedar City
Cedarville
Celillo
Chacci Oumas
Chachachouma
Chacchiuma
Chaco
Chaco Canyon
Chacato
Chadiere
Chaguaguas
Chahta
Chaiwa-Tewa
Chaloklowas

Chakankni
Chalkyitsik
Champagne
Chanchon's
Chanega
Chantorabin
Chapel Island
Chapen
Chapleau
Chappequiddick
Charah
Charew
Charley Creek
Chastacosta
Chatot
Chats
Chaushila
Chavi
Chawasha
Chayimanak
Chefornak
Chehalis
Chehaw
Chekalis
Chelan
Chelemela
Chemahawin
Chemainus
Chemakum
Chemapho
Chemehuevi
Chenakisses
Chenkus
Chepenala
Cher-Ae Heights
Cherokee
Cherow

Chesapeake
Cheslatta
Cheslatta Carrier
Chespiooc
Chesterfield
Chetco
Chevak
Cheveux on Port leue'
Cheveux relevez
Chewella
Cheyenne
Cheyenne River Sioux
Chiaha
Chi
Chichen
Chichimeco
Chickahominy
Chickaloon
Chickamauga
Chickasaw
Chickataubut
Chicken Ranch
Chico
Chicora-Siouan
Chictaghick
Chideh
Chignik
Chignik Lagoon
Chignik Lake
Chihokokis
Chilkat
Chilkoot
Chilliwack
Chilluckkittequaw
Chilocotin
Chilula
Chilucan

Chimakuan
Chimariko
Chimsean
Chine
Chinik
Chininoas
Chiniquay
Chinook
Chinookan
Chipewyan
Chippewa
Chiricahua
Chisasibi
Chistochina
Chitimacha
Chitina
Chilula
Chiwere
Chochiti
Chochnewwasroonaw
Choctaw
Choinumni
Chokonen
Chougaskabee
Choula
Choumaus
Choushatta
Chowan
Chowanoc
Chowwichan
Choya'ha
Christanna
Christian Pembina
Christiantown
Chuathbaluk
Chucalissa
Chukchansi

Chuloonawick
Chumash
Cibecue Apache
Ciboney
Cilan
Cicora
Circle
Citizen
Citizen Potawatomi
Clackamas
Clallam
Clark's Point
Clatskanie
Clatsop
Clayoquot
Clear Lake
Clearwater River Dene
Clifton-Choctaw
Cloverdale
Clovis
Clowwewalla
Coahuilteco
Coaque
Coast
Coast Miwok
Coastal Band
Coastanoan
Cocatoonemaug
Cochimi
Cochiti Pueblo
Cocopah
Cocopu
Cofan
Cofubufu
Coharie
Coka
Cold Lake

Cold Springs
Colorado River
Columbia
Columbia Lake
Colusa
Colville
Comanche
Combahee
Comox
Conchakus
Concow
Conestoga
Congaree Eno
Connecedgas
Connewaugeroonas
Conohasset
Conoy
Conoyucksuchroona
Constance Lake
Cook's Ferry
Coos
Coosa River Creek
Coosan
Copalis
Copper
Coquille
Coranine
Corchaug
Coree
Cortina
Cosmit
Costa
Costano
Costonoan
Cote
Coticyini
Couchiching

Couer d'Alene
Council
Courte Oreilles
Coushaes
Coushatta
Covolo
Cow Creek
Cowasuck
Coweset
Cowessess
Cowetaw
Cowichan
Cowlitz
Coyote
Coyotero Apache
Craig
Cree
Creek
Crees of Quebec
Croatan
Crooked Creek
Cross Lake
Cross Lake Cree
Croton
Crow
Crow Creek Sioux
Culpala
Cultoa
Cumberland Creek
Cumberland House
Cumumbah
Cupeno
Curyung
Cusabo
Cusetah
Cussabee
Cussetaw

Cussobo
Cut Head
Cuttacochi
Cuyapaipe
Da'naxda'xw Awaelatla
Dakota
Dakota Lake
Dakota Plains
Dakota Sioux
Dakota Tipi
Dakubetede
Dania
Darrington
Dassa Monpeake
Dauphin River
Day Star
Deadose
Dease River
Death Valley
Deeking
Deer Creek
Deer Lake
Dehcho
Delaware
Delaware-Muncee
Dena'ina
Denali
Dene
Dene Tha'
Deneh
Deschute
Devils Lake Sioux
Dewagamas
Dibaudjimoh
Diegueno
Digger
Dine'

Dineh
Diomede
Dionoudadie
Ditidaht
Dogue
Dog Creek
Dog River
Dogenga
Dogrib
Dogwood
Donnacona
Pat Lake
Douglas
Doustioni
Dresslerville
Dresslerville Washoe
Driftpile River
Dry Creek
Dubois
Duck Valley
Duckwater
Dudley
Dumanish
Duncan
Dunlap
Dwamishe Shingle
Springs
Eabametoong
Eagle
Eagle Bear
Eagle Lake
Eagle Village-Kipawa
Eano
East Cree
East Mesa
Eastern Cherokee
Eastern Shawnee

Eastman
Ebahamo
Ebb and Flow
Echota
Edisto
Eek
Eeyou
Eel Ground
Eel River
Eel River Bar
Egegig
Ehatteshaht
Eklutna
Ekok
Ekuk
Ekwok
Elasie
Elem
Elim
Elk
Elko
Elwha
Ely
Ely Shoshone
Embera
Emmonak
English River
Eno
Enoch Cree
Enterprise
Entiat
Epesengles
Epicerinis
Erie
Erie See
Ermineskin
Escaamba

Escamacu
Eskasoni
Esketemic
Eskimo
Esopus
Espogache
Esquimalt
Esselen
Essipit
Estotoe
Etchemin
Etiwa
Etocale
Etowah
Euchee
Eufaula
Eureka
Evansville
Eves
Exangue
Eyak
Eyeish
Faircloth
Fairford
Fall River
Fallon
Fallon Paiute-Shoshone
False Pass
Faroan
Federated Coast Miwok
Fernandeno
Fisher River
Fishing Lake
Flandreau Santee Sioux
Flathead
Florence
Florida Creek

Flying Dust
Flying Post
Folsom
Fond du Lac
Fond du Lac Denesuline
Foothills Yokuts
Forest County
Potawatomi
Fort Albany
Fort Alexander
Fort Ancient
Fort Belknap
Fort Bidwell
Fort Folly
Fort Hall
Fort Independence
Fort McDermitt
Fort McKay
Fort McMurray
Fort Mohave
Fort Nelson
Fort Peck Sioux
Fort Severn
Fort Sill
Fort Ware
Fort Williams
Fort Yukon
Four Hole
Four Winds
Fox
Fox Lake
Fraser Canyon
Fremont
Fresh Water
Frog Lake
Fuel
Fuloplata

Fushootseed
Gabrielino
Gaigwu
Gakona
Galena
Galice
Galisteo
Gambell
Gambler
Ganienkeh
Garden Hill
Gaspe
Gaspen River
Gaspesiens
Gayhead
Georgetown
Georgia
Georgia Cherokee
Gesgapegiag
Gila Bend Papago
Gila River Pima-
Maricopa
Ginoogaming
Gitanmaax
Gitanyow
Git-ga'at
Gitlakdamik
Gitsegukla
Gitwangat
Gitwinksihlkw
Gitxsan
Glen Vowell
God's Lake
God's River
Golden Hill
Good News Bay
Gordon

Goshute
Grand Portage
Grand Rapids
Grand River
Grand Ronde
Grand Traverse
Grand Village
Grassey Narrows
Grave Creek
Grayling
Great Serpent
Green River Snake
Greenville
Grigra
Grindstone
Grindstone Creek
Gros
Gros Ventre
Grouard
Guacata
Guadalquini
Guajiro
Guale
Guasco
Guidiville
Gulkana
Gull Bay
Gun Lake Village
Gwa'Sala-
'Nakwaxda'xw
Gwich'in
Hackensack
Ha'degaenage
Hadley
Hagwilget
Haida
Haihais

Hainai	Heiltsuk
Haish	Henya
Haisla	Herring Pond
Halalt	Hesquiat
Halchidhoma	Hidatsa
Halfway River	High Bar
Haliwa-Saponi	Hihantick
Halkomelem	Hilabia
Halqʼmeylem	Hileni
Halyikwamai	Hill Patwin
Hamilton	Hill Wintun
Han	Hinonoeino
Hanis	Hitchiti
Hannahville	Hocaesle
Hanneton	Hocak
Hano	Ho-Chunk
Hanuanos	Hocomawananch
Hare	Hoh
Hare Mountain	Hohokam
Hasinai	Hohuana
Hasinais Caddo	Hois
Haso	Hokan
Hassanamisko	Holikachuk
Hassenamesitts	Hollow Water
Hatchet Lake	Holy Cross
Denesuline	Homalco
Hathawekela	Honeches
Hattadare	Honellaque
Hattaras	Honniasont
Haudenosee	Hoomus
Havasupai	Hoonah
Hawoyazask	Honniasonts
Hayfork	Hoopa
Haynoke	Hoopa Valley
Haytian	Hooper Bay
Healy Lake	Hootznahoo
Heart Lake	Hopewell

Hopi

Hopland

Hornepayne

Horse Lake

Hostaqua

Horton

Hot Creek

Hothliwahali

Houeches

Houlton

Houlton Maliseet

Houma

Housetonic

Hownonquet

Hualapai

Huanchane

Huara

Huchnon

Hughes

Huichol

Hul'qumi'num

Humptulips

Hunkpapa

Hunkpatila

Hupa

Hupascath

Huron

Huron-Wendat

Huslia

Hutali

Huttlhunssen

Huu-Ay-Aht

Hwalya

Hydaburg

Ibihica

Icafui

Igiugig

Igiulivmiut

Igurmiut

Iichisi

I'isaw

Ima

Iliamna

Illiniwek

Illinois

Inaha-Cosmit

Inaja

Inde

Indian Birch

Indian Brook

Indian Canyon

Indian Island

Indian Knoll

Indian Township

Ingalik

Innocence

Innu

Innu-Aionun

In-shuck-ch/n'quatqua

Intielikum

Inuktitut

Inuit

Inuk

Inuna-ina

Inupaiq

Inutitut

Ione

Ioway

Iquluit

Iroquet

Iroquois

Isabella

Iskut

Iskutewizaagegan

Island	*Kahkewistahaw*
Island Lake	*Kahnawake*
Islandlittle	*Kahon:wes's*
Isleta	*Kahtonik*
Iswa	*Kaibab*
Itaba	*Kainai*
Itawan	*Kake*
Itazipco	*Kaktovik*
Itivimiut	*Kakumlutch*
Ituan	*Kalapauga*
Itza	*Kalapooian*
Ivanoff Bay	*Kalapuya*
Iviatim	*Kalgani*
Iwiktie	*Kalispel*
Jacal	*Kalnawake*
Jackhead	*Kalskag*
Jackson Rancheria	*Kaltag*
James Smith	*Kaluschian*
Jamestown	*Kamia*
Jamestown S'Klallam	*Kamloops*
Jamul	*Kampa*
Jatibonicu	*Kanaka*
Jeaga	*Kanalak*
Jemez Pueblo	*Kanankawa*
Jena	*Kanatak*
Jhee-challs	*Kanesatake*
Jicarilla	*Kaniagmiut*
John Day	*Kanien'kehaka*
Joseph Bighead	*Kansa*
Juamo	*Kaoutyas*
Juaneno	*Kapawe'no*
Jupe	*Kaposia Sioux*
K'omok	*Kappas*
Kadohadacho	*Karakwaw*
Kagita-Mikam	*Karankawa*
Kaguyak	*Kareses*
Kah-Bay-Kah-Nong	*Karluk*

Karok
Kasaan
Kasabonika Lake
Kashaya Pomo
Kashia
Kasigluk
Kasihta
Kaska
Kaska Dena
Kaskaskia
Kaskaya
Kaskinampo
Katlammet
Kato
Katzie
Kavelchadom
Kaviagmiut
Kaw
Kawacatoose
Kawaiisu
Kawchottine
Kaweah
Kawe'sqar
Kayapo
Kaytenta
Kealeychi
Keechi
Keeseekooenin
Keeseekoose
Kee-too-wah
Keewatin
Keewatinowi
Kee-Way-Win
Kehabous
Kehewin
Kenaitze
Kenisteno

Kenowun
Keres
Keresan
Kern Valley
Keroa
Ketchikan
Kettle Point
Keweenaw Bay
Key
Key Band
Keyauwee
Khotana
Khot-La-Cha
Kiabab
Kialegee
Kiana
Kiawa
Kichai
Kickapoo
Kigiktamiut
Kikiallus
Kilatak
Kilispel
Killisnoo
Kimsquit
Kina'matnewey
Kinbasket
Kincolith
King Island
Kingfisher Lake
Kingsclear
Kinistin
Kinuguit
Kinuhmiut
Kiowa
Kipnuk
Kiscakous

Kispoix
Kispoko
Kitamat
Kitanemuk
Kitasoo
Kitchie
Kitcisakik
Kite
Kitigan Zibi
Anishinabeg
Kititas
Kitkehahki
Kitlope
Kitsagh
Kitsai
Kitselas
Kitsumkalum
Kivalina
Kiwigapawa
Kiwistinok
Klahoose
Klallam
Klamath
Klanoh
Klasset
Klatklam
Klatsap
Klatskanie
Klatstonis
Klawock
Klickitat
Klodesseaottine
Kluskus
Kluti Kaah
Knik
Koasati
Koasota

Kobuk
Kobukmiut
Kodiak
Kogohue
Kolash
Kolchan
Kolomi
Kolomoki
Kolushan
K'omoks
Kongiganak
Konkonelp
Konkow
Konomihu
Kootenai
Kopagmiut
Koprino
Koroa
Koshare
Koskimo
Koso
Kotlik
Kot'sai
Kotsoteka
Kotzebue
Kouchiching
Koutani
Koutenay
Kowalitsk
Koyuk
Koyukon
Koyukuk
Ktunaxa
Ktunaxa/Kinbasket
Kuaua
Kugmiut
Kuitsh

Kuiu

Kullullucton

Kumeyaay

Kumiai

Kuskokwim

Kusso-Natchez

Kutchin

Kutenai

Kwadahi

Kwagiutl

Kwahada

Kwaiailk

Kwak'wala

Kwalhioqua

Kuitsh

Kwandahi

Kwantlen

Kwatna

Kwa-Wa-Aineuk

Kwayhquitlum

Kwethluk

Kwiakah

Kwicksutaneuk-Ahhwaw-
Ah-Mish

Kwigillingok

Kwinhagak

Kyuquot

L'Ecureuil

La Conner

La Jolla

La Posta

La Romane

Lac Courte Oreilles

Lac Des Milles

Lac du Flambeau

Lac La Croix

Lac La Ronge

Lac View Desert

Lac-Saint-Jean

Lac-Simon

Lacumeros

Laguna

Laich-kwil-tach

Lakahahmen

Lakalzap

Lake Babine

Lake Helen

Lake Manitoba

Lake Miwok

Lake Nespelem

Lake Nipigon Ojibway

Lake St. Martin

Lake Superior

Lake Traverse Sioux

Lakes

Lakmut

Lakota

Lakota Wowapi

Lamale

Langley

Lansdowne House

L'Anse

Laplako

Lapwai

Larsen Bay

Las Vegas

Lassik

Latgawa

Laurentian

Lax-Kw'Alaams

Laytonville

Leech Lake

Lemhi

Lenape

Lenechas
Lenni-Lenape
Lennox Island
Lesnoi
Levelok
Lheidli
Lheidli Tenneh
Lheit-lit'en
Liano
Liard
Likely
Lillooet
Lime
Lipan
Listigui
Listuguj
Little Black Bear
Little Black River
Little Grand Rapids
Little Pine
Little Red River Cree
Little River
Little Saskatchewan
Little Shell
Little Shuswap
Little Traverse Bay
Lkumbsen
Llaneros
Loafer/Sioux
Lochapoka
Lohim
*Lone Pine Paiute-
Shoshone*
Long Island
Long Lake
Long Plain
Long Point

Lookout
Loon River Cree
Los Coyotes
Lost Ranier
Louis Bull Tribe
Luiseno
Louisiana
Loup
Lovelock
Lower Brule Sioux
Lower Elwha
Lower Kalskag
Lower Kootenay
Lower Nicola
Lower Similkameen
Lower Sioux
Lower Umpqua
Lower Yanklonai
Loyal Shawnee
Lubicon Lake
Luckiamute
Lucky Man
Luiseno
Lumbee
Lummi Nation
Lumni
Lushootseed
Lutainian
Lyackson
Lynch's
Lytton
M'chigeeng
Macah
Macapiras
Machapunga
Machia Lower Creek
Mackinac

Magaehnak

Maha

Mahapony

Mahekanande

Mahican

Maidu

Maihais

Makah

Maklak

Makoutepoeis

Makwasahgaiehcan

Malataute

Malecite

Malecites of Viger

Maliseet

Malmiut

Mamaceqtaw

Mamaleleqala-qweqwa-sot-enox

Manahoac

Manakin

Manawan

Manchester

Mandan

Mangakekis

Mangas Apache

Manhattan

Manley Hot Springs

Manokotak

Manso

Manzanita

Marameg

Mariame

Maricopa

Marsapeague

Marshall

Marten Falls

Martha's Vinyard

Marti Gras

Mary's Igloo

Mascouten

Mashantucket-Pequot

Mashpee

Maskegon

Maskote Pwat

Maskutick

Maskwachee

Massachuset

Massapequa

Masset Haida

Massomuck

Match-e-be-nash-shewish

Mathias Colomb

Matinecock

Mattabesic

Mattachee

Mattapoist

Mattaponi

Mattole

Maumee

Mapuche

Mawihl Nakoatok

Mawiomi

Maya

Mazipskiwik

McDowell Lake

McGrath

McLeod Lake

Mdewakanton Sioux

Mdewakantonwon

Meadow Lake

Mechoopda

Medaywakanoan

Meherrin

Meit

Mekoryuk
Melochundum
Melunglons
Membertou
Membrino Apache
Menasha
Mendocino
Menominee
Mentasta
Mentous
Merherrin
Merrick
Mesa Grande
Mescalero Apache
Meskwaki
Meso-Indians
Mesquacki
Metepenagiag
Methow
Metis
Metlakahtla
Metoac
Me-wuk
Michigamea
Mi'Kmag
Mi'Kmaw
Miami
Miao
Miawpukek
Mibinamik
Mical
Miccosucci
Michif
Michigamea
Michipicoten
Micmac
Middletown

Mikamawey
Mikisew
Mi'Kmag
Mi'Kmaw
Mikmawisimk
Millbrook
Mille Lacs
Miluk
Mimbre
Minatarre
Mingan
Mingo
Miniconjou Sioux
Minisink
Minnesota Chippewa
Minquas
Minto
Misawum
Misga
Mishikwutmetunne
Mission
Mississauga
Mississinewa
Mississippi
Missosukee
Missouri
Mistapnis
Mistassill
Mistassini
Mistawasis
Mitchell Bay
Mitchigamuas
Mitgan
Mitla
Miwok
Mixe
Moallalla

Moapa Nevada
Mobile
Mocama
Mocogo
Modoc
Mogollon
Mojave
Mohawk
Mohegan
Mohican
Moingwena
Molala
Monacan
Monache
Moneton
Mongontatchas
Monie
Mono
Monshackotoog
Montagnais
Montagne
Montana
Montauk
Montaukett
Montgomery Creek
Montreal Lake Cree
Moor
Mooretown
Moosomin
Moratoc
Moravian
Moricetown
Morongo
Mosa
Mosakahiken
Moses
Mosookee

Mosopelea
Mosquito Grizzly Bear
Mouche
Mount Currie
Mountain
Mousonis
Mowa
Mowachaht
Muckleshoot
Mugulasha
Muh-he-ka-ne-ok
Muin Sipu Mi'kmag
Muklasa
Mukwema
Multnomah
Muache Utes
Munatagmiut
Munsee
Muscogee
Muscowpetung
Musgamagw
Mushagamiut
Muskeg Lake
Muskoday
Muskogean
Muskokee
Muskokeem
Muskowekwan
Muskwaki
Musqueam
Mussissakie
Mutsun
Muwekma
Mystic
N'laka'Pamux
Naausi
Nabari

Nabesna
Nacoochee
Nadako
Nadawaska Maliseet
Nadene
Nadoka
Nadouesteaus
Nahapassunkeck
Nahew
Nahua
Nahuatl
Nahyssan
Naicatchewenin
Naichoas
Nakhuston
Nakne
Nakoaktok
Nakota
Naltunnetunne
Nambe
Namgis
Nanasoho
Nanimoos
Nansemond
Nanticoke
Nanwalek
Napaimute
Napaskiak
Napgitache
Napochi
Narragansett
Nase-Gitksen
Nasharo
Naskapi
Naskapi of Quebec
Nassonis
Natchitoches

Natakmiut
Natashquan
Natchez
Natick
Nation Nueht
Nauser
Nauset
Navajo
Nawihl
Nazko
Neah Village
Nebedache
Neches
N'de
Nedhi
Neecoweegee
Nee-Tahi-Buhn
Neetlum
Nehkereages
Neketemeuk
Nekutameux
Nelson House
Nelson Lagoon
Nelson River
Nemaska
Nenana
Neo-Indians
Neosho
Nepissing
Nepnet
Nesaquake
Neskonlith
Nespelem
Netselia
Netsilik
Nettotalis
Neuse

Neusiok

Neutral

New Koliganek

New Stuyahok

New Westminster

Newark

Newhalen

Newtok

Nez Perce

Niagra

Niantic

Nicichousemenecaning

Nicola

Nicoleno

Nicomen

Nightmute

Niji Mahkwa

Nikolai

Nikolski

NI-MI-WIN

Ninilchik

Nio

Nipmuck

Nipewais

Nisenan

Nisga'a

Nishinan

Nishnabek

Niska

Nisqually

Nitinat

Noatak

No Bows

Noheum

Nohewee

Nokoni

Nomadic

Nome

Nomelaki

Nomtipom

Nondalton

Nongati

Nonowuss

Noohitch

Nooksack

Noorvik

Nooshalhlaht

Nootka

Noo-Wha-Ha

Noquet

Nor-el-muk

Norridgewalk

North Caribou Lake

North Spirit Lake

North Thompson

North West Angle

Northeast

Northern Cherokee

Northern Cheyenne

Northern Maidu

Northern Paiute

Northern Quebec

Northern Valley Yokuts

Northfork

Northlands Dene

Northway

Northwest Coast

Northwest Shoshone

Northwestern

Norway House

Norwottock

Notchee

Nottawaseppi

Nottoway

Nowitna
Ntlakyapamuk
Nuchatlaht
Nuchawanack
Nuiqsut
Nulato
Numa
Numamiut
Nunapitchuk
Nunivagmiut
Nunivak
Nunivakhooper
Nuu-chah-nulth
Nuxalk
Nuxalko Two Kettles
Nuyaka
O'odham
Oagan Toyagungin
Oahatika
Oakfuskee
Oaksoy
Oak Lake
Oaktashippas
Obedjiwan
Objibway
Ocale
Occaneechi
Ocean Man
Ochapowace
Ochese Creek
Ochiapofa
O-Chi-Chak-ko-Sipi
O'Chiese
Ochiichagwebabigo
Ocita
Ockhoys
Ocoma

Oconee
Octotate
Ocute
Odanak
Odawa
Odsinachie
Offogoulas
Ofo
Oglala Sioux
Ogulmiut
Ohio
Ohlone
Ohogamiut
Oil Springs
Ojibway of Onegaming
Ojibway of Pic River
Okelousa
Okanese
Okanogan
Okchai
Okfuskee
Okimakanak
Okinawan
Oklewaha
Okmulgee
Okwanuchu
Okwejagehke
Old Harbor
Old Masset Village
Omaha
Omaus
Onatheaqua
One Arrow
Oneida Nation of New York
Oneida Nation of Wisconsin
Ongmiaahranonon
Ongwanonsionni

Onieda

Onion Lake

Onodo

Onondaga

Ontonagon

Onyape

Oohenumpa

Oomaka Tokatakiya

Ooseooche

Oowekeeno

Opaskwayak Cree

Opatas

Opelousa

Opetchesaht

Oque Loussas

Oraibi

Ordovice

Oregon Jack Creek

Oriskany

Orista

Oromocto

Orutsararmiut

Osage

Oscarville

Osetto

Oshkaabewis

Osochi

Osoyoos

Ospogue

Osprey

Otapala

Otax

Otchagras

Otchentechakowin

Otesiskiwin

Otheuse

Oto

Otoe

Otoe-Missouri

Otomi

Ottowa

Oua

Ouabaches

Oufe Agoulas

Ouiagie

Ouje'Bougoumou

Oumamiouck

Oumas

Ounontcharonnous

Ouray

Ousita

Outachepas

Outaounones

Ouyslanous

Ouzinkie

Owanux

Oweekeno

Owenagungas

Owendats

Owens Valley

Oxford House

Oyale Lutapi

Oymut

Ozembogus

Ozette

Ozotheoa

Pabaksa

Pabineau

Pacaha

Pacheedaht

Pahrump

Pahvant

Paich-kwil-tach

Paimiut

Paiute

Pakana

Pakanii

Pakanoket

Pakit

Pakua Shipi

Pala

Pala Mission

Palaquessous

Paleanas

Palenque

Paleo-Indian

Palong

Palouse

Pamlico

Pampticough

Pamunkey

Pana

Panaloga

Panamaha

Panamint

Panana

Panara

Pani

Panimaha

Panis

Panivacha

Panka

Papago

Papenachois

Paquate

Parkeeaum

Parianuc

Pasca Oocolos

Pascsgoulas

Pascua Yaqui

Paskempa

Paskenta

Pasqua

Pass Cahuilla

Passamaquoddy

Patiri

Patofa

Patowomeck

Patuxet

Patwin

Paucatuck

Paugusett

Pauingassi

Pauloff Harbor

Pauma

Pauquachin

Pavioso

Pawhatan

Pawhuska

Pawnee

Pawokti

Pawtucket

Pays Flat

Payson

Peaurian

Peadea

Peauguicheas

Pechanga

Pecos

Pedro Bay

Peepeekisis

Peguis

Pehnahterkuh

Peigan

Pelican Lake

Pellault

Pemunkey

Penacook

Penatoka
Pend d'Orielles
Penelakut
Pennacook
Penobscott
Penotekas
Pensacola
Penticton
Penutian
Peoria
Peovis
Pepikokia
Pequawket
Pequot
Pera
Perfido Bay
Perryville
Person County
Peskadaneeoulkanti
Peter Ballantyne
Petersburg
Peticotras
Petun
Pheasant Rump Nakota
Piachi
Pianguichias
Piankashaw
Piapot
Pia Yuman
Pic Mobert
Pic River
Picayune
Picts
Pictou Landing
Picuris
PideeKadapau
Piegan

Piekann
Pigwacket
Pikanii
Pilot Point
Pilot Station
Pilthlako
Pima
Pimaquid
Pima-Maricopa
Piman
Pinal Apache
Pinal Coyotera Apache
Pine Creek
Pine Ridge Sioux
Pinkeshaw
Pinoleville
Pipestone Sioux
Piqua Sept
Piro
Piscataway
Piscataway-Conoy
Pit River
Pitaa
Pitahavret
Pitano
Pitka's Point
Piware
Pjobwe
Plano
Plat cotez de chiens
Plateau
Platinum
Pleasant Point
Plumas County
Poarch Creek
Pocasset
Pocomoke

Pocomtic	*Principal Creek*
Pocumtuck	*Prophet River*
Pohoc	*Pshwanwapan*
Pohogue	*Pswanwapam*
Pohoy	*Pte Oyate*
Point Barrow	*Puan*
Point Hope	*Pueblo*
Point Lay	*Pueblo Bonito*
Pojoaque	*Puget Sound*
Pokagon	*Punhuni*
Pokanokut	*Punka*
Polar	*Puntlach*
Pomo	*Puturiba*
Ponca	*Puyallup*
Ponocock	*Pyramid Lake*
Poosepatuck	*Qagam Toyagungin*
Poplar Creek	*Qagyuhl*
Poplar Hill	*Qahatika*
Poplar River	*Qawalangin*
Port Gamble	*Quabache*
Port Graham	*Quachita*
Port Heiden	*Quadichhe*
Port Lions	*Quahatika*
Port Madison	*Qualicum*
Portage Point	*Quanchas*
Potano	*Quanostino*
Potawatomi	*Quapaw*
Potomac	*Quara*
Potter Valley	*Quartz Valley*
Poundmaker	*Quassarte*
Poverty Point	*Quatoghies*
Povi-Tamu	*Quatsino*
Powhatan	*Quechan*
Prairie	*Queet*
Prairie Island Sioux	*Quiattanon*
Priest Rapids	*Quiattanous*
Pribiloff Island	*Quigualtam*

Quilcene
Quileute
Quimaieit
Quinaquous
Quinarbaug
Quinault
Quinipissa
Quinnepas
Quiripi
Quiripi-unquachog
Quohhada
Quonantino
Quon-di-ats
Quzinkie
Qwidicca-atx
Rainy River
Ramah
Ramapough
Ramona
Rampart
Rankokus
Rappahannock
Raritans
Red
Redding
Red Bank
Red Bluff
Red Clay
Red Cliff
Red Devil
Red Earth
Red Lake
Red Pheasant
Red Sticks
Red Sucker Lake
Redwood
Redwood Valley

Rees
Renais
Reno-Sparks
Resighini
Restigouche
Rincon
River
Roanoke
Roaring Creek
Robinson
Rockaway
Rock River
Rocky Bay
Rocky Boys
Rogue
Roherville
Rolling River
Rondaxe
Ronkokus
Roseau River
Rosebud Sioux
Round Valley
Ruby
Ruby Valley
Rumsey
S'Klallam
S'rntotchone
Saanich
Saboda
Sac
Sachdagughroonaw
Sacigo Lake
Saco
Saddle Lake
Sadlermiut
Sae
Saginaw

Sagkeeng
Sahap
Sahaptin
Sahohes
Saint George
Saint Johns
Saint Mary's
Saint Michael
Saint Paul
Sakonnet
Sakimay
Salamanco
Salamatoff
Salano
Salawik
Salchishe
Salina
Salinan
Salish
Salishan
Sallumiut
Salona
Salt River Pima-
Maricapo
Salteaux
Saluda
Samahguam
Samish
Sammanish
Samson
San Carlos Apache
San Felipe
San Ildefonso
San Juan
San Manual
San Nicoleno
San Pasqual

San Poil
San Xavier
Sand Point
Sandia
Sandy Bay
Sandy Lacs
Sandy Lake
Sans Arc Sioux
Santa Ana
Santa Clara
Santa Rosa
Santa Ynez
Santa Ysabel
Santee Sioux
Santiam
Santo Domingo
Sanutch
Sanya
Sapala
Saponi
Sapotaweyak Cree
Sara
Sarcee
Sarsi
Saschutkenne
Satsop
Satuache
Satudene
Saturiwa
Saugeen
Sauk-Suiattle
Sault
Sault Ste. Marie
Saulteaux
Saura
Savannah
Savanois

Savoonga
Sawokli
Sawridge
Saxman
Sayisa Dene
Scammon Bay
Scaticook
Schaghticoke
Schahook
Schefferville
Scotts Valley
Secatogue
Secotan
Secwepemc-Shuswap
Sewee
Seine River
Seip
Sekanai
Selawik
Selchelt
Seldovia
Semiahmoo
Seminole
Seneca
Senijaxtee
Sequim
Seri
Serrano
Setalcott
Setauket
Seton Lake
Sewee
Shackan
Shageluk
Shagticoke
Shagtoolik
Shakopee Sioux

Shakori
Shamattawa
Shamokan
Shasta
Shawanoe
Shawonese
Shawendadie
Shawnee
Sheep Ranch
Sheldon's Point
Sherry-dika
Sherwood Valley
Shi'sha'lth
Shibogama
Shield
Shingle Springs
Shinnecock
Shipaulovi
Shi'sha'lth
Shishmaref
Shoal Lake
Shoal Lake Cree
Shoalwater Bay
Shoccaree
Shoshone
Shubenacadie
Shungnak
Shuswap
Shutaree
Sia
Siakaieth
Sicangu
Sigesh
SiHa SaPa
Siksika
Sikyakti
Siletz

Simcoe	*Slave*
Sinkaieth	*Sleetmute*
Sinkakaius	*Sliammon*
Sinkiuse	*Smallon*
Sinkquaius	*Small Robes*
Sinkyone	*Smith River*
Sinodouwas	*Smohallah*
Sioux	*Snagua*
Sioux Valley	*Snake*
Sishiatl	*Snoqualmoo*
Siska	*Snowqualmu*
Siskiyou	*Snuneymuxw*
Sisseton Sioux	*Soacatino*
Sisseton-Wahpeton	*Soboda*
Sissipahaw	*Socorro*
Sitka	*Soda Creek*
Siuslaw	*Sokaogan*
Skagit	*Soke*
Skagway	*Sokoki*
Skal vian	*So-kulk*
Skam Swatch	*Solomon*
Skawahlook	*Songhee*
Skeedee	*Songish*
Skeetchestn	*Sonoma*
Skidegate	*Sooke*
Skidi	*Soque*
Skilloot	*Sorcier*
Skin	*Sotequa*
Skitwash	*Sothoues*
Skockuck	*Souchitiomi*
Skokomish	*Souriquois*
Skookumchuk	*South Bentick*
Skowkale	*South Fork*
Skull Valley	*Southeastern Cherokee*
Skuppah	*Southern Paiute*
Skway	*Southern Ute*
Skykomish	*Southern Valley Yokuts*

Southhampton
Sovzhnaknek
Spallumcheen
Specum
Spirit Lake Sioux
Split Lake
Spokan
Spplam
Spuzzum
Squ'ay
Squam
Squamish
Squaxin
Squaxin Island
Squomsquot
St Croix
Stehtsasamish
St Francis/Skokoki
St Francois
St George
St Helena
St Johns
St Lawrence Island
St Michael
St Paul
St Regis
St Theresa Point
Staitan
Stalo
Standing Buffalo
Dakota
Standing Rock Sioux
Stanjikoming
Star
Star Blanket
Stebbins
Steilacoom

Stevens
Stewart Washoe
Stewarts Point
Stikeen
Stillaquamish
Sto:Lo
Stockbridge
Stockridge-Munsee
Stone
Stoney
Stoney Point
Stono
Stony River
Straits
Sturgeon Lake
Sucker Creek
Sugar Bowl
Sugeree
Suiattle
Suislawan
Sukininmiut
Sulpher Bank
Sumas
Summcamy's
Summerville
Summit Lake
Sunchild
Supai
Suquache
Suquamish
Susanville
Susquehanna
Susquehannock
Surruque
Sutaio
Sutslmc
Swallah

Swampy Creek
Swan Lake
Sweet Mouth
Sweetgrass
Swift Creek
Swinomish
Sycuan
Table Bluff
Table Mountain
Tabeguache
Tacatacura
Tache
Tacibaga
Tacusas
Taensa
Tafacanca
Tagish
Tahagmiut
Tahnuemuh
Tahitan
Tahtan
Tahupa
Taidnapam
Taino
Takamiut
Takelma
Takotna
Taku river
Talaje
Talakamish
Talapenches
Talapo
Talax
Taliyumc
Tall
Tallcree
Tallissee

Talmuchasi
Taltushluntude
Tamathli
Tamescameng
Tamoroa
Tanacross
Tanaina
Tanana
Tanawas
Taneks haya
Tangeboas
Tanoan
Taos
Tapala
Taposa
Tapoussas
Tarahas
Tarahunara
Tarascan
Taskarorahaka
Taskigi
Taskikis
Tasse
Tatasi
Tataviam
Tatitlek
Tawakomie
Tawakoni
Tawasa
Tawehash
Tazlina
Tchannus
Tchinook
Tchulhutt
Tchulwhyook
Tchunn
Tekesta

Tocopa
Te'mexw
Tee-Hit-Ton
Teet
Tegesta
Tehah Nahma
Tehatchapi
Tehoanoughroonaw
Tehome
Teitton
Tejas
Tekesta
Tekinago
Telida
Teller
Temagami
Te'mexw
Te-moak
Temuno
Tenawa Widyunuu
Tenino
Tennuth Ketchin
Tentoucha
Teoux
Tepa
Tepehuan
Tesgi Canyon
Teskesta-Tiamo
Teslin
Tesuque
Tete de Brule'
Tetlin
Teton
Teton Lakota
Tewa
Texas
Teyosta

The Wet'suwet'en
Thins
Thlingchadinne
Thlopthlocco
Thomez
Thompson
Three Affliated
Thunderchild
Tia
Tiakluit
Tiaoux
Tichenos
Tidewater
Tidu
Tierra del Sol
Tigua
Tillamook
Timba-Sha
Timiquan
Timiskaming
Timucua
Tinde
Tionontati
Tiowitsis
Tipai
Tipsoe Tyee
Tiwa
Tlalam
Tlatlasikwala
Tl'etinqox-t'in
Tlingit
Tloohoose
Tlo-o-qui-aht
Tlowitsis
Tlowitsis-Mumtagila
Toa
Toannois

Tobacco
Tobacco Plains
Tobique
Tocabago
Tocobagan
Tocoaya
Togagamiut
Togiak
Tohome
Tohono O'odham
Tolowa
Tokpafka
Toksook Bay
Tolomato
Tolowa
Tomeas
Tomez
Tomkas
Tompiro
Tongass
Tonguah
Tongva
Tonica
Tonkawa
Tonowanda
Tonto Apache
Tookabatchas
Toosey
Tootinaowaziibeeng
Topachula
Topingas
Toquaht
Torimas
Torres Martinez
Tortuga
Tosawi
Totonacs

Towa
Towiache
Towila
Tribe of the Sells
Trinidad
Trinity Wintun
Tsa Keh
Tsalagi
Tsanchifin
Tsankupi
Tsartlip
Tsawatenok
Tsawathineuk
Tsawout
Tsawwassen
Tsay Keh
Tsay-Keh-Dene
Tseil-wamuth
Tsekani
Tselona
Tseshaht
Tsetsaut
Tsetsehestehese
Tsetseu
Tseycum
Ts'ilhqot'in
Tsiljqot'in
Tsimshian
Tsitsistas
Tskwaylazw
Tsleil-Waututh
Tsnungwe
Tsoo-yess
Tsoya'ha
Tsqescen
Tsu T'ina
Tualatin

Tubatulabal
Tufulo
Tugalo
Tukabahchee
Tukaduka
Tukuarika
Tulal
Tulalip
Tulare
Tule
Tuluksak
Tunahe
Tunica
Tunica-Biloxi
Tuntutliak
Tununak
Tunxis
Tuolumme
Tupiqui
Turtle Mountain
Tusatulabal
Tuscarora
Tuscola
Tuskegee
Tutchone
Tutelo
Tutora
Tutuni
Twana
Twatna
Twenty-Nine Palms
Twightwee
Twin Hills
Two Kettles
Tyandega
Tyge Valley
Ty-hes

Tyone Martinez
Tyorek
Tyigh
Tza Tinne
U'mista
Uashat Mak Mani-
Utenam
Ucachile
Ucheam
Uchee
Uchusklesaht
Ucluelet
Uculegue
Ugashik
Uintah
Ukakhpakht
Ulibahali
Ulkatcho
Umatilla
U'mista
Umkumiute
Umpqua
Unalachtigo
Unalakleet
Unaligmiut
Unallapa
Unama'ki
Unami
Uncas
Uncompahgre
Unga
Union Bar
Unitah
United Auburn
United Houma
United Keetoowah
United Shawnee

Unkchaug	Waccamaw-Souian
Upper Creek	Waco
Upper Kiskapo	Wagmatcook
Upper Lake	Wagmatcookewey
Upper Mataponi	Wahkiakim
Upper Nicola	Wahnapitae
Upper Similkameen	Wahpakoota
Upper Sioux	Wahpeton
Upper Skagit	Wahu
Upper Yanklonai	Wahunsonacock
Urebures	Wailaki
Uscamu	Wainwright Native
Usheree	Wakashan
Utalapotoque	Wakinyan
Utawawas	Wakokai
Utayne	Wakpa
Ute	Walapai
Ute Mountain	Wales Native
Utina	Walhominies
Utinahica	Walker River
Utu Utu Gwaitu	Walla Walla
Utukokmiut	Wallamotkin
Utraca	Walpi
Utsushuat	Walpole Island
Uxmal	Walua
Uzita	Wamanus
Venetie	Wampano
Vermillion Bay	Wampanoag
Viejas	Wanabaki
Village des Hurons	Wanapum
Waatch Village	Wando
Wabanaki	Wanniah
Wabash	Wapekeka
Wabasseemoong	Wapeton
Wabauskang	Wapingeis
Wabigoon	Wappinger
Waccamaw	Wappo

War Lake
Warao
Warm Springs
Warroad Chippewa
Warraskoyak
Wasagamack
Wasco
Wascopum
Washa
Washagamis Bay
Washepoo
Washoah
Washoe
Washone
Waskagamish
Waskalatchat
Wasoco
Wasses
Waswanipi
Waterbee
Waterhen
Waterhen Lake
Watlala
Waukeshan Waxhaw
Wauyukma
Wauzhushk
Wawakapewin
Wawyachtonoc
Waxhaw
Wayanouk
Waycobah
Waywayseecappo
Wazhazhe
We Wai Hun
We Wai Kai
Wea
Weanoc

Weapemene
Weapememeoc
Weaponeiok
Webequie
Wecquaesgeek
Weeden Island
Weeminuche
Weenatouchee
Weetumkee
Wells
Wells Indian Colony
Wemindji
Wenachee
Wenatchi
Wendat-Huron
Wendover
Wenrohronon
Weott
Wesley
Wesort
West Main Cree
West Moberly
Westbank
Westbank First
Western Shoshone
Western Woods Cree
Westo
Wet'suwet'en
Wewenock
Weymontachie
Whapmagoostui
Whee Y Kum
Whilkut
Whispering Pines
White Bear
White Earth
White Mesa

White River Utes.
White Mountain
Apache
Whitecap Dakota/Sioux
Whitefish Bay
Whitefish Lake
White River
Whitesand
Whitwater Lake
Whuaquum
Whymatmagh
Wichita
Wick-ram
Widdah
Wikwemikong
Williams Lake
Willopah
Wilono
Wiwohlka
Wimbee
Wimbre
Wind River Arapahoe
Wind River Shoshone
Wind
Winnebago
Winnefelly
Winnemucca
Wintoon
Wintu
Wiogufki
Wiscasset
Wisconsin
Wishmai
Wishram
Witchekekan Lake
Wichita
Wiwohka

Wiyok
Woccon
Wolaistoquyik
Wolf Lake
Wolinak
Wood Mountain
Woodbridge
Woodfords Washoe
Woodland
Woodstock
Wowapi Oti Kin
Wukchunmi
Wunnumin
Wusita
Wuskwi Sipihk
Wyam
WyanPatte
Wyiot
Wylackie
Wynochee
Wyogtami
Wyum
Xatalalano
Xatsu'll
Xeni Gwet'in
Yagua
Yaha
Yahi
Yahooskin
Yakama Cowlitz
Yakima
Yankton Sioux
Yanktonai
Yaminahua
Yamhill
Yampah
Yamparika

Yana
Yamhill
Yampah
Yankton Sioux
Yakonan
Yaminahu
Yanktonai
Yanomamo
Yaocomaco
Yanomamo
Yataches
Yatasi
Yaqui
Yellowquill
Yemassee
Yeopim
Yerington
Yewkaltas
Yfulo
Yaquina
Yavapai
Ybitoopas
Yea Patano
Yekooche
Yellowknife
Yoa
Yokayo
Yscanis
Yokotc
Yokut
Yomba
Yonkalla
York Factory
Youghiogheny
Young Chippewyan
Ysa
Yucanis

Yufera
Yui
Yuima
Yuki
Ysleta Del Sur Pueblo
Yuchi
Yuma
Yuman
Yumsai
Yuki
Yuohulo
Yupik
Yurok
Yustaga
Zaaging
Zapotec
Zia
Zia Pueblo
Zuni

EPILOGUE

Before the Europeans came to this part of the world an estimated seventeen to eighteen million indigenous people nurtured their land, with respect for Mother Nature. After those natives were mostly eradicated in four centuries of genocide, the invaders began a campaign that continues to the present to denude the land of its natural resources, pollute the water and create a situation where people are stacked on top of each other like boulders on a levee. Humans lack the intelligence to limit population. Emerging are the indications of too many people living in too close proximity to other people: deprivation, conflict, social tension and hostility emerge. Wildlife is more intelligent than humans because they urinate a scent around their domain and from that scent other animals know not to encroach.

When Indians became aware that resources were being depleted they held a powwow, discussed the situation then decided that some of the families should move farther away and begin a new village to stop overpopulation and the depletion of natural resources. People now build megalopolises where they exist in sardine-like proximity that augers trouble. To keep their minds from dire situations people drink alcohol and use drugs with conflict in direct proportion to the social degradation.

Years ago a study was conducted in a classroom with mice as subjects to learn how problems are created by overpopulation. A community was built with adequate food and water to provide for 150 mice. Additional food and water supply was not programmed into the study. Cubicles, wheels, ropes, and other devices were added for recreation and privacy.

Four female mice plus two male mice were placed in the environment with observations of their behavioral habits beginning immediately.

They played and cavorted around the compound. It was a scene of complete tranquility. The mice began to reproduce. While the population remained below 150 they were sociable with each other but as the population increased, with food and water insufficient to meet their needs, problems soon evolved.

With a huge increase in the mice population peace was replaced by gangs of mice marauding in search of food and water. The supply was soon depleted. When that happened they began to prey on each other, even engaging in cannibalism.

They developed a nervous disorder, indicated by habitually chewing their skin until they bled. The mice stopped breeding and within six months of the beginning of the study the mice were dead. The study is an example in miniature of conditions developing over the world. The population of the planet is projected to increase to ten billion inhabitants within fifty years. Predation will become a fact of life when desperate people without sustenance begin migrating to regions where food and water is available.

As the fissure between the rich and the poor widens desperation will increase and impoverished people will not just sit idly and starve but will begin predation on the wealthy and a replica of the study on mice will occur. The problems can be seen today in many regions in the world and will unfortunately end the same as that social study on rodents. A societal collapse is happening at this moment in America as those with little education or job skills prey on others as their method for survival. With the onslaught, our law and order agencies will be under even greater stress as lawlessness sweeps over the land.

Sees the mansions for the rulers
Safe in fortress like enclosures,
Use of dogs and stockade fences,
Chains and bolts to thwart intrusions,
And ward off the desperate masses.

Excerpt from 2nd Timothy 3:1–7 NASB

But realize this, that in the last days difficult times will come. For men will be lovers of self, lovers of money, boastful, arrogant, revilers, disobedient to parents, ungrateful, unholy, unloving, irreconcilable, malicious gossips, without self control, brutal, haters of good, treacherous, reckless, conceited, lovers of pleasure rather than lovers of God, holding to a form of godliness although they have denied its power. Avoid such men as these. For among them are those who enter into households and captivate weak women weighed down with sins, led on by deviant impulses, always learning and never able to come to the knowledge of the truth.

THE END